AFTER LIFE

A Raney/Daye Investigation

Rich Hosek
Arnold Rudnick
Loyd Auerbach

I0635500

PRESS

Sherman Oaks, California

Visit **RaneyAndDaye.com** for more information about
future Raney/Daye Investigations
and resources about the paranormal.

Copyright © 2023 Rich Hosek, Arnold Rudnick and Loyd Auerbach
All rights reserved.

No part of this book may be reproduced in any form whatsoever
without written permission from the publisher.
The characters and events in this book are fictitious.
Any similarity to real persons, living, dead or undead,
is coincidental and not intended by the authors.

Nifni Press
a division of
Paraphrase, LLC
P.O. Box 56508
Sherman Oaks, CA 91413

Read a Book, Read a Mind

ISBN: 978-1-953566-05-8

Printed in the United States of America
First Printing: January 2023

For Arnold and Kathy.
My best friends on this adventure called life.

—*Rich Hosek*

I'm not crying, you're crying.

—*Arnold Rudnick*

To my wife, Julie, for always supporting my work in and around the paranormal, and to all the families experiencing the paranormal I have worked with (and hopefully helped) over the years.

—*Loyd Auerbach*

also by Rich Hosek, Arnold Rudnick & Loyd Auerbach

Near Death - A Raney/Daye Investigation

also by Loyd Auerbach

ESP Wars: East & West (with Edwin C. May, Victor Rubel,
Joseph W. McMoneagle)
Self-Publishing: It Ain't Rocket Science (with Richard L. Wren)
Mind Over Matter
*Psychic Dreaming: Dreamworking, Reincarnation, Out-of-Body Experiences
& Clairvoyance*
A Paranormal Casebook: Ghost Hunting in the New Millennium
Ghost Detectives' Guide to Haunted San Francisco (with Annette Martin)
ESP, Hauntings and Poltergeists: A Parapsychologist's Handbook
Ghost Hunting: How to Investigate the Paranormal
Psychic Dreaming: A Parapsychologist's Handbook
Hauntings and Poltergeists: A Ghost Hunters Guide
Reincarnation, Channeling and Possession: A Parapsychologist's Handbook
Presenting the Paranormal to the Public (coming soon)

also by Arnold Rudnick

ESPete: Sixth Grade Sense
ESPete in ESPresident: Featuring *ESPete's Psychic Joke Book*
Little Green

also by Rich Hosek

The Dead Kids Club
Gaston Leroux: The Man Behind the Man Behind the Mask (as told by Lynn Santer)
The Tenth Ride (2023)
The Charlatan's Conundrum and other Bedtime Stories for Insomniacs
The Time Traveler's Dilemma and more Bedtime Stories for Insomniacs (2023)

And listen to Rich Hosek's *Bedtime Stories for Insomniacs* fiction podcast
on your favorite podcast app or Audible. Visit https://bedtimestories.studio

RANEY/DAYE INVESTIGATIONS

Det. Nate Raney
Dr. Jennifer Daye

Visit RaneyAndDaye.com
for more information about the
Raney/Daye Investigations
Paranormal Mystery
Book Series.

RING BELL FOR DELIVERIES

Sign up for
our email list
to receive a
FREE Bookmark!

If you like audiobooks, you'll love the

Bedtime Stories
For Insomniacs
FICTION PODCAST

Fresh, new, original stories to *not*
fall asleep by every week! Subscribe on your
favorite podcast app or Audible.

Visit **BedtimeStories.studio** to
listen to the latest stories and enjoy
unabridged audiobooks by Rich Hosek

Sign up for the *Insomniac's Snoozeletter*

PROLOGUE

Danville, California - 2007

The heavy steel door to the bank vault slowly swung open and the man and woman who opened it stared inside.

"Told you it was a piece of cake," Dale Everly said to his wife, Maureen.

"I never doubted you," she replied.

They smiled and embraced. So far, everything was going according to plan. They had spent most of the night working to open the vault, with Dale doing the bulk of the work and Maureen handing him the necessary tools while monitoring the police scanner.

Six months of planning. That's what it had taken to get this far.

Maureen had been the inside man—or woman, rather—working as a bank teller. She kept track of when the bank was flush with cash and cultivated a relationship with the assistant manager. He would often ask her to stay late and help him close the bank. She used those opportunities to memorize his security codes and make wax impressions of his keys.

With their share of the score, Maureen and Dale planned to escape their desperate situation. They would leave this one-horse town, move east, buy a house, and start a family.

"Come on, we have to hurry," Dale urged.

They entered the vault, each carrying an empty duffel bag. The large, secure area doubled as the safe deposit box room. A steel gate separated the walls of boxes from the cash.

Dale set a pager on a steel table in the middle of the room. He picked up a large circular saw and started cutting through the deadbolt between him and the stacks of bundled bills.

Meanwhile, Maureen took her bag to one of the walls of safe deposit boxes and pulled out a diamond-tipped power drill. They had purchased boxes like these on eBay and practiced breaking into them. It wasn't as easy as they made it look in the movies, but she managed to get the whole process down to three minutes or less.

First, she drilled into the keyhole. Then she inserted a jig that allowed her to remove the lock cylinder. Finally, by anchoring a threaded bit in the hole and using a tool that pulled on the door with incredible force, the small door protecting the box opened.

Dale finished cutting his way through the gate and filled his bag with cash as Maureen emptied the contents of her first safe deposit box—a few gold coins and some expensive-looking watches—into her duffel.

Their instructions were to target certain size boxes. The wide, flat ones most often held papers like deeds and insurance policies, while the largest ones were infrequently rented.

It was the ones that were the size of a shoe box where people kept jewelry, coins and other valuables.

Dale stuffed some of the cash that didn't fit into his duffel into Maureen's. "There's about two hundred grand in cash," he reported. Not what they had hoped for. During its busiest weeks, the bank would be holding nearly twice that. But that didn't bother them. They had been assured that it was the safe deposit boxes would make this job worth their while.

Soon, they fell into a rhythm, with Dale extruding the lock cylinders and Maureen popping open the doors and emptying the container's contents into her duffel.

On their way into the bank, they hadn't tripped any alarms—thanks to the codes Maureen had acquired. But a failsafe sent a silent alarm directly to the local police if the vault was opened outside of regular bank hours. There was nothing they could do to prevent that. They had roughly eight minutes to get away before the police arrived.

But they had an ace up their sleeves.

An insider with the police would delay that alert. He would page them if for any reason he could no longer keep the silent alarm silent.

If all went according to plan, the only thing limiting how much time they had was the early morning arrival of the bank manager.

"Maybe we should go," Maureen suggested. "Two hundred thousand is a lot."

"Not split four ways," Dale reminded her. In addition to their partner at the police station, there was another man due his share, the Mastermind who had planned and recruited them for the heist. Dale checked his watch. "We've got plenty of time. Besides, I think there's something in these boxes our benefactor really wants. If we don't get it, we might have bigger problems than being fugitives."

Maureen pulled out another container. It was empty except for what looked like a velvet covered jewelry box, something perhaps big enough for a necklace. She resisted the urge to peek inside, added it to the contents of her duffel bag and kept on working.

Chrissy Sanger was five years old. Old enough, she had decided, that if she got thirsty in the middle of the night, she could get up and get her own glass of water.

The sky was starting to turn a pretty orange color outside her bedroom window. She slid from her bed and walked quietly toward the door, but then turned quickly and grabbed the doll she had been sleeping with before she headed toward the kitchen.

Her favorite sippy cup was sitting in the dish rack. She carefully placed her doll on the kitchen table and pulled one of the chairs next to the sink to stand on so she could reach the cup. She snapped on the lid, but quickly realized she needed to remove it to fill it up from the dispenser in the fridge. Her tiny fingers struggled to pry it loose. When she finally pulled it free, the lid popped off and flew across the room, hitting their sleeping dog on the nose. The animal opened his eyes and saw Chrissy standing before him.

"Sorry, Boxer," she said.

Boxer decided it was time to wake up anyway, got up and pushed his way through the dog door.

Chrissy lost interest in her water. She traded her cup for the doll on the kitchen table and followed Boxer outside.

In the yard, Chrissy saw Boxer peeing on some flowers. "Ew, Boxer, not on the daisies!"

The dog glanced at Chrissy as he continued to pee.

Suddenly, a squirrel ran along the top of the fence.

Boxer's instincts kicked in. He barked at the squirrel and ran after it until he reached the gate. It was ajar. Boxer nosed it open and bounded after the squirrel.

"Boxer! Come back here!" Chrissy shouted. She ran after him through the open gate.

It slammed shut behind her with a clunk.

Chrissy suddenly felt afraid. She clutched her doll close as she continued into the front yard.

Boxer was staring up at the branches of a tree where the squirrel was sitting.

"Boxer!" she shouted, "Come on boy, come on."

Boxer looked back toward Chrissy, his tongue hanging out as he panted.

The squirrel made a run for it.

Boxer heard the creature scampering away and his attention shifted back to his quarry. He ran down the street after it.

Chrissy knew she wasn't supposed to leave the yard, but neither was Boxer. What if he got lost? Or hurt? She wasn't supposed to cross the street by herself, but if she just went to the end of the block, that would be okay, wouldn't it?

She ran after Boxer into the brightening morning light.

Liam McDonald sat at the 911 desk of the Danville Police Department, playing solitaire on the computer. Technically, he wasn't supposed to be doing anything other than waiting for calls and monitoring the incoming alarms from various businesses and the handful of banks and credit unions downtown. But tonight was slow, and there was really only one reason he had volunteered to cover for the overnight operator while she was on vacation.

The alarm on the vault at the Danville Bank had sent in an alert about twenty minutes ago. The standard procedure was to dispatch one of the overnight patrol cars. However, the system had an override. In case a bank employee forgot to turn it off, they could call in and let the police know it was a false alarm. The operator at the 911 desk would click the "dismiss" button when it popped up on the computer screen and the alarm would be paused for ten minutes.

So far, Liam had clicked that button twice. It was due to show up again in the next minute and he would click it again. The plan was to keep "snoozing" the alarm until shift change at seven. By then, the Everlys would be done and gone.

Normally, Liam would be in one of the patrol cars cruising around overnight. Danville was a good-sized town. It was usually pretty quiet and had avoided many of the big city problems that had affected other communities in the more metropolitan areas.

The chief had been surprised when Liam offered to fill in for the vacationing operator. Usually, Liam was asking his boss for more "real" police work. Liam's partner didn't seem to mind being on his own temporarily, and the chief saw it as an easy way to fill the vacancy.

The only other people in the station were Sergeant Cooper, who manned the front desk in case there were any walk-ins, and Isaac, the janitor, who gave the station and the small jail in the back a good cleaning every night. Cooper was struggling over a Sudoku puzzle, and Isaac was currently running a vacuum between the empty desks.

It had been an uneventful night. Sometimes you'd get a drunk or two, or a domestic disturbance that had escalated to the point where one or both of the parties needed to be arrested.

But tonight there was nothing.

Liam scanned the cards of the Solitaire game on his screen as he clicked through the virtual deck, looking for a play he could make. Frustrated, he clicked on the button to start a new game.

The 911 line lit up and started beeping.

Liam was startled. He closed the Solitaire window and put on the headset resting around his neck. He waved at Isaac to kill the vacuum and then pressed the button on his keyboard to answer the call.

"911, what's your emergency?" he asked as the caller's address appeared on his screen.

Cooper lifted his head from his puzzle and turned to watch Liam from across the room.

"Okay, slow down," Liam said to the caller. "Are you sure she's missing? She's not hiding in a closet or something?" he asked.

The distraught parent loudly assured Liam in very colorful language that their little girl was indeed missing.

"All right, I need a description of what she looks like and what she was wearing. We'll put out an alert." Liam typed the information onto the screen.

"No, just sit tight in case she comes home, and we'll have someone come to you," he instructed. "You might want to start calling her friends' parents. Let them know to be on the lookout as well."

Liam tapped the button that switched the headset over to the police band radio and issued an all-points bulletin, repeating the description the parents had given him.

He sat back, wondering how this unexpected situation would affect the Everlys' escape. The little girl lived a few blocks from the downtown area. All the cars on duty would be converging there, but they would be focused on looking for the little girl, wouldn't they?

Then again, a couple driving around in the early morning hours might warrant a stop by an eager patrolman to see if they might have a five-year-old in the backseat.

He contemplated dialing the pager number from the disposable cell phone he had in his pocket. But he could do little more than alert them that something was wrong, not what precisely was going on. It might do more harm than good to deviate from the plan at this point.

"McDonald, what are you doing sitting there?" Sergeant Cooper asked. "Get your ass into a car and get out there. It's all hands on deck for a missing kid. You know that."

"Who's going to man the phones?" Liam asked.

"I'll take care of that," Cooper replied, tossing Liam the keys to his cruiser.

Liam caught them awkwardly, then took off his headset and stood up. He was staring at the spot on the screen in which the silent alarm from the bank would show up shortly.

"Get a move on, McDonald," Cooper said as he ambled over to the 911 station.

Liam nodded, padding his pockets and looking around the desk as if he was searching for something, stalling.

Just as Sergeant Cooper arrived, the alert appeared on screen and Liam quickly clicked the "dismiss" button. He nodded to the sergeant, then headed for the front door.

"Can I help?" Isaac asked.

"Just keep on doing what you're doing," Cooper answered as he sat down and put on the headphones. He started pressing buttons on the keyboard until he heard a dial tone in his ears. He punched in a number and waited for someone to answer. "Sorry to wake you, chief, but we have a situation."

Chief Williams listened as Sergeant Cooper told him about the 911 call regarding the missing girl. "Well, I guess I better get over there," he grumbled. "Send one of the cars over to pick me up in ten minutes, Coop."

The chief hung up the phone and looked over at his wife, Barb. She was already out of bed and slipping into her robe. "No need for you to get up," the chief said to his wife.

"Nonsense, I'd be up in ten minutes anyway. I'll put some coffee in a thermos for you," she said, then padded off toward the kitchen.

The chief sighed, lifted himself out of bed and headed over to his closet. He had been hoping his last month on the job would be quiet. An abducted—or God forbid, murdered—little girl was not how he wanted to end his career.

He grabbed a clean, pressed uniform from the closet. Barb was meticulous about making sure he always had several ready. He tossed his pajamas into the hamper and got dressed.

Liam walked slowly out to the cruiser. When he was sure he was out of view of anyone in the station—and no early morning dog-walker or delivery man was looking his way—he pulled out the disposable cell from his pocket. He flipped it open and hit the number one key and the asterisk to speed dial the pager.

Nothing happened. The screen was dark. He held his finger over the power button and there was a flash of light as the screen came to life. It started displaying logos and messages and then shut off. He pressed the power button again.

This time, there was nothing.

When was the last time he charged it? Had he even bothered to plug it in since he bought it at the truck stop off the Interstate?

He unlocked the car and checked to see if Cooper had a phone charger plugged in. There was nothing. He checked the glove compartment and found a cigarette lighter adapter with a short cord attached. He inspected the plug at the end and saw that it was the same shape and size that would fit into the jack on his phone.

He plugged it in. It took only a few seconds for the screen to light up again, but it felt like minutes. He smashed his thumb down on the power button and an icon showing that the battery was charging appeared along with a message: "Battery level too low. Try again later."

Liam snapped the phone closed and squeezed it in his hand until it felt like he was going to crush it. Then he dropped it on the passenger seat, started the car, and drove off into the early dawn.

The patrol car pulled up in front of Chief William's house just as he was walking out the front door, a thermos of hot coffee in one hand. The driver got out to open the passenger side.

"Get back in the car. I can open my own door," the chief ordered.

The young officer ran back to the driver's side and slid behind the wheel.

The chief settled in beside him, held a hand up indicating he wanted the driver to wait until he took a sip from his thermos before driving off. "Do you know where we're going?" the chief asked.

"Yes, sir. The family's house, over on Arroyo," the officer answered.

"All right," the chief said, squeezing his thermos into a cup holder. "Let's go."

They pulled away from the curb and made a U-turn on the empty street.

A voice crackled over the radio. "Chief Williams, are you out there?" asked Sergeant Cooper.

The chief grabbed the microphone for the radio and pressed the talk button. "Yeah, I'm on my way to the family's home. What's up, Coop?"

"I've got a silent alarm at the Danville Bank," he said.

"Jesus, when it rains…" the chief said. He checked his watch and then pressed the talk button again. "Larry probably went in early and forgot to disable it. Who's the closest unit?"

"It's actually on our way, sir," the driver said.

The chief nodded. "All right. We'll take a peek through the windows, see what's going on." He addressed Cooper over the radio. "I'll take a look on my way over to the family. Do we have anyone else with them yet?"

"Yes, sir. Lewis is there."

"Okay, let him know we'll join him as soon as we can." The chief unclipped a key ring from his belt. The Chief of Police kept a key for all the major businesses in town. He flipped through them until he found the one for the front door of the Danville Bank.

Liam drove down Main Street and pulled over a block from the bank. Another patrol car passed him, driving slowly in the opposite direction. He exchanged a nod with the officer, then reached down and picked up his phone. He flipped it open and pressed the power button. The phone cycled through the startup screens until it was ready. Then he hit the speed dial sequence again.

The pager service answered. He punched in a single number, zero, then the pound key, and disconnected the call. He immediately turned the phone off, unplugged it from the charger, and shoved it in his pocket.

The pager buzzed.

Dale and Maureen stopped what they were doing and turned toward the table.

It buzzed again, the vibration causing it to topple over onto its side.

Dale checked his watch. "Shit, something's wrong."

They listened for a moment. "I don't hear any sirens," Maureen said.

Suddenly, the police scanner squelched to life and voices crackled over its speaker, exchanging updates about a missing girl.

"Doesn't sound like they're talking about us," Maureen remarked.

"Not yet. Let's move," Dale said, a tone of panic in his voice. They were supposed to have a good half-hour lead before the police knew they had been in the bank. Now they had at most eight minutes — probably less if there happened to be a patrol car close to downtown.

Maureen dropped her tools in the duffel bag with the cash and valuables and zipped it up. Dale grabbed the other one as well as the equipment bag. He turned off the scanner and added it, too. They headed for the back door of the bank. Their car was parked in the alley a few doors down. Maureen looked out the door. The alley was deserted.

"Shit!" Dale whispered.

"What is it?"

"The pager. I forgot the pager."

"Go get it, I'll wait here."

"No, you go get the car and then swing by to pick me up."

Maureen nodded, grabbed her bag and walked out of the back door of the bank.

Dale left his duffel bags and doubled back to the vault. Although the pager was an anonymous burner, there might be fingerprints, maybe DNA. Perhaps the page could be traced. He wasn't going to take any chances that the police might put the squeeze on Liam to spill the beans on them.

He reached the vault, grabbed the pager, and spun around to leave.

"Freeze. Hands in the air," a deep, smoker's voice ordered.

The police chief was standing in the bank lobby, holding his gun in both hands.

It crossed Dale's mind to make a run for it, but Maureen still had a chance to escape if he could stall them. He raised his hands in the air.

Another officer entered behind the chief, one hand hovering near his holster. He spotted the pager clutched in Dale's hand and immediately drew his gun.

"He's got a weapon," the younger officer said.

Dale held his hands higher. "It's a pager," he shouted back in a tone he hoped conveyed he was not armed or dangerous.

"Drop it," the chief said.

Dale let the pager fall from his hands. It hit the ground and broke apart.

"On your knees!" the officer ordered.

Dale kneeled, still holding his hands high.

The officer grabbed Dale's arm and twisted it behind his back. Then he grabbed the other and cuffed both wrists together.

"Anyone else back there?" the chief asked warily.

Dale shook his head.

While the younger officer kept Dale restrained, the chief cautiously entered the vault. It was empty. He grabbed the radio from his belt. "Cooper, this is the chief. We've got a suspect in custody at the bank. Send backup."

"We found the girl. She was at a park, cold and scared, hugging the family dog," Cooper reported. "I'll send over all available units."

The chief sighed, relieved. "Okay, have them set up roadblocks around downtown."

"Roger," Cooper replied.

Chief Williams scanned the interior of the vault. About two-thirds of the medium sized boxes were empty. He looked around the vault and didn't find what he was looking for. Where was the cash and the contents of the boxes?

The chief walked up to Dale. "Where's your partner?" he asked.

"I was working alone," Dale replied.

"Then where's the money?" the chief asked.

Dale stared at the floor. Hopefully, Maureen could still get away if he kept them preoccupied long enough. He prayed that she was smart enough to drive to safety when he didn't return.

The chief kept his gun at the ready as he walked down the hallway that led to the back door.

Out in the alley, Maureen walked the fifty yards to the car with quick, purposeful strides. She didn't want to draw more attention than necessary by running. The car was parked down the alley behind the barber shop—which didn't open until noon.

Maureen made it to the station wagon without being seen. She opened the back of the car and tossed the duffel bag in among two other identical bags. She grabbed a baseball hat and a black satin jacket with red and gold lettering and slipped them on, pulling the hat low on her forehead.

Once behind the wheel, she glanced at the rear view mirror. No sign of Dale. She started the car and headed out of the narrow alley to turn around and pick him up. The plan was to head straight for Diablo Road and then I-680 and head north, then west. They had told their friends and family they were planning a trip to Vegas, so their absence wouldn't draw any immediate suspicion.

Maureen eased out of the alley into the street, planning to make a U-turn and drive through the alley in the opposite direction to pick up Dale. It would add a couple more left turns to their escape route—not something she was comfortable with. She checked her watch. How long had it been? One minute, maybe two?

She waited as a bread truck making early morning deliveries passed. Then she started to make a sweeping counterclockwise turn back where she came from.

From the far end of the alley, a police car approached, its lights flashing.

She slammed on the brakes.

Her heart was racing.

The police cruiser pulled up to the back door of the bank and two officers got out. They drew their guns and approached the rear entrance.

Maureen sighed with relief, realizing they hadn't noticed her. But now there was no way she could pick up Dale without getting caught.

Maureen eased off the brake and continued down the street instead of making the full U-turn into the alley. She listened for the sound of gunshots, so concerned and distracted she didn't notice the vehicle that appeared in front of her.

Another police car.

There was a single officer inside.

"Hey, careful there," he shouted to her.

Maureen recognized him as a regular customer at the bank.

The officer got out of his vehicle and walked up to her car. Maureen quickly gathered her thoughts and rolled down the window. "Sorry, I didn't see you there. What's going on?" she asked innocently, nodding down the alley. "I was going to cut through to avoid the light."

The officer regarded her suspiciously. "What are you doing out this early?"

"Heading over to get set up for soccer practice," she said, tilting her hat so the office could see the team logo for the Danville Nuggets on it.

"You get those girls out of bed this early?"

"Believe it or not, they usually get there before me," she answered with a forced smile.

The officer's eyes roamed from Maureen to the back of her car. It was filled with soccer balls and duffel bags. "Mind if I take a look in the back?" he asked.

"Sure, go ahead."

"Can you step out of the car, ma'am?" he asked politely.

"Okay," Maureen said, then asked again, curious, "What's going on?"

The officer waited for her to get out of the car before answering. "There was an alarm at the bank," he told her. "Can you open up the back, please?"

Maureen walked around to the rear of the car and opened the hatch. It swung open, and she stepped back.

The policeman reached inside and pulled the nearest duffel bag toward him. He unzipped it and looked inside. It was full of orange rubber cones and some netting.

He reached for the next bag and opened it up. There were extra cleats, a collection of dirty red vests, and a foot pump.

Maureen scanned the street, looking for an escape route, some place she might be able to run to before getting shot, some way to survive.

The officer reached for the third duffel. His radio crackled. "Jones, where are you?" a voice asked through the tinny speaker of the walk-ie-talkie.

Maureen thought she recognized it. It sounded like Liam McDonald, their accomplice.

The officer pressed the talk button on the microphone clipped to his shoulder. "Alley, west end."

"Secure the rear bank exit, over."

"Ten-four, over." He pushed the bags back in place in the rear of the car and closed the hatch. "Have a good practice," he said to Maureen, then walked briskly back to his own car. He climbed in and drove into the alley.

Maureen got back into her car and pulled away, confident that with all of Danville's police converging on the downtown area that once she was out of the city center, she could blow through the stop signs and red lights to get far away as quickly as possible.

They had planned for this contingency, for dozens of situations. Maureen had estimated their chances of success at nearly one hundred percent.

Nearly.

Obviously, there was a chance something could go wrong. And it had. The missing girl they heard about on the scanner had thrown all of their assumptions out the window.

Maureen knew Dale would keep the police off her trail for as long as possible—she would do the same for him. Right now, she needed to get out of town and out of the state. She'd take I-80 to Reno, blend in with the crowds of the casinos. Once she was safe, she'd find some way to help him.

But she needed to go home first. She needed to stash the money and the contents of the safe deposit boxes. If she was caught with it, she had no chance.

There was some money at the house that couldn't be traced back to the bank. She would pack it and some clothes, maybe grab some keepsakes. Maureen couldn't return to Danville or her family home ever again. That was no longer an option. She'd find a lawyer for Dale and wait till they could be together again.

The chief approached the back door of the bank.

It started to open. He raised his gun, his heart pounding.

Two police officers entered, their guns drawn as well. They saw the chief and lowered their weapons.

"Did you see anyone out there?" the chief asked.

The officers shook their heads. "No, the alley was clear," one of them answered.

The chief put his gun away and approached the two duffel bags sitting in the hallway. He opened one of them up. It was filled with tools and equipment, likely the means of opening the bank's vault.

The second bag was stuffed full of cash.

The chief stared at the two bags, thinking.

"What is it, chief?"

"He emptied about forty safe deposit boxes in that vault," he replied.

"Yeah, so?" the officer shrugged.

"Where's the stuff from the boxes? I've only got cash and tools here." He grabbed his radio. "All units, we have a suspect on the loose from the bank robbery. Be on the lookout for… someone."

Liam listened to the broadcast from the chief.

Everly's wife had managed to get away. She was smarter than he gave her credit for—though he wondered if she knew he was the one who had called that eager patrolman off of her while she was making her escape.

It would be crazy to try to follow her at this point. There was a rendezvous out of state where he was supposed to meet up with the Everlys and the Mastermind, but he didn't see that happening.

How long did they have before Dale talked? Or would he do everything he could to protect his wife? How long before they found out who he was and converged on the farmhouse they had on the outskirts of town?

Would she be crazy enough to go there?

Maybe she had left something behind. Some indication of where she might go, what she might be thinking. He turned off the radio and put the car in gear, trying to remember how to get to the Everly house.

Dale was escorted into the police station, his hands cuffed behind his back.

He had screwed up. Not in the execution of the plan, but in thinking it was a good idea in the first place. And his biggest regret was involving Maureen.

"This way," one of the officers instructed, leading Dale to a small room at the back of the police station where there was a fingerprinting station and a camera for mug shots.

They uncuffed Dale and fingerprinted him. "Do we have a name?" one of the officers asked.

"Not yet. He's taking the whole 'You have a right to remain silent' thing seriously. We'll have to wait for his prints to come back before we get an ID—that's if he's in the system."

Dale was offered a hand wipe to clean the ink off his fingers. An officer refastened his cuffs and positioned him in front of the camera. The flash went off. "Turn to your left," the officer instructed. Another flash.

Isaac passed by, pushing his mop as an excuse to see what all the fuss was about. "Hi, Dale," he said when he saw the prisoner.

The officers exchanged a look.

"Isaac, you know this man?"

"Sure, that's Mr. Everly." Isaac replied. "We get our hair cut at the same place. Mr. Ruben, the barber, is really nice," he added.

Chief Williams saw the small crowd in the records room. "What's going on over here? Why isn't the prisoner in a cell?" he asked.

"Well, chief, it turns out Detective Isaac here cracked the case for us. This here is Dale Everly," one of the officers explained.

"Is that right?" the chief asked, smiling at the janitor, who shuffled sheepishly. "Well done, Isaac. Well done."

Maureen arrived at the old farmhouse, half expecting it to be surrounded by police. Maybe they hadn't identified Dale yet. But Danville was a small town. It wouldn't take long to find out who he was, that he was married, and where he was living. Soon the old house would be crawling with cops.

She pulled the station wagon into the driveway and stepped out, taking a moment to brush off the dirt and underbrush she had accumulated hiding the duffel bag. She ran to the front door, opened it, rushed inside and up the stairs.

From her bedroom closet, she removed a large backpack that was stuffed with a few days' clothes and toiletries. She pulled a small, flat box from a bottom drawer and stuffed it into the top, then added the contents of her jewelry box to a side pocket.

Maureen stepped up onto the bed and took a framed painting hanging above the headboard off the wall. Taped behind the landscape were several thin bundles of cash in various denominations. Not even Dale knew about this stash. It was the money she was saving for her baby fund. She wouldn't be needing it for a long while, now.

Maureen stuffed the bills into another side pocket of the backpack and zipped it shut. She hefted the backpack onto her shoulders and raced back down the stairs, looking around one last time.

This was the house she had grown up in, the one she had once hoped to raise her own family in.

She pulled open the front door to find Liam standing in front of her.

"Going somewhere, Maureen?" he asked.

She didn't respond, not knowing if she could still trust him.

"Lucky I caught you. I got lost on the way over."

The two of them stared at each other for a moment.

"We need to talk," he said.

"What's there to talk about? Dale got arrested because of you," she replied.

Liam shook his head. "It wasn't my fault. I paged you as soon as I could."

Maureen regarded him suspiciously, wondering if their "inside man" had turned on them. But what would he have to gain? Instead of his share of their haul, he'd end up with nothing, and risk getting exposed as an accomplice. "Well, now Dale is going to jail."

"Unless he talks and gives us up."

Maureen shook her head. "He won't do that."

"How much did you get out?"

"One bag, half cash, half safe deposit boxes."

"Is that it on your back?"

"No. It's in a safe place."

"They're going to search the house."

"They won't find it."

Liam looked down at her boots and noticed the remnants of leaves and dirt. "Does Dale know where it is?"

"He'll know," she said confidently, and moved to leave the house.

The man blocked her way. "Just tell me where it is. In case something happens to you."

"Yeah, right," she said.

A siren sounded in the distance. Maureen glared at Liam.

"Hey, it wasn't me. Someone down at the station must have recognized him."

Maureen pushed her way past Liam toward the car.

"That's a mistake," he warned. "If they know who he is, they know who you are and will have a BOLO out for your car." Maureen froze.

"Go out the back," Liam suggested. "Can you make it up over the mountain to the fire road?"

She nodded.

"Then go, I'll stall them," he said.

Maureen retreated back into the house, closing the door behind her and raced toward the kitchen. She wasn't used to navigating the house with a backpack on and when she tried to pass through, the frame of her pack caught on the doorway and knocked her off her feet.

Her head smacked into the hardwood floor, stunning her for a moment.

Outside, Liam drew his gun, letting it hang at his side, and stepped down off the front porch just as two cars pulled up with more on the way.

"McDonald, what are you doing here?" one of them asked.

"I heard the BOLO on the radio. She must have gotten here just before me."

"We'll cover the back," one of the officers said, signaling to his partner. They each moved in a different direction to circle around the house.

Had she gotten out? If they caught her, would she talk? "She might be armed," Liam warned the officers.

They acknowledged his warning and drew their guns as they continued around the sides of the house.

Inside, Maureen cursed. She had overheard Liam. What was he trying to do, get her shot?

The question was its own answer.

She never really had trusted Liam, but Dale had insisted they could count on him. And according to the mysterious Mastermind, they had needed someone inside the police department to make the whole thing work.

A lot of good that did them.

What was he hoping to gain by killing her? Split the money with Dale? Were they in it together?

No, that wasn't possible.

Maureen shook off the pack and got to her feet. She grabbed the bundles of cash from the side pocket and shoved them in her pockets. She dug out the cardboard box and took a moment to peek under the lid. It was filled with family photos, some going back to her great-grandparents. She tucked it under her arm and stepped toward the kitchen. Through the windows, she could see the police converging on the back door.

Maureen turned toward the front door. The sound of additional sirens approaching was loud and clear. She grabbed a pen and a pad of paper from next to the phone and ran through the living room back up the stairs to the landing on the second floor.

She pulled on the chain that lowered the steps to the attic and climbed up into the hot, musty space, pulling up the ladder after her. She stepped over the jumble of boxes and old furniture toward a window.

Just outside were the thick branches of an old oak tree between the house and the woods next to it. It was an escape route she had used as a teenager to sneak out after her parents' curfew.

Now, it was her last chance to get away.

Maureen tucked the box of photos in a space between the wallboards. She'd come back for them someday, but she couldn't take them with her now. She scribbled a note on the pad, folded it and dropped it into the same hole. It was a hiding place she had used for a scavenger hunt she had created for Dale on their first anniversary. He pretended to hate having to follow the clues around the house but didn't complain when he solved the last one that led to their bedroom. Hopefully, he would think to look here in case she didn't make it.

She lifted the sash and cautiously looked outside.

There was no one in the side yard. She crawled out onto the

branch, clutching the rough bark with her hands while she crawled out onto the bough. It bore her weight easily.

Maureen took a moment to evaluate her options. The old oak's canopy would help hide her while she made her way to the adjacent trees. She could then descend into the forest while the police still searched for her in the house. By the time they discovered her means of escape, she would be miles away, hopefully in the cab of a trucker not averse to picking up a hitchhiker.

"She's not in the kitchen," a voice shouted. "Get some men in the yard! When are those dogs getting here?"

"She's got a gun!" a voice warned.

Maureen spun around, trying to hold her hands up to show that she wasn't armed. There was someone looking up at her. She couldn't quite make out who.

Then, a loud crack.

"Shots fired!" one of the officers shouted.

Maureen felt a sharp pain in her chest. She looked down and saw a red spot on her shirt. It grew as blood from the bullet hole soaked into the fabric.

The world went dark.

The last thing she remembered was falling.

CHAPTER ONE

San Francisco - Present Day

Dr. Jennifer Daye guided her Volkswagen Microbus through an upscale neighborhood on the outskirts of San Francisco. The sun was setting. She peered over the top of her cat eye sunglasses at the house numbers as she slowly navigated the tree-lined street. Dr. Daye was a tenured professor of Anthropology at Cal State East Bay, but this evening she was conducting an investigation beyond the normal bounds of her field. The pendant she wore around her neck, the Greek letter Psi, was a symbol representing parapsychology. She had a passion for studying the paranormal, both in connection with anthropology, and also as an investigator of various psi phenomena.

Whenever her activities were mentioned by the press, she was invariably labeled a "Ghostbuster," a comparison she didn't shy away from. She used it as a point of reference to describe how her work differed from the exploits of Peter, Ray, Egon and Winston and their proton pack powered adventures.

In the passenger seat was her undergrad intern, Emily Vargas. Where Jennifer tended to stay with earth tones in her usual outfit of a light turtleneck paired with tweed slacks and punctuated with bright red Vans shoes, Emily was a study in black, from her hair and heavy eyeliner, to her baggy T-shirt, jeans and black leather boots.

"Are we there yet?" Emily asked in an impatient monotone.

"Should be. We're on the right street. I think."

Emily sighed. "Tell me again why you didn't bring Dave?"

Dave Edwards was Jennifer's graduate assistant. He normally accompanied her on preliminary investigations, but tonight she could tell his reluctance was more than his usual default protestation. He had been making progress on research for his Ph.D. thesis, and Jennifer decided not to disrupt his momentum. So, she recruited Emily to join her instead.

"Dave is working on his dissertation. And when he graduates and moves on, I'm going to need to rely on you even more."

"He'll never graduate. He likes being a student too much."

Emily was usually pretty good at getting out of things she didn't want to do, but Jennifer was better at getting people to do what she wanted. In this case, the immovable object gave way to the unstoppable force—though Jennifer suspected that Emily was not as resistant to joining Jennifer as she let on.

"Why didn't you bring Detective Raney?" Emily asked, somewhat rhetorically.

Nate Raney was a retired police detective Jennifer had teamed up with in hopes of making her paranormal investigations more of a business rather than a hobby. Their partnership seemed like a sure thing, especially after all the publicity surrounding a sixty-year-old cold case they helped solve in which the spirit of a wrongly accused man helped them catch the real killer.

Nate, nonetheless, was a confirmed skeptic, and didn't credit anything but luck and good police work with cracking the case. It was also the reason she didn't usually involve him in the preliminary investigations. The few times she had persuaded him to come along he spent the whole time shooting down any suggestions the incidents were paranormal in nature.

Although they still hadn't gotten any high-profile cases, Jennifer was an optimist at heart. She knew it was just a matter of time and hoped Nate had as much patience as she did.

"There it is," Emily said, pointing to a large gray house surrounded by walnut trees.

Jennifer almost missed the driveway. She slammed on the brakes. The contents of the van shifted noisily, pressing against the curtain separating the rear compartment from the passenger area.

"What did you bring?" Emily asked. "I thought this was just a preliminary interview."

"Be prepared, that's my motto," Jennifer answered.

"Isn't that the Boy Scouts' motto?"

"They lent it to me for the week."

Jennifer turned into the driveway and approached the house. A woman appeared at the front door and stepped out onto the porch. Dr. Daye parked the van and turned off the engine.

"Do I need to grab any gear?" Emily asked.

Jennifer reached through the part in the curtain and pulled out a medium-sized case. "This is all we'll need." She handed it to the intern.

Emily climbed out, dragging the case with her.

Jennifer waved to the woman waiting for them. "Mrs. Young? I'm Dr. Daye." She looked to Emily, who was lugging the case. "This is my assistant, Emily Vargas."

"Hello," Mrs. Young said. "I wasn't sure you would make it in time." She glanced at the rapidly dimming sunset. "It usually happens just after sunset. Please, come in."

Mrs. Young held the door open as Jennifer and Emily entered the house. The living room was large and filled with stylish furniture. Emily found an empty spot to set the equipment case and opened it up.

Jennifer noticed that there was a pile of bedding on one of the chairs.

"Thank you so much for coming," Mrs. Young said. "It's been getting worse."

"Tell me what's been happening," Jennifer said, approaching the nearest sofa and inviting Mrs. Young to join her. "When did it start?"

The older woman sat down, perched on the edge of the sofa as though prepared to leap up and flee at any moment. She took a deep breath, briefly glancing upward. "It began the first night we moved in. We were so exhausted and stressed. I thought the noises were just something I was sensitive to because we were in a new place. We moved from New York city, where it's noisy all the time. Gerald said we'd have to get used to a whole new set of sounds living in the suburbs."

She smiled meekly, as if embarrassed to have such a high-class problem. "When the noises happened again the next night, I knew the footsteps were not coming from the outside."

"Footsteps?" Jennifer asked.

"They sound like footsteps to me. Gerald thinks they sound like someone tapping. The first thing we did was look around the house to see what it might be. There were several branches from the walnut trees close to the house, so we had someone come by and trim them back."

"But the noises continued," Jennifer guessed.

"Yes," Mrs. Young replied, nervously clasping her hands in her lap. "I know it sounds silly, but I'm at my wit's end. I don't know if I can spend another night in this house."

"It's not silly at all," Jennifer assured her.

"Do you know if anyone died in this house?" Emily asked, off-handedly.

Mrs. Young gasped.

Jennifer shot her intern a look.

Emily shrugged. "Don't we usually want to know stuff like that?"

Jennifer addressed Mrs. Young. "It is something we consider. What do you know about the history of the house?"

"Just the basics, when it was built and such. I do remember Gerald jokingly asked the real estate agent if anyone had been murdered here. He thinks he's amusing."

"Had there been?" Emily asked, ignoring another warning glare from Dr. Daye.

"Oh, goodness no," Mrs. Young declared. "We never would have bought the house if something like that had happened in it."

"Maybe no one knew," Emily suggested. "Did you have cadaver

dogs check out the yard? They can smell if there are any bodies buried out there."

"Oh, my," Mrs. Young exclaimed.

"Emily, do you want to wait in the van?" Jennifer pointedly asked.

"No," replied Emily.

"Is it possible there are dead bodies in my backyard?" the older woman asked.

Jennifer placed a reassuring touch on Mrs. Young's nervously clasped hands. "No, I'm positive."

"They could be in your basement," Emily added. "I saw this show on the Discovery channel where this guy had—"

"Emily, perhaps since this is your first time filling in for Dave, maybe you should just observe," Jennifer suggested.

"Fine," Emily conceded. She pulled out her laptop and started typing notes. The undergrad was very intelligent, and Jennifer saw a bright future for her, if not in anthropology, then anything else she set her mind to. But Emily was prone to speaking her mind in an unfiltered way—just like Jennifer. It was a trait which had gotten her into a lot of trouble, both personally and professionally.

Jennifer turned to Mrs. Young, who was growing visibly more anxious. "We did a thorough historical check on the property," she said. "If there was anything to be concerned about, we would have found it."

The older woman cautiously breathed a sigh of relief, but still seemed nervous. She checked her watch and glanced at the large front window. It provided a view of the sunset and rapidly approaching dusk.

Jennifer sensed Mrs. Young's unease. "This is the time you usually hear the footsteps?"

"As soon as it gets dark," she replied with an emphatic nod.

Jennifer looked at the ceiling, then over at the staircase that led to the second floor. "I'd like to take a look upstairs. Can you show us around?"

"I suppose," Mrs. Young replied tentatively.

Normally, Jennifer would arm herself with her a few sensors that measured magnetic fields and other environmental metrics to try to get a baseline for the house. She decided to forgo them this time to focus on helping the homeowner feel more at ease. Jennifer rose from her seat and waited for Mrs. Young to follow.

Emily rose as well, setting aside her laptop and grabbing a camera. She looked at Dr. Daye, then moved her fingers across her lips in a zipping motion, promising she would keep her thoughts to herself.

Jennifer led the way, climbing the stairs slowly, listening carefully, but also taking in the classical architectural features of the old house. The ornate banister, topped by a dark walnut rail, looked to be carved from a single piece of wood and curved elegantly to the second floor. There was also a stunningly crafted crown molding wedding the flat off-white paint of the ceiling to the delicately textured wallpaper.

When they reached the landing, Jennifer paused and looked up and down the hallway. A long runner covered most of the hardwood floor, and half a dozen or more doors stood closed.

"Which one is your bedroom?" Jennifer asked.

Mrs. Young pointed to a door towards the end of the hallway.

Jennifer began walking slowly in that direction.

The homeowner followed closely behind.

The window on the far wall revealed how dark it was getting outside.

They approached the bedroom door. Mrs. Young opened it. There was a carefully appointed bedroom featuring a perfectly made king-sized bed and a pair of ornate dressers. While Jennifer and Emily took in the room, Mrs. Young glanced nervously at the ceiling.

"When was the last time you slept in here?" Jennifer asked.

Mrs. Young seemed surprised by the question.

"I noticed you have bedding downstairs. I'm guessing you might be trying to be as far away from whatever's going on as possible. I'd feel the same way," Jennifer said.

"About a week," Mrs. Young confessed. "I couldn't take it anymore. I told Gerald I was going to move to a hotel if you couldn't get rid of him."

"Him?" Emily couldn't help but ask.

"It sounds like a man's footsteps to me. So that's how I think of it." She looked upward once more. "There's a man pacing in the attic. Gerald has checked several times and insists there is no one up there—which doesn't reassure me at all."

"How do you get up to the attic?" Jennifer asked.

"There's a door in the hallway that leads up there," Mrs. Young replied, pulling an antique key from a pocket. "Gerald thought I would feel better knowing I had the only key."

Jennifer looked at the brass key in Mrs. Young's palm. She could hear the voice of her skeptical partner, Nate, muttering, "You can find a skeleton key like that at any flea market, and anyone with a paper clip could pick a lock that used a key like that." But she was sure that the locks on the outside doors to the house were not guarded by nineteenth century hardware.

"Let's take a look," Jennifer said.

Mrs. Young seemed surprised by the request. There was a fear behind her eyes that grew stronger the darker it got outside. The sunset was now just a soft glow on the horizon. She led Jennifer and Emily from the master bedroom down the hallway to a narrow door. She inserted the key into the old-fashioned lock and turned it until there was an audible click and stepped back without opening it.

Jennifer reached out and turned the knob. The door opened outward, and beyond it was a narrow staircase leading up into the dark. She pulled out her phone and switched on the flashlight. Its bright light illuminated the exposed rafters of the attic at the top of the steps. She turned to Emily. "Let me have the camera."

"You don't want me up there with you?" Emily asked, a little disappointed.

"No, stay downstairs with Mrs. Young. Set up one of Bits' omnisensors."

"Okay, chief," Emily said with a mock salute.

Jennifer ignored her intern's not-so-subtle rebelliousness. She started up the steps. Each one seemed to squeak at a different pitch as she climbed up into the attic. She heard Emily reassuring Mrs.

Young that Dr. Daye had done this thousands of times, and not to worry.

The attic spanned the entire width of the large house. Jennifer saw a pull chain hanging and gave it a tug. A bare bulb lit up the space, casting eerie shadows behind boxes and unused furniture. She wondered if it was the property of the Youngs, or if it had been left by the previous owner.

A fine layer of dust covered the floor. There were footprints—likely left by Mr. Young—centered under the attic light. It didn't look as if he had ventured very far past the top of the stairs.

Jennifer used the light from her phone to illuminate the dark corners that the bare bulb from the ceiling didn't reach. She noticed rodent feces in some spots—which wasn't uncommon in a Northern California attic—but she doubted the scurrying of a small animal could be mistaken for a man's footsteps.

Upon closer inspection, she spotted a trail across the floorboards from whatever creature had taken up residence in the attic. There were multiple tracks, likely the same animal moving back and forth between its nest and whatever opening there was to the house—probably an uncovered vent.

But there were also wobbly, broken lines traced in the dust. A rat's tail?

Jennifer shivered at the notion. She wasn't afraid of encountering anything paranormal—actually, she hoped she would—but rats were one fear she shared with Indiana Jones's father.

As unlikely as it was that a rat was responsible for the sounds causing Mrs. Young so much consternation, it was the only lead she had so far. "Emily, I'm going to stay up here for a while," she called down the steps. "Close the door for me, will you?"

"Ten-four, boss," Emily replied.

Jennifer searched the attic for a chair among the furniture. She found an upholstered dining chair, wiped off the dust on the seat and set it at the end of the animal trail that led to a pile of boxes. Then she pulled the chain to turn off the overhead light, sat down and shut down her phone's flashlight.

Next, she turned on the camcorder, switched it to its night-sight mode and positioned it so it faced the attic before her. She then folded the attached screen against the body of the camera so its light wouldn't interfere with her observations.

Once the room became dark, she noticed a red light on the camera creating a surprisingly bright glow. She covered it with her thumb and the attic became completely black.

Jennifer wondered to herself how long she would need to wait. Mrs. Young was quite sure that the footsteps occurred shortly after dark. Hopefully, she wouldn't have to wait long. Fortunately, the chair was quite comfortable.

Her patience didn't need to be tested for long.

Something chittered in the dark, followed by a light scraping sound.

Then she heard a faint rumbling sound underneath what sounded like footsteps, thumping across the attic floor.

Footsteps walking directly toward her.

Jennifer held her breath.

Who was it? How did they get up here?

The footsteps came right up to her, then stopped.

She heard scratching noises behind her, as if something was scrambling over the stack of cardboard boxes.

Something brushed against her ankle.

She screamed.

There was a rapid scrambling sound.

Jennifer jumped up and swiped her phone flashlight to life. There was movement at the far end of the attic, but she didn't see what it was.

Her phone pinged with an incoming text message. It was from Emily. "Have you been murdered or dismembered or something?" She ignored it.

Jennifer reached for the dangling chain for the overhead light and turned it back on. She scanned the attic.

There was no one there.

The door at the bottom of the stairs opened. "Are you all right, Dr.

Daye?" Mrs. Young asked. "Did you see who it was?"

"I'm fine," Jennifer called down, but didn't want to respond to the other questions until she had some answers.

Jennifer flipped out the screen of the camcorder and pressed the rewind button. The recording zipped by in reverse. Jennifer didn't see any ghostly figures in the frame, but didn't expect to. It was her belief that the reason there weren't any conclusive photographs of apparitions was that they couldn't be photographed—at least by traditional chemical or electronic means. She was convinced that when they were visible, it was by a psychic mechanism requiring a human brain to interact with.

Hopefully, the video revealed some other type of clue.

Jennifer hit the play button and studied the grainy black and white infra-red video on the small screen.

"Dr. Daye? Should we come up?" Emily shouted from the bottom of the stairs.

"Hold on," Jennifer shouted back.

As she watched, she noticed a white speck crossing the floor toward the camera. As it got closer, Jennifer could discern that it was some sort of animal, but not a rat. The bushy tail identified it as a squirrel.

There was something else. Something dark that the squirrel was rolling along the floor.

Jennifer looked over at the chair she had been sitting on, and the stack of boxes behind it. She moved the chair aside and started taking boxes off the stack. Most of them were empty.

When she reached the bottom box, however, there was something inside. As she shook it, it sounded like a box of rocks. Something fell out of a squirrel sized hole in the bottom.

A handful of walnuts.

Jennifer bent over and picked one of them up.

It didn't look like the walnuts in a shell you'd buy at the grocery store, it still had a mottled green fruit around the large pit that was the actual nut.

Then she looked down at the floor. It wasn't covered with plywood, but rather floorboards that over the years had warped and separated.

Curious, she bent down and gently rolled the walnut across the floor.

As it hit the edge of each floorboard, it popped up into the air and landed noisily as it continued rolling toward the next one.

Sounding surprisingly like footsteps walking across the attic.

"Oh my God, that's him! Do you see him? Who is it?" Mrs. Young shouted from the bottom of the steps.

"Come on up!" Jennifer shouted back.

"Are you sure? No creepy ghosts up there with you?" Emily asked for the benefit of Mrs. Young.

"I'm alone," Dr. Daye assured them.

Emily appeared at the top of the steps, then nodded to Mrs. Young, who followed her up into the musty open space of the attic.

Once they were both there, Jennifer picked up another of the green walnuts at her feet and gently rolled it across the floorboards.

Mrs. Young gasped as she heard the sound of the mysterious footsteps recreated by the bouncing nut. "Are you sure that's what it was?"

Jennifer held up the camcorder. "I have the culprit on video. There's a squirrel who's been using your attic to store up for the winter."

"That is so cool," Emily said, uncharacteristically impressed.

"Oh, my. I almost feel silly that I ever was afraid," Mrs. Young said, relieved, transformed from a woman gripped in fear, to someone relaxed and calm. "How can I ever thank you?" she asked.

Jennifer shrugged. "I'm just glad we could help," the parapsychologist said.

Emily cleared her throat. She rubbed her fingers together in a gesture to remind Jennifer that Nate would expect them to return with a paycheck.

"Although now that you mention it, there is the matter of a small fee for our time..." Jennifer added, smiling uncomfortably.

CHAPTER TWO

Nate Raney sat in his SUV, staring out the window from behind his sunglasses. He wore a sports coat with matching slacks and a dress shirt, but no tie. In his previous line of work as a police detective, he always made sure to be impeccably dressed. But he had somewhat relaxed his personal dress code in the months since an injury had forced him to retire.

A younger Asian man sat in the passenger seat. He had a bag of white cheddar popcorn in his lap, and there were open and partially eaten packages of cookies on the dashboard in front of him. Max Lee was Nate's last partner on the job and had been a steadfast and loyal friend since.

"You know, Max, you didn't have to come on this stakeout with me."

"Hey, what are friends for?" he asked, grabbing a handful of popcorn and lifting it to his mouth.

Nate cringed as he watched bits escape and drop down into the space between the center console and the seat.

"Besides, it's my day off, and I hardly see you these days."

"I've been busy."

"Well, not too busy to take this case—which you still haven't thanked me for getting you, by the way," Max said.

"I'll thank you when I get paid," Nate replied.

Max looked out the window across the street to the dog park they were staking out. He saw a woman walking an Afghan Hound enter the park. She was middle-aged, rather attractive and well dressed.

"That's her," Max said, rolling up the top of the popcorn bag and wiping the cheese dust off his hands on Nate's leather seats. He picked up a pair of binoculars.

"You want to shout it a little bit louder? I don't think she heard you," Nate said. He picked up a camera with a long telephoto lens from his lap and framed the woman and her dog in the camera's screen. He started snapping photos.

"This is exciting," Max whispered. "Just like old times, right?"

"The last stakeout we were on was for a case we had been building for two years against one of the city's top crime bosses."

"Was it? I just remember that was about the time they released the Mega-Stuff Oreos." Max reached toward the packet of overstuffed sandwich cookies on the dash, plucked one out and twisted it open. He licked the creamy filling, then tossed the chocolate cookies out the window. "I don't know why they don't just sell the filling," Max wondered.

"It is a mystery," Nate agreed sardonically. He kept his focus on the woman and her dog, as she made her way to where a large tree shaded a portion of the park.

Standing there was a man and his dog, a lab-collie mix. The two of them struck up a conversation while their dogs sniffed each other.

Max picked up his binoculars and searched for the woman, spotting her talking to the man beneath the tree. "Well, well," he said. "Looks like we caught her red-handed."

Nate sighed. When he had started Raney/Daye investigations with Dr. Daye, he knew he might be exposing himself to some unorthodox cases. But he never expected that the work would challenge his credibility.

Yet here he was, at a dog park, snapping photos through a telephoto lens of a clandestine rendezvous, while Max littered his car with cookie crumbs and popcorn.

To make things worse, it appeared the woman's dog was in heat, and the man's mutt was taking full advantage of her condition.

Nate clicked off a few more shots. "Okay, I think we have enough," he said to Max. Nate twisted around and put the camera into the bag resting on the back seat. The movement sent a twinge of pain up his right shoulder, aggravating the injury that had cost him his career as a police detective.

He paused to let the worst of it pass.

Max noticed. "Shoulder still bugging you, boss?"

"No, it's fine. I just twisted it a little."

"Want me to drive?" Max asked.

"That would be a hard 'no,'" Nate replied.

He started the car and pulled away.

They didn't have far to go. Nate's client owned a pet shop near the dog park. Luckily, they found a parking spot in front of the store. Nate popped the memory card out of the camera, grabbed a laptop computer and got out of the car.

Max got out on his side. "Not a bad day's work," he said, trying to cheer Nate up.

Nate grunted. He just wanted to get this over with.

Max held the pet shop door open for Nate, then followed his old partner inside. They headed straight for a counter at the back. Nate rang the old-fashioned brass bell sitting on the Formica.

A man emerged from behind a curtain. He was covered in white fur. "Ah, Detective Raney, Max, I didn't expect to see you so soon."

Max patted Nate on the back. "Hey, Burt. I told you my boy was the best."

Burt seemed nervous. "Do I want to know?"

"You might as well see the photos," Nate advised. "You pay the same either way."

"All right, let's get this over with," Burt said.

Nate opened his laptop and slid the memory card into a slot on the side. A photo viewing app opened automatically, bringing up the first picture of the woman walking her dog into the park.

"Oh, Ghiselle," Burt lamented.

Nate tapped the arrow key to advance through the photos. They showed Ghiselle as she made her way through the park toward the tree, and her meeting with the man and his mixed-breed dog.

Burt's eyes filled with tears.

"Do you want me to stop?" Nate asked.

"No, I need to see this," Burt insisted.

"Be strong, pal," Max urged.

Nate scrolled through the photos of the man and the woman laughing jovially with each other, on to the pictures that included the two dogs humping.

Burt looked away from the screen, sobbing. "I can't believe it. I feel so betrayed."

Nate followed the man's gaze to a framed photo on the wall of the shop, a portrait of the Afghan Hound.

Burt walked over and took the photo down from the wall. "I had such plans for you. You were going to be the dam of champions."

"To be fair," Max interjected, "it was your wife that took her to the dog park…"

"I thought I raised her better," Burt replied, shaking his head, placing the photo face down on the counter.

"I'm very sorry it turned out like this," Nate said. "And I hate to appear insensitive at such a moment, but I do need to ask you to settle the bill." He pulled a folded sheet of paper from his inside jacket pocket. "As Max told you, my rate is five hundred a day plus expenses, but there weren't any expenses for this case, so an even five hundred will cover it. You can make the check out to Raney/Daye Investigations."

Burt took the invoice from Nate and stared at it.

Max nudged Nate and whispered in his ear. "What do you mean 'no expenses'? What about my stakeout snacks?"

Nate ignored Max's question.

"Wow, the whole five hundred? I mean, how long did it take you to get these photos? Ten, fifteen minutes, tops?"

"That's not the way it works," Nate tried to explain.

"I thought maybe it would be around forty or fifty dollars." Burt looked to Max. "I only agreed to hire you as a favor to Max. I could have taken these photos myself for free."

Nate shook his head. He was hoping this payday would help offset the humiliation he felt for taking the job in the first place. He was a detective with twenty years of experience who had to stoop to staking out a promiscuous dog. Could things get any worse?

"You know, Burt, Nate has a dog himself. What do you say we work out some kind of trade?" Max suggested in answer to Nate's silent question.

CHAPTER THREE

Nate pulled up to his house and parked.

His home was a large, four-bedroom, two-story frame building with a downstairs den, which was now an office he shared with Dr. Daye. He had inherited it from his great-uncle Bill, who, along with his wife, Lillian, hosted Nate and his cousins there for long weekends and extended summer stays. Bill and Lillian never had children of their own, but enjoyed spoiling all their nieces and nephews whenever possible.

After Lillian passed away, Bill found it difficult to live in such a large house by himself and moved to a convalescent home. Nate had been able to afford the property taxes on his detective's salary, but since he'd taken an early disability retirement, money was starting to get tight.

Nate had decided to hang out his shingle as a private detective in the hope that his friends in the department might throw some consulting work his way from time to time. His partnership with Jennifer was supposed to round out that business plan, bringing in a steady case load.

Jennifer did have a robust backlog of cases to investigate. But he quickly discovered that most of the people didn't have the means to pay for their services. The divorce cases and corporate background checks he'd been avoiding were looking more and more appealing as his bank account dwindled.

Nate noticed that Jennifer's van was not parked in its usual spot. This wasn't one of her teaching days, so he expected to find her here. More importantly, he was hoping the fee they were expecting from her investigation at the Young house would offset his own disappointing experience.

He walked around to the rear of the SUV and opened the back. There were three giant bags of dog food stacked there. He had been reduced to bartering his services for kibble.

The idea of lifting the heavy bags and hauling them into the house was daunting. Dr. Daye's graduate assistant, Dave, could bring them in later. Or maybe someone at the gas company would be willing to trade the dog food for the balance on this month's bill.

As he approached the house, he became aggravated to see the front door open. Although the storm door was closed, his dog, Madge, was an accomplished escape artist. She would exploit any opportunity to get outside and explore.

Nate opened the door, entered and let it close loudly, hoping that whoever had left it open would hear him.

The living room was empty of any of Dr. Day's college student staff.

He crossed through the kitchen to the office he shared with Jennifer at the back of the house.

Both rooms were similarly vacant.

Except for Madge, snoring away in her spot on the couch in the office.

Nate stared at the oversized vintage poster of Harry Houdini hanging on one wall, then to the equally large poster across from it of The Mysterious Professor, Dr. Daye's alter ego from her own days as a professional magician. He always felt that she was giving him a judgmental stare.

On his side of the large partners desk that filled most of the room, Nate noticed a check. He breathed a sigh of relief. One of Jennifer's investigations finally paid off.

He picked it up and looked at the amount.

Instead of the three-hundred-dollar minimum fee he and Dr. Daye had agreed on, it was made out for fifty dollars.

"Hey, Detective Raney. What are you doing here?"

"This is my house," Nate answered. "I live here."

He turned to face Dave Edwards, who was standing in the doorway to the office holding a Hot Pocket in one hand, while his other arm hugged a stack of binders. The graduate assistant seemed nervous and embarrassed, shuffling his weight from foot to foot, trying to decide if it was better to walk away or not.

"I-I know," Dave stammered. "I meant I thought you would be at your appointment with Dr. Daye and your mother."

Nate glanced at his watch. "Is that today?" he asked.

"Yeah," Dave answered. "I put it on your calendar."

Nate had completely forgotten that this was the day he was supposed to meet his mother's favorite psychic. He and his mother had frequently fought over the money she spent on mediums who claimed they were putting her in contact with Nate's deceased father. At the moment, the two of them had reached a state of détente, but it was Nate's ultimate goal to convince his mother that these people were charlatans and frauds.

He had agreed to meet the psychic as long as Jennifer was there too. Insisting on having Dr. Daye there was a risk—she truly believed that people could make contact with the dead. But he had also witnessed her debunk a psychic who was trying to bilk a millionaire who was pledging a major donation to the university's anthropology department. Her actions derailed the endowment—along with her already shaky relationship with her dean. That was part of the reason she had moved her operation to Nate's house.

"Should I call and tell them you're not coming?" Dave asked.

Nate shook his head. He didn't want to put this off, and with any luck he could make it to the storefront parlor the psychic used in time. "No, I'll text them on my way over. Thanks for the reminder, Dave," Nate added.

"No problem, detective," Dave replied.

Nate tossed the check back onto the desk. He would discuss that with Jennifer later.

CHAPTER FOUR

The room was small and dimly lit by candles placed at random throughout. In the middle of the chamber was a round table, surrounded by four upholstered antique chairs. Soothing, atonal music played.

Sitting in the largest chair was Harmony Fortuna, a heavyset woman with pure white hair. She wore a generous amount of makeup, her ears were pierced from the lobe all the way up to the top, and she had layers of chains draped around her ample neck.

Eleanor Raney sat to her left, smiling nervously. She was plainly dressed but her hair was immaculate, straight from the hairdresser as if she wanted to make sure she looked her best.

Jennifer sat opposite Nate's mother. She checked her phone.

"Anything from Nate?" Eleanor asked.

"No, but I'm sure he'll be here any minute."

Harmony seemed unperturbed by the delay as she sat with her eyes closed. She had told Eleanor that it would be an extra charge to have more people at the session, and the woman had eagerly agreed, so she didn't mind if one of the party was a few minutes late.

The bell on the front door tinkled. "Hello?" Nate called from the other room.

"Back here, dear," Eleanor called back.

A moment later, Nate parted the beaded curtain that separated the

41

two rooms.

Eleanor smiled at him.

Jennifer gave him a look that conveyed just how lucky he was that he made it there in time.

"Come, sit here," Eleanor said, waving at the empty chair opposite Harmony.

"Sorry I'm late," he said, but offered no further explanation. He looked around the room, seeing all the clichéd trappings of a side-show fortune teller. "Seriously?" he whispered to Jennifer.

"I know it's a little kitschy, but some mediums find it helps set a mood that their clients expect," she whispered back.

"Well, I already know what I expect," he replied.

Harmony opened her eyes. "Are we all ready?" she asked in a deep, soft voice.

"I'm ready," answered Eleanor, who closed her eyes, tilted her head back slightly and took a deep breath of the incense-filled air.

"Yes," added Jennifer. She had promised Nate she would watch for any signs of deception but encouraged Nate to keep his mind open to the possibility that many mediums did actually communicate with the deceased. At the very least, she extracted a promise that he would be respectful. She shot an expectant look at Nate.

Nate took a breath, swallowing the sarcastic comment that he wanted to utter. He glanced at his mother, who looked like she was meditating. "I'm good to go," he finally said.

Jennifer gave him a steely glance, warning him to behave.

Harmony placed her thick arms on the table, reaching toward El-eanor and Jennifer with her palms up. "Let's join hands and com-plete the circle," she said.

The two women each placed their hands in Harmony's, then reached out to Nate. Nate sat up straight and took their hands, sup-pressing his annoyance at having to participate in the absurd ritual.

Harmony took in a deep breath. "Please close your eyes."

Eleanor already had hers closed—an obvious veteran of the expe-rience—and Jennifer joined her. Nate kept his eyes open until Jen-nifer peeked to check on him. He rolled his eyes, then closed them.

Harmony began moaning in a soft, melodic tone. "We call upon the spirit of Benjamin Raney, beloved husband of Eleanor, devoted father of Nathaniel. Your family wishes to hear from you, Ben. If you're here, please make your presence known."

As Harmony moaned, a gust of cold wind passed over them.

Eleanor shivered and smiled.

Nate shook his head.

Jennifer listened for the telltale sound of a fan spinning, but the music obscured any ambient sounds.

"Is that you, Ben?" Harmony asked.

A tinny bell rang.

"Oh, Ben, my darling," Eleanor said, smiling even broader.

"I can feel him. He is with us." The medium paused for a moment, as if listening to a voice only she could hear. "He wants to know... he senses conflict. It's making it hard for him to... Ben, stay with us."

"Ben," Eleanor pleaded, "I'm here. And so is Nate. He doesn't believe you can speak with us, but if you talk to him, I know you can convince him. We both miss you so much."

Harmony sighed and moaned.

Eleanor squeezed Nate's hand. "Tell him, Nate. Tell your father that you love him."

Nate paused before responding, remembering Jennifer's advice to at least accept that his mother believed she was talking to his father. "Hi, Dad," he said, then added, "How are you doing?"

Eleanor's grip on Nate's hand relaxed. Jennifer gave his other hand an appreciative squeeze.

Harmony's moans subsided. "He wants you to know that he's been watching over you," she said. "He's glad that you... that you didn't join him in crossing over. It wasn't your time. Does that mean anything to you?"

"Oh, yes," Eleanor said excitedly. "Nate was shot on duty. We nearly lost him."

"Ah..." Harmony said, pleased. "I can sense that in his aura."

"Or you can read a newspaper," Nate added snidely under his breath.

"Stop it," Jennifer warned him in a whisper.

Eleanor ignored the comment. "Ben, please talk to your son, convince him."

Suddenly, the table wobbled.

Harmony sucked in a breath.

"Oh, my," Eleanor exclaimed. "Ben, is that you?"

The table slowly rose a few inches, then sort of hovered in place, as if it was a raft resting in a pool of water.

"Oh, Ben. Thank you," Eleanor said. She opened her eyes and looked over at her son.

Nate took his hands back and bent over, lifting the cloth that was draped over the table to peer underneath.

"Mr. Raney, please don't break the circle!" Harmony cried.

The table sank back down to the floor.

"What do you have under there?" Nate asked. "A couple of switches under the rug you press with your feet to blast the cold air, ring the bell and raise the table? I've seen better magic shows at kids' birthday parties."

Harmony sighed and sank back in her chair. Her head collapsed forward, her chin on her chest. "He's gone. I'm sorry, Eleanor, I tried to hold on."

"I know you did, dear," Eleanor said consolingly.

"Oh, come on," Nate pleaded. He turned to Jennifer. "Don't you have anything to say? I know you didn't fall for this Vegas lounge act. You're too smart for that."

"This is not the way I wanted to handle this, Nate," Jennifer replied.

"I'm afraid all of this negative energy is driving away the spirits. I don't think we'll hear from Ben or anyone else today." Harmony turned to Eleanor. "I need to go lie down. I'm sorry, but I have to ask you all to leave." She reached into a pocket and pulled out a collection of twenty-dollar bills folded up together. "Here, you should have this back." She offered the money to Eleanor.

Eleanor pushed it away. "Oh, no, dear. It wasn't your fault, you keep it. Thank you for trying."

"Oh, for goodness' sake, Mom, take the money," Nate said.

Eleanor looked at her son reproachfully. "You promised you wouldn't misbehave," she said to him. "I'm very disappointed."

Those words shut Nate up. He had agreed to sit through the whole thing, allow Jennifer to do a complete evaluation, and consider her opinion. And he had broken that promise.

"I'm sorry, Mom, but I couldn't just sit there—"

"I'm not the one you need to apologize to," Eleanor admonished.

Nate looked at his mother. Eleanor nodded toward Harmony, who sat back in her chair, expectantly. He shifted his gaze to Jennifer, who offered no support. "Forget it," Nate said. "I can't believe you two are so gullible, but I'm not playing along with this charade." He looked at Harmony. "You're a fraud. My mother may not believe it, and Dr. Daye may not want to say it out loud, but you're a fake, phony huckster, and I have nothing to apologize for."

Harmony's eyes started to tear. Her mouth turned down into a frown and she started to shake with sobs.

"Great, now the waterworks start," Nate added.

"I think you should go," Eleanor said to her son while reaching out a comforting hand to Harmony's shoulder. She looked at Jennifer. "Dr. Daye, would you be able to give me a ride home?"

Jennifer cast an I-told-you-so glance at Nate, then smiled at the elderly woman. "Of course."

Nate shook his head. He pushed his chair back, stood up and exited through the beaded curtain.

"Why can't he see that his father is trying to reach out to him?" Eleanor asked Jennifer.

Jennifer shrugged. "I know he can be stubborn, but he's just looking out for you."

Eleanor sighed. "I just want him to be able to talk to Ben like I do."

"Maybe it's not something he wants," Jennifer offered.

"But why wouldn't he?"

"Maybe you should ask him."

CHAPTER FIVE

Nate entered his house, still furious over how he had somehow become the bad guy when all he was doing was trying to prevent his mother from getting conned by a side-show palm reader.

The room was filled with the sounds of warfare. Machine gun rounds and grenade explosions emanated from the television.

Sitting across from it were two college-age kids. Emily sat with her legs folded under her, hunched over a video game controller, staring unblinkingly at the screen.

The young man sitting next to her, Bits, exuded nerd. He was skinny and always seemed to be suffering from one skin condition or another.

Bits wasn't a student—as far as anyone could tell. He was Dr. Daye's tech guy and built and maintained the equipment she used in her investigations. Judging from the expression on his face, the virtual battle he was in with Emily was not going in his favor.

"This is not a dorm room, you two," Nate said over the din.

There was no response.

Madge trotted into the room, sat at Nate's feet, and whined pleadingly.

Nate looked down at the poodle and glowered. "Shut up, dog," he said harshly.

Madge bowed her head, then trotted off to a nearby corner. She curled up into a furry ball and closed her eyes.

Nate returned his attention to the gamers on his couch. "Can you guys take that somewhere else? This is my home, not an arcade."

"Almost done," Emily responded in a dispassionate monotone.

There was a big explosion on the television. Bits threw up his arms in exasperation. "You were so lucky," he said defensively.

"If by lucky you mean superior to you in every way, then yes, I was lucky," Emily responded.

"Rematch," Bits said, pressing buttons on his controller.

"No match," Nate said as he turned off the television. "You guys have your own rooms. Why do you need to invade my space?"

"We're taking a break," Bits explained.

"I thought this was like a common area," Emily offered. "You never made a big deal about it before."

"Yeah, well, from now on the living room is off limits," Nate declared.

"Fine. No problem. We'll make sure to stay off your lawn, too," Emily added sarcastically.

She and Bits tossed their game controllers onto the coffee table and slunk out of the living room, heading up the stairs to the bedrooms that had been converted into offices for them. Previously they had been using space provided by the university, but Dr. Daye's ongoing conflict with the dean had gotten them kicked out of the department offices despite her tenure. Two of the most recent were a basement and a gymnasium equipment room, so it wasn't too much of a loss.

Madge lifted her head from her corner exile, emitting a soft whine.

"Not now, Madge, I'm not in the mood," Nate admonished.

The dog rested her chin on her paws and watched as Nate crossed over to the couch and inspected the empty wrappers stuck between the cushions and the crumbs covering them. He brushed some away.

He cringed as the motion caused a pain deep in his shoulder, a reminder of the gunshot wound that cut short his career. He had been on his way toward recovery, but then one rainy night, on top of an apartment building roof, he had aggravated the injury during a confrontation with an octogenarian serial killer. In the struggle to save himself and Jennifer, he had torn muscles and detached ligaments, kicking off a whole new round of surgeries.

Weeks earlier, he had finally shed the sling his arm had been cradled in for months, and even though he religiously followed the instructions of his physical therapist, his range of motion and strength were still greatly diminished. If he slept on it wrong, the next day he would have constant pain.

Nate reached into his jacket pocket and pulled out a prescription bottle. He opened it and tapped two pills into his palm, tossed them to the back of his throat and swallowed them dry.

"Careful, you don't want to get hooked on those things," Emily warned from the base of the stairway.

"Thanks for the unsolicited advice," Nate replied dismissively.

Emily walked over and grabbed the notebook she had left behind on an end table. "You should be tapering off those by now," she added.

"When did you get your medical degree?" Nate asked with a smirk.

"The day I found my cousin dead in his bed from a fentanyl overdose," she replied.

Nate turned away, hiding his embarrassment. But he wasn't in the mood to be lectured by some college kid. "I'm fine," he assured her. "And I'd appreciate you keeping out of my personal business as well as my living room."

Emily shrugged, then turned around and went up the stairs.

Nate closed his eyes. This day was not getting any better. He took a deep breath, trying to let go of his stress. After a moment, the pain started to ebb, and his head cleared. He went to the kitchen.

At the counter, Dave put a sandwich on a plate, and then started to carry it toward the office.

Nate cleared his throat.

Dave turned around, looked at Nate, then followed the detective's gaze to the mess he had left behind. "Sorry," Dave said. He put the sandwich down and started closing up the various bags and containers he had opened.

"If you can't keep this place clean, I'm going to revoke your kitchen privileges," Nate warned.

"I know, you're right. I don't usually leave a mess, but Dr. Daye wants me to file a grant proposal that's due in..." he checked his watch, "... less than three hours."

"A grant proposal? I hope it's enough to cover our expenses."

"Well, it's supposed to be used exclusively for field work, so I'm not sure it would apply," Dave explained nervously.

"Maybe you'd be more useful finding us clients who can actually pay," Nate countered.

"I'm trying," Dave said. He carried an armful of sandwich fixings to the refrigerator and put them away. "But Dr. Daye is always more interested in the other kind."

"The kind where the people are broke, and we end up losing money?" Nate asked rhetorically.

Dave shrugged and put away the last of the sandwich supplies. "I'm trying, Detective Raney, but you know Dr. Daye."

Nate nodded.

"What about Dr. Daye?" Jennifer asked from the passage to the living room. Madge was at her side, excitedly wagging her tail as Jennifer scratched behind her ears.

"You need to have a word with your staff about respecting my home," Nate said to her.

Jennifer looked at Dave, who shrugged. "My staff? What's wrong?" she asked Nate. "Are you still upset about—"

"Why do you assume this is all about me? Your *kids* are making a mess of my home. I can't walk around this place without tripping over someone's backpack or a box of photos, or that damn dog."

"Madge is your dog," Jennifer pointed out.

"That's not the point," Nate countered.

"What is the point?"

"This is not how things were supposed to be," Nate said. His eyes were wide with anger and frustration. "We're not taking in any money. There are messes everywhere. People come and go at all hours, seven days a week, and when I ask you for one thing. One little thing: tell my mother that the psychic scammers she's giving all her money to are ripping her off, you can't even do that."

Jennifer paused to let Nate cool down. "I agreed to assess Harmony and give Eleanor my professional opinion. *You* were the one who interrupted the séance before I could do it," she pointed out calmly.

"Come on, you know all that stuff with the cold breeze and the rising table were just parlor tricks."

"Agreed," Jennifer replied. "But sometimes genuine psychics add a little showmanship if they think their clients expect it. But that doesn't exclude them from having a legitimate connection to the consciousness of those who have passed."

Nate rolled his eyes. "Fine. I give up. You and my mother can go on talking to my dead dad. I wash my hands of the whole thing." He turned to Dave. "Find us a client who can pay. That's what you're here for. Do your job."

Nate opened the fridge, pulled out a bottle of beer, and twisted off the cap. He felt a twinge as the effort reawakened the pain in his shoulder. He took a swig and waited, daring anyone to say something. When no one did, he strode out of the kitchen and headed upstairs to his room.

Madge nuzzled against Dr. Daye's leg. Jennifer kneeled down and scratched the dog's muzzle with both hands. "Don't worry, girl, he'll be okay."

"Sounds like the séance didn't go well," Dave said.

"Nate's got a lot on his mind, and he's not the type of man who likes to talk about his feelings or share his burdens. But he does have a point. Do we have any potential paying clients?" she asked.

"I don't know. I've been working on the grant proposal."

"Forget about that. Start going through our inbox and see if you can find something—anything—so at least he doesn't need to worry about the bills. Come on, I'll help."

Jennifer led the way to the office.

Dave and Madge dutifully followed.

CHAPTER SIX

Greg and Marcia Foreman loved their old Victorian farmhouse. They had picked it up for a song, considering how close it was located to San Francisco. It was a bit of a fixer upper. The previous owner had done very little to update it, and there were rumors in town that a woman had died in the house. But Marcia was in love with its idyllic and isolated setting. There were woods right outside the back door for the kids to play in, like she remembered doing as a child. Despite its condition and history, it was worth the effort.

They had gutted the kitchen and bathrooms to update the plumbing and most of the electrical. As much as Marcia liked the rustic exterior, she absolutely needed a modern kitchen and bathrooms. The rest of the house needed some rehab as well. She and Greg had stripped the walnut trim and molding to the bare wood, steamed off the multiple layers of wallpaper, and tore out the musty carpeting. Luckily, most of the original flooring was still intact and just needed to be refinished.

The exterior of the house was Marcia's pride and joy. After scraping off all the loose paint, she put a fresh coat on the wood siding, the ornate balustrades and the hand-carved pieces adorning the gables and eaves. She used a colorful, eclectic palate, and you couldn't help but notice the house as you drove by.

Greg had spent the spring planting a flower garden in front of the wide porch. He found some perennials that complimented the colors Marcia had picked out. Their blooms were fragrant and beautiful. It had taken them over a year to complete all the work, but it paid off. They had made a home.

Greg worked in town managing the local warehouse store. Marcia worked from home, doing web development. They had two children, Danny was ten and loved to read and draw, and Daisy, who was six and idolized her brother, but most of the time preferred to play with the dollhouse her father had built that was a scale model of their home.

It was a typical morning in the Foreman household. Greg and Marcia shared the chores of cleaning up after breakfast—cereal with fruit today—and packing lunches for the kids and Greg.

Marcia checked her watch. "You need to get going soon. Where are the kids?"

"Probably playing. Do you really expect them to be standing at attention by the front door waiting to go to school?" Greg asked playfully.

She sighed. "A mom can dream, can't she?"

Greg smiled. "I'll finish here. You go wrangle the kids."

Marcia gave him a peck on the cheek and then went off in search of the children. Just to make sure, she checked by the front door to see if they were perhaps standing there, waiting patiently with their book bags and their clothes all properly buttoned and zipped. They weren't.

She continued on through the living room and up the stairs to the second floor where the bedrooms were. There were four of them, a reasonably sized master bedroom for Marcia and Greg, smaller rooms for the kids and an extra they had set up as a guest room.

Marcia went to Daisy's room first. The little girl was kneeling in front of the dollhouse, posing her dolls—some of whom were far too big for the tiny structure—and providing the voices for a conversation in which they were all exchanging compliments about how lovely they looked today. Marcia paused to watch her daughter at play. Daisy had a rich imagination, a trait both kids inherited from their mother.

"Miss Violet, wherever did you get that wonderful hat?" Daisy asked in what sounded like a southern accent. "Oh, this old thing?" she replied with a bit of an English lilt. "Thank you, that's very kind."

"Daisy," Marcia said, interrupting. "Time to go. Do you have your things together?"

The little girl, wearing a gingham dress and long white stockings, looked up at her mother and nodded. "Uh-huh." She stood up and grabbed her *Frozen* themed Disney backpack off the bed and rushed past her mom down the stairs.

Marcia continued on to Danny's room. The door was ajar. She pushed it open, expecting to see him reading on his bed, or at his desk drawing some fantastical alien monster. But he wasn't there. "Danny?" she asked, wondering if he was hiding from her under the bed or in his closet. "Time for school!" she said.

There was no answer.

She exited the room and checked the upstairs bathroom. He wasn't there, either.

"Danny?" she called out.

Again, no answer.

Leaning over the banister, she called downstairs. "Daisy, is your brother down there?"

"Nope," her daughter answered.

Marcia was going to head down the stairs to check for herself when she noticed the door to the guest room at the end of the hall was open partway.

As she approached, she could hear her son engaged in a one-sided conversation.

"Danny?" she asked, softly.

He either didn't hear Marcia or was ignoring her.

Marcia pushed the door open and peeked inside.

The guest room was the one room in the house that hadn't gotten a modern makeover. Marcia wanted to keep it close to the original, she even found an antique wallpaper to decorate the walls, and the carpeting had been ripped up and replaced by a large area rug.

Danny was perched on one corner of the four-poster bed, his feet dangled off the edge. He was staring at a rocking chair in the corner of the room.

"She's okay, for a little sister," he said, answering a question Marcia didn't hear. Danny continued, "Kind of, but I'd have to share my toys with a brother, so having a sister is okay."

Marcia stepped into the room. "Danny, time to leave for school."

Danny looked at his mother and hopped off the bed. "Okay." Then he turned to the rocking chair. "I have to go to school now. I'll see you later." Then he walked out of the room, squeezing past his mother as if nothing unusual had happened.

An imaginary friend? Marcia wondered to herself. She followed Danny to his room and watched as he stuffed books and notepads from his desk into his backpack.

"Who were you talking to?" she asked.

Without looking at her, Danny answered. "Maureen."

"Is Maureen a friend from school?"

"No, she's an old lady, like you. She says she used to live here. We're friends," he said, then slung his backpack over his shoulders and squeezed by her once again on his way downstairs.

Marcia took a moment to absorb what Danny had told her. First of all, she wasn't "old," but a not-quite-middle-aged woman was still an odd choice for an imaginary friend.

"We're off," Greg called from downstairs.

Marcia left Danny's room and hurried down the stairs to wish them all a good day. Greg and the kids headed for the minivan as Marcia watched them go from the front door.

Once they disappeared down the street, she closed the door and looked back upstairs, wondering if she should be concerned about Danny. She brushed the thought aside and turned her attention to the backlog of work piled up on her desk.

CHAPTER SEVEN

The quarterly Department of Anthropology meeting was held in a medium-sized lecture hall even though the number of instructors and administrators present was far below the room's capacity.

Jennifer sat a few rows back on the aisle. She had the meeting agenda in her hands and was obviously angry. The specific topic she had submitted was not on the list of new business.

To be honest, she hadn't expected it to be considering her strained relationship with the dean, but it still stung.

They had been hired as young adjunct professors at the same time. She went on to earn her tenure as a full professor, he became an administrator. Along the way, his disdain for her pursuits in the field of the paranormal grew, and he weaponized any media attention that tied her "ghost hunting" to the university against her.

Dr. Daye remained silent throughout the meeting, but stared directly at the dean as he ran the proceedings from the dais. Whenever he would look up at the audience, if he met her glare, he would quickly look away.

The meeting proceeded through old business, updates on university policies and then on to new business. When the published agenda had been exhausted, the dean asked perfunctorily if there was any other new business.

Jennifer stood up. "Yes, there is. I have a new course I've proposed for the fall semester that is missing from the agenda," she said, holding up the stapled papers.

"I don't believe all the requisite forms have been submitted," the dean replied, shutting down her complaint. "If there is no other new business, the chair moves—"

"Oh, they've been submitted." Jennifer picked up a thick folder from the seat next to her. "I have all the required documentation, along with all the requisite confirmations and signatures. I jumped through all your hoops, dotted all my I's and crossed all my T's. I even submitted a list of over one hundred students who are interested in taking the course."

"And which course would this be?" the dean asked, making a show of shuffling through the papers scattered in front of him.

"Anthropology and the Paranormal."

The dean gave up looking. "I can't seem to find my copy. Perhaps we can address this at the next—"

"I have a copy for you," Jennifer said, and pulled a sheaf of collated and sticky-note annotated forms and printouts from the folder. She made a show of walking down the aisle, up onto the dais and placing them in front of the dean.

He smiled at her, the smile of a toad eying a passing fly. "Well, like I said, maybe we can discuss it at next quarter's meeting. There is no motion before the chair to consider it at this time."

A young woman, seated near the rear of the auditorium, rose to her feet. "I make a motion to consider Dr. Daye's course," she said loudly.

Everyone turned around to see who had spoken.

It was Heather Long, a recently hired adjunct professor. She smiled supportively at Jennifer.

Another member of the audience, an older woman, Helen Abara, rose to her feet. The whiteness of her hair and the darkness of her skin were a striking contrast. "I second the motion," she said. "If Dr. Daye has a course that will boost enrollment for the department, I say we should hear about it, Robert."

The dean took a deep breath, realizing he wasn't going to get away with just dismissing Jennifer's course out of hand. "Very well. A motion to consider is before the chair. All those who support the motion say 'Aye.'"

A loud chorus of "ayes" issued forth.

"Opposed, say 'Nay.'"

A much less enthusiastic collection of "nays" followed.

"In the opinion of the chair, the vote is in the negative and the motion to consider is defeated."

A murmur of disagreement rumbled through the audience.

The dean banged his gavel. It sounded more like a weak door knock than a resounding call to order.

Helen raised her voice above the growing din. "I move for a hand count," she said. Her authoritative voice commanded respect, and everyone quieted down.

Jennifer smiled. Dr. Abara had always been a supportive mentor, both in her anthropology work and her parapsychology investigations.

"I second the motion," Heather added from the back of the room.

The dean looked at the assistant dean and the department secretary. They didn't seem eager to provide him with a way out of counting each vote. "All those in favor of considering Dr. Daye's course, raise your hand," he said reluctantly.

More than two-thirds of the attendees raised their hands. The department secretary counted them and wrote the number down.

"All those opposed," the dean said, the arrogance that normally dominated his tone now absent.

An obviously lesser number of hands was raised. The secretary counted, put the number next to the other and handed it to the dean.

The dean didn't bother to look at it. "The motion passes. The proposal for Dr. Daye's course will advance to the curriculum committee." He consulted a sheet of paper. "The next meeting is scheduled for December."

Jennifer glared at him.

"Is there anything else, Dr. Daye?" he asked smugly.

Jennifer shook her head and returned to her seat.

Once the meeting concluded, she gathered up her things.

Dr. Abara approached her. "Chin up. In case you forgot, I am the chair of the curriculum committee," she told Jennifer. "I have a feeling we're going to be meeting well before December," she said with a conspiratorial smile.

"Thanks," Jennifer said. "Honestly, what do you think the chances are?"

"Well, Robert is definitely capable of putting up obstacles, but I think we'll get it through, if not for next semester, soon. Be patient. This is academia, not Silicon Valley."

Heather Long approached the two women. "So, are these department meetings always so exciting?" she asked. Heather was a great "get" for the department. She had studied at Princeton and had already published a few papers on indigenous tribes in Australia. Jennifer knew her in passing, but based on her actions in the meeting, she wanted to get to know her a lot better.

"Get used to it," Helen said. "'Science moves, but slowly, slowly...'" she quoted.

"Tennyson sure knew what he was talking about," Jennifer added. "Can I buy you a coffee? Or better yet, a drink?" she asked.

"Not me. It's almost my bedtime. You two go out and celebrate. Every step forward is a victory."

"George Bernard Shaw?" Heather asked.

"That one is all Helen Abara," the older professor answered.

CHAPTER EIGHT

Dale Everly lay in the cot where he had spent much of the last fifteen years. The possessions he had accumulated during his incarceration had been distributed among the few men he had called friends, and a few others whom he owed favors.

Fifteen years.

He probably could have gotten far less if he had been cooperative, but they had killed Maureen. His wife had been murdered by those trigger-happy cops, and he wasn't interested in helping them find the money and valuables she had hidden. He hadn't even participated in his defense. There was a trial. The judge had entered a plea of not guilty during his arraignment, and his public defender tried to present his case. Dale was content to just let the justice system carry him along with it, condemn him, and cart him off to prison for what added up to a third of his life.

He had been offered deals, a shorter sentence if he cooperated in recovering the missing loot. Apparently among the items they had emptied from the safe deposit boxes was a diamond necklace worth undisclosed millions that the owner—or rather the owner's insurance company—was desperate to recover.

He couldn't care less.

The truth was, he had no idea where his wife had left the money. If he had to guess, it was buried in the woods behind their house, but where exactly he had no idea. And any thoughts he did have, he wasn't going to share with the system that had killed the love of his life. No time outside of prison, no amount of money was going to bring her back.

He was twenty-nine the day he entered prison.

Maureen was twenty-five the day the Danville Police killed her.

When he was caught, and the chief had ordered him to raise his hands, the first thoughts that ran through his mind was that he had been double-crossed by their inside man.

Then, after they had taken him to the station and booked him, he overheard a radio call that the suspect was dead. They had blown it. Any leverage they might have had over Dale, the opportunity to exploit the doubt he felt about being betrayed went right out the window.

Dale never saw Maureen again. He wasn't even allowed to attend her funeral.

He never told anyone about the third person that was part of the heist, or the Mastermind who had recruited them all. Not out of any sense of loyalty, but because he didn't want to help the police in any way.

Their plan had been a good one. They had timed their egress from the bank to coincide with the morning roll call—which occurred an hour before the bank opened. The majority of the police would be attending the daily briefing, while the overnight shift would be heading back to the station.

Dale had managed to piece together the events of that morning that contributed to him getting caught and Maureen killed. They never could have anticipated a young girl going missing, drawing virtually all of Danville's police to the downtown area.

But even with that, there should have been enough time for Deputy McDonald to send a message to warn them. Something had gone wrong.

When they received the page, instead of the eight minutes they were counting on, the police were able to converge on the bank from multiple directions in less than two.

Maureen had gotten away from the bank. The contingency plan she had, "Operation Soccer Mom," had obviously worked that far.

With the unfortunate happenstance of the station janitor recognizing Dale, it didn't take long for them to discover that he was married, and the couple was living in Maureen's old family home on the outskirts of town.

It still should have been enough time for Maureen to make her escape, but the police had caught up to her while she was still in the house. Her attempt to escape into the woods through an attic window was thwarted by a bullet.

Liam had not reached out to Dale personally, never sent him a letter or came to visit. But he did manage to get messages to Dale via other prisoners. He'd pay off family members of other inmates to pass along notes. But Dale never responded.

After a while, the queries stopped. Either Liam had given up—maybe even died—or perhaps had discovered where Maureen had hidden the money and valuables after all. Though if that had happened, he had a feeling he would have heard about it one way or another.

Dale's time in prison hardened his soul. He went through all the motions of all the rehabilitation programs, but none of them really took. He made no efforts to shorten his sentence with the repeated requests that he tell law enforcement where the money was. Of course, he had his theories, but he kept them to himself.

He sometimes wondered if someone had come across the loot and just walked away with it. He would have.

"Let's go, Everly," a guard said.

Dale sat up, careful not to bump his head on the bunk above him.

The cell door was open at this time of day. He stood up and offered his wrists to the C.O. for handcuffs.

"Put your hands down, Everly," the guard told him. "You're a free man as of two minutes ago. Time for you to get your ugly mug out of my prison."

Dale lowered his arms and found himself standing a little taller. He smiled and walked toward the door to the cell block that connected it to the corridor leading to the intake and outtake areas.

They passed through several doors, each of which buzzed and clicked in succession as he got closer and closer to freedom. He could swear the air was getting sweeter with each step.

Finally, he was led up to the counter of the property room. The guard read the number off his prison issued shirt and then disappeared into a maze of shelves. When he returned, he held a basket that contained the clothes Dale was wearing when he was sentenced—a second-hand suit his second-rate lawyer had bought for him—and an envelope. "You can change over there," the guard told him, nodding toward a door that opened into a closet sized room.

When he emerged, the basket now held his prison grays. The watch that had been a little tight when he went in, hung loosely on his wrist. The wedding ring still fit perfectly.

They handed him a check that represented payment for his work over the years at various prison jobs minus the funds to cover his infrequent purchases at the prison commissary.

"You going to dig up that treasure?" the corrections officer who had escorted him from his cell asked.

"What treasure?" Dale asked.

"Yeah, that's what I thought," the C.O. replied. "Go on, get out of here."

Dale looked at the door marked "Exit." It buzzed and clicked, waiting for him to step through it. He did so. It led him down another short hallway to one final door. He waited in front of it for that harsh buzz and the motorized click, but there was none.

He pushed on the door.

It opened.

The air on this side of the wall was different somehow from the air in the prison yard. The sun was warmer, and a cool breeze reminded him he was still alive.

And free.

CHAPTER NINE

Jennifer pulled up to Nate's house. It was Saturday morning, and after a week dominated by the aftermath of her battle with the dean, she was ready for a break. Robert Patterson had a talent for making her life miserable. If only he would apply some of that energy to improving the department.

She stepped out of the VW and walked up the cement path that led to the broad wooden porch. The name of their joint venture, "Raney/Daye Investigations," was painted on the frosted glass of the front door. It was barely noticeable from the street, but as you walked up to the house, it let you know you were at the right place.

Jennifer pulled the outer storm door open and reached for the door handle. Instead of the round knob she was used to, there was a lever atop a big, bulky keypad. She pushed down on the lever, but discovered it was locked. There was a keyhole on the new digital lock. Jennifer tried her key, but it was a completely different shape. Had she missed a memo?

She rang the bell and heard the chime sound inside the house.

A few moments later, the door opened, revealing Nate wearing what Jennifer had come to think of as his weekend uniform. Pressed khakis, a plain polo shirt and polished loafers. She wondered if he ever wore shorts and a T-shirt.

"What's with the new security?" she asked. "Were we robbed?"

"No, of course not. Unless you count the constant raiding of my re-frigerator by your people."

Jennifer was surprised by Nate's statement. He had always made it clear that Jennifer's staff was welcome to anything in the fridge — although much of it was more suited to Nate's taste rather than the less sophisticated palate of a college student. He always made sure to include more dorm room friendly fare as well.

But that wasn't the part that really bothered her.

"My people?" she asked. "I thought we were a team. Dave does as much work for you as he does for me."

"He also leaves papers and books and files all over the house. Emi-ly thinks my sofa is her dining room, and Bits has rewired everything to the point that I can't even turn my own lights on and off. I gave them all spaces of their own. All I ask is that they respect mine and remember that this is also my home."

"Okay, that sounds entirely reasonable," Jennifer agreed, sensing that there was a growing fury behind Nate's words. "I'll have a talk with them. But that doesn't explain the keypad lock. Are you going to make us all ring the bell when we want to come in? That sounds like a lot of up and down for you."

"You'll each have individual access codes, but they won't work on weekends."

"You don't want us here on weekends? That's when we get the most done. I have obligations at the university during the week. The weekends are the only time we can catch up on our investigations, and all our equipment is here."

"Well, maybe you could keep it at your place."

Jennifer paused. She looked at Nate, concerned. "Can I come in and talk with you about all this? I need to pick up some notes for the *Sunday in San Francisco* show."

Nate stood aside and allowed her to enter.

Madge trotted up to Jennifer and was rewarded with a double scratch behind the ears. She could tell Nate had been cleaning. The house smelled fresh, the coffee table was gleaming with a selection of magazines atop it spread out in mathematical precision. "Getting ready for a photo shoot in *Home Beautiful*?" she asked.

Nate ignored the comment and took a seat in a chair. She could see that he must have been straining his shoulder with all the work he was doing around the house by the fact that his right arm was hanging loosely by his side. He cringed when he placed it on the armrest of the chair.

Jennifer walked toward the sofa and sat on the end closest to Nate. She leaned forward, resting her elbows on her knees with her chin perched on her folded hands. "Is this about the séance?" she asked.

"No," he replied instantly.

She waited for him to expand on his curt answer, but no additional explanation was forthcoming. "Have you talked to your mom? Maybe apologized?"

Nate became offended. "What do I have to apologize for? *You* were the one letting her get bamboozled by that phony psychic."

"I told you, Nate, I didn't have enough information to make a judgment at the time."

"That's bullshit," he insisted. He looked away from her, shaking his head almost imperceptibly.

"So, it's just the extra people in your house seven days a week, not respecting your property and privacy?"

"That's it," he said.

Jennifer nodded. "It has nothing to do with the fact that from all the cases we've investigated over the last six months, we've made only a few hundred dollars?"

"Two-hundred and seventy-five," he corrected.

"All of which has gone toward expenses," Jennifer pointed out. "Dave's salary comes from a grant, and Emily works for class credit and Bits doesn't believe in money—so he's easy."

Nate grunted.

"I understand your concerns. We entered this as partners. And I know I promised we'd be able to turn this into a viable business, but you just need to be patient. Dave and I are chasing down some very promising leads.

"I need you to talk to me when things like this come up. You can't just lock us all out without any warning."

Madge walked up to Nate and placed her chin on his lap. He tried to ignore her, but gave her a scratch on the forehead, anyway.

Jennifer asked a question she didn't want to know the answer to. "Do you want to end this partnership? We can find someplace else. Bits is always offering to hack us into a rent-free penthouse office suite in the Prudential Building."

Nate chuckled at the idea, letting go of some of his frustration and anger. He turned and looked at Jennifer. She was being a friend, just what he probably needed right now, and he was too stubborn to allow himself to take advantage of her empathy and compassion. "No, I don't want you guys to go. And you're right, I should have handled this better. I'm sorry. I've just been feeling a little overwhelmed."

"By the money?"

"No, I get enough from my disability to keep the lights on, though a paying case or two would help."

"Your mother?"

"She and I have been down this road before. We'll sort it out. It's that I'm…"

Nate trailed off.

"Not a cop?" Jennifer asked.

Nate looked at her and then nodded. "Yeah. I really miss it."

Jennifer couldn't help but feel a twinge of guilt over that. It was Nate's effort to save her while she was falling off the roof of a twelve-story apartment building that had led to him taking early retirement from the San Francisco Police Department, the only job he'd ever known. Because of his selfless actions, she was alive, and he was falling down a well of depression.

Jennifer sat up straight and looked around. "What can I do?" she asked.

"About what?" Nate asked back.

"To help you get this place back into shape. I can see you've been ignoring the doctor's advice to use your arm sparingly. I'm your maid for the day," she declared.

Nate smiled skeptically. "You'd be the most highly educated maid in history."

Jennifer rose to her feet. "One of my jobs when I ran a non-profit during college was cleaning the bathrooms."

"That certainly sounds like a very frugal non-profit. I can manage the kitchen, but if you really wouldn't mind taking on the bathrooms—"

The front door opened. Bits stepped in, saw the two of them on the couch.

"How did you unlock that? I haven't given you the codes yet," Nate said.

Bits smiled. "It's kind of cute that you think that an off-the-shelf lock like that could keep me out. I'm going to choose not to be offended, though." He walked through the living room and up the stairs.

Jennifer looked at Nate, expecting a response to Bits' comment.

Nate shrugged. "I thought he might at least try knocking first."

CHAPTER TEN

Maureen Everly knew that she was dead. She no longer felt the passage of time like she used to. She didn't get tired, or hungry, or experience any of the physical needs that used to mark the hours of her day. Exactly how and when that had happened wasn't quite clear.

Memory was a tricky thing. She knew her name, knew that she had lived in this house, and when she wandered from room to room, she could recall specific events that had happened in each of those places. Little by little she had been collecting those memories and piecing back together her life.

Maureen looked out the windows, but never ventured outside. She had a fear that she only existed this way inside the house, and if she left it, she would lose her tenuous hold on this... whatever it was. Was she a ghost? She had a sense that there was some purpose for her, some reason why she hadn't gone to heaven... or maybe hell. But what that reason was, she didn't know.

Maureen couldn't help but smile as she watched Danny sitting at the small desk in his room, drawing intently. He had taken several sheets of paper, folded them in half and was making a comic book. She tried to follow along with the story. Danny was into pirates, and this story featured a very unlucky one named Eric. He had two peg-legs, two hooks for hands and an eye-patch.

It took some time for her to realize the boy could see and hear her. It wasn't until he had turned to her one day and asked if she was a friend of his mom. She told him that she wasn't, that she used to live in the house and was happy to see a new family making it their home.

So far, Danny was the only one who could see or hear Maureen. She had tried talking to other members of the family, but none of them seemed to be aware of her in any way. When he wasn't there, time seemed to skip around. She would watch him go off to school, and then in what seemed like the blink of an eye, he would be back, playing with his sister in the back yard until dinnertime, and then diligently working on his homework and then his drawings until bedtime.

Sometimes, if she focused, she could take in the house around her like she did when she was alive. She would watch a fly buzz around on a windowpane or the sunbeams light up dust motes as they floated across the room.

Moving through the house was different. It was more of an act of will than a physical effort. She would imagine herself across the room, in the hallway, down the stairs, and then find herself in that very spot.

For a long time, before the Foremans moved in, Maureen only remembered being in the room at the end of the hall. It had been her room when she was a child. Although her memories were fuzzy and incomplete, that was something she was certain of. She couldn't remember leaving that room until the day when Marcia and Greg started remodeling the house. She was grateful that they left her room mostly like it was, though the bed was much nicer than the ratty old twin mattress on a rickety frame she remembered.

It was around that time that she began exploring the rest of the house. The changes Marcia had made were very nice and revealed a beautiful house under the layers of paint and wallpaper that had been added over the generations. But she remained fearful to go outside.

One afternoon, she was watching the children play under the large oak through the window of her old room. Danny was making an effort to climb the tree but was unable to grab hold of the lowest branches. He tried to scale up the rough bark of the trunk to get himself closer, and his fingers almost made it around the thick branch, but he came up short and fell to the ground—much to Daisy's amusement.

A memory came to Maureen. She was in that tree.

She fell.

She looked up at the ceiling and a moment later found herself in the attic. Next to the attic window, she could see the foliage of the oak tree within arm's reach.

Then she remembered something else. The attic had been cleaned, and it was now filled with Christmas decorations and other odds and ends, but the Foreman's renovation efforts didn't extend to this space. Below the window, there was a board missing, exposing a space between the studs.

Maureen went to Danny's room, eagerly awaiting his return. The clock told her it would be time for dinner soon, and as if reading her thoughts, she heard Marcia call out to the children to come in and wash up.

A few moments after that, Danny raced into his room. "Hi, Maureen," he said when he saw his friend perched on his bed.

"Hi, Danny. Can you help me with something?" she asked.

"I gotta get ready for dinner," he answered.

"It will only take a minute."

Danny smiled. "Okay." He was curious. Maureen had often talked to him, telling him stories about her childhood and she was a good listener, but she had never asked him to do anything for her before.

"Grab your chair and follow me into the hallway," Maureen said.

Danny obediently picked up the wooden chair in front of his desk and carried it out of his room. Maureen was standing in the middle of the second-floor hallway, below a rectangle in the ceiling that had a chain dangling down from it. Danny had asked his father about it, and he told him it was the attic.

"Come here and stand on the chair. You should be able to reach the chain," Maureen told him.

The boy placed the chair beneath the spot she indicated. The end of the chain was an inch too high, but Danny gave a little jump and managed to grab onto it.

He pulled, and the door swung down, revealing a ladder tucked up inside.

"Move the chair," Maureen instructed.

Danny did so. He inspected the ladder and saw that it unfolded like a grabber toy he had. He grasped the bottom step and pulled it back. It extended much more easily than he had expected. "Are we going up there?" he asked.

"Yes, don't be afraid. It's just like another room."

"I'm not afraid," Danny declared, then started trudging up the steps. There was enough light coming in for Danny to see the piles of boxes and old furniture.

"Over here," Maureen said from the window.

Danny walked over and looked outside. "Wow, I can see the whole yard from up here."

"Yes, it's beautiful," she said.

"Why did you need me to help you get up here? Can't you like walk through walls and ceilings?" Danny asked.

"Kind of," Maureen answered. "But what I need you to do is see if there's a box in that space under the window."

Danny kneeled down and inspected the gap. "I think I see something." He reached inside, oblivious to the cobwebs and dust, and pulled out a slender box.

Maureen had another flash of memories. Of her stuffing the box in the hole before crawling through the window and out into the tree.

"What's inside?" Danny asked.

"Why don't you open it and find out?"

Danny sat on the floor, placed the box in front of him and lifted the lid.

Daisy skipped into the kitchen and sat down at the table.

"Did you wash your hands?" Marcia asked her.

Daisy held up her freshly washed hands for her mom to see.

"Where's your brother?" Greg asked.

"He went up in the ceiling," Daisy told them, as if it was something he did every day.

Marcia and Greg exchanged a puzzled look.

"I'll go see what's going on," Greg offered. He wiped his hands on a dishtowel and walked briskly toward the stairs. About halfway up, he caught sight of the extended attic steps. Then, as he got closer, he saw Danny's desk chair pushed off to the side.

"Danny? Are you up there?"

There was no answer. Greg climbed the ladder to the attic. It only took a few steps for him to spy Danny at the far end of the narrow space, looking through photographs from an old, dusty box. What worried him more was that he appeared to be having a conversation with someone.

"Danny? What are you doing?" he asked as he completed the ascent into the attic and crossed over to where his son was sitting.

"Hi, Dad," Danny said, smiling. "I helped Maureen find her old pictures."

"Maureen?" Marcia had told Greg about Danny's odd imaginary friend, but they had both written it off to his active imagination.

Danny pointed to a photograph of a man and a woman sitting on a porch that looked very much like the one in front of their own home. He tapped the face of the woman. "That's her," he said.

Greg sat down across from Danny and picked up the photo. He turned it over and saw written on the back in casual script, "Maureen and Dale, Summer, '99." He glanced down at the floor. There were a multitude of other photos spread out. Some were contemporaries of the one he held, most of them were much older, black and white snapshots mixed with a few faded Polaroids.

Is this how Danny had come up with his imaginary friend? Had he found these photos and used them as inspiration to bring her to life?

He felt something cold on his shoulder, but when he looked, there was nothing there.

CHAPTER ELEVEN

The town had grown considerably while Dale had been in prison. He barely recognized the downtown area—though the bank he was caught burgling was still there. It had received at least one major makeover and was now part of a larger national financial services company.

The computers he had access to in prison were mostly used in the context of learning skills for his life after incarceration. They were old, outdated and their internet connection was severely locked down. The unrestricted high-speed access he found at the local library blew him away. It was a far cry from the slow-painting screens of the America Online account he had shared with Maureen. And the fact that he could stream videos for free, of almost anything imaginable, had exceeded his expectations. He likened it to a child who had spent his summers in a small splash pool in his backyard, being introduced to the ocean. There was just so much of it.

Although iPhones and Androids weren't available when he went into prison, Dale still knew what a smart phone was. The newer inmates complained about how much they missed them. After the library, he stopped by a mobile phone store. The walls were lined with dozens of variations of the full-screen devices, playing the same content he was able to access in the library, but without any wires tethering them to a specific location.

He remembered when he had bought a flip phone for Maureen on her birthday, one that had a color screen atop the physical keypad. At the time, it was the latest tech and even could take grainy photographs.

The one piece of advice he had taken to heart from the other inmates was to get himself one of the modern devices. These days you couldn't do anything without one. He picked out the cheapest Android model they had, along with a bargain-priced service plan, and returned to the halfway house he had been assigned outside of town near Walnut.

He settled into his room. It was tiny—not much larger than the cell he had recently vacated—but there were no bars, no toilet in the corner and he didn't have to share it with someone who might kill him if he snored too loud. The bed was too soft. It felt like he was lying in a pile of marshmallows. He had a chair and a small desk which he sat down at to unbox the phone.

There was no instruction manual, just a miniature pamphlet that illustrated how to insert the tiny SIM card the salesperson had given him and then turn it on. He declined setting up an email account and skipped the screen where it asked if he wanted to add any contacts.

The icon that indicated the signal strength bounced between one and two bars, but he was still able to use the web browser. Out of curiosity, he plugged his name into the box that asked him what he wanted to search for.

The results that showed up were mostly news articles about the bank job.

One of them had a picture of him with Maureen, his arm around her, both of them smiling for whoever took the photo. He didn't recognize it. But it looked like it was from before when things went bad.

When they were happy.

He turned the phone off and slumped back in his chair. He hadn't thought about what he expected, but life on the outside was nothing like it had been before the robbery. And it was different still from the years he had spent behind bars.

When Dale first arrived in prison, he didn't talk to anyone. He found the narrow social groove between the gangs and lifers with guys like him who just wanted to do their time in peace. Getting to that place wasn't easy. He had endured numerous assaults, some of which left him in the infirmary. But once it was known that he was not interested in participating in the dominant social structure and that he wasn't a threat to anyone, he was mostly left alone.

One exception was Hakim, the jailhouse lawyer. He was a lifer, convicted of killing six rival gang members, and he freely admitted that he was guilty of those crimes. He had discovered the small group of inmates that spent their time among the law books the prison provided in the library and found he could make sense of the convoluted text. He helped other prisoners with appeals, deciphering correspondence with their attorneys and filing frivolous civil rights complaints, which at the very least got them a free trip to court even if the cases were summarily dismissed.

Hakim had approached Dale after he had settled into his I-just-want-to-do-my-time lane, asking questions about Maureen. He had researched Dale's case and knew the man had lost his wife in the aftermath of the robbery. He also learned that she was a full-time employee of the bank. And that many companies offered their personnel life insurance as part of their benefits package.

Dale insisted he didn't care about any of that.

Hakim assured him he understood and offered to look into the matter on Dale's behalf—for a small commission if he was able to collect.

Dale agreed, assuming nothing would come of the matter. But nearly a year later, Hakim notified Dale that he had settled with the bank's benefits provider for the full balance of Maureen's life insurance policy, nearly fifteen-thousand dollars—of which Hakim took his ten percent—and offered to set up an investment account for Dale minus another small percentage.

The account had grown to nearly fifty-thousand dollars since then. So he was relatively secure, financially. It wasn't the need for money that caused him to obsess about the fact that somewhere out there Maureen had left him a duffel bag filled with cash and valuables, but that it represented a connection to her, a chance to complete what they had started.

He no longer had the same goals as when Maureen and he had made plans to start a life and a family. In all likelihood, if he did discover where she had hidden it, he probably would give it all away to a charity or youth group Maureen had worked with. She had always wanted to be a mother, and this would be a small way he could honor her memory.

When the police and later the prosecutors had asked him where she had stashed it, he kept quiet, not even denying he knew where it was. The truth was, he didn't have any idea. That was something they had skipped in their meticulous planning.

Nevertheless, Dale had a strong feeling that Maureen had stashed it some place he, and perhaps only he, would be able to figure out.

But where?

There had only been a short amount of time, less than an hour between when she had escaped out the back of the bank and when she was shot by the police trying to evade capture at the house.

When he had been processed out, Dale was advised that he didn't need to return to Danville. He could have chosen to meet the requirements of his parole in a different judicial district. And although the thought of returning to any place near the town that took Maureen from him was painful, he wasn't going to leave until he found what she had left behind.

Dale paced the length of his room. He found himself counting the steps. It was an activity he used to pass the time while in jail. He memorized his cell so completely that he could navigate it with his eyes completely shut.

There was a knock at his door.

"Come in, Mrs. Laughlin," Dale said. In the short amount of time he'd been staying at the informal halfway house, his landlady stopped by, it seemed, almost hourly, checking to see if he needed anything. At first it was annoying, but then he realized it made her feel good to be useful, so he accepted her invitations to join her for dinner or watch her stories on TV and helped her with things around the house.

Mrs. Laughlin had been married to an ex-con who had gone straight after serving his time, so she had a soft spot for men in similar situations. Mr. Laughlin had died of stomach cancer some years earlier, but the house was littered with photographs of him and Mrs. Laughlin at various tourist traps around Northern California.

The door opened. Only instead of Mrs. Laughlin, there was a man in a Danville Police Officer's uniform, Liam McDonald.

"Good afternoon, Dale. Mrs. Laughlin was kind enough to let me in."

Dale's eyes narrowed and his muscles tensed.

The officer smiled. "No need to get riled up," Liam said. "I just came by to see how you are doing."

Dale didn't reply.

"Come on, you don't still blame me for what happened to Maureen, do you? I tried to talk to you, I sent you messages, you never gave me a chance to explain."

"There's nothing to explain," Dale answered. "We knew there was a chance something could go wrong. We all knew the risks."

"That's right," Liam agreed. "I just can't help but feel you hold me responsible. I was the one who was supposed to send you that page. But when the call came in about the missing girl, everything went to shit. Instead of being at the station in the middle of shift change when the alarm came in, the whole force was downtown.

"I helped her escape, you know. If that janitor hadn't recognized you, she would have made it. If there's anyone you should be mad at, it should be him. He's still around. I could get you his address, you could pay him a visit, get a little payback..."

Dale ignored the suggestion.

Liam took a step into the room so he could close the door. "I tried to get to the farmhouse ahead of them, to warn her, but I was too late."

Dale shook his head. "I don't understand why she went back."

The officer shrugged. "We found a backpack with some clothes, money and personal items. I'm guessing she didn't want to leave without them."

"Money?"

"The money wasn't from the bank, if that's what you're thinking. She must've had her own emergency stash. If she ditched the bank money, she would have needed something to go on the run that wouldn't be traced back to the robbery."

Dale nodded. "Maureen was always thinking ahead," he remarked.

Liam continued. "She was in the house when the posse arrived. Some trigger-happy rookie spotted her trying to escape out the attic window into that old oak. If she had made it to the woods…"

Dale closed his eyes, surprised to feel a tear rolling down his cheek. He knew the rest of the story. The coroner testified she was likely dead before she hit the ground. The cops had searched the house, her car, the woods for any sign of the missing money and valuables but had found nothing.

"You never found it," Dale said with his head bowed.

"The money? Not for lack of trying. You think I'd still be an underpaid civil servant in this town if I had? I waited. Fifteen years for my partner to get out so we could find it together."

Dale didn't respond.

"Unless, of course, you already know where it is…"

Dale looked up. "What makes you say that? I'm living in a ten-by-eleven-foot room a stone's throw from the town that took my wife. If I had my hands on that loot, I would be in the wind by now."

"Without cutting me in for my share?" the officer asked.

Liam crossed over and sat on the bed, closer to Dale, so he could speak in a lower voice. "Don't forget, I'm not the only one who was expecting a cut of that haul. Do you really think if we found it, our friend wouldn't show up to collect?"

"Is he…" Dale started to ask about the anonymous Mastermind who had planned the job but stopped himself.

Liam shrugged. "All I know is he's not the kind of man who would forget a ten-million-dollar payday. And I always had the feeling he was just a middleman. There was someone else, higher up, pulling the strings."

This was the first Dale had ever heard of any sort of boss behind the Mastermind, and for some reason the thought of it scared him. He had heard stories on the inside of shadowy organized crime figures orchestrating big payday thefts, hiring low-level crooks to carry them out, and punishing failure with death. Could he have gotten caught up in such a situation? Is that why Maureen had died?

"So, what do you say… partner?" Liam asked.

"Fine," Dale said after a moment.

"So, where is it?"

"I have no idea. If you haven't found it by now, I don't know where else to look. Maybe she threw it into a culvert on the side of the road and some passerby picked it up."

"That doesn't sound like something Maureen would have done. It took her nearly an hour to make the twenty-minute drive from the bank to your house. Somewhere along the way, she hid that money someplace where she knew you would find it."

Dale agreed with Liam but didn't want to admit it out loud.

"Come on, think," Liam urged. "You must have the answer somewhere in there," he said, rapping Dale's head with the knuckles of his right hand.

Dale grabbed the officer's wrist and twisted it into an uncomfortably painful position.

Liam locked eyes with Dale. "Not a smart move, my friend. Assault on a police officer with your record will get you ten more years behind bars."

Dale let him go. "What makes you so sure I have the answer?" he asked.

"Because," Liam said as he rose and crossed to the door. "She loved you."

Dale watched the man go. The unspoken conclusion to the conversation was that their partnership wouldn't be over until he found that money.

CHAPTER TWELVE

Nate woke up Sunday morning well past the time his alarm would have normally roused him. Madge was on the bed, licking his ear. He pushed her away and checked the clock, noting that the alarm was set, but he had apparently slept through the insistent buzzing for whatever period his clock decided was long enough.

He thought back to the day before. Jennifer had expressed her concerns about his reaction to the situation with his mother and the failing business that Raney/Daye Investigations was turning out to be. In the beginning he thought he would welcome the presence of Jennifer and her staff, but a trio of college kids shuffling around his house leaving messes in their wake was not the same as a bustling bullpen of police officers.

Jennifer was right. He missed the job. And it ate at him more than he was willing to admit.

The physical exertion from the previous day's cleaning had also taken its toll. With Jennifer's help, he was able to get the house back to a level of cleanliness it hadn't seen since before her crew had arrived. He had taken an extra pain pill that night and had a vague recollection of waking with a dull ache and needing an additional couple of pills to get back to sleep. That was likely why he had slept through his alarm.

Nate went through his morning routine, appreciative of the fact that he was alone. Most days, either Emily or Dave or both were already there, eating Hot Pockets and whatever else they could find.

In truth, he really didn't mind having them around. He imagined it was like when he would visit his Uncle Bill and Aunt Lilly in this very house. Lillian would be sitting at the kitchen table, sipping at her morning tea while a houseful of kids helped themselves to heaping bowls of sugary cereals, jam-laden slices of toast and large tumblers full of orange juice and chocolate milk.

Now it was his turn. Only the children were college students and a quirky parapsychologist with more energy than he could remember any of those cousins having.

He fed Madge, then took a large cup of heavily creamed coffee and a freshly warmed, lightly buttered croissant to the living room where he turned the television to the final day of the week's golf tournament. He wasn't really a big fan of golf and rarely played, but he needed something sedate and lacking drama to wind down his week. Normally, he would be dressed by now, but today he felt like lounging about in his pajama pants and t-shirt, enjoying the peace and quiet and solitude.

The channel changed to a local Sunday morning talk show.

Bits plopped down on the sofa.

"Where did you come from?" Nate asked.

Bits ignored the question and answered a different one. It was a frustrating habit of his. "Isn't it time for that TV show the Doc is on today?"

Nate remembered Jennifer telling him something about being interviewed on a local Sunday morning show, promising it would drum up some paying business for their struggling enterprise.

Bits popped open a can of Red Bull and tore through one side of the wrapper on a granola bar. Nate watched each crumb that escaped when Bits took a bite from the crunchy snack, fall to the freshly cleaned couch and drop into every crack and crevice. He put it out of his mind and decided to ignore Bits. Just pretend he wasn't there.

The show was hosted by a popular local news anchor, Hanna James, and was a traditional, casual show on a set that consisted of a couple of chairs, a small table and a plant. The anchor smiled as the theme music wound down.

"Good morning, everyone, and welcome to Sundays with Hanna. I'm Hanna James."

"Obviously," Bits commented.

"This morning my guest is Dr. Jennifer Day, professor of anthropology at Cal State East Bay and a parapsychologist."

The shot widened to encompass both women. Jennifer was wearing her usual wardrobe with the addition of a stylish jacket, her bright red Vans sneakers conspicuous in the wide shot. Her hair was pulled back, tucked into a low bun, and her ever-present Psi pendant hung around her neck. The TV station's makeup artist had obviously had a go at her, she was wearing more cosmetics than Nate had ever seen her in before, but it was subtle enough that she still looked like herself.

"Did I get that right?" Hanna asked.

"Yes, Hanna. Thank you for having me on the show," Jennifer replied.

"That's quite an interesting combination," Hanna remarked.

"Well, from my point of view, it's not an unusual pairing at all. A good portion of anthropology is the study of human cultures and their development. What's interesting to note is that every society, from the most primitive to the highly advanced, indulges in some belief in the paranormal. My focus on parapsychology through an anthropologist's lens is only natural."

"Or 'supernatural,'" Hanna added with her trademark smile.

Jennifer grinned back. Nate wondered if they had scripted that introductory moment.

"Tell me," Hanna continued. "What does a parapsychologist do? Is it anything like Ghostbusters?"

Nate cringed at the question. He had been around Jennifer long enough to hear that comparison made more times than he thought possible. But Jennifer took it in stride.

"Not quite. We're more interested in trying to capture evidence of paranormal activity with cameras and sensors and recording devices."

"You take photographs and videos of ghosts?"

"No, though that is a popular misconception promoted by a lot of the ghost hunting TV shows. What we're looking for are changes in the environment that connect to what a person is experiencing, data that supports that they may be actually witnessing a ghost."

"Any luck?"

"Yes," Jennifer answered brightly. "We have a large amount of evidence gathered by my team and other paranormal investigators."

"Why haven't we heard more about it then?"

"Well, to be honest, it's not quite as exciting as getting slimed by some mischievous spirit. There's a lot of evidence that our minds, or at least some aspect of them, can tap into a perception that transcends our physical senses and allows us to experience more than what we see and hear in our everyday lives.

"That form of perception, which people have called the sixth sense, is not something we're able to replicate with a camera, so even though people 'see' apparitions, it's not necessarily a vision that they're processing with their optic nerve, but rather a psychic impression being shared to their minds by the disembodied spirit. Since a camera is just a mechanical object, it can't perceive the world the same way a receptive human mind can."

"So, do you believe in the soul?" Hanna asked.

"In a way," Jennifer replied, "but we use the term 'consciousness.'"

"What about Heaven and Hell?"

"That's a little too theological for me."

"Where do you draw the line? Isn't the concept of a soul part of religion?"

"It is, and it isn't. I think what form an afterlife might take is pure speculation."

"Let me play devil's advocate for a moment. If everyone has a soul—sorry, consciousness—and that consciousness persists after death, wouldn't the earth be absolutely overrun with the billions of people who have died throughout history?"

"Well, you're assuming they're all bound to Earth. It's a big universe, maybe the afterlife endows our consciousness with the ability to transcend our existence here to something bigger.

"However, some may not want to transition, they may feel they have unfinished business, or are even afraid to move on. Those are the ones some people experience."

"I was reading in your book that there's actually a difference between ghosts, poltergeists and hauntings. I thought they were all basically the same thing."

"Well, the terms are used somewhat interchangeably, but they technically describe three different phenomena."

"Really? So, what is the difference between them?"

"Let's start with what we think of as your typical ghost. Many ghosts do appear to us as apparitions, but what makes them different from a haunting is that we can interact with them to varying degrees. Some apparitions like to talk to us, some like to appear to us, and some can do both if a person is especially receptive.

"A haunting, on the other hand, is more like a recording of an event, something that leaves a powerful psychic impression."

"So, it's like a movie," Hanna observed.

"Pretty much. It might be tied not only to a place, but a certain time of day, or it could be associated with an anniversary of some kind."

"But you can't talk to a haunting."

"No, it'd be like trying to have a conversation with Humphrey Bogart while watching *Casablanca*."

"So that leaves…"

"Poltergeists, which we believe aren't associated with spirits at all, and are more closely tied to living people who are exerting an unrealized psychic ability on their surroundings."

Marcia and Greg sat on their sofa watching the *Sundays With Hanna* show. Daisy was playing in the yard, and Danny was up in his room, creating the next edition of his comic book about Eric the Pirate.

Greg had been doing some research on the internet, looking for some answers about what was going on with Danny, and came across the website of a parapsychologist who taught anthropology. She seemed to approach the topic from more of a scientific point of view rather than a spiritual one, and he knew Marcia would be more at ease with that. He was particularly excited to see a media alert at the top of her website about her appearance on a local television show. He convinced Marcia to watch the program with him. She was reluctant at first, but Greg made all sorts of ridiculous promises, and she eventually relented.

On the television, Jennifer completed her explanation of the distinctions between different paranormal phenomena. Hanna zeroed in on the ghosts.

"So, the apparitions are actual dead people that we can see and hear?" she asked.

Jennifer nodded. "Yes, though to be specific, it isn't the actual person, just the psychic aspects of them."

"And are they still them? I mean, do they remember who they are without…"

"Without their bodies? Their brains?" Jennifer finished.

"Well, I guess I'm wondering how that works," Hanna explained. "I mean, our memories are in our brains, and when we die, don't our thoughts just… stop?"

"But what is consciousness? What are our thoughts and memories? We know the brain uses electrochemical signals, but what consciousness actually is, what our minds are, is widely argued across many fields of science. Even how memory works is still up in the air. So, who's to say consciousness cannot itself survive the death of the body? There's a lot of how it works that we can only guess at, but since the apparitions we do have evidence of can recall memories of their corporeal lives and the personalities seem not to have changed, the evidence supports a mechanism for survival."

Hanna nodded. "So, you're starting with a hypothesis, and searching for the evidence that proves it."

"Or disproves it," Jennifer added. "If there's some other explanation, some other theory that explains the phenomena I've researched and experienced myself, I want to know what exactly consciousness is."

"Do you think you'll ever prove your theories?"

"To everyone's satisfaction? Well, I'm an optimist at heart. But there are still people out there who believe the Earth is flat. I hope that someday, technology will evolve to allow us to capture irrefutable proof of the paranormal. Until then, I'm going to work to continue to expand our understanding of psychic phenomena, and consciousness in general."

Hanna shifted in her seat as she changed gears in the conversation. "So that brings me to your website. I was reading through some of your case studies, and I was surprised to find that you listed just as many, if not more, incidents that turned out *not* to be paranormal at all."

"Yes. I think it's helpful for people to see that we really try to get to the bottom of the cases we investigate."

"I'm particularly interested in a case you looked into a few months back that was a big deal around here for a while. You helped solve a sixty-year-old serial killer case."

"Well, usually the incidents we take on are not that dramatic."

"You were working with a police detective on that case."

"Yes, Detective Nate Raney."

"There wasn't much in the papers about his involvement, nor in the account on your website. I understand the case you solved was one that was originally investigated by his grandfather?"

"It was his great-uncle, who was just a rookie at the time and happened to be on the scene when the man they thought was the killer had died."

"I wouldn't expect a cop to be… well, aren't they usually all 'just the facts, ma'am'?"

Jennifer smiled, thinking back to when she and Nate had first met, and he was a hard-core skeptic. He still was, but she liked the way it forced her to think like him, to look at things from all angles and be prepared to counter his arguments. "Oh, he's very much a skeptic, which is often the exact point of view our investigations require. I'm lucky to have him as a partner."

"How much of a partner?" she asked suggestively, raising an eyebrow with curiosity.

"A business partner," Jennifer explained. "His experience as a detective is invaluable."

"All right, we'll leave it at that, then. I want to talk more about some of your cases, but we need to take a break." Hanna smiled to the camera. "We'll be right back."

The commercials started playing, and Greg hit the mute button on the remote.

"What do you think?" he asked Marcia.

"I don't know," she said with a sigh. "What if it's just a..."

"A what?" Greg asked. "A phase? An imaginary friend? How do you explain that box of photos?"

"He found it in the attic and invented a story around them."

"But you told me that he had described her and even told you her name before he found them."

"As far as we know," Marcia clarified.

Greg looked at her challengingly. "You honestly think he had been poking around in that attic for the last few weeks without us knowing about it?"

"I think it's more likely than a ghost. You know what kind of imagination he has."

Greg considered. She was right. Finding an old box of photos and making up a story about a woman who was featured in them would be something their ten-year-old would be capable of. But still, even if he had managed to get into the attic previously, how could he have managed to push the folding steps back up inside and close the door?

"You heard what she said about how they find out that a lot of their cases are not ghosts at all," he said.

Marcia nodded.

"And she is a scientist."

Marcia nodded again.

"And she works with a retired police detective. Who's probably more skeptical than you are."

Marcia smiled. "You really want her to see if we have a ghost?"

"It would be nice to rule it out, don't you think?"

"I have ruled it out," she said.

"Okay, it'd be nice to have someone get it past my thick skull that we don't have a ghost, just a very imaginative fifth grader."

Marcia sighed. "All right. But I don't want her putting Danny on her blog or website or anything."

"I agree completely," Greg assured her. "Look, we send her an email, see if she's interested in looking into it, and if she is, we set the rules."

She considered. "What do we tell Danny?"

Greg shrugged. "The truth. She's a Ghostbuster."

Marcia laughed. "Let's go with she's a scientist."

"So, you're okay with me reaching out to her?" Greg asked.

"I'm okay with it," she assured him.

The commercial break ended, and Greg turned the volume back up and put his arm around Marcia as Jennifer continued talking about some of the more interesting phenomena she had investigated.

At the top of the stairs, Danny sat with his legs poking through the gaps in the balusters. "What's a parapsychologist?" he asked Maureen, pronouncing the word slowly.

"I'm not sure. Maybe someone who can help," Maureen replied. Then she added, more for herself, "Maybe someone who has answers."

"Do you think she really is a ghostbuster? And wants to trap you and send you away?"

Maureen wasn't sure if such a thing was possible. It was obvious that she had been dead for some time. She couldn't remember ever seeing things like the tiny computer screens Greg and Marcia kept with them that seemed to work like phones, too. And their TV was just a flat panel. She'd remembered seeing something like it, but also remembered that such things cost a fortune. But the Foreman's didn't seem like they were very rich. Both of them worked, and they had done almost all the remodeling themselves.

The woman on the television seemed nice. She was a college professor, so maybe she did have some answers. And maybe Maureen would be able to talk to her as well as Danny. The truth was, she was just as curious as Greg to find out what she was and why she was here.

"I'm gonna go work on my comic," Danny stated, then pulled his legs back and scurried off to his room.

Maureen sighed, watching him skip back to his room, determined to appreciate her connection to Danny no matter how or why it had come about—or how long it might last.

CHAPTER THIRTEEN

Dave sat in front of the panoramic screen on Jennifer's side of the large, wooden partners desk. When he turned on the computer, the small badge on the icon for the email, as he was expecting, showed over two hundred messages waiting.

He looked up over the screen at Detective Raney, who was focused on something on the laptop on his side. Ever since the blow up the previous week, Dave had been afraid to even set foot in the house, let alone do any work here. But he could understand why Detective Raney was upset. Emily, Bits and he had taken Nate's hospitality for granted. After the dean of the Anthropology Department had shuttled them from office to office, some of them little more than a cleared-out space in a basement—and that was one of the nicer ones—having a quiet place to work without fear of needing to move every day was a welcome change of pace. He resolved to be a better guest and be more respectful of the retired policeman's hospitality. After all, Dr. Daye's conflict with the dean could have just as easily ended with Dave losing his position as Jennifer's graduate assistant and the tuition waiver and stipend that accompanied it.

"Dr. Daye was pretty good on the *Sundays with Hanna* show, didn't you think?" he asked in as friendly a voice as he could manage.

The detective acknowledged him with a grunt.

Dave decided that was enough small talk for the day and opened the email program on Dr. Daye's computer. Evidently, the number on the icon hadn't been refreshed recently, as there were nearly twice as many messages waiting for him as he had been promised.

Dr. Daye had called in a lot of favors to get booked on the popular local show. She had done television appearances in the past, but usually it was for some Halloween puff piece, or a brief interview after one of her cases made the newspapers or went viral on the internet. This was a long form interview, the kind she excelled at, mostly because it was very much like the lectures for her Introduction to Anthropology course at the university. It gave her a chance to connect with her audience and share her enthusiasm.

Her appearance was part of a concerted effort to find a case that could not only help pay the bills but demonstrate that Dr. Daye's partnership with Detective Raney was viable. Despite the fact that she was engaged, once again, in an academic conflict with the dean—this time regarding a course she wanted to teach focusing on parapsychology—she was determined to prove to Nate that they could make a go of their joint venture, and that she and her staff were not just freeloading in his home.

To that end, Dave had set aside his own renewed efforts at making progress on his doctoral thesis to help her find a case that would achieve those goals. He started sorting through the emails, dropping many of them into folders based solely on the subject line. He had developed a knack over the years working for Dr. Daye for separating the crazies from the people who were genuinely in need of her help.

"Are you doing the email?" Emily asked.

Dave and Nate both turned and looked toward Emily, who was standing in the doorway, her own laptop resting in the crook of her arm.

Nate turned his attention back to his own work, ignoring the interruption.

"Yes," Dave answered. "Are you here to help?"

Emily didn't answer with words. She responded by walking into the room, setting her laptop down next to Dr. Daye's computer and tapping a few keys.

"What are you doing?" Dave asked.

Emily rolled her eyes, sighed and nodded toward the screen where Dave had been sorting emails.

He looked at the program and was struck with a note of panic as he watched all the messages rapidly disappear from the inbox. "What's going on?" he asked. "I haven't sorted those yet! How are you doing this?"

"Relax," Emily replied. "I'm running an AI app on Dr. Daye's inbox to sort the incoming messages."

"I have a system," Dave protested.

"I know. It's based on your system."

"What do you mean?"

"I've been training a machine learning algorithm with your choices of how to categorize the incoming emails from the website for the last few months."

Dave started clicking through the folders he usually directed the incoming messages to and sampled some of the messages in each.

"I set the confidence threshold to ninety-nine percent, so you may see a few messages that aren't sorted."

Dave looked at the badge of unread emails left in the main inbox. It was down to four.

"You created an artificial intelligence that sorts Dr. Daye's incoming emails?"

"Just the ones from the website."

"And it does it exactly how I would do it?"

"Within ninety-nine percent."

"And you've had it for months?"

Emily nodded.

"Then why have I been busting my butt to sort these emails every day?"

"I told you, I needed to train the algorithm."

"Why couldn't you do that?"

"Then it would sort the email like me, not you. And I know you prefer it done your way."

Dave closed his eyes and took a deep breath. "Only when I have to do it over because you're so lazy."

"Exactly. And you're welcome." Emily snapped her laptop shut, turned and left the room.

Dave watched her go, then returned his attention to the email program. He couldn't decide whether to be angry at Emily for using him as her own personal lab rat, or grateful that one of his most tedious jobs had been reduced to the click of a mouse.

"She doesn't make it easy to say thank you, does she?" Nate asked.

"Hmm?" Dave asked, engrossed in an email.

"We had a woman like that in the records room. A whiz on the computer but treated us all like we were five-year-olds who were incapable of understanding anything she said. Drove me nuts, but she got the job done."

Dave looked across the desk at Nate. "Yeah, she's all that wrapped up in an annoying little sister."

Nate laughed.

"I assume we're talking about Emily," Jennifer said from the doorway. She breezed into the office, dropping a collection of envelopes in front of Nate and stepping behind Dave to peer over his shoulder at the screen. "Anything promising?"

"And by promising, you mean any that don't start with, 'I can't afford to pay you anything, but...'?" Dave asked.

Dave and Jennifer both glanced over the desk at Nate, checking his reaction.

Nate held up the envelopes Jennifer had dropped on his side of the desk, fanning them out like a poker hand. "Got anything that beats a full house?"

Dave looked back at the screen. "Millionaire whose wife recently died and is wondering if the psychic he hired is the real deal?"

"Pass," Nate and Jennifer said in unison, recalling the event that crashed Jennifer's academic career square into Nate's house.

Dave continued scanning the list. "Here's one. There's a family out in Danville who seem like they're not a total charity case."

"What's going on with them?" Jennifer asked.

"They have a ten-year-old son whose best friend is the ghost of a woman who used to live in their house."

"Pass," Nate said.

"Pass?" Jennifer asked.

Dave went on, "The father says the boy can see and hear the ghost, and she's told him things he couldn't possibly know."

"Imaginary friend, internet," Nate replied. "Next."

Jennifer stood up straight, crossed her arms, and looked at the detective. "Nate, I hate to be the practical one, but we can't bill them if we don't actually investigate. You may be absolutely right, but we're not selling snap judgments. We're selling our best professional efforts and hopefully peace of mind."

He considered for a moment, setting the bills down on his side of the desk. He shifted them around with his fingertips. She was right, of course. He couldn't just dismiss every case out of hand without doing the work.

The life of a private investigator was different from being a cop. As a policeman, he got the same salary no matter how long it took to clear the case. Now he needed to have clients and generate billable hours and ask for retainers. He could understand why Uncle Bill hadn't done it for very long. But for his great-uncle, it was more of a hobby, something to do after his retirement. Nate needed a new career, and if he wasn't willing to give this arrangement with Jennifer and her crew a serious effort, then what was he doing? At the very least, it would be more interesting and appealing than following cheating spouses and chasing down workman's compensation fraudsters and spying on promiscuous dogs.

"Okay," Nate said. "Let's do it. And make sure they know there's a fee involved. Get a retainer in advance."

Jennifer smiled. She placed her hands on Dave's shoulders and leaned over to read the screen. "Great, let's email the Foremans and schedule a phone interview. Then start compiling any information we can find out about the town. Do they mention anything about how old they think the ghost is?"

Dave scrolled down. "They found a box of photos in the attic. The most recent ones go back about fifteen or twenty years, give or take."

"Okay. Find out what happened in that town fifteen years ago and let's see if we can connect any events of interest to this apparition." Jennifer checked her watch. "I better leave. I'm going to be late for lunch with Eleanor," she said, offhandedly.

"You're having lunch with my mother?" Nate asked, surprised.

"We've been chatting. I think I can convince her to see a psychic friend of mine whom I trust."

"Great, more séances."

"He's not really like that," Jennifer assured Nate. "Do you... want to join us?" she asked tentatively.

Nate considered. It was a little strange to think that Jennifer was developing a better relationship with his mother than he had, but at the same time, he'd known his mother his whole life, and knew that it was still too soon to reach out to her. He'd apologize, but with everything else going on in his life, he didn't trust himself to be able to contain his emotions. "That's all right. Maybe next time," he replied.

"Okay," Jennifer said with a reassuring smile. Then she looked back at Dave as he tapped the keys on the computer that sent the email to the office printer. "I've got a good feeling about this case," she said. She turned back to Nate. "It's all going to work out. You'll see."

Nate watched her go, understanding that her words weren't just about the Foremans and their alleged ghost, but his mother as well. He glanced back over at Dave, who retrieved some pages from the printer and slipped them into a new manila folder. "Well, I guess I'm off to Danville," he said to Nate.

"Can't you do this research online?"

"Possibly, but I can only find online what there is online. A lot of these small-town newspapers don't have an internet presence and don't have the resources to digitally archive all their old articles. The local library is the best place to start."

"Want some company?" Nate asked.

Dave froze in his tracks. It had never occurred to him that Nate would be interested in doing the type of background research Dave did.

"Um," Dave stuttered. "Okay. Th-that would be great."

Nate smiled, aware that his offer both caught Dave off-guard and made him a little uncomfortable. "While you're paging through old newspapers, I can chat up the local cop shop. There's always someone there who knows everything that's ever happened and is happy to tell you all about it."

"Sounds good," Dave said. "Do you want to take my car, or—"

"I'm driving," Nate replied. He shut down the Sudoku puzzle he'd been solving on his computer and stood up from this desk. He slipped into the jacket draped over his chair and adjusted his tie. "Road trip," he said with a borderline maniacal smile that was enough to kick Dave's anxiety into high gear.

CHAPTER FOURTEEN

Maureen never felt bored. Time passed in flashes, like she was skipping through it. Unless she made an effort to pay attention to what was going on around her, she was like a leaf in the wind.

When Danny was around, she sort of anchored herself to him. She enjoyed watching him play, either alone or with his sister. She wasn't sure if he could always see or sense her and tried not to pester him when he was otherwise occupied. She didn't want to become annoying and risk losing their connection.

He was at school now, but ever since she'd overheard the conversation between his parents, she didn't skip the time when Danny was away. She watched and listened to Marcia when she was home, read over her shoulder when she worked on her computer, listened to the radio and watched the television when it was on.

Today, Marcia seemed engrossed in some work she was doing on the computer. Maureen had determined that she did something related to making websites, and from what she had seen, Marcia was good at it.

Like most days, Marcia worked with the radio or television on in the background. Today it was the television, and there was a midday news program playing. At first, Maureen didn't recognize the photograph that appeared on the screen.

Then she realized it was herself.

The reporter was telling the story of a bank robbery fifteen years earlier. One of the thieves had been caught, but his partner had tried to make a run for it and was shot trying to escape.

The story lit up memories for Maureen. She could remember that day, being in the bank vault, driving away, making it to the house.

But it was only pieces, fragments with large gaps between them.

The reporter went on to explain that the surviving robber had recently been released from prison.

There was another photo on the screen.

A name came to her.

Dale.

More memories came back in a flash.

He was her husband. They were going to use the money to move and start a family.

Then she died.

She turned her attention back to the news story. The reporter was showing a photo of a bank in downtown Danville. "The daring robbery was foiled when a young girl went missing in the middle of the night, flooding the area with law enforcement at a time when police presence normally would have been sparse. When the robbers triggered the alarm, one of them was caught in the bank, while the second one managed to slip past the police. She had taken tens of thousands of dollars in cash as well as the high-value contents of dozens of safe deposit boxes. The money and goods were never recovered. Dale Everly insisted throughout his trial and incarceration that he had no idea where his partner had hidden them. Among the valuables stolen was a diamond necklace valued at the time at nearly ten million dollars."

Maureen didn't pay much attention to the words. She was focused on the photo of Dale that was now on the screen. He was older than the picture in her mind, but it was the same face.

The graphic changed to an old photograph of a house.

This house.

It was from before the Foremans had moved in, before they had painted the weathered exterior different colors and planted flowers in front of the porch.

Before she realized what was happening, Maureen found herself on that porch.

It was the first time she could remember being outside the house since...

... since the day she had died.

She looked out over the front yard. The Foremans' minivan was parked in the driveway.

Then the minivan was gone, and it was a station wagon parked there.

The flowers were gone now, too. The house was whitewashed, and the lawn was burned brown from a hot summer dry spell.

There were police cars parked on the street, and officers streamed out of them, drawing their guns.

It was like watching a movie trailer. She felt like she was seeing the highlights, enough to capture her interest, but it also felt like there was something missing. Something important.

"There she is," a voice shouted.

"She's got a gun!" another voice warned.

A shot rang out.

Maureen could feel the wound in her chest.

She looked up at the large oak tree that grew up against the house and remembered clinging to the branches near the attic window, then falling to her death.

CHAPTER FIFTEEN

Eleanor Raney sat across the table from Jennifer in the quiet tea house. A delighted smile appeared on her face when the server appeared with a multitiered stand filled with various finger foods and delicate desserts and set it between the two women.

"You must try the cucumber sandwiches," the older woman suggested. "They're my favorite."

Jennifer picked up one of the small triangles of carefully constructed layers and popped it into her mouth. "Delicious," she said before her mouth was empty.

"Nate doesn't enjoy tea. He doesn't like that they just bring you a lot of tiny things you can try. He thinks a meal should 'tell a story.' Have you ever heard anything so silly? I think a meal should fill your belly and make your tongue happy."

"I agree," Jennifer said.

"Is that why he didn't come? Because we were eating here?" Eleanor asked.

"I didn't invite him," Jennifer lied. "I just wanted it to be a girl's lunch."

"Well, it's all for the best. I'm still mad at him," Eleanor confessed.

"I don't blame you. I'm upset with him as well. I never would have asked him to join us if I thought he wouldn't behave himself."

Eleanor took a bite of a miniature pie. "I know he only does it because he's trying to protect me," she said. "I just wish he would trust me."

Jennifer sipped her tea. "You know why he worries, don't you?" she asked Eleanor.

Eleanor looked away, embarrassed. "I know. But I don't care about money and things the way he does."

"I don't doubt that," Jennifer said, recalling their recent conversations about the bills.

"I just miss Ben so much. It makes me feel better to know he's with me, that I can talk to him, tell him about Nate."

"I understand."

"I just wish Nate would accept that I can speak with his father. That he could too."

Jennifer nodded. "I think the problem is that when Nate was on the police force, he saw a lot of people who called themselves psychics, but who were really just con men, frauds exploiting grieving people."

"This isn't like that," Eleanor insisted.

Jennifer nodded. "You may trust them, but all Nate sees is someone out to squeeze the last buck from an unsuspecting, vulnerable old lady."

"Harmony would never do that to me," Eleanor insisted.

"I'm sure you're right."

"She tells me things only Ben would know. And when I talk to him through her, I know it's him. I know him."

Jennifer reached out and placed a hand on Eleanor's. "I have no doubt that's true, Eleanor, but Harmony has a certain... personality that makes it difficult for Nate to consider your side."

"So," Eleanor began, "you're the expert. What do you think I should do?"

"Well, I happen to know someone who is very good at this sort of thing. And he presents in a way that may be more palatable to Nate."

Eleanor shook her head. "I don't know if that's possible. He's not very open-minded about psychics."

"Yes, I know. But I think I'm wearing him down."

The older woman smiled knowingly. "I'm sure you are. I never would have thought he would become a—what did you call it?—a paranormal investigator."

"Well, the arrangement is that I'm the parapsychologist, he's the private eye. I hope that by working together, I can get him to look at the world around him and his own experiences from a different point of view."

"Oh, I don't know about all that. What I do know is that a man will do almost anything for a pretty girl."

Jennifer tried unsuccessfully not to blush. "Nate and I are just friends and colleagues."

"Dear, I've known Nate all of his life. I can count the number of women he's brought home on one hand, and you've already moved in with him."

"We don't live together, Eleanor. We just share an office."

"You don't have to pretend with me, Jennifer. Has he made his tiramisu for you?" Eleanor asked.

Jennifer thought back to a stakeout she and Nate conducted not so many months earlier. He had volunteered to bring the food after she teased him about buying donuts and Red Bull. It turned out he was quite an accomplished chef. The assortment of gourmet treats he provided included a decadently delicious tiramisu.

The pause in her reply was all the confirmation Eleanor needed. "I thought so."

Jennifer blushed.

"Trust me, dear. We don't have as much time on this Earth as you think. You shouldn't spend it making excuses."

"Why don't we just work on getting Nate to come see my friend with us?"

Eleanor poked at her food with her fork. "I don't know. I mean Ben expects me to talk to him through Harmony."

"I promise you, Ben is with you wherever you go. I know you like Harmony, but Nate is never going to take her seriously."

"And you think he might be more… open with your friend?"

"I do."

"And I don't have to stop seeing Harmony?"

"How about you just take a break?"

Eleanor put down her fork and placed her hands in her lap. "Well, if Nate trusts you, I guess I can give it a try."

CHAPTER SIXTEEN

Nate drove while Dave tapped away at his laptop.

A GPS app on the phone mounted to the dashboard showed the route to Danville, a small community east of San Francisco in a valley at the foot of Mount Diablo. Formerly home to ranches and wheat farms, then later fruit and nut orchards, it had grown into a nice little high-end suburb.

Dave's computer gave a terse warning about running out of power. He rushed to save the document he was editing before the screen went black, then closed his computer. He looked out at the passing scenery. "Have you ever been to Danville before?" Dave asked.

Nate nodded.

"Work or pleasure?"

"Both."

Dave took Nate's limited response as a sign that he wasn't interested in having a conversation to pass the time. They still had almost twenty minutes before they reached their exit.

"I've been there to question witnesses, and my dad used to take me to the national park to go hiking when I was a kid," Nate said. "What about you?"

Dave was caught off guard. "Me? I've never been there."

"Really? You live less than an hour away and you've never come out here? I know there are some archaeological sites in the area."

"Yeah, native American history isn't my thing. And I grew up in New York. Central Park is about all the nature I can take."

"I didn't know you were from New York," Nate said.

"Really? I thought you were supposed to be a detective," Dave said sarcastically. He glanced at Nate, but he apparently didn't find the comment funny. He wore a stern expression and stared straight ahead. "Sorry," Dave said reflexively, "I didn't mean—"

Nate smiled. "I'm just messing with you, Dave."

The grad student laughed nervously.

"I know you did your undergrad at the University of Iowa, finished second in your high school class, collect Chia Pets and have seven unpaid parking tickets."

"I do?"

"No, just messing with you again on the last one."

"You did a background check on me?"

"Of course I did. You're practically living in my house. And, as you pointed out, I am supposed to be a detective."

"Yeah, I guess that makes sense." Dave paused for a second. "What did you find out about Bits?"

"I found out that he is a digital black hole. There is nothing about him after the eighth grade."

"That's... kind of disturbing."

"But, not illegal."

"What about Emily?"

"What about her?"

"Anything... interesting?"

"Like does she have a boyfriend?"

"No. I'm not interested in her," Dave replied, a bit too defensively.

"She shot you down, huh?"

"None of your business."

"I don't blame you. She does have an air of mystery," Nate remarked.

"Not that difficult when you don't really talk to anyone," Dave added.

"She is a hard nut to crack."

"Yeah, the complete opposite of Dr. Daye."

"What do you mean?" Nate asked.

"You know. It's obvious that she's into you," Dave said.

"Excuse me?"

"I mean, you two are a thing, right?"

"No," Nate said emphatically. "We just work together."

"Oh," Dave replied, surprised. "We thought that you two were..."

"We?" Nate asked.

"Well, me, Bits, and Emily. And your old partner Max—"

"When do you talk to Max?"

"He calls once in a while. Mostly asks how you're doing."

"Really? Why doesn't he just ask me?"

"He says you don't tell him anything interesting."

Nate grunted. "What do you tell him?"

Dave shrugged. "Nothing."

"Dave, you know I can tell when you're lying."

Dave had suspected as much. Nate always seemed to regard Dave with suspicion whenever he was keeping something from the detective. "He just wants to know how you're doing. How your shoulder is doing. I think he hopes you might come back."

Nate knew that wasn't the whole story. Max had been there when Nate was shot, and the younger detective had put a lot of the blame for Nate's injury on himself. He'd seen a marked difference in his old partner. Whenever they'd gotten together for lunch or went out for drinks with some of the other guys from the force, Max was less the brash, rule-breaker he had been as Nate's partner, and more professional, often picking Nate's brain about some case or another.

The one thing that didn't change was Max's preoccupation with Nate's love life.

"So, are we stopping by the family's house first," Nate asked his passenger in an unsubtle attempt to change the subject.

"Not this trip," Dave said. "Dr. Daye likes me to get as much background as I can before we actually visit anyone."

"So just the library?"

"Always the best place to start. Librarians are notorious gossips."

Nate laughed. "I can't picture you dishing dirt with some middle-aged bibliophiles."

"Usually Emily handles that part."

Nate tried to form a mental picture. "Nope, can't picture that one, either."

"She's actually a theater minor. Not always the broody goth girl, she can turn on whatever personality she needs when she wants to."

"Makes you wonder if the whole dark misanthrope is just a role."

"Yes, it does," Dave agreed.

They passed a sign on the side of the highway letting them know they had entered the city limits. A short while later, they took an off-ramp and found themselves rolling through the usual collection of small shopping centers until they reached a residential section.

The architecture shifted from a modern utilitarian style to an eclectic collection of rustic farmhouses and ranch-style homes. The GPS guided them through an older part of the city until they reached a cluster of buildings, one of which had a sign out front indicating it was home to the Danville Public Library.

Nate pulled into the parking lot. "How long are you going to need?"

"I have no idea," Dave replied. "I don't suppose you want to... help?"

"I think I'll be more use chatting up the local constabulary."

"Nobody says constabulary."

"I do. Give me a call when you're done."

"Okay." Dave gathered his things and opened the door. He stepped out and then turned back to Nate, checking his watch. "Do you want to meet for lunch? Maybe?" he asked tentatively.

"Call me when you're done," Nate repeated.

Dave nodded, closed the car door, and headed for the library.

Nate reached over and tapped the screen on his phone to pull up the address for the family that had reached out to Jennifer. He cringed when a bolt of pain shot through his shoulder. The injury hadn't bothered him during the drive, but when he reached for the phone, it felt like there was a shard of glass scraping along every nerve. He fought through the discomfort and programmed the GPS.

Usually, a couple of deep breaths were enough to get past these moments, but this time, the pain settled in and refused to let go. With his left hand, Nate pulled out the prescription bottle from his jacket pocket. He placed the bottom of the bottle against his leg and pressed down on the lid, and with a practiced twist, opened it.

He held the bottle up to his mouth and shook out a pill directly onto his tongue. The taste was bitter, even more so after he crunched down on it and used the small amount of saliva in his mouth to swallow it.

He knew it would take a moment to take the edge off the pain, but just the promise of relief was enough for him to continue on his way.

CHAPTER SEVENTEEN

Nate took his time winding his way through the town toward the Foreman's house. He didn't take the route his phone suggested, but instead took a more circuitous path, experiencing the different aspects of the town. There were examples of older ranch houses that had at one time stood alone at the center of a farm or orchard, but were now surrounded by newer homes and businesses, remnants of a previous age.

When he reached the Foreman residence, he didn't stop. He just slowed down a bit, taking in the freshly painted exterior and its impressive garden. There was a car parked in the driveway, and Nate thought he saw a woman through one window hunched over a computer. It was a weekday, so the children were in school. From all outward appearances, it was a normal rural household.

As he roamed the area, he saw signs of a burgeoning neighborhood, with new construction nearby—though the Foreman house still remained fairly secluded as it was nestled against a forest and backstopped by wooded foothills.

Nate waited until he reached a stop sign before entering his next destination. The pill had done its work, and the pain in his shoulder was now a dull ache accompanied by a little stiffness. Soon he was on his way back into the heart of Danville, toward the municipal building that the city government shared with the police station.

He parked and found the entrance to the newly renovated station at the side of the building. It led to a small lobby that felt like an air-lock to a bunker. There was a thick metal door with a digital keypad lock, and next to it a window like you might see at a bank-drive through. It had glass that was inches thick and a drawer one could use to pass items back and forth. There was no one at the window, but there was a button labeled "Press for assistance." Nate pressed it.

He didn't hear anything, but a moment later, a uniformed woman appeared. Her voice came across an intercom. "How can I assist you?" she asked in an officious monotone.

Nate pulled out his Private Investigator credentials and held them up to the window. "Hi, Nate Raney. I'm retired SFPD. I may be working a case in town, and I thought I'd drop by and check in. I was wondering if there was anyone I might be able to talk to? Just want to get some background."

The officer behind the glass gave the credentials a quick glance, then pulled a lever on her side, causing the drawer to open on Nate's. "Put it in the drawer," she said.

Nate placed the wallet that held his ID into the drawer.

It retracted, and the officer took his credentials and disappeared behind another door.

Nate spotted a pair of chairs in the corner and decided to wait in one.

The door opened much sooner than he expected. An older man in uniform, a bit thick around the middle, stepped forward, scanned the room and spotted Nate sitting in the chair. "Holy shit, it is you. What is all this Private Detective crap?" he asked, tossing the badge to Nate.

It took him a moment to place the brash police chief, a face from his past. "Captain Lewis?" he asked. "What are you doing here?"

"It's Chief Lewis, detective, but since you're no longer on the job, make it Brian." Nate rose, and the two men shook hands heartily. "How's that old uncle of yours doing?"

"He's hanging in there. Enjoying his retirement. I see him every week."

"Good, good. I heard about your heroics," Lewis said.

"More like stupidity. I acted like an impulsive rookie."

"You saved lives," Lewis said, clasping Nate's left shoulder in a meaty hand. "That's never stupid."

"Thanks," Nate said. He knew that was true, but it was nice to hear it from his old captain. "So, how did you end up here? I thought you and Nancy were riding off into the retirement sunset."

"Yeah, that lasted about a month. Then I heard about this job. I actually got my start here before I moved to the big city. The pace isn't as crazy, and I've got a lot of great men and women working under me. Come on in."

Lewis held the door open and allowed Nate to precede him into the station. They passed a bullpen of nine-one-one operators, then entered a hallway that led past a series of offices. There was an open area that resembled some of the open plan tech offices Nate had seen, but instead of hipster coders, it was filled with uniformed and plain-clothes officers.

They entered the chief's office. The older man made his way behind his desk to an over-sized chair and motioned for Nate to take a seat at one of the plush armchairs set in front of it. "Let's get down to business. What brings you and your shiny new P.I. badge to our neck of the woods?"

Nate realized he hadn't prepared for how he was going to explain that he was here gathering background for Jennifer's investigation. "Favor for a friend," he said. Not a lie, but not exactly the whole truth, either. "Do you know anything about a house out on Pine? Four-fifty-five. Farmhouse, new family, looks like they did some major renovations."

"The Foremans," Lewis answered without hesitation.

Nate reacted with surprise. "You know them?"

"The wife, Marcia, did some work for us, updated our website design, streamlined our workflow, tweaked our UI and UX and all sorts of other stuff I can repeat but couldn't explain if you held a gun to my head. I believe her husband, Greg, works over at the Costco. What's going on with them?"

"I can't go into it," Nate said. "Confidentiality and all that."

"Can you tell me if it's anything I need to be worried about?"

"No, it's not a police matter."

"Because if it's anything to do with Dale Everly, you really should let me know."

"Dale Everly?" Nate asked.

Lewis nodded. "I guess he's not a big enough of a story to make it out to the bay."

"What is the story?"

"Oh, it's a doozy. He and his wife broke into a local bank vault, nearly got away with it, too, but Danville's finest managed to stop their getaway."

"When was this?"

"About fifteen years ago. I was a brand spanking new patrolman at the time. When the burglary went down, I was taking a missing person's report on a lost kid."

"I guess you missed all the excitement," Nate said.

"Well, I more than made up for it when I joined SFPD," Lewis replied.

"So what's the story with Dale Everly?" Nate asked.

"He just got out of prison."

"What about the wife?"

"Dead. She was shot by officers at their home trying to make her escape."

"Did she fire on them?" Nate asked.

"I don't remember the details, but apparently before she died, she hid part of the loot from the bank."

A violent death on the property. Nate knew this was something Jennifer would seize on to bolster her assumption there was a ghost hanging out with the boy. "The husband didn't know where it was?" Nate asked.

"If he did, he's kept his mouth shut for fifteen years."

"Obviously they searched the house."

"Yeah, I think if the Foreman's had found a diamond necklace hidden in the walls of that old place when they remodeled, we would have heard about it."

"A diamond necklace?" Nate asked.

"Among other things, including nearly a hundred thousand in cash."

Nate whistled, impressed. "I'm guessing Everly came back to town when he got out."

"He's down near Walnut. We're keeping an eye on him."

"Anyone else around who was with the force at the time of the robbery? Maybe someone who was at the house?" Nate asked.

"There are a couple of old-timers. Liam McDonald comes to mind. He entertains the rookies with stories of that day. It was the biggest thing to happen to this town since the gold rush. He was there when she was shot."

"Can I talk to him?"

"Sure, I think I saw him just before you got here." Lewis got up and walked over to the door, where he had a view over the bullpen area. "McDonald. Got a sec?" he asked, returning to his desk without waiting for an answer.

A moment later, Liam McDonald entered. "What's up, Chief?" he asked, offering a friendly smile to Nate.

"Have a seat," Lewis said. "This is Nate Raney, formerly of the San Francisco Police Department. He was asking about the old Everly place."

"Yeah, the Foremans," Liam said as he eased himself into the other chair in front of the chief's desk. "Marcia did that computer work."

"You think Dale Everly has any reason to give them any trouble?"

Liam scratched his head. "Are you talking about that missing money?"

"Well, from what I've heard, it never turned up."

"I can tell you we searched that house from top to bottom, even used metal detectors in

the yard, the orchard across the road and the woods behind the house. Never found anything. And I'm sure Everly knows it. If you think he might pay them a visit thinking it's there, there's no chance of that."

"Yeah, that's what I thought," Lewis agreed.

"Did you know the Everlys?" Nate asked.

Liam seems surprised by the question. "No," he answered, shaking his head.

Something about the deputy's response made Nate suspicious.

He stared the officer down.

Liam shrugged. "I'm sure I walked by them in town now and then—Danville was a bit smaller back then—but I didn't know them enough to say 'hi.'"

Nate nodded. "That house looks like it doesn't have many neighbors. I guess they kept to themselves, mostly."

"Yeah, I guess so."

"You were there? When the police caught up to Everly's wife?"

Liam nodded.

"Why do you think she didn't just turn herself in?"

Liam shrugged. "Who knows?"

Nate smiled. "Indeed," he said, nodding in agreement. "You were born in Danville?"

Liam reacted with surprise. "What makes you say that?"

"Well, not many people would be satisfied being an officer for over fifteen years unless they had ties to the community."

"I like it here," Liam replied.

Nate considered the man's response. There was obviously more to the story. "Well, thanks for talking to me." Nate offered his hand and he and Liam shook.

"That's all, McDonald," Lewis said.

Liam nodded to his boss, then got up and exited the office.

Once he was gone, Lewis asked Nate, "Any help?"

"Yes, big help. Thanks," Nate replied.

There was something about Liam McDonald that rubbed Nate the wrong way. He felt like the officer was lying about something, but he wasn't quite sure what it was.

CHAPTER EIGHTEEN

Jennifer sat at her end of the partners desk, grading exams with Emily. Emily was marking the multiple-choice questions, while Jennifer graded the essay portions of the test. It was a daunting stack, but Emily was nearly done with her task.

"Do you think Nate will bring Dave back alive?" Emily asked.

Jennifer grinned. "I think the two of them can manage a one-hour road trip together."

"I would have killed Dave and buried him in the desert after ten minutes," Emily said.

"It's not like they're spending the whole day together. Dave will be in the library and Nate will be off doing his ex-cop thing with the locals."

"If he does kill Dave, can I have his stuff?"

"No one is killing Dave."

"They still have the drive back."

Bits appeared in the doorway to the office. "Have you seen my six-G router?" he asked.

"There's no such thing as six-G," Emily said.

"Right, and the NSA isn't reading all your text messages."

"What does it look like?" Jennifer asked.

"It looks like my five-G router, only smaller."

"That doesn't help, Bits," she said.

"It's about the size of your phone, but twice as thick, six fold-out antennas equidistant around the perimeter."

Emily and Jennifer looked around the office. "Where was the last place you saw it?" Jennifer asked.

"On the Handelman stakeout."

"Maybe it's still in the van," Emily suggested. "I'll go take a look."

Emily walked over to where Jennifer had left her satchel to get the keys.

Jennifer leaped out of her chair and snatched it out of Emily's hands. "I'll get it," she said, fishing the van keys out of a pocket in the bag. "You guys stay here. I'll be right back."

Jennifer left the office and walked out through the kitchen toward the front door.

"That was odd. Does it seem like she's acting strange to you?" Emily asked Bits.

"How would I know?" he replied.

Emily started after Jennifer.

"So, we're not waiting for her?" Bits asked rhetorically as he followed Emily to the front door.

Jennifer opened the passenger side of the Microbus and stepped between the seats into the cargo area in the rear. There was an air bed set up along the side, and a clothes rack opposite it.

Another small set of shelves held a collection of red Vans sneakers.

At the back of the van were a few crates stacked on top of each other. Jennifer walked through the makeshift living quarters and started searching through the collection of gadgets, cables and cords in the top crate.

She lifted the top one off of the stack and set it aside so she could search the next one. She found a rectangular device and inspected it. There were tiny arms folded around the edge. She lifted one up. "This must be it," she said to herself.

Jennifer opened the back of the van and stepped out into the daylight.

Emily and Bits were standing there.

Jennifer looked at them, then looked behind her at her makeshift living quarters. She turned back to her assistants and handed the router to Bits. "Found it," she said. She closed the rear door to the Microbus and headed back to the house.

"Dr. Daye, why are you living in your van?" Emily asked.

Jennifer froze. After a moment, she turned around and faced them with a forced smile. "What makes you think I'm living in it?"

"You have a bed and all your clothes inside," Bits answered.

"I thought you lived on the other side of campus," Emily added.

"Look, you can't tell Nate or Dave about this," Jennifer implored.

"About what?" Emily asked.

Jennifer walked back toward them and leaned against the van. "When the dean cut off my office privileges, he also ended the funding for Dave's position."

Emily nodded. "Right. But you found a benefactor."

"Exactly," Jennifer said, then stood up straight and held out her arms.

"*You're* the benefactor," Bits deduced.

"And you can't afford your rent and Dave's tuition and salary," Emily added.

"And neither of you can tell Dave. Or Nate."

"Why?"

"Because I'm going to fix all of this soon, and it won't matter. But if Dave knew, he'd drop out, and he's so close to finishing his dissertation."

"He's been close for five years," Emily reminded her.

"And it'll be just another thing for Nate to worry about. So, you two have to promise me you won't say anything."

Emily and Bits nodded.

"That was easier than I expected. Thanks." Jennifer checked her watch, then turned to Emily. "Let's finish that grading. I've got a meeting with Dr. Abara and Dr. Long this afternoon to get ready for." She headed back for the house.

Bits turned to Emily. "Five bucks says Detective Raney figures it out in a week."

"You're on."

CHAPTER NINETEEN

Dale carried his grocery bags down the street on his way home. His heart skipped a beat when he saw Liam waiting for him on the front porch of Mrs. Laughlin's halfway house.

"Hello, Officer McDonald," Dale said. He walked up to the house, climbed the steps and took a seat on one of the weathered chairs on the deck. "I thought you weren't coming by until tomorrow," he said.

"There was a P.I. at the station this morning asking questions. The chief said he was working for the family who moved into your old place. Any chance they might have discovered some hiding place we missed?"

"Well, if they did, we'll find out soon enough."

Liam regarded Dale, trying to divine if there was something he was keeping back. "Yeah, I guess we will. You have any other ideas why they would be hiring a private eye who's asking questions about you and Maureen?"

Dale shook his head. "I've been stuck in prison for the last fifteen years. You would be the one with the answers to questions like that."

"Well, the only other answer I can come up with is that she maybe left a map behind, or some clue as to where she stashed the loot. And maybe the family found that and hired the detective to help them track it down."

"Maybe," Dale answered.

"So, the real question is, where haven't we looked? There's a lot of ground between the bank and the house. And she had an hour to stash the money somewhere. We need to narrow that down," Liam said.

Dale nodded. He'd thought about that as well. Why didn't she stick to the plan? It was smart of her to ditch loot, if she had been caught with it, the both of them would have been in jail.

Instead, her life ended.

"Dale, are you listening?" Liam asked.

Dale shook himself out of his daydream. "Yeah, yeah, I'm way ahead of you." He reached into one of the bags he had brought back and pulled out a folding paper map of Danville.

"I didn't know they still made those," Liam commented.

"They were next to the paperback books."

"I didn't know they still made those, either," he said. "You know, you can get maps online."

"Yeah, I met a lot of guys inside who planned their jobs on a computer."

"A little paranoid, are we?"

"You don't think there's anyone out there who's watching my every move to see if I lead them to the money? Fine, let's use your phone."

Liam reconsidered. "All right, we'll do it your way." He stood up. "You start thinking of where we have to look. I'm going to see what I can find out about that detective, Raney."

Dale stuffed the map back into his bag and entered the house.

Liam looked up and down the street, checking to see if there were any cars or vans that might be staking out Everly.

Nothing stuck out.

He got into his own car and drove away.

CHAPTER TWENTY

Nate looked at his phone to see if Dave had checked in. There were no messages, so he pulled up the address for the Danville Bank and navigated the downtown streets until he found it.

He had pulled up some news stories on his phone about the bank robbery. There was a lot of current information recapping the heist on the occasion of Everly's release, and one of them had a photo of what the Danville city center had looked like back then. There were a lot of changes in that relatively short amount of time, but the bank building was just the same as it had been — aside from a new logo on its sign.

Then he tapped in the Foreman's address and allowed the mapping app to generate the route for him. He examined it closely, trying to note any logical detours Everly's wife might have taken to hide the cash and valuables. There was an alternate path indicated that was of a slightly longer duration but avoided much of the town. Nate suspected that Everly's wife would have wanted to avoid the direct route, and instead circle around using the roads that cut through the foothills.

Nate started driving, making his way across the Interstate, past a patchwork of subdivisions that looked like they were fairly new, and onto a narrow winding road.

In his rearview mirror, he could see Mt. Diablo towering over the city. As the terrain grew rougher, the houses and farms were fewer and farther between until he was alone on the faded blacktop.

As he rounded a sharp bend, a dark gray Hummer appeared on the road ahead of him, taking up most of the single lane. Nate slowed and hugged the shoulder as the giant vehicle passed. He glanced down at the GPS, checking the time to get to the Foreman house from here. He'd been driving for about ten minutes, and there were fifteen minutes still to go, so wherever Everly's wife had hidden the loot could be no more than a ten- or fifteen-minute detour. These hills were riddled with old fire and logging roads. Nate kept an eye out for any gaps in the trees that might lead to a possible hiding place.

Something smashed into the back of his SUV.

Nate took his foot off the gas and gripped the steering wheel firmly with both hands. He looked in the rearview mirror and saw the grill of the gray hummer right on his tail.

What the hell? he thought to himself.

He honked his horn, then rolled down the driver's side window and did his best to indicate that they should pull over to check out the damage.

The Hummer slammed into him again.

The SUV swerved, and Nate had to fight to regain control as he pressed down on the accelerator.

The engine of the Hummer roared as it raced to catch up to him and hit the rear corner of the SUV, causing it to spin out of control.

Nate watched the world turn through his windshield as his vehicle left the road and started tumbling down the steep slope.

The last thing he remembered was seeing the glass shatter into a spiderweb of cracks.

CHAPTER TWENTY ONE

Dave packed up his computer and the stack of photocopies he had made from the archives of the local newspaper into his backpack. He pulled up Detective Raney's phone number and dialed.

After four rings, it went to voice mail.

"Detective Raney, it's me, Dave. I'm all done here at the library, so whenever you can pick me up, I'll be waiting. Just give me a call when you get here. Thanks."

He headed for the entrance to see if the detective was already waiting for him in the parking lot.

"Dave, is that you?" a familiar voice asked.

Dave looked up at an Asian man in his late twenties, with spiked hair and stylish sunglasses. He wore a suit jacket with the sleeves rolled up over a colorful shirt and clashing tie that hung loosely around the open neck.

"Yes," Dave answered, tentatively.

"It's me, Max," he said.

"Max?" Dave asked. He had never met Max in person and was not so much surprised by the man's identity, but by the fact that he was in the Danville Library. "What are you doing here?"

"Emily told me you would be here," Max explained.

"Why would you need to know where I was?"

Max took off his sunglasses and stuffed them in his jacket pocket. "There's been an accident," he explained.

"Accident?"

"Nate's car went off the road up in the foothills."

"Holy cow," Dave exclaimed. "What was he doing up there?"

Max shrugged. "I'll guess we'll ask him when he wakes up."

"Where is he?"

"At the hospital. He's going to be okay, but I figured I would come and get you before you started to worry."

"What about Dr. Daye?" Dave asked.

"She's meeting us there. Come on."

Max led Dave out of the library to his Dodge Charger. He popped open the trunk so Dave could store his backpack, then got behind the wheel while the nervous graduate student slid into the passenger seat and fastened his seatbelt.

The car started with a poorly muffled roar, then Max put it into gear and tore out of the library parking lot.

Dave pressed his hands against the dashboard.

"Nate used to do that, too," Max said. "But I think he learned to appreciate and even trust my driving skills."

"How long did it take?" Dave asked.

"A couple of years."

Max backed off a bit, wanting to put his passenger at ease, and started driving more like Dave was used to with Detective Raney.

"Do you know who Nate was talking to in town?"

"He said he was going to visit the local constabulary," Dave answered.

Max laughed, shaking his head. "I wouldn't want to take him on in Boggle. He didn't happen to mention any names, or if he was going somewhere else?" he asked.

"No, that's all he said. And to call him when I was done."

Max nodded. "Did you tell anyone at the library you were here with Nate?"

Dave shook his head. "No. No one. Why?"

"Just trying to think like Nate, covering all my bases," Max answered.

They drove the rest of the way to the hospital in silence.

CHAPTER TWENTY TWO

Nate opened his eyes.

The light was blindingly bright. He squeezed his lids shut, raising his arm to shield his eyes.

"Relax, you're in the hospital. Again. I thought you hated the food," Jennifer said.

Nate turned his head and squinted at the blurry figure seated to his right. His neck only turned part way, and he realized he was wearing a cervical collar. "What happened?" he asked.

"For some reason you decided to drive off the side of a mountain," she replied.

He remembered driving along the narrow road along the crest of the foothills, but nothing that would explain him ending up in a hospital.

"Do you remember any bright lights? Any voices calling out to you?" Jennifer asked.

Nate rolled his eyes. "No. I did not have a near-death experience. Not today, not ever," he replied firmly.

Jennifer shrugged. "That's not surprising. You were just unconscious, not clinically dead. This time."

"What are you doing here?" Nate asked, changing the subject.

"Wow, I didn't know you'd be so glad to see me."

"How did you know I was here? How long have I been out?"

"A few hours. No major injuries. Thank goodness for all the air-bags in your car. But the doctors were worried that you were out for so long. They were asking how many pain pills you usually take."

"I did not lose control because I took too much oxycodone."

"Do you remember what happened?" Jennifer asked.

"No. But I was not impaired," Nate insisted.

"Okay."

"You didn't answer my question."

"Oh, right. Max called me."

"Max? How did he know I was here?"

"Because," Max answered from the doorway, "I'm still your emergency contact."

Nate's old partner entered, followed by Dave.

"Hey, Doc," Max said to Jennifer. "Did you have to kiss him to wake him up?"

"No, I just read him the hospital menu," she said.

"That'll do it," Max grinned.

"All right, you two," Nate said as he struggled to sit up in the bed. "Who do I have to speak with to get out of here?"

"You think that's a good idea, boss?" Max asked.

"No broken bones, no internal injuries, just got a three-hour nap… I'm good to go. Besides, I'm so hopped up on Oxy I can't feel a thing."

Jennifer's eyes widened.

"I'm kidding. I feel like shit. But I don't need to stay here to do that."

Jennifer looked up at Max. "He can't remember what happened."

"Well, that doesn't sound like someone ready to walk out of a hospital."

"I remember what the deductible on my health insurance is, and I'm not going to see if I can hit it in one day." He searched for the call button for the nurse and pressed it. "Where are my clothes?" he asked, realizing he was wearing a hospital gown.

Max nodded toward the closet.

Nate swung his feet over the side of the bed. He felt a little dizzy but sat still for a moment until it passed.

A nurse walked in. He saw Nate trying to get out of the bed. "Sir, I don't think that's a good idea," he cautioned, as he rushed to Nate's side to catch him in case he fell.

"Well, I haven't had a good idea in months, so that's nothing new." He hopped off the bed and held out his hand where an IV needle was taped in place. "Would you mind removing this?"

"You can't let him go like this, can you?" Jennifer asked the nurse.

"Legally, I can't stop him if he wants to check himself out. But I do strongly suggest that you wait for the doctor to see you."

"No thanks, I want to sleep in my own bed and eat my own food. I'll make an appointment to see my doctor in the morning."

The nurse looked at him skeptically.

"I promise," Nate added.

The nurse shrugged, then carefully removed the needle from the back of Nate's hand and taped some gauze over the wound.

Nate removed the neck brace, then shuffled over to the closet and pulled out his clothes. He looked at everyone staring at him. "A little privacy, please?"

They all filed out of the room, including the nurse.

Nate slipped out of the gown, then put on his pants and shirt and sat on the chair Jennifer had been in to pull on his socks and shoes. He pulled the rest of his belongings out of the plastic bag his clothes had been shoved into, put on his watch, and shoved the rest of the items into various pockets.

He stood up and walked into the bathroom where he ran the water until it was cold, then splashed some on his face. He looked into the mirror.

A memory came back to Nate, of looking in the rearview mirror of his car and seeing the grill of the gray Hummer. "Max!" he called.

Max ran into the room. "Are you all right?" he asked.

Nate dried off his face and looked at his old partner. "I didn't drive off that road. Someone forced me off. A gray Hummer. I didn't get the plate."

"What?"

"I said, someone tried to kill me. Or scare me. But he didn't do either one."

"Nate, are you sure?"

Nate nodded. "We should go up to the accident site, take a look."

"It's getting dark, Nate. Why don't we just tell the local cops and let them figure it out."

"Tell the local cops what?" Chief Lewis asked. The police chief stood in the center of Nate's hospital room, still in uniform. "I heard about the accident, but just found out it was you ten minutes ago. What the hell happened?"

"Someone ran me off the road," Nate replied.

The chief didn't seem to find the information urgent. "That was the first thing my guys checked. There were no other tire marks up there, no debris except what you left tumbling into that ravine."

"Gray Hummer. Passed me going in the opposite direction, then turned around and bumped me off the road," Nate said with certainty.

"Look, Chief," Max interjected, "I've known this guy for years, he's not one to make something like that up."

Lewis nodded. "I've known him a long time, too. Okay, I'll put out a BOLO for a gray Hummer, but unless we find one with paint from Nate's SUV on the front bumper, I've got nothing else to go on except the word of a man who suffered a severe concussion."

"Brian," Nate pleaded.

"Nate, I spoke to the doctor. You shouldn't have been driving with that much Oxy in your system," he said in a low voice. "Out of friendship, I'll keep that off my report."

Max looked at Nate questioningly.

Nate shook his head. "I wasn't high, I wasn't impaired. Someone ran me off that road."

"Okay," Max said. "Let me get you home and we'll sort it out in the morning." He turned to Chief Lewis. "Thank you, Chief. I'm sure he'll be more appreciative once he's gotten a good night's rest."

"I have no doubt," Lewis assured him. "Nate Raney's a stand-up guy. Just take care of him, will you?"

"I will," Max promised.

Nate looked at the two men as if they had just betrayed him, then walked past them into the hall.

CHAPTER TWENTY THREE

Nate sat in the passenger seat of Jennifer's van as they drove through Siesta Valley toward Oakland. She was uncharacteristically silent on the trip back. Nate had expected her to grill him about whether he had had any psychic experiences while he was unconscious, but instead she turned on the radio, and they listened to a pop music station that fuzzed in and out until they made it past the mountains and were in sight of the Bay Bridge.

"Sorry to make you come all the way out here," Nate said. "Dave mentioned that you had some meeting you were supposed to go to."

"It was just a strategy session with some of my friends in the department about getting a new class on the schedule. Nothing urgent."

Nate nodded. "Did Dave tell you if he found anything interesting at the library?"

"I didn't talk to him about the case," Jennifer replied. "Did you find anything interesting? Before you got run off the road?"

He appreciated that she accepted his story about what happened without question. "Maybe," he answered. "But I want to see what Dave dug up before I tell you about it."

"Okay." She changed the subject. "From what I heard your car is pretty much totaled," she said.

Nate sighed. "Yeah, I wasn't expecting to add a new car payment to my budget."

"You have insurance, don't you?"

"Yes, but it's not going to cover a new car."

"So, get a used one. This old thing has been working for me since I started school." Jennifer patted the dash of the VW affectionately. "She's got another hundred thousand miles in her."

The vehicle's engine sputtered as if in reply.

Nate looked at Jennifer with a raised eyebrow.

"Okay, get a new car, then," she said, smiling. "We'll switch to tap water and peanut butter and jelly sandwiches."

"I'll be able to manage. I have some investments I can tap into," Nate said. He wanted to avoid revisiting the topic of dissolving their joint venture—at least until after this case. The angle of a recently released convict and unrecovered cash and valuables from a heist intrigued him. He wondered if it had anything to do with whatever was going on with the Foreman family. There probably wasn't a connection, but it felt like a real case, and the prospect of putting his detective's hat back on after investigating unfaithful pets pushed aside his worries about money and—he was surprised to discover— the chronic ache in his shoulder.

"Ooh, I like this song," Jennifer said, responding to the pop tune playing on the radio. She turned up the volume and began singing along and dancing in her seat. "Come on, you know the words," she said, urging Nate to join in.

Nate didn't recognize the song. He didn't really follow any new artists or listen to the radio. When he did find himself listening to music, it was something from his teenage years, but he found Jennifer's absolute abandonment of any decorum to lose herself in the lyrics and the melody a welcome distraction from the weight of the day's events.

When they arrived at Nate's house, he thanked Jennifer and opened the passenger side door.

"Do you need a hand with anything?" she asked.

"No, I'm fine," Nate assured her. He started to slide out of the van when Jennifer put a hand on his arm.

She had a sincere look of concern on her face. "Nate, do you think whoever ran you off the road is going to try it again?"

He shook his head. "No. It was probably just some off the books weed farmer who thought I was a fed."

Jennifer seemed unconvinced.

"The last two guys who tried to kill me are in jail, and there's nothing about this case we're on that would put me in danger."

"Dave mentioned he found out something about a bank robbery," she said.

"A fifteen-year-old robbery. I don't think it's connected. My incident was just a random act of violence. And I thought you didn't talk to him about the case."

"Maybe a little," she said. Her look still conveyed a degree of worry.

Nate smiled. "Hey, I can handle myself. I promise, it's nothing, but thanks for worrying about me."

Jennifer grinned. "I was actually thinking what an inconvenience it would be to have to find a new office."

Nate shook his head. "Good night, Dr. Daye."

"Good night, Detective Raney."

He slid out of the van and offered a curt wave as Jennifer drove away.

Nate entered his house and headed straight for the refrigerator. He didn't have the energy to cook anything, but he hadn't eaten since that morning, so he decided to fix himself a sandwich.

As he layered provolone cheese and Genoa salami on a pumpernickel rye with Dijon mustard and a homemade rémoulade, Madge pressed her muzzle against his leg and whined. Nate looked over at her empty food and water bowls. "Did no one feed you?" he asked.

Madge trotted over to the bowls expectantly.

Nate put the sandwich aside, fed the dog, and filled her water bowl. Then he plated his sandwich, grabbed an Evian and carried them into his office.

There was a stack of papers on Jennifer's side of the desk, likely the materials Dave had gathered from the library. He wasn't surprised that the graduate assistant and Max had made it back to San Francisco faster than he and Jennifer had. Max had offered to drive Nate home, but Nate decided he would rather risk Jennifer's interrogation over having to suffer under Max's judgmental attitude. He told Max, sarcastically, that he and Dave could catch up on Nate's social life.

Nate slipped out of his jacket and draped it over his chair, then sat down and ate half the sandwich, washing it down with the sparkling water.

He opened his computer and called up the website for an online car dealership he had seen on TV. He found the same make, model and a later year of the SUV he had wrecked. The price was more than he was expecting, but the convenience of arranging financing and delivery to his home offset his usually frugal instincts. It took less than an hour to confirm his financial information, and apparently the income from his police pension was enough to get him approved.

Once he confirmed a delivery window for the next morning, Nate turned his attention to the blank whiteboard behind him. He stood up, grabbed a red marker and wrote in the upper left corner, "Gray Hummer," then underlined it several times.

Next, he picked up a black marker and drew a line down the middle of the board. One side he labeled "Foremans" and the other "Everlys."

Under the Foremans' side, he began making a bulleted list of what he knew about them—which wasn't much.

FOREMANS
- **Marcia - IT/Web Design**
- **Greg - works at big box store**
- **Son - talking to ghost?**
- **Other children?**
- **House remote**
- **Recently remodeled**

Then he turned his attention to the Everlys' side.

EVERLYS
- Dale - released convict
- Wife - killed trying to escape
- Former owners of Foreman house
- Broke into bank
- Missing money and valuables
- Route between bank and home

He drew a line between "Route between bank and home" and "Gray Hummer."

Nate noted that he didn't know the name of Dale Everly's wife. He turned on his phone and pulled up one of the news articles on the robbery, then wiped away the word "wife" and replaced it with the name, "Maureen."

He stared at the board. It was just a start. Once he began his research, he would be adding to the lists and creating others. Then he looked at the stack of copies and photostats resting on Jennifer's side of the desk. He capped his marker and flipped open the file folder sitting on top of the papers. Inside was a printout of the initial email they had received from Greg Foreman. He scanned the text until he found what he was looking for, but hoping he wouldn't.

The name of the ghost the boy, Danny, said he could see and hear.

Maureen.

Nate took a drink from his Evian before returning to the whiteboard, wiping away the word "son" and replacing it with "Danny."

Then he drew a dotted line between the name "Maureen" and the word "ghost" on the opposite side. He knew that Jennifer would infer all kinds of meaning from this link, confirmation that the boy was talking to the ghost of a woman who had died at the house.

But Nate's mind went in a different direction.

He turned on his laptop computer and began searching for all the information he could find on the Everlys and their foiled bank robbery. There was a lot. He printed out some of the articles, many of the pictures, and added them to the board, along with additional lists in different colors and sizes. Some were facts that he had drawn from various sources, others were questions that needed to be answered.

He erased a spot in the middle of the dotted line connecting Danny and Maureen and drew a heavy question mark there and circled it. Then beneath that, he wrote, "Diary?" The email from Greg Foreman had specified that the boy had discovered a box of photos in the attic, but had there been a diary there as well? Is that how he knew details about the woman's life?

Nate rubbed his right shoulder. The pain meds they had given him at the hospital were beginning to wear off, and the aggravation to his injury from tumbling down the side of a mountain, coupled with all the activity he had engaged in since returning home, were beginning to make themselves felt. He knew he was going to pay for it in the morning.

From inside the pocket of his jacket, he pulled out his prescription bottle and shook out two pills. He didn't want to admit it, but Max's concern about Nate's increasing dependency on the medication was warranted. Nate promised himself he would see his doctor about it soon. He had seen coworkers, fellow officers, fall into the well of addiction following injuries before and was acutely aware that he was teetering on the edge.

Madge nudged him. He looked down at the dog, then at his watch, surprised to discover it was well past midnight. "You're right, sweet girl, it's getting late." He tossed the pills in his hand to the back of his mouth, swallowed the remainder of the Evian and turned off the lights as he and Madge headed off to bed.

But as he passed through the kitchen, he second guessed his plan to lie down in his bedroom and try to drift off. He spent a good part of the day unconscious and didn't really feel tired. He returned to the kitchen and pulled a bottle of wine from a rack on the counter. It had been months since he had had more than a sip from his modest collection of vintages, but the growing ache in his shoulder promised to keep him from any opportunity to rest unless he supplemented the pills with a glass or two of the Cabernet Sauvignon he was holding in his hands.

Nate pulled a glass from the cabinet, and a corkscrew from the drawer then carried his midnight libation to the living room. He sat down on the sofa, opened the wine, picked out an old movie on the television, and put his feet up on the coffee table. Madge jumped up and nestled down beside him. Nate ruffled the hair atop her head as he sipped from his glass, watching Laurel and Hardy wrestling a piano up an impossibly steep hill.

CHAPTER TWENTY FOUR

Jennifer drove up to Nate's house under the late morning sun. Her hair was still damp from the shower she had taken at her health club, and she rubbed at the crick in her neck she developed from sleeping on an air mattress that slowly deflated every night. The van life definitely didn't agree with her.

As she stepped out of the Microbus and walked up to the front door, she fished around in her backpack for the key. She pulled open the outer door and reached for the lock before remembering that Nate had replaced it with a keypad. She put the key away and entered the code he had given her. The lock flashed a red light and emitted what she interpreted as a disappointed beep.

Wrong code?

She tried again and was once more met with a flash of red and a scolding tone. She reached into her pack and rummaged around for the slip of paper she had written the entry code on.

But before she could find it, the inside door swung open. Nate was standing there, still half asleep, uncharacteristically ruffled and wearing the same clothes from the previous day. The sun was at Jennifer's back, and Nate squinted at her. "Oh, it's you," he said, then turned around and trundled off.

"Good morning," Jennifer said as she stepped inside and watched as Nate wandered over to the sofa and collapsed on it, face first. He must have fallen asleep there the previous night. "Rough night?" she asked, not expecting an answer.

There was an empty bottle of wine on the coffee table, and next to it was one of the prescription bottles Nate kept close at hand since his last surgery. He wasn't a very open person to begin with, but anything that made him appear vulnerable in any way he was especially guarded about.

He started snoring.

Jennifer grabbed a blanket that had fallen to the floor and draped it over Nate. She heard a whine from the kitchen and spotted Madge standing over an empty bowl. She scooped out some food from the bin Nate kept Madge's kibble in and dumped it in, then topped off the dog's water.

"I wish you could talk, Madge. You are probably the only one who knows what he's going through."

The dog ignored her, hungrily gobbling up her breakfast.

Jennifer continued on through the kitchen to the office. She noticed the whiteboard right away, glad to see that Nate had taken such an interest in the case. She crossed around to her side of the desk and opened the folder sitting there. Dave's work, clearly. A stack of copies made from the Danville News-Gazette's microfilm records as well as other documents, with handwritten comments on sticky notes throughout.

She sat down and started reading through them, starting with some older stories about legends handed down from the local indigenous tribes, other articles about the Gold Rush days, and then a series of clippings about a foiled bank robbery. Dave had highlighted the portion of one of the stories that indicated an address.

Jennifer compared it to the address mentioned in the email from the Foremans.

They were the same.

She looked up at the board Nate had filled with his lists. The names at the top caught her attention. She looked back at the newspaper story and scanned down until she saw where Dave had circled the name of one of the robbers.

Maureen Everly.

Emily sauntered in, sat down in a chair next to the desk, holding a super-sized cup of coffee. "What's with sleeping beauty in the living room?" she asked.

Jennifer shrugged. "You know how it is. Sometimes there's a Twilight Zone marathon on cable and you fall asleep on the sofa in front of the TV."

"*I* know what how it is. I didn't know you had cable in your van."

Jennifer shot her assistant a glare. "You're keeping that between us, remember?"

Emily made a show of looking around the room. "Yeah, I remember." Her eyes lingered on the whiteboard. "Looks like Nate didn't kill Dave after all."

"Why would Nate want to kill me?" Dave asked as he entered the office. He had a sheaf of papers in his hand and his backpack slung over one shoulder.

"Have you met you?" Emily asked.

"Very funny," Dave said.

"What do you have there?" Jennifer asked, eyeing the papers. "More research on the Everlys?"

Dave nodded and placed the stack in front of Jennifer.

"Yeah, I pulled up some recent articles from the internet. It's quite a story."

"Nate thinks so too," Jennifer said, nodding toward the whiteboard.

Dave stepped around the desk to get a closer look. "Looks like we might have a case."

"Let's get the ball rolling on this one. See if they'll allow us to come out and talk to Danny this weekend," Jennifer said.

"Are we taking any gear?"

"Yes, but we won't need the full stake-out package. Just the video cameras, mobile sensors, the usual first contact stuff."

"I'll go see what we have in the van already," Dave suggested.

"Good idea," Emily said, more to Jennifer than Dave.

Jennifer's eyes went wide. "Wait," she said, almost shouting.

Dave froze, turned back toward Dr. Daye.

"That can wait till later," Jennifer said, covering.

"Okay," Dave said. "I'll go up to my office and email the Foremans."

Dave left, heading up to the bedroom on the second floor that served as his private workspace. He used it primarily for his thesis research, but also for the work he did for Dr. Daye, and the bookkeeping he did for Nate.

On his way up, he checked to see if Nate was still asleep on the sofa. He was gone, and Madge had spread out across the warm spot Nate had vacated. As Dave climbed the stairs, he heard the shower in the master suite turn on.

Nate let the hot water cascade over his head. It lessened the headache pounding away inside his skull to a small degree, but not enough for him to forget the reason for it. The only positive thing about his hangover was the fact that it masked the pain in his shoulder. The hot water also served to loosen the stiffness in his damaged joint. He gently moved it in increasingly larger motions, stretching the repaired muscles and ligaments.

He had complained to his doctor that it felt like there was broken glass in his joint, and occasionally it would light up a sharp point of pain. The doctor had told him it was possible there was some damage to the cartilage, but he didn't want to do the procedure to check it out until he had healed more from his last surgery. The advice was to keep the movement to a minimum. So much for that.

He had grown used to showering with his left hand during the months after the shooting, when his right arm was in a sling. He would position his body so the shower spray would rain down on his right side, while he used his left arm to gently clean the rest of himself. It was one of the few moments in the day when he got some relief from the pain that hadn't come from a bottle of one kind or another.

Nate turned off the water, then draped himself in a towel while he stood in front of the bathroom mirror. He used his left hand to wipe part of the fogged glass clear. His eyes were still red, and the morning stubble darkened his chin. He started the process of shaving.

When he was done, Nate picked out a suit and shirt, deciding to forego a tie. He slipped into some loafers and headed downstairs to face Jennifer.

"Trouble sleeping?" Jennifer asked.

Nate sat down before answering. "Just a bit of insomnia," he said as he opened his computer to check his email.

"Nice work," she said, nodding at the whiteboard.

"I thought you'd like that," he replied.

"You really can't allow yourself to believe it could be a ghost?" she asked.

"I know you do, but there is a much more likely explanation."

"That Danny found a diary along with Maureen's photos and is pulling the details about her from that?"

Nate nodded.

"You know what I'm going to ask you," Jennifer said.

"Keep an open mind," Nate replied dryly.

"And not only about the Foremans. I managed to get an appointment with a friend of mine for Eleanor. He's a professional psychic."

"Good. I wouldn't want you to take my mother to an amateur."

"He's very well respected," she replied defensively.

"Well, so much for trying to get her to see that this whole thing is a waste of time." Nate started swiping and tapping at the trackpad on his computer, attempting to end the conversation.

"So that's what it was for you?" Jennifer asked. "You thought I would help you debunk some psychic and destroy your mother's belief that she's communicating with your father?"

Nate felt embarrassed hearing Jennifer reflect his attitude back at him. It made him sound arrogant and uncaring. "Sorry. You're right," Nate admitted. "I just don't want people to take advantage of her."

"Sam isn't like that. And he won't charge her."

"Okay. Whatever you think is best. I trust you," he said dismissively.

140

"Well, I'm afraid I'll need more than just your trust," Jennifer said.

Nate regarded her suspiciously.

"You should come with us. It would mean a lot to Eleanor."

He sighed, resigned. "When?" he asked.

"This afternoon. We should probably take an Uber. The van is still full of gear from the last gig."

A horn honked just as Nate's phone dinged with a notification chime.

"No need. My new SUV is here. God bless the Internet."

CHAPTER TWENTY FIVE

Marcia read the email on the iPad Greg had handed her. It was from someone connected to the parapsychologist they had seen on television responding to the form they had submitted on her website. The message let them know that Dr. Daye was interested in investigating their case and included a list of questions they needed to answer, ending with a very politely worded request for an on-site visit.

"I don't like the sound of that," Marcia said when she finished. "'On-site visit'? We're not some science experiment."

"She is a professor."

"I don't want Danny to be poked and prodded."

"Dr. Daye's not like that," Greg insisted. "I've looked at her website, most of the cases are completely anonymous."

"But not all of them."

"I guess some people want the notoriety."

"Well, I don't. And I don't want Danny to be known as the 'ghost boy.'"

"Neither do I," Greg agreed. "She also exposes frauds and debunks potential paranormal incidents when they have perfectly non-supernatural explanations. If this woman has answers, we should do whatever we can to get them."

Marcia knew he was right, but she was still wary of bringing a stranger into their home. Danny was her little boy.

She didn't know what Maureen was, a ghost or a manifestation of Danny's imagination. But if it was the latter, Maureen was quite a sophisticated fantasy for a ten-year-old boy. Danny was smart and creative, but usually a boy's imaginary friend was a talking bear, or an alter ego who was the one who stole Oreos from the cookie jar. The details Danny told Marcia about Maureen were more than a pre-teen's impression of an adult.

They had consulted their pediatrician, but he was of the imaginary friend school, insisting that he would grow out of it, eventually.

"Okay," she relented. "But she has to keep our names, where we live and work, all of it completely confidential. And no hooking him up to any machines or putting him in any sort of sensory deprivation tank."

"Look, if Dr. Daye and her people make you or Danny the least bit uncomfortable, we pull the plug," Greg assured her.

Marcia looked at her husband, a gaze that was both prodding and pleading. "Okay," she finally said. "Let's do it."

Maureen was getting very adept at moving around the house at will. She was still reluctant to go outside but did venture on to the porch from time to time, and the small patio the Foremans had constructed off the back door so she could more easily watch Danny and Daisy play in the yard.

The conversation she overheard between Danny's parents made her concerned, though she didn't exactly know why. She went up to Danny's room where he was drawing.

"Hi, Maureen," Danny said without looking up from his drawing.

Maureen smiled. It seemed Danny was able to sense when she was in his room without needing to see her. "Hi, Danny, what are you drawing?"

"A pirate spaceship," he replied. He put aside his pencils and held up the sheet of paper for her to inspect.

Maureen marveled at Danny's creativity—though there was a consistent pirate theme to most of his creations, even when they took place in outer space.

"That's fantastic."

"Space pirates are good," Danny explained. "They wouldn't hurt you."

"Why would they want to hurt you?"

"They don't. And I don't think the lady mom and dad want me to talk to would either. She's not really a Ghostbuster."

"Oh, that's good," Maureen replied. "But you shouldn't worry about me. I can take care of myself."

"Okay," Danny said, apparently satisfied with her explanation, as he began coloring his creation.

CHAPTER TWENTY SIX

The house belonging to Jennifer's psychic friend was large and luxurious without being extravagant. Nate assessed it to be worth millions, considering it was not only a spacious building, but sat on a large plot of land.

They pulled up and parked near the front door. The three of them got out of the car and took in the impressive home.

"Are you sure this is the right house?" Eleanor asked.

Jennifer laughed. "Yes, this is it. I've been here before. It looks like a lot, but Sam inherited it."

"I would have been more impressed if you told us he made a killing in the stock market—being a psychic and all," Nate commented.

"His abilities don't include precognition," Jennifer told him. "He's a medium and also can do psychometry."

"Psychometry?" Eleanor asked.

"He has the ability to get impressions from objects by touching them," Jennifer explained.

"Especially if it's money," Nate remarked under his breath.

Jennifer elbowed him in the side.

"You promised me you would behave this time, Nathaniel," Eleanor warned.

The only reason Eleanor agreed to come to see Jennifer's friend was because Nate had apologized and promised to keep his skepticism to himself.

Exacting the apology and promise from Nate was the easy part. Getting him to keep it was what worried Jennifer.

Before she could remind Nate of what he agreed to, he turned to Eleanor and put his arm around her. "You're right, Mom. I'm sorry," he said. "I promise I'm going to just sit back, watch, listen, and be here for you. Okay?"

"Thank you," Eleanor said.

Nate pulled her into a hug. It seemed to Jennifer that there was so much more communicated between them in that moment than in the years of their tumultuous relationship since the death of Nate's father.

"Ready?" Jennifer asked.

Nate and Eleanor separated, and Nate offered her his arm. She slipped her own around it and they followed Jennifer up the steps to the front door.

Jennifer rang the doorbell, and a short moment later it opened to reveal a tall, athletic man who was, from Nate's point of view, obnoxiously handsome.

"Jennifer, so good to see you," he said the instant his eyes fell upon her. He stepped forward and gave her a quick kiss.

The gesture caught the Raneys off guard.

"Hello, I'm Sam," the man said. "You must be Eleanor and Nate. Please, come in."

Nate gave Jennifer a curious look.

Jennifer looked away, embarrassed. It didn't take a detective to figure out that there was some history between them she hadn't fully explained.

Their host led them through a sparkling clean foyer into an expansive living room. The walls, ceilings, floors and furniture were different shades of white, even the hardwood floors were a bleached oak. The only color was found in the various plants and flowers placed around the room, some live in pots, others colorful bouquets set in vases.

"I hope you had a pleasant drive," Sam said.

146

"It was fine," Jennifer assured him.

They arrived at a large sectional sofa littered with throw pillows, another study in white. Sam sat down in the center of it. Nate noticed that he was barefoot when he folded his legs up on the cushions. He held his hands out to guide Jennifer and Eleanor to spots on either side of him. Nate took a seat a few cushions away and was shocked to see that his mother was even more dreamy-eyed around this new-age Adonis than Jennifer was.

Nate was glad to see that Sam didn't bring them into some dark, incense-scented room and seat them around a felt-covered table with crystal balls and tarot cards. This was a step up from the class of psychic his mother normally visited.

"Please, make yourselves comfortable. Would anyone like anything to drink?" he asked.

Jennifer and Eleanor shook their heads.

Sam smiled, then turned to Eleanor and took her hands in his. "So, Jennifer has told me about your journey, Eleanor. I feel I should warn you that my gifts don't guarantee that you will find what you want, but hopefully you'll receive what you need."

Nate struggled to keep himself from rolling his eyes and concentrated on keeping the friendly smile on his face.

"Did you bring what I asked?" Sam inquired.

Eleanor nodded. She took her hands back and reached for her purse. From within, she pulled out a pocketknife. Nate recognized it as the one that his dad always had with him. He had wondered if his mother had saved it and was glad to know she had.

She placed the pocketknife on Sam's open palm, and he closed his fingers over if for a second. Then he placed it onto the coffee table and took Eleanor's hands back into his.

"I can't reach Ben right now," he told Nate's mother. "I'm sorry."

Eleanor became suddenly agitated. "No, that's wrong. He's always with me. He told me so. I talk to him all the time."

Sam smiled to her, comfortingly. "I'm sure you do. But he's just not talking to me."

The explanation seemed to comfort Nate's mother.

Nate struggled again to keep the sarcasm that was welling up within him at bay.

Sam cocked his head as if listening to a voice unheard by the rest of them. He smiled. "I do hear the voice of the person who gave your husband that pocketknife. Betsy," Sam said simply. "Is that Ben's mother?"

"Grandma gave dad the knife for his thirteenth birthday," Nate said without thinking.

Eleanor nodded. "Is she with Ben?"

"Yes," Sam assured her.

"Can I speak with her?"

"She is sending love," Sam answered.

"Tell her I want to talk to Ben," Eleanor pleaded.

Sam shook his head. "I'm sorry. That's not going to happen right now. I know when the spirits are willing, and for some reason, they just don't want to speak at this time."

Eleanor and Jennifer looked over at Nate.

He kept his expression frozen.

Sam closed his eyes and drew in a deep breath. "They exist in their own way, outside of time." He squeezed Eleanor's hands, then looked at her with deep compassion. "You are right to believe Ben is always with you, but from his point of view, a moment passes, but it's been days in your life. Do you understand?"

Eleanor shook her head. "No. I don't. Are you saying he's in a different time zone?"

Sam smiled. "In a matter of speaking. But instead of being off by an hour or two, it's constantly slowing down and speeding up, and sometimes we're moving at the same speed at the same time in the same place and we can make contact."

"It sounds so confusing," Eleanor admitted. "Harmony just lets me talk to Ben."

"She must be in the right place at the right time," Sam assured her. "It's just not today, and not here."

Eleanor nodded. "Thank you for trying. You're a very nice man," she said.

"I was very much looking forward to meeting Ben. Maybe next time," Sam offered.

"Thank you, Sam," Jennifer added.

"Always glad to make time for my favorite professor," Sam said. "Can you stay for dinner?" he asked.

Jennifer was about to reply, but Eleanor cut her off. "Actually, Nate promised to take me and Dr. Daye out."

Jennifer and Nate looked at her with surprise.

Nate had the distinct impression that Eleanor was trying to keep Sam away from Jennifer, and knowing his mother, push Jennifer closer to Nate. He cast a glance at Jennifer, wondering if she was thinking the same thing.

"Rain check?" Jennifer asked.

Nate stood up, eager to take advantage of the semi-awkward moment to move on from this weird experience. "Yes, thank you for your hospitality," he said. Out of habit, he took a step forward and offered his hand to Sam.

Sam shook Nate's hand, then gripped it firmly and wrapped it with his other hand while looking into Nate's eyes.

Nate pulled his hand free.

"You've been to the other side," Sam said.

Nate smiled knowingly. "You mean when I was shot? It was on the news."

Sam nodded. "The figure you saw, the one that told you it wasn't your time. That was your father," Sam stated.

Nate swallowed. He hadn't told anyone about that part of the dream from when he had been under anesthesia while the doctors stitched him back together. Sam was shooting in the dark. Jennifer had likely told him about the conflicts he had with his mother over the years. Injecting a comment like that was merely him doing a cold read trick, trying to catch Nate off guard.

"Sure," Nate said, remembering his promise to his mother and Jennifer. "That's nice to know." He turned to Jennifer. "Well, it sounds like I'm taking you two to dinner."

CHAPTER TWENTY SEVEN

Dale Everly stared at the map taped to the wall of his room. There was a lot more on the map than there was the last time he had been in Danville—new roads, subdivisions and parks. The town had grown quickly in the years since he'd gone to prison. The edge of the town had grown closer to the old farmhouse he had shared with Maureen, and the road that led there was now home to clusters of retail stores, fast food restaurants and car dealerships.

For the last few days, Dale had been comparing his recollections of the area to what it looked like now. More importantly, he was checking for any of the places only he and Maureen knew. If Liam was right, and Maureen had left her loot from the bank somewhere he could find it, he should be able to figure it out.

The obvious locations, the ones he considered during noisy nights in his cell, he quickly ruled out. One was an old roadside bar they used to hang out at that had a gazebo at the back of the parking lot. No one used it much, but Maureen liked hanging out there on warm summer nights. There was a space underneath it that she could have easily tossed the duffel bag.

The site of the bar was now one of those chain restaurants. Chances are when they knocked down the old place, they would have noticed a duffel bag full of cash and valuables under the old wooden structure.

Then there was the bowling alley. They were in a league—not a very competitive one, it was more drinking than bowling—on Thursday nights. The bowling alley had a back room that he and Maureen would sneak off to for some alone time. And in that back room, there was a storage area that held discarded items that were decades old.

The bowling alley was still there but had undergone a major renovation of its own and was now part of a chain that included high-tech automated scoring and pizza. If she had hidden the loot there, it would have been discovered as well.

He went down the list of other possibilities, but either they were gone, or when he and Liam visited them, their prize was not to be found.

There were just a few more possibilities left on the list Dale had made. One was their old high school—the building had been condemned shortly after they had graduated, but it was still standing pending the funding for asbestos removal. There were several hiding places in the old building, a locker, the space under the stage in the tiny auditorium, the cabinets in the kitchen. They were planning an expedition of sorts to search the school, but Dale was not optimistic.

The last place on Dale's list was a long shot. An old sawmill that they had come across while hiking. It was behind a barbed wire fence, but they had found a gap in the barrier. Maureen loved exploring the old building. It was fairly dangerous, a good 4.0 earthquake away from splintering into kindling.

The problem was the timeline. Dale couldn't figure out how she could have made it from the bank to the sawmill and then on to the farmhouse in anything less than an hour and a half. And that didn't include time to find a good hiding place for the duffel bag.

Maureen had a lot of places like the sawmill. Little abandoned shacks in the woods, peaceful, isolated meadows, out of the way trails leading to mountain top vistas. Any one of them could have been a place where she might have felt like she could stash the bank loot, and not one of them was on any map.

There was a knock on the open door.

Dale turned and saw Liam leaning against the frame, an expectant look on his face.

"How's the treasure hunt going?" he asked.

Dale replied by waving at the map.

The bank and the farmhouse were represented by white pushpins. Dale had drawn arcs around the two points, representing roughly how far one could travel in about half an hour. The house's pin was well inside the arc centered on the bank and vice versa. The two of them formed a shape that reminded Dale of an open eye.

Somewhere in that eye was a treasure.

A treasure that Maureen had died for.

"I've narrowed it down to a few hundred square miles," Dale answered.

Liam whistled. "That sounds like a lot. Hope you've got extra batteries for your metal detector."

Dale shook his head. "A lot of it we can rule out. Houses, stores, parking lots." He pointed to some squiggles on the maps that were highlighted in yellow. "Those are the trails that intersect with the possible routes she might have taken from the bank to the house. That's probably where we're going to find it. She loved hiking these hills and woods. I remember going on some of them with her, and I can recall some spots that might have been good hiding places."

"What about those satellite photos of the area I printed out for you?"

Dale shrugged. "Everything is so different, and it was a long time ago."

"Are you sure we should rule out the house?" Liam asked. "The family that's living there hired a private detective for some reason."

Dale shook his head. "If there was a full duffel bag hidden in there, it wouldn't take much to find it."

"I still think she could have left a note or a map or something, explaining where it was," Liam suggested. "Was there some hiding place you guys had?"

The idea that she had gone back to leave him a note of some kind was something that Dale had considered. There were several spots he could think of, but if what Liam had told him about the extent of the remodeling the Foremans had done was correct, there was little chance it would have gone undiscovered. Still, if he could get inside, maybe it would stir his memory. "It's possible," he conceded. "But if they found something like that, why keep it quiet? And why would the P.I. go to your chief and tip his hand?"

Liam shrugged. "I just find it hard to believe that it's not connected somehow." He looked the map over. "I'll keep an ear out, but in the meantime, we can hike these trails ourselves, see what we can find."

"Hope you've got a good pair of boots."

CHAPTER TWENTY EIGHT

Nate took his mother and Jennifer to a restaurant he had been meaning to visit for years. It was expensive, but he needed the extravagance, a departure from his daily grind to take his mind off the events of the last couple of days. He had money put away for a rainy day, and recently it was a never-ending deluge. Maybe dipping into his investments and pulling out some cash would help relieve the stress. He'd already tapped some funds for the new car, but there were a few holdings that had done exceedingly well for him over the years, and with his current income level, the capital gains tax wouldn't be too hard a hit.

Jennifer and Eleanor had allowed him to order for them. Eleanor said she'd always wanted someone to do that for her and was delighted with Nate's selections. Jennifer was a little more hesitant about the idea, but Eleanor persuaded her to trust Nate's taste and she was surprised at how perfectly the dishes Nate picked out for her went together.

But what really impressed her was his wine choices. Jennifer had worked as a sommelier in her younger days, but Nate's knowledge went far beyond what she would expect from a man on a police detective's salary.

They spent most of the meal listening to Eleanor tell stories about her and Ben, and the meals she used to put together by clipping coupons and buying giant cans of things like tapioca pudding and lard.

The memories made Nate cringe.

The meal left all of them in a great mood, especially Eleanor, who had more wine than Nate and Jennifer put together. The disappointment of not being able to talk to Ben had fallen away.

They dropped Eleanor off at her house. Nate walked her inside and made sure she locked up after him. When he got back to the car, he turned to Jennifer with a somewhat shocked expression.

"What is it?" Jennifer asked.

"I just realized I don't know where you live. I've been to your offices—when you had them—I've been on stakeouts with you. You've been to my house almost every day for the last few months, but I've never been to yours. Where to?" he asked like an eager Uber driver.

Jennifer froze. She had given up her apartment and was sleeping in her Microbus, so there was nowhere to take her.

"Your place," she said. "I can drive myself home."

"Actually, if I were to breathalyze you right now, I'd have to arrest you."

"I'm okay," Jennifer insisted.

"You can grab an Uber in the morning. Or Dave can give you a ride."

"I guess," Jennifer agreed, not wanting to push it any further. She remembered an apartment building she had looked at a few years ago when she was thinking about moving closer to campus. It wasn't too far from where they were now. "It's over on Geary, by the campus," she told him.

"Okay." Nate put the car back into gear and steered them on a route toward the heart of the city. He noticed that Jennifer had become suddenly silent and wondered if his offer to drive her home was inappropriate, something she considered beyond the boundaries of their friendship.

The conversation he had had with Dave on the drive to Danville had gotten him thinking that maybe Jennifer was interested in him. And to be honest, it had gotten him thinking that maybe he was interested in her, too.

"Thanks for letting me order for you. I know it's kind of a throwback thing to do, but my mom—"

"It was nice," Jennifer assured him. "I got to try something I would never have ordered myself. Thank you."

"You're welcome," Nate said. "I'm glad you enjoyed it."

There was another period of awkward silence as Nate tried to come up with something else to say. It was strange. Normally, during the times they were both in the office they shared in Nate's house, they were never at a loss for something to talk about. Nate actually found her academic field of anthropology intensely interesting. And her excitement about the topic was contagious.

He wondered about her and Sam, and whether she would have accepted his invitation to dinner if Eleanor hadn't contrived an alternative. But she did decide to join them and appeared to have a good time. But now, she seemed like she was in a different place. Maybe her good mood was just an act for his mother.

"You want to turn here," Jennifer said, breaking the silence.

"Thanks," Nate replied. He steered his car onto another road and kept driving in silence. He glanced over and saw Jennifer nervously nibbling at her cuticles.

After another couple of miles, they arrived at a high-rise apartment complex. The first level was floor to ceiling windows, and in the corner where the entrance was, there was a guard or concierge manning a desk, where he could screen visitors and accept packages. It was a nice building, and Nate was glad to see that a tenured college professor made enough to afford a place like this.

"Do you… want me to walk you in?" Nate asked, instantly regretting how forward it sounded.

"I'm fine," she said. "I'll see you tomorrow. Oh, I almost forgot to tell you. Dave heard back from the Foremans. They've decided to let us visit this weekend."

"Great," Nate said.

"Yes," Jennifer agreed. Then she took a deep breath and let herself out of the car.

Nate waited at the curb for her to enter, making sure she got in safely, still debating whether she thought he was being a gentleman or just creepy.

Jennifer walked to the building entrance and gave Nate a little wave. He waved back, but remained at the curb, waiting.

She entered the building and walked up to the concierge.

"Hello," she said.

"Good evening. How may I help you?"

Jennifer considered telling him the truth, that she was trying to deceive a friend who thought she lived here, but that sounded a bit on the pathetic side. "Do you see that SUV parked on the curb?" she asked.

The concierge looked out the window at where Nate was still parked. "Yes."

"Tinder date. I know, bad idea, but he seemed nice. He was getting a bit clingy, so I kind of told him I live here, so he doesn't find out where I really live."

The concierge nodded. "Do you want me to call the police?" he asked.

"No, no, I don't think that's necessary, but I think he's going to wait until I go inside. So, do you think you can buzz me to the elevators? Once he's gone, I'll be out of your hair."

The concierge considered her request and nodded. He pressed a button on the underside of his desk and the door buzzed. Jennifer walked toward it, not stopping to look back at Nate. She waited on the other side for a good five minutes, using the time to call Heather Long, her new friend in the anthropology department, and ask if she could crash on her couch.

When she re-entered the lobby, Nate was gone. She smiled to the concierge. "Thank you."

"No problem. Careful who you swipe right."

"I will." She called up the Uber app on her phone and requested a trip to the address Heather had given her and stepped out into the night air, thinking this actually wouldn't be a bad place to live. Maybe once she got things straightened out with Dave's stipend, she'd take another look.

CHAPTER TWENTY NINE

Marcia and Greg were outside working in the garden. Maureen let Danny know the coast was clear.

Danny followed his friend down to the living room in the corner where Marcia had her home office. The boy became reluctant when he saw where Maureen was leading him. "I'm not supposed to play around mommy's stuff," he said.

"It's okay," Maureen assured him. "We're just going to go online for a minute."

Danny backed away. "I'm not allowed to go on the internet," he said. "That's for grownups."

"Well, I'm a grownup," Maureen pointed out. "But I need your help to do something on the computer." She showed Danny how her fingers were unable to affect the keyboard.

Danny considered her logic. It seemed okay. His parents always told him how important it was to help people. "Okay," he said. "But I don't know my mom's password."

"That's all right, just type what I tell you," Maureen said. She had watched Marcia log on to the computer and memorized the password that she had typed in. She instructed Danny to tap each of the characters on the keyboard and the computer unlocked. "Okay, we need to open the web browser. It's that icon on the bottom that looks like—"

"I know what it is," Danny told her, and he used the mouse to click open the browser. "What do you want to search for?"

"Dr. Jennifer Daye," Maureen told him. She spelled the last name for him.

"That's a funny way to spell it," Danny said.

The search results came up with a page of links. The first one was to her website. "Click on the first one," Maureen said.

Danny moved the mouse over the blue underlined text and clicked.

The website for Jennifer Daye filled the screen. It featured a blog of the cases she investigated mixed in with articles and commentary from other sources. Maureen saw the link at the top of the page she was looking for labeled "Staff."

"Click on the staff link," she told Danny.

Danny scanned the page and found the word Maureen had mentioned. He clicked on it and the new page snapped onto the screen. In the center of it was a picture of Dr. Jennifer Daye and her staff.

It was obvious which one was the college professor. She was confident and professional. She wore a jacket over a turtleneck top and tweed slacks. The only thing that stood out were the red shoes, a sharp contrast to the muted tones of the rest of her clothes. The other element that stood out was the necklace that hung around her neck with a symbol that looked like a pitchfork or a trident.

To her right was a young man, a couple of inches shorter than her and prematurely balding. He had a closed-mouth nervous smile and wore a plain sweatshirt over his very new looking blue jeans. The caption under the photo identified him as Dave Edwards.

To her left was a younger woman who had a very dark look. Her hair was black, her eye-liner heavy, and her dark clothes matched her overall mood. Her expression was completely blank, as if being in this photo was a burden. Her name was Emily Vargas.

There was another person in the photo—sort of. He was standing behind the rest of them, wore an unbranded baseball cap and dark sunglasses. According to the text below the picture, his name was Bits.

Maureen took a moment to memorize their faces.

There was something else on the site that caught her attention. It was a link referencing Raney/Daye Investigations. "Click on those gold letters on the right," Maureen said to Danny.

He moved the mouse to the text she was talking about. "This?" he asked.

"Yes."

Danny clicked on the link, and it opened on a new website. This one a little less cluttered. It was for what looked like a private investigation firm. "Can you scroll down?" Maureen asked.

Danny used the wheel on the mouse to move the page down.

There were side by side portraits of Raney and Daye.

Daye, she knew. It was Dr. Jennifer Daye, PhD, Parapsychologist.

Raney was a man who looked to be about the same age as the professor. He wore an expensive-looking suit. The caption under it identified him as Nate Raney, Private Investigator.

That explained Raney/Daye Investigations.

"Anything else?" Danny asked.

Maureen had what she needed. She wanted to know what the people Marcia and Greg had invited to talk to Danny looked like. "No, that's all. Thanks, Danny."

"You're welcome," he said, then ran off back up to his room.

In many ways, Maureen was still learning about what being a ghost meant. She had discovered that she could go outside the house, but she hadn't really tested the limits beyond the front and back yards. How many years had passed in the living world while she was in that bedroom, it felt like the blink of an eye to her, but she wondered if she had been there the whole time since she had died, or if she was somewhere else, and the presence of the Foreman's had drawn her back or woke her up.

She had learned that she didn't need to physically move through the house. She could follow Danny as he walked from his room to the kitchen and out to the backyard, but if she thought of herself downstairs, or outside, that's where she would be.

The notion of venturing outside the property frightened her. She was afraid that she was somehow tied to Danny and would lose that connection if she were too far away from him. But she was also afraid of the people the Foremans had invited to their home to investigate her. Would they be able to see her like Danny could? Did they have the means to send her away?

According to what she overheard between Marcia and Greg, they would be here today. And Maureen would be ready.

CHAPTER THIRTY

Dave inspected the large foam padded case that held their video and audio recording equipment to make sure everything was there. He checked off a couple of lines on the list on his clipboard, then closed and secured the lid. He stood it on end and tilted it forward so he could position a hand truck underneath it and wheel it out of Nate's house.

"Can someone get the door for me?" he shouted.

There was no reply. He knew Emily and Bits were both around getting ready for the field investigation. They were supposed to be leaving for Danville soon.

"Emily? A hand?" he called out.

Again, either she couldn't hear him, or, more likely, was ignoring his pleas.

Dave left the large case in the middle of the room, then went to open the front door and prop open the storm door. Once he had a clear path, he tilted the crate back on the hand truck and started rolling it out of the house.

It stopped when he hit the raised threshold of the front door, the weight of the crate keeping it from easily rolling over the obstacle. Dave backed it up and made the approach at a higher speed. The hand truck bounced over the threshold and the crate tipped precariously. Dave tried to wrangle back control, but the momentum pulled it forward and the crate rocked, nearly breaking the glass of the outer door.

He managed to regain his hold on the crate and settle it back into the crook of the hand truck. After easing it down the steps, Dave guided his load along the cement path until he hit the street.

Dr. Daye's van was parked at the curb. Dave set the crate on its edge on the grass nearby and walked up to the van to open the rear doors. They were locked. He walked around to the front of the van to try the passenger side door, but it, too, was locked. He scratched his head, puzzled. Dr. Daye normally left the van open for Dave on mornings when they had a trip into the field. He was reluctant to leave the case of video gear just laying out on the front lawn, so he tilted it back on the hand truck and pushed it up the walkway to the front door. He carefully pulled it up the steps and up and over the threshold into the house.

He saw Emily on the sofa in the living room, flipping through a magazine. "Where were you?" Dave asked. "I needed a hand getting this gear out to the van."

Emily raised an eyebrow when he mentioned the van, remembering the fact that Dr. Daye had sworn her to secrecy about her current living conditions as it related to Dave's stipend and tuition reimbursement.

"You went in the van?" she asked back.

"No, it's locked. Do you know where the keys are?"

"No," Emily replied.

"Do you know where Dr. Daye is?"

"No."

"Do you know what time we're supposed to leave?"

"No."

Dave gave up talking to Emily and shouted at the top of his lungs. "Does anybody know what's going on around here?"

"Dave, lower the volume," Nate said, emerging from the kitchen with a cup of coffee. He saw the crate blocking the front door. "Shouldn't that be out in the van?"

"The van's locked. Have you seen Dr. Daye?"

"She hasn't come in yet?" Nate asked.

"Her van's here," Dave answered.

"We went out to dinner with my mother last night. I dropped her off at her apartment. She was planning on getting a ride back here in the morning."

"Her apartment?" Emily asked in surprise. "You dropped her off?" Emily wondered if she somehow had gotten a new place in the last few days.

"Yes," Nate said, as if the question was offensive.

"And she went inside?"

"Of course."

"Did she ask you up?" Dave asked.

Nate and Emily shot Dave a look.

"What?" he said to Emily, "you were thinking it, too."

"He's right," she said. "I was thinking it. Did she?"

"No. And frankly, if she had, it's none of your business."

"True, but technically I work part time for a private detective, so the snooping kind of comes with the territory," Emily said.

"Any idea when she's coming in?" Dave asked. "I'd like to get the gear loaded."

"I think there's a spare set of keys in the office," Nate said. He set down his coffee and turned to head to the back of the house.

Emily cut him off. "She wanted to take your SUV," she said to Nate.

"She did? She didn't say anything last night."

"She mentioned it a couple of days ago. The van's been making weird noises."

"It always makes weird noises," Dave said.

"Plus, it's almost an hour's drive. No back seats, no seat belts. Safety first," Emily added.

Dave and Nate both looked at her inquisitively. Nate could sense there was something going on, but he couldn't quite put his finger on it.

Jennifer entered the house, squeezing past the equipment crate.

"Why isn't this in the van?" she asked.

"It's locked," Dave explained.

Jennifer opened her purse to fish out her keys.

"Dr. Daye," Emily said, "I thought you said you didn't want to take the van. You know, because of the strange noises that may be coming from the stuff in the back."

Jennifer froze, remembering that even though she had spent the night in a real bed for the first time in months, her actual bedroom was in the Microbus. And she hadn't had time to stuff it into the tiny storage locker where some of her other stuff was.

"Of course," Jennifer said. She turned to Nate. "Do you mind if we use your car?"

"Not at all," Nate said. He pulled his keys out and tossed them to Dave. "What time are we leaving?"

"You're coming?" Jennifer asked.

"Sure. Last time I checked the front door, this was still Raney/Daye Investigations. Plus, I've already got a contact at the local police station."

"Yes, of course. That would be great. I always want you to come along, but you usually…"

"Don't want to go," Emily said, finishing Jennifer's sentence.

"Seem to be busy," Jennifer corrected.

"Well, I want to, and I'm not busy. I think maybe it's time I lend a hand more directly."

"You're curious about the whole bank robbery connection," Jennifer said.

"That, too," Nate admitted.

"Great."

Nate looked at Jennifer. "Aren't those the same clothes you were wearing last night?"

Without skipping a beat, she replied, "same shoes, different top and slacks." She made a point of looking at her clothes.

"I guess they are similar."

"Your wardrobe is so boring," Emily agreed.

Bits walked by, carrying a crate of cables. "I thought you just wore the same thing every day. Like Jeff Goldblum in *The Fly*."

Everyone watched Bits pass through and out the front door.

"Yay, road trip," Emily added.

CHAPTER THIRTY ONE

Marcia pulled into the grocery store parking lot and checked her watch. She hadn't planned on making a food run, but it occurred to her as she and Greg were making breakfast for the kids, that they really didn't have anything to offer Dr. Daye and her staff when they came over this afternoon. So, she left the kids with Greg and headed into town to stock up on some fresh fruit, maybe some cheese and crackers and soft drinks and coffee.

The market was one of the big chain stores. She usually preferred the organic market on the other side of town, but she was pressed for time. She walked in, grabbed a cart and pushed it straight toward the produce.

A man in a police uniform, carrying a sack in one hand and a Diet Coke in the other, eyed her as she walked by. Marcia noticed him watching her. He looked familiar.

She started selecting apples and pears and grabbed a bag of the mini oranges the kids liked.

"Mrs. Foreman?" a voice asked.

Marcia turned around and saw the policeman standing just behind her. She smiled, digging through her memory for his name.

He extended his hand. "Liam McDonald, we met when you were working on the department website."

The face and situation registered in Marcia's mind, but not the name. She had gotten the contract to revamp the Danville P.D. site shortly after they had moved to town. Liam was one of the officers there who knew a little about everything. Her interactions with him were brief and unmemorable. She couldn't even recall if he had ever told her his name.

"Officer MacDonald, of course. It's nice to see you again."

"I hope I'm not bothering you," he said.

"Well, I'm kind of on an emergency shopping trip," she told him.

"Oh," Liam replied, reconsidering whether this was the right time and place to engage Mrs. Foreman. But he and Dale needed to know what was going on with them. Had they found the money, or some clue? Why was that detective snooping around and asking questions about the house? He decided to take an indirect approach. "Well, I won't keep you. I was just curious why there was a detective at the station the other day asking questions about you."

Marcia suddenly lost interest in the produce. "About me?"

"Well, not you specifically, but your family. He said his name was Raney."

Marcia thought back to the website she and Greg had visited when they had initially reached out to Dr. Daye. She remembered that name was part of it somehow. Of course, it was the thing that Greg used to sell her on reaching out to the parapsychologist. She worked with a private detective who was an ex-cop, and his name was Raney. She didn't know if she should feel offended or reassured that he was checking up on them.

"I think I know what that's about," she told him.

"Anything I can help with? I mean, if you want me to look into him, find out—"

"No, that's not necessary. It's someone my husband and I reached out to. We've been having a bit of a situation at the house."

"I hope it's nothing bad."

"No, it's just..." Marcia considered whether she should say anything else but decided it might be better to reassure Officer McDonald that it was nothing he needed to worry about. "It's kind of a personal matter. My son, Danny, has been—well, his best friend is a ghost," she said.

The expression on his face was pure surprise. Whatever he thought she was going to say, this was the farthest thing from it.

"Oh," was the first word out of his mouth. "You mean like Casper?"

Marcia laughed. "Kind of. But instead of a little boy ghost, he's made friends with a grown woman."

"Well, that's interesting," Liam replied. "I'm at a bit of a loss as to what that has to do with a detective from San Francisco."

"He works with a parapsychologist."

"A what?"

"Dr. Daye. She's an expert on ghosts and hauntings and stuff like that. Detective Raney apparently gives the cases a skeptic's point of view. My husband is convinced it's really a ghost, but I'm not so sure."

"What do you think it is?"

She shrugged. "Just an imaginary friend. He found a box of photos in the attic, and maybe he just made her up, imagined what it would be like to know her. He has friends at school, but we live so far out of town, he doesn't see them a lot."

"I'm sure that's what it is," Liam said.

"The doctor and some people from her staff are coming over today. I have to do a little last-minute shopping so they don't think I'm a rude hostess." Marcia glanced down at her watch, then offered a hasty goodbye. "Nice to see you again, Officer McDonald, but I've really got to get going. I'll tell Maureen you said hello," she added as a joke. She grabbed her cart and started to push it toward the deli counter.

"Did you say Maureen?" Liam asked.

Marcia answered as she walked away. "Yes, that's the name of Danny's friend," she replied, offering him an embarrassed smile. "See you around, Officer."

Liam stood completely still.

Maureen.

He slipped the bottle of Diet Coke into his bag, pulled out his phone, and tapped on one of his recent calls. When the party on the other side answered, Liam said, "Dale, we need to talk."

CHAPTER THIRTY TWO

Maureen stood on the front porch of the house. She looked out at the orchard across the road. She hadn't really paid it any attention until now. The trees had just been planted by an almond grower a few years before the robbery, and now they were twenty feet tall.

In the house, Greg and the kids were getting ready for their guests while Marcia had gone off to run some errands. She knew if she was going to attempt her plan, she would have to do it now.

Even though she had spent time outside the house in the yard and on the porch, she hadn't dared make her way to the road. But today, she needed to go much further than that. Would she be able to leave? Would she be able to return?

Maureen thought back to the robbery. She thought about the bank, and the counter where she worked as a teller. Then she closed her eyes.

When she opened them, she was standing there in the bank. Not behind the counter, but in the middle of the lobby, the exact point she was thinking of just a second ago.

She looked around. The bank was busier than she remembered it. The tellers had mostly been replaced by automated terminals and people stood in line in front of them, impatiently looking at the tiny video screens that Maureen knew, now, from watching Marcia and Greg, were their phones. It amazed her that they could play games and watch videos on them.

No one noticed her. She had wondered if there were other people like Danny, who could see and hear her, but it was becoming more apparent that what they had was unique. She was deciphering the rules of being a ghost as she went along. So far, she knew that she could change her clothes by just imagining herself wearing something different. And likewise, she didn't need to walk from one place to another. She could just see herself in a different location and she was there. Traveling to the bank was a test of just how far she could take that ability. But it was a place she knew, a place she had a connection with. Could she go somewhere she hadn't been before?

At the same time, how was she able to see? Why was her interaction with the world so one-way? She could see the people around her, but they couldn't see her. She could see the things around her, but couldn't touch them. She felt like she had to shake the notion that she was using her eyes to see. There had to be something else at work, a sense that she didn't have when she was alive, or if she did, wasn't aware of.

And if that was the case, was that wall really keeping her from seeing the street outside?

It turned out it wasn't. For the first time, she felt disconnected from the image she had of herself. She wondered if she could see the whole town at once, and then she could. As she expanded her awareness, it became less focused, individual people became crowds, but she could still sense them.

She thought about Marcia, wondering where she was in that sea of people.

The grocery store, she knew instantly. And then she could see her pushing a cart filled with bags toward her minivan in the parking lot.

But she knew Marcia and maybe had a connection with her through Danny. Would it work with someone she hadn't met?

With Dr. Jennifer Daye?

She pictured the photo from the website. Was that face out there somewhere? Could she see it with her "ghost sense"?

Then she became aware of something in the distance.

It resolved into an SUV speeding down the highway.

And in the passenger seat was Dr. Daye.

Maureen was pleasantly surprised to find herself in the back seat between two people she recognized as members of Dr. Daye's staff. Dave and Emily, she remembered. And driving was Detective Raney.

Dave and Emily shivered. "Can you turn the air down a bit?" Dave asked.

"It's not on," Detective Raney replied. His gaze was focused on the rearview mirror, trying to figure out if he really did catch a glimpse of a dark gray Hummer on the highway behind them, or if he was just imagining it.

"You haven't answered my question," Dr. Daye said, continuing a conversation they were having before Maureen joined them.

"What? Will I be open to the possibility that the boy is actually talking to a ghost?"

"I believe I used the word 'apparition.'"

"It's just not the first explanation I jump to. Or the second." He thought for a moment. "Or tenth."

"Well, I don't buy your theory that he found some diary and is making the whole thing up. He's ten."

Detective Raney nodded. "So, what you're telling me is that *you're* not open to the idea that kids sometimes go to great lengths to get attention."

"If he wanted attention, he could have just set the house on fire," Emily said in a dry monotone. "That worked for me."

Jennifer and Dave looked at her, curious.

"Kidding," she said in the same flat voice.

"Look," the detective said with an authoritative tone, "I've seen kids who were not much older than ten who were running some pretty sophisticated rackets in their schools, selling drugs, stealing phones—"

"This isn't some disadvantaged youth trying to survive on the streets. He's a normal suburban fifth grader," Dr. Daye said to him.

"I'm just pointing out that kids are smarter than we give them credit for sometimes," he replied.

Danny is certainly pretty smart, Maureen thought. *But he's not lying about me.*

Dave chimed in from the back seat. "According to his dad, Danny has a lot of details of her life. Cultural references that he would have no exposure to."

"Maybe he's watching reruns of *Seinfeld,*" Detective Raney suggested.

"All the ten-year-old boys I know are watching Rick and Morty," Emily droned.

"You know ten-year-old boys?" Dave asked.

"Cousins," she explained.

"I'm just saying there are alternative explanations that are much more likely than conversations with a dead woman," Detective Raney reiterated.

"Only if you don't believe we can have conversations with a dead woman," Dr. Daye countered.

Maureen smiled. She was really starting to like Dr. Daye.

CHAPTER THIRTY THREE

Marcia watched nervously as Emily set up a couple video cameras on tripods and Dave unpacked a selection of sensors and started pairing them with a laptop computer.

"Is all this really necessary?" she asked.

Jennifer put a reassuring hand on her shoulder. "I promise. This is just for our use. Nothing we record here today will be shared with anyone unless you give us explicit permission."

Marcia looked across the room at Nate. The detective had been quiet after introducing himself when they had first arrived. He didn't seem interested in what Dr. Daye and her assistants were doing. He walked around the living room, checking out the family photos they had hanging on the wall and looking out the windows.

"Is that true, Detective Raney?" she asked, calling across the room.

Nate turned his attention to the concerned mother and smiled. "You can believe Dr. Daye," he told her. "I'd trust her with my life."

"And he has," Emily added dryly.

Nate could see that Marcia was truly concerned. He crossed the room and gave her a reassuring smile. "In all the time I've known Dr. Daye and her staff, they have always been completely professional."

Marcia seemed unpersuaded. "A lot of her cases end up in the newspapers and on the web," she said.

Nate nodded. "Dr. Daye has never commented publicly without

the consent of her clients. And everything published on her website has any personal information redacted. If you want answers, she's the right person to ask the questions."

The tension in Marcia eased. "What do you think about all of this?" she asked Nate.

Nate eyed Jennifer, who raised a cautioning eyebrow. "I'm a detective," he answered. "I try to wait until I have all the facts before I make a determination."

"And what facts did you gather from the local police?" Marcia asked.

Nate didn't seem surprised that word of his visit with Chief Lewis had made its way back to the Foremans. "Nothing you need to worry about," he replied.

"Nothing makes a person worry more than telling them they don't need to worry," Marcia countered.

"I have to agree with Mrs. Foreman on that one, Detective Raney," Dave said. "It's like telling someone not to think about elephants."

"I like elephants," said a young voice from the stairway to the second floor.

Everyone turned toward the sound.

Daisy, the Foreman's daughter, was dancing down the stairs, followed by Greg and Danny. The children were dressed as if they were going to school, and Danny didn't seem too pleased.

"Elephants are kind of stinky," Emily said.

Daisy paused and looked at Emily. "But they can pick things up with their noses."

Emily thought about it, then replied, "Yeah, that is kinda cool."

"My name's Daisy," the little girl said to Emily. "Like the flower. What's yours?"

"My name's Emily," Emily said. "Like other people named Emily."

Daisy laughed. "You're funny."

"Not on purpose," Emily assured her.

"Hello everyone, this is Danny," Greg said as he and his son entered the living room.

Danny gave a shy wave.

Jennifer waved back, then reached into her pocket and pulled out a small white paper bag. "Do you like candy corn?" she asked as she pulled out an orange and yellow candy from the bag and popped it into her mouth.

Danny looked up at his dad. "Can I?" he asked.

Greg patted him on the head. "Sure."

"Not too much," Marcia warned.

Jennifer bent over and offered the bag to the boy.

Danny picked out four of the candies. He put two in his mouth and slipped the other two into his pocket.

"Can I have some?" Daisy asked.

"Sure," Jennifer replied. She held the bag out to Daisy and the girl reached inside to find it empty.

"There isn't any left," she said, pouting.

"There isn't?" Jennifer asked. She looked inside the bag. "I wonder where they went."

Daisy shrugged.

Jennifer looked at the girl, inspecting her face. "Oh, I see them."

"Where?"

Jennifer reached out for Daisy's nose with one hand while holding the empty bag below. She made a show of shaking Daisy's nose as the bag filled up with candy corn.

The little girl's eyes widened in surprise. Jennifer took her hand away from her nose and held the bag out for Daisy, who eagerly filled her small hand with the colorful treats and started eating them, one by one.

"Watch out for the boogers," Danny warned.

Daisy stopped, then looked up at Jennifer.

"Don't worry, I promise they are booger free," Jennifer assured her.

Daisy stuck her tongue out at Danny, then ran to her mom and pressed herself against Marcia's leg.

Jennifer put the candy away and turned back to the boy. "My name's Jennifer," she said. "It's very nice to meet you, Danny." She extended her hand and Danny shook it.

Nate marveled at how quickly and completely Jennifer charmed the kids. The magic trick for Daisy put the little girl at ease. And shaking Danny's hand let him know she would take him seriously. The way the kids accepted her in turn caused the parents to relax.

Danny eyed the camera Dave was setting up. "Am I going to be on TV?"

"No," Jennifer answered. "We just use those because sometimes it's hard to remember everything. But if we have a video, we can just watch it again."

Danny nodded his understanding.

"Do you know why we're here?" she asked.

"Because of Maureen," Danny answered. "You're not going to try to catch her like they do on *Ghostbusters*, are you?" he asked. "I promised her you were nice."

Jennifer lowered herself on one knee to Danny's level so she could look him straight in the eye. "No, not at all. I'm a scientist, Danny, a parapsychologist. We study things like ghosts and people with special abilities. And it's not too often that we find two of them in the same house."

"You think I have special powers?"

"Kind of. You know how some people can hear or see better than other people?"

Danny nodded.

"Well, you can see and hear ghosts better than other people."

"So you think Maureen is real?"

"That's what I'm here to find out," Jennifer assured him. "Why don't we all sit down and get comfortable?"

The Foremans and Jennifer moved toward the sitting area of the living room. The family sat on the sofa, Danny in the middle with Marcia and Greg on either side and Daisy on her mother's lap.

Jennifer sat in an armchair across from them.

Nate remained standing. He took a position where he could observe the whole scene, see everything going on including a view of Dave's laptop showing the sensor widgets and video camera feeds. He didn't really think that this was some elaborate setup by the

Foremans to get attention, but he didn't want to miss anything in case he was wrong.

Emily took a seat on a chair against one wall behind Jennifer. She looked disinterested and bored but used that as a cover to be hyper-observant. The undergrad was much smarter than anyone except Nate and Jennifer gave her credit for, and she used that to her advantage. Her low-key attitude gave her a kind of social invisibility, and sometimes people said and did things around her without realizing she was there. Nate knew cops who adopted a similar strategy.

Dave finished double checking that everything was working and recording, then picked up the laptop and walked over to join Jennifer and the family, heading for another empty chair.

Danny followed Dave, and when he saw where he was headed, his eyes grew wider.

Jennifer noticed Danny's reaction to Dave. "Dave, hold on a second," she said to her assistant, just before he sat in the chair.

"What's wrong?" Dave asked.

Jennifer smiled at Danny. "She's here, isn't she?"

"Yes," Danny answered.

"And she's sitting in that chair that Dave was going to sit in."

Danny nodded and looked over at the empty chair.

Dave took a step back and spied a loveseat. "I'll just go sit over there," he said.

"Has she been here the whole time?" Jennifer asked.

Danny's head bobbed affirmatively.

"How long have you been able to see Maureen?"

The boy shrugged. "I don't know. Ever since we moved here."

"How come you didn't tell your mom and dad about her then?"

"I didn't know who she was."

"But now you do."

He nodded. "She's my friend."

Jennifer smiled reassuringly. "Does Maureen have a last name?"

"I guess so. Everyone does. But she never told me what it is."

"Can she tell you now?"

Danny looked over at the chair but didn't get a response.

"Tell you what, let's play a game. I'll try to guess, and you tell me when Maureen says I have it right. Is it Smith? Jones?"

Danny shook his head no.

"Anderson? Snodgrass? Hufflelump?" Daisy giggled at the last one.

Danny shook his head again.

"Everly, Johnson, Flynn?"

Danny's attention was drawn to the chair. "Everly," he confirmed.

Jennifer cast a glance in Nate's direction.

He avoided returning her gaze. "Danny, do you watch the news with your parents?" Nate asked.

"Sometimes," Danny admitted.

Nate looked at Jennifer. Her glare was decidedly scolding, now.

"Maureen says she saw a picture of herself on the news."

Jennifer returned her focus to Danny. "You can hear Maureen, too?" she asked.

"Yeah, but not the same way I can hear you. It's kind of inside my head instead of in my ears." Then he turned toward Nate. "I don't watch reruns of Seinfeld," he added.

Nate remembered back to the car ride when he suggested that Danny might be getting some of the cultural references he attributed to Maureen from old television shows. He shot a look at Dave, who appeared surprised by the revelation.

Emily and Jennifer didn't betray their reactions, if they had any.

Danny turned toward Maureen's chair. "It's a cartoon about a weird family that travels through time and space. But it's mostly for grownups."

"What is, dear?" Marcia asked.

"I was just telling Maureen what *Rick and Morty* was," Danny explained.

Emily and Dave exchanged a look.

"Why did she ask you that?" Jennifer asked him.

"She heard you guys talking in your car when you were coming here. She wanted to make sure you weren't going to try to trick her."

"How did she know who we were?" Nate asked.

180

"That's actually a good question," Emily added.

Danny bowed his head.

"It's okay, Danny," Greg said. "You can tell us."

"You won't be mad?" he asked, looking sheepishly at his mother.

"Of course not," Marcia assured him.

Danny looked down at his shoes. "I helped her look you up on Mom's computer." He instantly looked at his mother, expecting her to be angry, but she only smiled.

"It's okay, Danny," she promised him.

"Danny, does Maureen know she's a ghost?" Jennifer asked.

He nodded. "She figured it out."

"What does she look like?"

Danny shrugged. "A lady. Like you."

"What color is her hair? Can you tell me what she's wearing?"

"Her hair is darker and shorter." He looked at the chair. "She's wearing blue jeans and a lumberjack shirt."

"Is that what she always wears?"

"No, sometimes she has a dress on. Or wears a t-shirt."

"And she used to live in this house?"

"She still does. She uses our guest room."

"More like a 'ghost' room," Dave whispered to Nate.

Jennifer ignored the comment. "Do you see her all the time?"

"Only when she's with me," Danny answered.

"So, she's not with you all the time?" Marcia asked.

Danny shook his head.

Marcia breathed a sigh of relief.

"Can you ask her what she does when she's *not* with you?" Jennifer asked the boy.

Danny turned his head toward the chair for a long moment, then looked back to Jennifer. "She says most of the time she doesn't do anything. The time just sort of disappears. But if she wants to, she's figured out how to go other places."

"Like our car."

Danny listened again to his invisible friend.

"Yeah, she said that wasn't as hard as she thought it would be. At first, she thought she could only move around the house. But when she wants to go somewhere, she just thinks of that place and she's there. When she thought of your picture, and your friends, she just… found you."

Jennifer took in the information from Danny. If it was true, it explained a few things that had always puzzled her about how some spirits were able to be present in different locations. "Does she know why she hasn't moved on?"

Danny seemed confused. "What does that mean?" Then he turned again to the empty chair. "Oh, do you mean why she hasn't gone to heaven?"

Jennifer nodded.

Danny seemed sad. "She's not sure. She can't remember some stuff and is afraid she might go to the other place."

"Smart move," Emily said quietly.

"What does she remember?" Jennifer asked.

Danny listened for a minute. "She remembers growing up in this house. She remembers that she died here. And she remembers that she did something bad." He looked at the empty chair.

"She says she thinks she robbed a bank."

Jennifer smiled at Danny, then looked sidelong over at Nate.

"Like the bank robbery they've been talking about on television lately?" Nate asked.

"I don't know. I only get to watch an hour a day, and I like the Disney channel."

"But you hear the news when your parents watch it, right?" Nate asked.

Marcia looked at Nate, glaring at him protectively. "Danny is not a liar," she insisted.

"I'm sure he's not," Nate said.

Greg gave Danny a reassuring pat on his head, then looked at Jennifer. "Do you think it's her? I mean, who else could it be?"

"That's what we're here to find out," Jennifer said.

"What more proof do you need?" Greg asked.

Jennifer took in a breath. "In matters like this, when we don't have anyone to confirm Maureen's presence and verify what Danny's telling us, we can only record what he says and look for confirmation of what she tells him afterwards."

"She already told you what she heard you talking about during your drive here. Isn't that confirmation?" Greg asked.

"It's very convincing," Jennifer admitted, "but unfortunately, it wasn't under any controlled circumstances. Danny may have overheard something, a conversation among my team members."

Nate looked at Jennifer, surprised that she wasn't jumping at the opportunity to rub that little revelation Danny had dumped on them in his face.

Out of the corner of her eye, Jennifer saw Dave suddenly sit up straight, his eyes wide open. He shivered. "Danny, where is Maureen right now?" she asked.

Danny looked over at the empty chair, then at Dave. He giggled.

"What do you see?" Greg asked.

"She's dancing around Dave, moving through him. It's funny."

Dave held perfectly still. "Please ask her to stop," he asked.

Danny passed his gaze across the room as if watching someone walking around.

Emily felt a chill on the back of her neck.

Something tickled Jennifer's ear.

Danny looked at Nate. The detective was looking right at him, smiling confidently.

"Do you feel anything?" Dave asked Nate.

Nate shook his head.

"He already has ice in his veins," Emily said.

"What just happened, Danny?" Jennifer asked.

"Maureen walked through the weird girl, then touched your ear and now she's standing next to the policeman. She says there's something about him that's different. That he's more like her than anyone else she's met."

"Freaky," Emily said in her low monotone.

"What does that mean?" Greg asked.

Jennifer looked at Nate, expecting him to admonish her not to reveal her theories about his near-death experience. But he gave an amused smile instead. She took that as permission to share his story. "Detective Raney was in a situation six months ago where he was shot and had died for a short period until the doctors revived him."

Everyone looked at Nate.

"Can you see her?" Greg asked.

Nate shook his head. "No, I don't see anything except for the living people in this room. I don't feel a chill in the air, or the hairs going up on the back of my neck."

"This is why we call him Detective Buzz-Kill," Emily droned.

"Why would Maureen say that to Danny?" Greg asked Jennifer. "Danny wouldn't know anything about Detective Raney's past. Isn't that proof?"

"It's nothing," Nate answered before Jennifer could speak. "You could interpret that a hundred different ways."

"He's right," Jennifer said. "No one thing that's happened is in itself proof—"

"But added up together?" Greg suggested.

Jennifer shrugged. "I'd like for Danny to ask Maureen to show us around, take us to the places in the house that have meaning to her, that have triggered memories of her past."

"I don't know," Marcia said. "I don't feel comfortable asking him to do too much of whatever this is. Maybe another time."

"It's okay, Mom," Danny said, smiling at Marcia. "I want to. And Maureen says she likes Dr. Daye."

"We'll keep it short," Jennifer promised.

Danny and Greg both looked to Marcia, pleading.

"All right," she finally relented. But there was something bothering her, a nagging thought in the back of her mind, something she hoped she could find an opportunity to talk to Detective Raney about before he left.

CHAPTER THIRTY FOUR

Dale stepped out of the house into the afternoon sun.

Standing on the sidewalk, hands in his uniform pockets, was Liam.

"Okay, what?" Dale asked.

Liam walked toward Dale and joined him on the front porch. They sat in a pair of wicker chairs off to one side. Liam spoke in a low, conspiratorial voice. "I ran into the mother from the family that moved into your old place."

"So?"

"They hired some psychic to check it out. Apparently, the little boy sees dead people."

Dale swallowed. A feeling overcame him, like a long-forgotten premonition that suddenly came true.

Liam, seeing the reaction in Dale, continued. "Supposedly, the kid has made friends with a ghost. A ghost named Maureen."

Dale felt suddenly dizzy. That was impossible. "There are no such things as ghosts," he said.

Liam shrugged. "Maybe. But what if she is there? What if we don't need to wander the back trails around here for months, maybe years, looking for the loot that Maureen hid?"

Dale closed his eyes. Could it be true? Could he speak with Maureen again? Tell her how sorry he was that he got her mixed up in that crazy heist? Sorry that he got her killed, and all her dreams of growing old together with children and grandchildren would never happen.

He had often teased Maureen when she made any remarks about the feelings she would get from time to time that her grandmother was hanging around the house, how she would get excited whenever they saw a television show featuring psychics who claimed they had a pipeline to the spirit world.

His own mother had been a die-hard believer and even claimed she had what she called the second sight, the ability to sense the future—though to be honest, most of her predictions were vague and general. But when he had first brought Maureen home to meet her, she had told him she would become the love of his life. Of course, he knew that already, but to hear it from his mother, with more surety than he had ever gleaned from any of her predictions, cemented his love for her. If only his mother had lived long enough to warn him about how disastrous the bank robbery would be.

"Dale, you still with me?" Liam asked.

Dale nodded. "It could be a trap," he suggested.

"What, you think the District Attorney placed a family of secret agents in your old house to trick you into revealing where Maureen hid the loot?"

"Not the D.A. I'm guessing some insurance company paid out a large benefit for that necklace you mentioned. And they aren't known for just walking away from that kind of loss."

Liam shook his head. "I know the mother. She did some computer work for the department. The father works over at the Costco. First thing I did was check to see if they had any connection to the bank or the safe deposit box victims. They're clean. Just an all-American family living the dream in rural California."

"What about the Mastermind?"

Liam shuddered at the mention of the man who had set up the ill-fated heist. He thought about the accident the detective had had on the mountain road. The investigator claimed he had been run off the narrow strip of asphalt by a gray Hummer. Was that more than just a possible road rage incident? "Maybe," Liam conceded. "It is strange that we haven't heard from him yet."

Dale nodded in agreement, then looked at Liam. "Do you really think it could be Maureen talking to the boy?"

Liam shrugged. "In my experience, things like that end up being someone trying to get attention. He could be faking the whole thing, spinning a tale, trying to get back some of the status he had before his younger sister was born."

"How old is he?"

"Ten."

Dale whistled. "Kind of a sophisticated grift for a fifth grader."

"Not unheard of, though. All kinds of crazy stuff going around the internet these days. Probably a couple dozen YouTube videos alone on how to pull that kind of scam."

"And I thought fifteen years in prison made me a cynic," Dale said.

"Sometimes I think you're the one who had it easy. I've been looking for that stash and plugging away in this two-bit town when I should be living it up on a Caribbean island," Liam replied. "Let me ask you. You knew her best. Do you think it's possible?"

Dale thought for a moment. "She did believe in all that afterlife stuff. And if anyone would have the sheer stubbornness to stick around, it would be Maureen."

Liam nodded. "Either way, if he's talking to her ghost, or stumbled upon some clue she left behind, he could short-cut this whole treasure hunt for us."

"So, what do we do? Pay them a visit? Get the kid to convince Maureen to tell us where she stashed the bag?" Dale asked.

"Let me do a little more snooping around. I'll find out exactly what's going on, and if it turns out that the kid does know something, we'll figure it out from there."

Dale nodded. It was moments like this when Liam scared him the most. When they were at a fork in the road. He always seemed to follow Liam to the path that led them over a cliff.

CHAPTER THIRTY FIVE

For nearly half an hour, Emily followed Jennifer, Nate and Danny with a hand-held video camera, and Dave trailed behind with an array of sensors, taking and recording readings in the various rooms they went in and out of. Greg followed along, while Marcia stayed with Daisy in the living room, watching TV.

Dave got excited when they checked out the guest room where Maureen claimed she had spent much of the time between her death and the Foremans moving in. His sensors were recording something unusual.

Nate wasn't convinced that the reading meant much of anything. Electromagnetic fields and background radiation were everywhere these days. After everyone else had filed out of the room, he went to the bedroom window and found what he was expecting. The electrical line for the house came in from a pole along the street and was attached just outside the window.

Nate caught back up to them as they were congregating in Danny's tiny bedroom. Danny's back was to the door, but when Nate arrived, being careful to be quiet, the boy looked behind him with an amused smile. "Dave tells me that you had found some old photos up in the attic," Nate said.

Everyone turned to look at Nate standing in the doorway.

"How did you get up there?" the detective asked the boy.

"Maureen told me how," Danny answered. "She told me to put a chair under that chain hanging from the ceiling and pull it down so the stairs could slide out."

Nate looked down the hall. He saw the chain that Danny was talking about. It was indeed too high for the boy to reach without something to stand on. He walked over and pulled on it. It didn't require much force. The mechanism was counterbalanced. A good tug pulled the trapdoor open and allowed the telescoping ladder to extend to the floor.

Nate climbed the stairs and poked his head up in the attic. Sunlight crept in through the windows on either side of the gabled roof. He stepped up and saw that the window that was right in front of him had some tree branches pressing up against it. He walked over and looked down at the yard where a very old oak tree stood, spreading its boughs in a wide circle that extended all the way up to the window.

"That's where she died," Danny said.

Nate turned around and found that the rest of the party had followed him up into the attic. "Here, in the attic?" Nate prompted.

Danny shook his head. "No, she went out that window and thought she could climb down the tree and get to the woods. But she didn't make it."

Nate took a closer look at the tree branches and noted that someone could indeed possibly gain purchase on the thick limbs and make their way toward the massive trunk.

"The pictures were in that hole," Danny said.

Nate bent down and saw the gap in the wall boards Danny was talking about. He pulled out a penlight from his jacket pocket and shined it in the dark space. There was something in there. He reached his hand inside and pulled out a piece of paper covered in years of dust.

It was a single sheet, folded over. On the outside was a name. Dale. He unfolded it and read the message inside. "Stashed the bag, heading on to the place we discussed if I can. *Wish* you were here, Maureen." The word "wish" was underlined.

Nate handed the note to Jennifer. She held it up to the camera for Emily to record. "Guess she never made it to wherever they had discussed," Dave said.

"Would have been nice if she said where she stashed the bag of loot," Emily added.

They all looked at Danny.

"Say, Danny, does Maureen remember where she left the money?" Emily asked.

Danny looked toward the window—not where Nate was standing, but next to him. "No, she doesn't," he said simply, but kept his attention on the space by the window.

"Is there something else, Danny?" Jennifer asked.

"She says there's someone she's afraid of."

"Is it Dale?" Dave asked.

"She doesn't know. She can't remember," Danny replied. He looked over at Jennifer. "Can we go back now?"

Jennifer nodded and led the group back down the steep ladder.

Dave and Emily finished packing up the gear.

Jennifer did a few more magic tricks for the kids, and then Greg sent them both upstairs to change so they could go outside and play. The two kids ran up the stairs to their rooms.

Nate approached Marcia, who was sitting alone on the living room sofa. She greeted him with a friendly smile. Of the two parents, she was the one who was more like Nate, more skeptical. "Can I talk to you for a minute?" Nate asked her.

"Sure." She moved over to one side so Nate could take a seat next to her.

"So, now that you've seen Dr. Daye and her crew at work, what do you think about all this?" he began.

She shrugged. "I don't know what to think. Danny has always been creative and imaginative, but some of this... I just don't know where it could come from."

Nate nodded. "How has Danny adjusted to your move? I know you guys came out here from the city. It must have been a big change for him. Has he been able to make new friends at school?"

"He's not a very outgoing boy," Marcia told Nate. "He likes to read and draw, mostly. His teachers say that he gets along well with everyone and there haven't been any incidents of bullying."

"What about his relationship with his sister? Was it a big adjustment for him to go from being an only child to a big brother?"

Marcia shook her head. "He loves it. He's very protective of her, and they actually play together quite well."

"If you don't mind me asking, what made you move?" Nate asked.

"My mother," Marcia replied. "Well, actually, she was the reason we had put off moving for so long. She was living in a nursing home, late-stage Alzheimer's. When she passed away, we didn't have any other reasons to stay in the city."

"Was Danny close to his grandmother?"

"When he was younger. When she could still remember who he was. We didn't take the kids to visit the last year. I could barely stand to go myself, but she was my mother. And even if she didn't recognize me, I wanted her to know that someone loved her."

"What about the funeral? Did the kids go?"

Marcia nodded. "The funeral home had a room set aside for the kids, but Danny was curious, and wanted to look inside the coffin. I was reluctant at first, but the funeral director, and our pastor, assured us that it could be helpful for a kid Danny's age to know about death." Marcia looked up at Nate. "Do you think that might have something to do with why he says he's seeing a ghost?"

"I don't know. I'm just trying to get the whole picture. I guess I still fall back into interrogation mode sometimes. Occupational hazard of being a policeman for so long."

"So how did you end up working with Dr. Daye?"

"The shooting," he replied, referring to the incident that had come up earlier. "I had to take early retirement. Teaming up with Jennifer was a business decision."

"Have you ever..." Marcia struggled to formulate the question she wanted to ask, but Nate knew instinctively where the conversation was going.

"In the time I've worked with her, I have never seen anything that I couldn't explain with logic and common sense. She, of course, would argue otherwise but from my point of view there is always an explanation that is rooted in reality no matter how paranormal the circumstances seem."

Marcia nodded.

Nate sensed that there was something bothering her.

Jennifer and Greg approached them. "I think we've got everything packed up," she told Marcia. "I just wanted to thank you again for allowing us to meet Danny. He's a great kid."

Marcia nodded and offered a polite smile.

"So, what's next?" Greg asked.

"Well, with your permission, I'd like to bring a friend of mine over. A medium to see if he can confirm what Danny is telling us."

"Is that really a good idea?" Marcia asked. "Don't you have enough?"

"We have a lot," Jennifer confirmed. "But this would be different. Sam is very sensitive to spirits. If he can confirm what Danny is seeing and hearing, it would give us more definitive answers."

Nate tried not to cringe at the mention of Sam's name. He was hoping he would never have to deal with that psychic Ken doll again.

"What do you think?" Greg asked his wife.

Marcia considered. "We'll talk about it," she promised.

"I hope you'll really consider it. Regardless, like we discussed, we'll keep everything confidential."

"Thank you," Marcia said, relieved.

Emily and Dave carried the cases containing the cameras and sensors out of the house, followed by Jennifer. Greg tagged along, talking to Dr. Daye, peppering her with questions about Sam.

Nate offered a parting smile to Marcia and turned to follow the rest of the team.

Marcia put a hand on Nate's arm to stop him.

Nate looked at her. "Is there something else?" he asked.

"My computer," she said.

"What about it?"

"I don't understand how Danny could have used it to look up you and Dr. Daye. It has a password."

Nate looked over at the desk tucked away in one corner of the living room. "Do you have it written down on a sticky note? Maybe under the keyboard or something?"

"No, I work in IT. I don't keep passwords lying around. It's been bugging me ever since he told us he used it. And I believe he did. He knows he's not supposed to play with it, and I could see he felt guilty."

"Maybe he watched you type it in a few times. Kids pick up a lot more than we give them credit for."

Maureen shook her head. "I never log on while the kids are at home, only after they go to school, and rarely in the evenings." She folded her arms as if warding off a chill. "Do you think she was watching me? Could this be real?" Marcia asked, looking pleadingly to Nate, hoping for an answer.

But he didn't have one.

CHAPTER THIRTY SIX

The front door to Nate's house opened and the staff of Raney/Daye Investigations piled through, all of them speaking simultaneously and excitedly, continuing a conversation started on the ride back.

All of them except Nate. He held the door open as they carried the cases of equipment from their visit to the Foremans back into the house. Dave and Emily dropped the gear in the living room and continued their conversation into the kitchen where they grabbed bottles of water from the refrigerator.

"Are you going to leave these crates in my living room?" Nate asked.

The discussion stopped. Emily and Dave cast a quick glance toward Jennifer, who shrugged her agreement with Nate. That was the rule. Keep the equipment where it belongs and out of his living space.

"Can't we just take a minute to hydrate?" Emily asked. "Mr. Frugal didn't let us run the air conditioner on the way back. My mouth feels like I gargled with sand."

"It would have been nice if we had stopped for something to drink on the way back," Dave agreed.

"They charge two dollars for a ten-cent bottle of water at those convenience stores," Nate countered. "Finish your waters, then get this stuff put away." He walked past them, through the kitchen to the office in the back of the house.

"Is it just me, or is he a level or two grumpier than usual?" Emily asked.

"He's got a lot on his mind," Jennifer reminded her.

"I can't believe he really thinks everything we saw and heard with Danny Foreman was all a scam by a ten-year-old," Dave added. "I swear, when he said that Maureen could sense Nate had been dead…"

"Would he ever admit it even if he did feel her presence like we did?" Emily asked.

"It's not his job to think the same way we do," Jennifer replied. "He's a cop."

"Ex-cop," Dave said.

"I don't think he'll ever think of himself as anything else. I want him to be a skeptic. I want him to challenge everything we see and record and force us to look at it from his point of view. Trust me, it's easy to be fooled by misdirection. I did a lot of it when I was a magician."

"What do the Foremans have to gain?" Emily asked.

"I don't know. But we just met them. They're strangers to us. He's right to be skeptical."

"I can't believe you're on his side," Dave said. "I totally believed Danny. There's no way a kid would come up with that detailed a lie. And it's not like we haven't seen situations like this before," he reminded Jennifer. "There was that woman we met in San Jose who could see and hear the spirit of a little girl."

"I never said I was on his side," she replied. "I can't remember a case where we had this type of connection with a spirit where we can verify the subject's information. If it is Maureen Everly who is communicating with Danny, there are enough of her contemporaries available to confirm what he says."

"You know what Nate thinks. The boy probably found a diary along with those photos and is just pretending to talk to her," Emily said.

"And he might be right. That's something we still need to rule out."

"Well, I can't believe you can compare Danny to a professional con artist," Dave insisted.

Jennifer walked up to where Emily and Dave were sipping at their waters, then looked back at the equipment in the living room. "Get this stuff put away, then start transcribing the interview and writing up your impressions. And get Bits to correlate the sensor readings with the video. Then, find all the publicly available information on Maureen Everly and anyone who knew her. If Danny is somehow tricking us, we want to find out."

Without waiting for a reply, she crossed through the kitchen toward the office.

Dave and Emily watched her go, then Emily raised an eyebrow at Dave. "Rock-paper-scissors for who does the transcript?"

Dave nodded.

They each pounded their palms three times. Emily showed a flat hand to Dave's balled fist. She wrapped his hand with hers, claiming her victory, then went into the living room to grab the smaller of the cases piled up there and take it upstairs.

Dave sighed, then grabbed the remaining cases and trudged after her.

Jennifer entered the office and found Nate sitting at his end of the partners desk, staring at his phone.

Madge was sleeping on the couch off to the side.

Jennifer gave the sleeping pooch a quick scruff behind her ears. Madge opened her eyes to see who was disturbing her midday nap, then closed them again and let out a satisfied grunt.

Nate looked over at Jennifer as she sat on her side of the desk and leaned back. She was looking at him with a challenging gaze. "What?" he asked.

"You didn't say anything during the ride back."

"I didn't have anything to say."

"There's something on your mind. What is it? The bills? The car? Did the guys leave a mess in the kitchen again?"

Nate decided to cut off her inquiry before it became annoying. He picked up his phone and showed it to her. "I get alerts when my mom uses her credit card. She saw Harmony today."

Jennifer shrugged. "It's only natural after Sam couldn't reach Ben that she would return to someone who she's had success with in the past."

Out of nowhere, Nate rose to his feet, swung his arm and banged the desk with his fist.

The sound shocked Jennifer, but she was more distressed by the look in his eyes. They were filled with pain and on the verge of tears.

Nate had used his right arm to express his frustration, and the force of the blow created a wave of agony in his reconstructed shoulder. He wasn't supposed to be picking up anything heavier than a sandwich, let alone smashing his fist into a hardwood desk.

A moment later, Dave and Emily appeared in the doorway to the office, expressions of concern on their faces. They looked at Jennifer, who gave them a reassuring nod and silently signaled them to go back to what they were doing.

After they left, Nate collapsed into his chair and looked over at Jennifer. "I'm sorry," he said. "That was totally inappropriate."

"It's okay," Jennifer told him. "I'm injecting myself into your relationship with your mother, and I have no right to—"

"No, you have been nothing but understanding, supportive and generous with your time. I just..." Nate trailed off as another wave of pain swept through his shoulder.

Jennifer looked at Nate sympathetically. "The only thing I want to do is find a way that you and your mother can accept each other."

"I know," he said. "I just miss her."

His response surprised Jennifer. "I know you two haven't been on speaking terms in the past, but things are better now, aren't they?"

"My parents were high school sweethearts. There was no one else either of them had ever loved. And I can understand why my mother would want to hang on to that, but..." Nate closed his eyes.

Jennifer walked around to Nate's side of the desk, sat down on the edge, and placed her hand over his.

Nate continued. "It was like I lost them both." He looked up at Jennifer, wondering what her reaction to his confession would be.

She nodded. "I get it," she told him. "How can I help?"

Nate shrugged with his good shoulder. "Just keep being you. And have a little more patience for an old cop who has a problem expressing his emotions."

Jennifer squeezed his hand. "I can do that," she said. "And I really think Sam can help. Let that play out, see if it doesn't change Eleanor's expectations. He won't charge her anything and won't try to scam her."

Nate raised an eyebrow. "That's quite a favor."

"We're old friends," she replied, then quickly changed the subject as she gave Nate's hand a final pat and returned to her chair. "So, back to the case. You still think everything we saw today you can credit to a young boy's imagination?"

Nate let her dodge of his question about Sam go, then nodded and answered hers. "Yes, I do."

Jennifer shook her head. "You did notice how excited Dave and Emily are? I know that wouldn't escape the notice of an accomplished detective like you."

Nate cocked his head, silently asking her to make her point.

"This is the most promising case we've had since they've been working for me. An actual communicative spirit, manifesting visually and aurally to probably the most reliable witness I've ever interviewed."

"Reliable?" Nate challenged.

"Yes, he's a kid. He's innocent. No ulterior motives, no apparent psychoses, no reason to try to deceive us."

"Kids are impressionable," Nate countered. "They're not reliable witnesses. They have a hard time distinguishing fantasy from reality."

"Where would the fantasy come from? There aren't a lot of kids' shows that feature the spirits of people who died fifteen years ago."

"Kids pick up a lot more than we give them credit for. At that age, they are learning machines. And the father…"

"What about him?"

"He's all in on the paranormal stuff. The mother is on the fence, but the dad really believes that his son is talking to a ghost. Boys idolize their fathers," Nate said.

He paused, thinking about his own dad, remembering that larger-than-life figure who loomed over him, clasping his giant hand over his son's shoulder, that gesture of praise that meant everything to a young boy eager for approval.

Nate returned his thoughts to the case. "Greg reinforces his son's delusions. Gives the boy approval whenever he reports something this dead woman says or does and shows disappointment when he doesn't."

"I noticed that, too," Jennifer said. "But that doesn't explain how he could know so much about her life."

Nate started to answer her, but Jennifer cut him off.

"Yes, yes, I know. Maybe she hid a diary in that hole in the attic wall too. Do you really believe that's likely?"

"His mother said he's at the top of his class, but a bit of an introvert, an outsider. He saw the opportunity to be the center of attention for once and seized it.

"You see that a lot in families with multiple children. The youngest always gets most of the attention and the older siblings sometimes act out."

"This doesn't seem like that," Jennifer asserted. "His parents say he's a perfectly adjusted big brother. You were an only child. Your point of view on sibling relationships is more academic."

Nate nodded, acknowledging her point. "I've seen how divisive rivalries in families can be."

"This isn't a Cain and Abel situation," Jennifer protested.

"No, I'm not saying that. But you can't know everything going on in a family by spending just a few hours with them."

Jennifer sighed. "Sometimes I feel like you reach for explanations just to be contrary. There really aren't too many fifth graders who know who Jerry Seinfeld is, let alone that he had a TV show. How do you explain how he could have known what we talked about during the car ride there?"

"He overheard some chatter between Dave and Emily."

"See?" Jennifer countered. "You always have an alternate explanation and discard the most direct and obvious answer."

"That a ghost hitched a ride with us, like in the Haunted Mansion at Disneyland."

Jennifer smiled, imagining Nate sitting in one of the iconic cars from the famous attraction and sliding along the final stretch of the mechanical track that pulled them past mirrors that made it look like there was a ghost sitting next to you. "Yes," she said simply. "If people can project their consciousness out of their bodies while they're alive, then it just makes sense that if that consciousness can survive death, that part of them would have the same abilities."

Nate rolled his eyes. "I don't know how many unproven assertions you made in that sentence," he said, "but it certainly doesn't qualify as a more likely explanation in my book."

"I can show you some of my case notes on out-of-body experiences. I've had them myself. Maybe reading about them will stir up your own memories."

It had been some time since Jennifer had made a direct reference to her belief that during the time his heart had stopped and he was clinically dead, he had a near-death experience. She had tried to connect a couple of coincidental incidents in which it appears that Nate had acquired information to help him track down the shooters. There was a logical explanation of what had happened all those months ago, but she kept on trying to convince him that he somehow left his body, and that the vivid dreams he had experienced under the influence of a cocktail of painkillers and anesthesia he was administered during his hospital stay were more than just inventions of his subconscious mind.

"So, you think we should write this off as just a kid with an overactive imagination and sibling rivalry?"

"Yes," he said simply. "After we send them a bill for our time."

"Well, we're not going to bill them without giving them an answer. Despite your doubts, I am convinced there is something going on there. We have a chance to verify communication with an actual spirit of someone who lived recently enough to be able to corroborate what Danny tells us. We need to find people who knew her, people who can give us questions and answers that can verify that Maureen is who Danny says she is. Things that wouldn't be in a diary, no matter how detailed."

"Have you considered this may actually be a scam that goes beyond the Foremans?" Nate asked.

"What do you mean?"

"Maybe they're conspiring with these people you think you can find to verify that there is a ghost in that house. If a noted parapsychologist such as yourself gives your stamp of approval, then they can cash in. Maybe even get one of those reality shows."

Jennifer shook her head. "That's not what this family is after. They just want answers, not their fifteen minutes."

"We'll see," Nate said.

Emily entered the office, sat down next to Madge and rubbed her hand up and down the dog's back.

Madge moaned with pleasure.

"Dave sent me down to see if you still have that memory card we swapped out of the camera."

"I thought I gave it to Dave," she said in a small panic.

"He says you must have it."

Jennifer searched her pockets, then smiled when she found a small plastic square tucked away in one of them. "Here you go," she said, handing it to Emily.

"Thanks," Emily said, taking the memory card. She turned to Nate. "So, what if she does remember where it is?"

"Who remembers where what is?" Nate asked.

"Maureen and the money. Seems to me if Danny can get her to remember where she stashed it, it would answer a lot of questions and solve a lot of problems," Emily said, eyeing the stack of bills next to Nate's computer. She got up and walked out of the office.

Once she was gone, Jennifer raised an eyebrow at Nate. "Don't tell me that wouldn't convince you," she said.

Nate started to open his mouth.

"And don't try to tell me that her last entry in this mythical diary was a confession of where she hid the money," she added.

Nate considered, then offered a tepid, "Maybe."

Jennifer sighed and turned on her computer, deciding to write up her notes rather than engaging Nate any further.

Nate got up from his chair, and without another word, walked into the kitchen where Dave was deciding which flavor of Hot Pocket he was in the mood for in front of the open freezer door. They exchanged polite nods, and Nate continued into the hallway and ducked into the downstairs bathroom.

He locked the door, then collapsed against it and slid down to the floor, trying not to audibly express the utter agony he was in. He had thought the pain would ebb after the initial shock from pounding the desk, but it was getting worse, like someone had stuck a knife into his shoulder joint and was twisting it.

Nate pulled the prescription bottle from his pocket and shook the contents into his right hand.

There were three pills left. He set the bottle on the floor, then picked up two of the pills and held them over the open bottle to drop them back in, but instead, he popped them into his mouth and swallowed them dry.

Then he eyed the last pill resting in his palm, picked it up and tossed it to the back of his throat and swallowed that one, too.

It took a moment for the medication to take effect. His breathing slowed and became less shallow, and the pain finally faded to a dull ache.

CHAPTER THIRTY SEVEN

Liam sat in the booth of the downtown diner that was his usual lunchtime stop, staring at the half-eaten burger on his plate nestled among the untouched French fries and that god-awful sprig of parsley that Kenny's Restaurant dropped on every dish. Next to the plate was the pocket notebook he always carried with him open to the page of potential hiding spots where Maureen Everly may have hidden the duffel bag full of loot.

"Ten million dollars," was scribbled at the top of the page and underlined heavily.

Liam picked up one of the cold fries from his plate and popped it into his mouth. He sighed and stared out at the midday crowd. He saw a man he recognized get out of his car and walk toward the barbershop. It was Marcia Foreman's husband. Liam searched his memory for his name. Greg, he recalled. After he had run into Marcia last weekend at the market, he had done a little snooping into the family that lived in the house that Dale and Maureen had once called home.

The deputy pulled a few bills from a money clip and tossed them on the table, then made his way out of the diner and onto the street. He dodged light traffic to jaywalk across to Gary Reuben's barber shop.

It was the type of establishment you would expect to find in a small, rural town. There were two barbers manning three chairs, backed by a mirror that ran the length of the shop. Opposite them was a row of seats where a few other men sat, one of them completely bald, so obviously not there for a haircut.

There was a conversation going on, a debate on the latest season of *Survivor*.

"Afternoon, Liam," one of the barbers said. The others in the room grunted their own greetings.

"Hey, Gary."

"There's a bit of a wait if you want a trim."

"I got a little time to kill," Liam said, running a hand through his hair that didn't really seem like it needed a trim at all.

Gary had just draped the giant bib over Greg Foreman and was running a comb through the man's hair, getting a feel for the way it laid on his head.

Greg looked over at the deputy.

Liam pointed a finger at him. "You're Marcia Foreman's husband, aren't you?"

Greg seemed surprised to be recognized by the deputy. "Yes, I'm Greg."

"I'm Liam McDonald. Your wife did some work for the department a while back."

"Yes, she did. I hope there's nothing wrong with it," he asked jokingly.

"Nope, made things a hundred percent easier—though to be honest, that wasn't a very high bar to jump over."

"Well, I'll let her know you're happy with her work."

"Actually, I just saw her on Saturday. She was running out of the market like a madwoman, said you guys were having some psychic over to do an exorcism or something."

Liam settled himself into one of the empty seats across from the barber chairs.

Greg looked around, feeling a little self-conscious as the *Survivor* debate ceased and everyone's attention turned to him.

"It wasn't anything like that," he assured them. "She's a parapsychologist, not a psychic. She only investigates paranormal phenomena. She doesn't talk to spirits."

"Para-what?" one of the regulars said from behind the newspaper he was holding in front of his face.

"Paranormal, it's another word for ghosts and stuff like that," Greg explained.

"Marcia said that your boy was talking to one," Liam said.

Everyone leaned in expectantly to hear the answer. Even Gary the barber paused, wetting down Greg's hair.

Greg nodded slightly. "Yes. He does appear to have made contact with a spirit."

"Huh," the old man behind the newspaper said. "Don't surprise me, none. Lots of ghosts in these parts. Bunch of forty-niners still roaming the hills looking for gold."

"Football players?" the bald man sitting next to him asked.

"No, you idiot. Prospectors."

"Which is your boy talking to?" the old man asked.

"Actually, it's a woman," Greg replied.

"A woman?" the bald man echoed back.

"Yes, we think she was the previous occupant of the house. Maureen Everly."

"Oh, you're the sucker that bought that old place, huh?" the newspaper guy asked.

The others chuckled.

"My wife and I are big DIYers, and we love Danville."

Liam steered the conversation back to Maureen's ghost. "Do you think that's who it really is?"

Greg nodded. "Seems to be. Dr. Daye and her crew gathered some pretty convincing evidence."

"Hey, Liam," the bald man shouted, "weren't you out there on the day of the robbery? Seems I remember you talking about it a time or two."

Liam felt himself blush. He hadn't wanted to turn the topic back on himself.

"Did you know her?" Greg asked.

The deputy shrugged. "I'm sure I ran into her around town before she died."

"Would you mind if I give your name to Dr. Daye? She mentioned that if we can find people who knew Maureen when she was alive, they might be able to confirm whether or not it's actually her that Danny's talking to."

"I'm afraid I probably wouldn't be able to help you in that regard. We didn't run in the same social circles," Liam answered with an apologetic tone.

Greg sighed with disappointment. "Well, if you think of anyone who might be able to help, please let us know."

"Will do," Liam replied.

Another one of the old-timers spoke up. "If your boy is really talking to Maureen Everly, he should get her to tell you where she hid the million bucks she got away with in that bank robbery."

Greg smiled. "She mostly entertains my son with stories about what things were like when she was alive. For him, it's all ancient history."

Liam made a show of pulling his phone out of his pocket and staring at the screen. "Gary, looks like I'll need to get that trim another day. Duty calls." He stood up and nodded goodbye to the barbershop crowd and left.

The deputy placed a call on his phone and held it to his ear as he walked toward where he had left his car. After waiting a moment for Dale to answer his call, he said, simply, "It's her. Time to make our move."

CHAPTER THIRTY EIGHT

Eleanor Raney checked her purse, making sure she had everything she needed before she left the house. She could make out her keys, wallet and phone nestled in among the collection of tissues, lozenges, lipsticks and other odds and ends. She checked the smart watch Nate had given her. Aside from telling her the time, it complained that the battery was getting low, but it should last till she got home. If she delayed any longer, she would miss the bus that took her to Harmony's storefront parlor—and keeping Harmony waiting was not something she wanted to do.

She looked around to make sure she had turned out the lights and shut off the television, then opened the front door. She gasped when she saw Dr. Daye standing before her, seemingly frozen in the act of knocking.

"Sorry, didn't mean to frighten you," Jennifer said.

Eleanor paused to catch her breath. She offered a reassuring smile. "You just surprised me, deary."

"I tried to call, but there was no answer. Is everything all right?"

"Sometimes I don't hear the cell phone. And I have no idea how to get the messages," Eleanor explained.

"Well, did you forget about our meeting with Sam?" Jennifer asked.

"Sam?"

"We were expecting you an hour ago. I came by to make sure you were okay."

"Yes, yes, I'm fine," Eleanor reassured her. She glanced at her watch. "I really must be going. I don't want to miss my bus."

"Where are you headed?"

"I have an appointment," Eleanor said.

"What about Sam?"

Eleanor looked away from Jennifer.

"What is it? I thought you liked Sam."

"Oh, it's not me."

"What do you mean?"

Eleanor looked anxious.

"What's wrong? You can tell me."

The older woman clutched the straps of her purse. "It's Ben," she said.

"Ben?"

"Maybe *he* doesn't like Sam. I've always been able to talk to him when I see Harmony, but with Sam…"

Jennifer smiled. "I see. You know, in my experience, it's not always the medium a spirit is attracted to, but the loved one."

Eleanor seemed confused. "But the other time we met your friend, he said Ben wasn't there."

Jennifer shrugged. "Sam explained about that, remember? How someone who has passed doesn't experience time and space the way we do?"

Eleanor shook her head, unconvinced. "That's not what Harmony says."

"Oh? What did she say?"

The older woman hesitated. "She thinks maybe Ben doesn't trust Sam."

"Ah. And you trust Harmony."

"Of course. She's always been there for me. And for Ben."

"Do you trust me?" Jennifer asked.

Eleanor seemed suddenly embarrassed. "Of course I do. You've been very nice to me, and I know Nate trusts you."

"I've been working with mediums for years. Sam is probably the best I've ever seen. If I were to trust anyone to help you speak to Ben, it would be him."

"But the last time we tried…"

"So, we try again. And if Ben doesn't appear, we try once more. I promise you, Ben is not going to refuse to speak to you because of the medium you choose. If the roles were reversed, would that stop you? Wouldn't you want to communicate with Ben by any means possible?"

That argument seemed to reach Nate's mother. "I suppose so."

"Let me drive you to Sam's place. Give him another chance. At the very least, you'll make Nate feel better that you tried. That's worth something, isn't it?"

"All right," Eleanor conceded. "But I really should call Harmony. She's not going to be happy. Melody has been driving her mad lately. Maybe I should go see her…"

"Why don't we stop by on the way, to let Ben know that Nate would like you to try using Sam?" Jennifer asked.

The older woman shook her head. "I don't know if Harmony would like that," she answered fearfully.

Jennifer stepped closer and put her arm around Eleanor. "If Harmony really cares about you and Ben, she'll understand. She'd want you to be close to him any way you could."

Jennifer's argument made sense. Harmony was her friend. Surely, she would understand how important it was to Nate that she give Sam another chance. "Okay."

"Great. I'm sure everything will be just fine," Jennifer assured her.

CHAPTER THIRTY NINE

"You really think it's possible?" Dale asked Liam.

The deputy paced, deep in thought. He paused and ran a hand through his hair. "Personally, I still have my doubts. But the father sure was convinced."

"If Maureen was a ghost or spirit or whatever is haunting that old place, why is she suddenly making herself known now? Maybe it's just a publicity stunt. They found out who the house used to belong to, saw the story on the news and they're playing it up for attention."

Liam stopped pacing and looked out the window. "They don't seem the type. The wife, Marcia, doesn't want any part of it. Greg, the husband, seems all in, but he's got two young kids. Doesn't feel like he's trying to cash in from the way he was talking about it at the barbershop. He just wants answers."

"Did you ask him about the duffel bag?"

Liam turned his stare away from the mountains in the distance and directed it at Dale. "I didn't have to. Old Henry Cooper brought it up. Asked him straight up if Maureen had told the kid where she hid the loot."

"And...?"

"He kind of side-stepped the issue."

"So, what do you want to do? Go to the house and ask if we can speak with Maureen?"

Liam shook his head. "Apparently, the boy is the only one who can see or hear her."

Dale watched as the deputy walked from one end of his tiny room to the other. "It can't be a setup. The feds are smart, but to put an entire family in that house, have them renovate it for months and then hope that the story trickles out to us is a completely crazy idea."

"Any more crazy than Maureen actually haunting the old place?" Dale asked.

Liam held up his hand to silence Dale. "Listen, they say the boy is the only one who can talk to her, but how many people have actually tried? I mean, if she was going to haunt anyone, it would be you, wouldn't it? The love of her life?"

"What are you saying?"

"What if she can talk to other people? You were her husband. If anyone has a connection to Maureen, it should be you."

Dale shrugged, still skeptical of the notion that Maureen was a ghost. "So, what do you propose? We go there and I strike up a conversation with Maureen. Get her to tell me where she hid the loot?"

"We're not getting anywhere poring over maps. It's worth a try."

"And what if I can't?" Dale saw the answer to his question in Liam's determined eyes, and he didn't like it.

"Then we're going to have to take him."

CHAPTER FORTY

Harmony stood before the stove in the room behind her parlor, waiting for the kettle to boil. She heard the bell attached to the front door of her waiting room tinkle faintly, pulled a phone out of her pocket and tapped open an app.

On the screen appeared a fisheye view of the entrance to her establishment. She pressed the button on the side of her phone that raised the volume so she could hear her guests as well as see them. Harmony truly did have the gift—she was sure of that. But it didn't hurt to get a little help from technology once in a while.

The kettle started to whistle, and Harmony quickly picked it up off of the burner and poured the steaming water into a cup with a waiting tea bag. She dunked the bag several times before returning her attention to the video feed on her phone.

There were two people, Eleanor Raney and another woman who Harmony recognized as the same one who was present when Eleanor's skeptical son had attended one of her sessions. So much negative energy in that man, so much doubt and distrust.

Harmony breathed a sigh of relief when it became evident he had not accompanied them this time.

She sat down at a small table, holding her tea in one hand and her phone in the other. It was her experience that leaving her guests to wait a while helped them settle their minds and loosen their lips. She never had trouble receiving messages from the spirits—as frustratingly vague as they sometimes were—but it made her job a bit easier if she had a jumping-off point to get started from.

The woman with Eleanor—Harmony couldn't remember what her name was—walked around the waiting room, examining the assortment of statues and candles and crystals displayed on shelves and small tables. She picked up one of the candles and discovered the price tag stuck to the bottom. Her eyes widened at the cost of the seemingly commonplace item. The medium scoffed at the woman's reaction. Obviously, she didn't realize that all of those candles were personally blessed by Harmony.

Eleanor sat on the small couch where she usually waited. This time, she seemed nervous. She clutched her purse in her lap with both hands, her gaze furtively darting around the room. "Maybe we should come back another time."

"Okay," her companion answered. "Let's go."

Eleanor hesitated. "But I really should talk to Ben."

The other woman smiled warmly. "Of course. Whatever you want. Does she usually keep you waiting?" Eleanor's companion looked around the room, her eyes settling on the spot where the camera lens was hidden in the eye of an ebony owl statue. She smiled, then crossed the room to sit next to the old woman.

Eleanor's tension eased. "I don't mind. It gives me a chance to tell Ben things in private. I know he can't talk back to me without Harmony, but I hope he can hear me, anyway."

The other woman glanced back at the camera. "I'm sure he can," she assured Eleanor.

Harmony sipped at her tea. There was something about her client's friend that made her uneasy.

"Are you afraid he might not want to talk to you if you go see Sam?" the woman asked Eleanor, purposefully.

Harmony sat up in the flimsy kitchen chair, holding up her weight. She put aside the tea and held the phone with both hands. So, this was who was trying to convince Eleanor to take her business to another psychic.

Eleanor shrugged. "I don't want things to change."

"What about Nate?"

The old woman sighed. "I'm so worried about him," she confessed. "I just wish he would try to be…"

"More open-minded?" Eleanor's companion suggested.

Eleanor smiled. "You too?"

The other woman nodded. She took one of Eleanor's hands into hers and gave it a gentle squeeze.

"Thank you, Jennifer."

Jennifer. Yes, that was the name she had given. Jennifer Sunshine, or Bright… Day! Jennifer Daye was the other woman's name. Harmony tapped back to the home screen on her phone. "Siri, who is Jennifer Daye?" she asked.

The phone answered by pulling up search results from the internet, including Jennifer's Wikipedia page. "A parapsychologist…" Harmony noted. Well, at least she wasn't one of those skeptical debunkers, or a cop—not that Harmony had anything to hide. Maybe she fudged a few numbers on her taxes, but that didn't count.

Harmony continued reading Jennifer's condensed biography as she sipped her tea.

Jennifer checked her watch. "How long does it usually take?" she asked Eleanor.

Nate's mother took a deep breath. "I don't think she uses clocks. Harmony relies on the spirits to tell her when someone's here."

Jennifer glanced again at the black owl statue resting on a high shelf that had one glass eye different from the other.

An enormous cat scurried out from under the beaded curtain that separated Harmony's salon from her waiting room. Jennifer didn't remember it from her last visit with Nate and Eleanor.

"Hello, who are you?" Jennifer asked as the large feline rubbed up against her ankles.

Eleanor smiled as she saw the cat so obviously approving of Jennifer's presence. "That's Melody, Harmony's sister. She generally doesn't like people."

"Her sister?" Jennifer asked.

Before Eleanor could explain, there was the sound of rustling beads as Harmony pushed her way through the colorful curtain, making a grand entrance. "Welcome," she said, then bowed her head. "The spirits are ready." She held out a hand in Eleanor's general direction.

Eleanor gave Jennifer an embarrassed smile, then fished into her purse for a credit card, which she handed to Harmony.

Jennifer remembered Nate's last reaction to discovering that his mother was still paying psychics with her credit card. She stood up and pulled out her own wallet. "Let me take care of this," she insisted, then turned to Harmony with a stack of twenties in her hand. Jennifer counted out five of the bills and paused.

Harmony smiled.

Jennifer added one more to the collection of bills and Harmony deftly snatched it and tucked it somewhere under the neckline of her dress.

"Come," Harmony said, "they are waiting for us." And then she disappeared into the darkness of the room beyond the curtain.

Eleanor pushed her way through the beads, and Jennifer followed. When they entered the séance room, it was much as Jennifer remembered. Harmony was seated in her "throne," and her guests took the remaining two seats that had been placed around the table.

Harmony placed her hands on the felt covering, palms up.

Eleanor put her own hand into one of the medium's, and Jennifer did the same with the other, then they took each other's hands, completing the circle.

Harmony's breasts heaved as she drew in a deep breath. "I sense conflict," she began. "Something is bothering you, Eleanor."

The older woman shot Jennifer a look, then lowered her gaze. "I need to ask Ben something," she replied. "Something that he—and you—might not like."

Harmony kept her eyes closed and lifted her chin as if smelling something in the air. "He knows. You seek his blessing to talk through another medium," she said plainly.

Jennifer smiled, recalling the conversation she had with Eleanor in the parlor.

"Yes," Eleanor confirmed. "My son—our son—Nate wants me to try someone else."

"Ben wants to know why this is different." Harmony wanted to know as well. "Does it have something to do with your guest? Dr. Daye?"

Eleanor sucked in a breath, trying to remember if she had ever told Harmony that Jennifer was a professor.

Harmony smiled. "The spirits are familiar with her. She is a friend..." she said, smiling at Jennifer in a way that could have been a warning.

Eleanor settled a bit. "She has a friend she'd like me to use. And since Nate trusts her, I thought I'd maybe give it another try."

"I see," said Harmony. "I will ask, but I must warn you, in my experience once a spirit forms a bond with a medium, they are sometimes reluctant to communicate through others." She started swaying, humming random notes to herself.

And then there it was. The voice of the spirits in her mind, unmistakable and emphatic. *Yes, I will speak with my wife through anyone.*

Harmony's eyes sprung open. An expression of shock and surprise took over her face. She looked at Eleanor, then at Jennifer, fixing on the younger woman's eyes with an inquisitive gaze.

"What is it?" Jennifer asked.

"What did he say?" Eleanor added.

Harmony let go of the women's hands. The voice had been so clear, so direct, she felt compelled to relay the message despite what it might cost her. "He said that you have his blessing," Harmony replied, as much surprised by the words coming out of her mouth as her guests were.

"Oh, thank you, Ben," Eleanor said to the air above the table. "Nate will be so pleased."

The medium averted her gaze from Jennifer. She wondered if the parapsychologist had somehow planned this, somehow manipulated the spirits, but that was ridiculous. Part of her was disappointed knowing that she wasn't the exclusive conduit between Eleanor and her deceased husband, but another part of her was thrilled that the voice had been so clear, so convincing. It had been a long time since she had made that strong of a connection. "If you'll excuse me, would you mind seeing yourselves out? I must rest," she said, then stood up from her chair and passed through the sliding door that separated the business portion of the space from the small residence in the back.

"I wasn't expecting that," Eleanor confided.

"Neither was I," Jennifer said. "Neither was I."

CHAPTER FORTY ONE

The Shanty, a cop bar about a block from Nate's old precinct, was fairly typical of the type of establishment off duty law enforcement would frequent in the movies and television shows, only a lot bigger and not quite so dark as you would imagine. The owner had acquired the lease on the space next door about ten years earlier and had expanded it into a dining area with booths along the wall and a pair of pool tables in the back.

Nate sat at one of the booths, a legal pad on the table before him, a glass of wine off to the side. The selection of vintages at The Shanty was small, but the owner always had a couple of bottles on hand that Nate could enjoy. His former coworkers would tease him at times about his choice of adult beverage. There were plenty of times when a cold beer hit the spot, but on most occasions, he preferred wine. And if he was being honest, it worked better at taking the edge off the pain that lived deep in his shoulder.

The other thing he liked about The Shanty was that it wasn't filled with a deafening soundtrack. In the evenings it got loud from the sheer volume of people who crowded in at the end of the day shift, but right now, in that time between lunch and happy hour, it was quiet except for a television playing a ballgame behind the bar.

Nate gazed down at the pad, twiddling a pen between his fingers as he stared at the empty page. Normally it would be filled edge to edge with lists, bullet-pointed facts, observations, questions and conclusions. But today his mind was on other things, his mother most prominent.

Jennifer was taking her to see her friend Sam again. The "psychic" she knew—Nate couldn't help thinking of the word psychic in quotes—to hopefully convince his mother to at least lessen the frequency of her visits to the storefront mediums she usually visited. Lately it had been mostly one woman, Harmony, who in Nate's mind was a complete and obvious fraud. The cheap parlor tricks she had done when he, Jennifer and his mother had visited her had sent him over the edge—something he wasn't proud of—but his frustration had built to a point that he had to let it out. Why couldn't she see how these people were taking advantage of her?

And then there was the encounter with the Foremans. He didn't know what their angle was, but Nate was convinced everyone who claimed to see ghosts had one. Nate had been watching the family closely, like he would if he were observing an interrogation, searching for the telltale signs of deception. But with Danny and his parents, he couldn't see any. There was tension among them, especially between Greg and Marcia, but as far as he could tell, no one was lying.

He scratched a few words at the top of his pad.

"Explanations for Danny's hallucinations," he wrote.

Jennifer would excoriate him for writing such a judgmental heading, but then again, that was the reason why she insisted that Nate work with her team. To bring a skeptical eye to their investigations.

For Nate, the notion that the boy was actually communicating with a ghost was the least likely explanation of all. Emily would probably throw that Sherlock Holmes' quote in his face in her annoying monotone, "Once you eliminate the impossible, whatever remains, no matter how improbable, must be the truth."

Well, he hadn't eliminated the possible let alone the impossible, yet, so he wasn't close to accepting that a dead woman had befriended a fifth grader.

He started filling out a bullet point list:

- **Mental illness - schizophrenia**
- **Drug use - found his parent's stash of mushrooms?**
- **Possible trauma from**
  - **loss of grandmother**
  - **move**
  - **new school (Something happening there? Check with teachers...)**

"Do you make a list of all the lists you make?" a voice asked.

Nate looked up and saw Max Lee smiling down at him.

"Hello, Max," Nate said.

"Hey, boss," Max answered as he slid into the booth opposite his old partner. Today he wore jeans and a t-shirt, his jacket hooked over a finger and slung over his shoulder. He tossed the pale rose-colored linen sports coat into a heap next to him on the bench, causing Nate to reflexively cringe as he imagined all the wrinkles he had just made. There was such a thing as too casual.

"You know I never really was your boss. We were partners," Nate reminded him.

Max shrugged. "Whatever you say, boss."

Nate couldn't help but laugh. "Listen, Max, I'm sorry about how things went out in Danville. I really appreciated you showing up and making sure I was okay."

"Don't mention it. By the way, when's your next surgery?" Max asked, nodding at Nate's right shoulder.

"Two months," Nate replied.

"You going to tell your mom this time?"

Nate shook his head. "She has other things on her mind."

"Well, the next time she calls me, I'm not going to cover for you."

"You didn't cover for me the last time."

"Yeah, I can't lie to moms."

"How's the job going?" Nate asked, changing the subject.

"Translation, 'Do I miss you?'" Max asked back.

Nate smiled. "How could you not? How's the new partner working out?"

Max sat back and sighed. "Well, I'm stuck with the rookie. Guess the captain still has it in for me. Maybe she blames me for letting her best detective get shot."

"Wasn't anyone's fault, Max."

Max nodded.

"Anyway," Nate went on, "if you need any tips on working with a new, annoying partner, I'd be happy to tell you about this guy I got stuck with a few years back."

"Ha. Not too smart of you throwing jabs at the guy you need a favor from."

Nate feigned offense. "Why do you assume that if I needed a favor, I'd come to you?"

Max took a thumb drive out of his pocket, placed it on the table, and set it spinning. "Guess you don't need this, then."

Nate reached out and slapped his hand over the drive and held it up in front of his face. "It's not filled with porn this time, is it?"

Max rolled his eyes. "Jeez, I mix up the drive one time… and you never gave that one back to me, by the way."

Nate shook his head. He slipped the drive into his jacket pocket. "What are the highlights?"

"My buddy over at San Quentin said Dale Everly was a bit of a celebrity in prison. He was offered a reduced sentence several times over the years if he told them where his wife hid the stuff they stole."

"Why did he hold out?"

"He swore up and down that he had no idea what she did with it. Either he's playing the long game, or they weren't as close as he thought."

Nate nodded.

"Why the interest?" Max asked. "You joining the treasure hunt? One of the safe deposit boxes they emptied had a diamond necklace in it. It was appraised at ten million at the time of the robbery. I'll bet Dale Everly could fence it for a million or two, easy."

"I heard that," Nate said. "With the cash he could score for the diamonds, he could easily disappear to a non-extradition country. If he knew where it was, he wouldn't be hanging around at some halfway house."

"Is that why you were out in Danville last week?"

"It's related to a case that Dr. Daye is working on."

Max smiled knowingly. "I like how you call her Dr. Daye to try to make me think there's nothing going on with you two."

"There's not."

"Is that why you haven't invited me over to watch a game in months?"

"I haven't invited you over because you leave watermarks on my coffee table and fart into the sofa cushions."

"That was your dog. Seriously, why are you playing hard to get? Ask her out."

"What makes you think that I haven't, and she turned me down?"

"Because I've known you for over five years."

Nate opened his mouth to respond, but hesitated.

"I knew it," Max said. "Man, you have someone who would be perfect for you, who obviously likes you, and you're too chicken to pull the trigger."

"Well, you're wrong about that."

"Which part?"

"She doesn't like me. It's purely a professional relationship."

"She told you this?"

Nate paused, considering whether he should tell Max the whole story. He was oddly curious as to what his old partner's take on Jennifer's actions was.

"We went out to dinner one night…"

"Wow, big step, bro."

"With my mom."

"There's the old Nate."

Nate ignored the comment. "Afterward, we dropped my mom off then I took her back to her place."

"Wow, that sounds like a move I would do. Did she invite you up?"

Nate gave him a "what do you think?" smirk.

"Oh, right, otherwise you wouldn't be telling me the story. Sorry, dude."

"That's bad, isn't it? I mean, if she was interested, she would have at least invited me up for a drink or offered a rain check."

"Not even a peck on the cheek?" Max asked.

Nate shook his head.

Max winced. "I don't know what to tell you, buddy. I called that one all wrong. I thought for sure you were in after the fifth time she turned me down."

"*You* asked her out?" Nate asked, surprised.

"Of course. I got tired of waiting for you to make a move."

Nate moaned. "Well, I guess we're both not her type."

"I usually give it ten tries before I write someone off."

"I got the message in one."

CHAPTER FORTY TWO

Eleanor struggled to make herself comfortable on the great white couch in Sam Lightman's living room. She felt like a little kid in a big chair, unsure where to put her arms and ended up gripping the straps of her purse tightly in her lap.

Jennifer sat in a chair off to the side, offering moral support. Eleanor had insisted that she be there during her session with Sam.

It felt strange to Eleanor, sitting in someone's living room rather than an incense-filled, dimly lit chamber.

Sam sat across from her. He was distractingly handsome with a disarming smile and a casual manner. Instead of finding it comforting, it added to her anxiety.

Sam sensed her discomfort. "Let me take your bag," he offered, reaching out his hand.

Eleanor looked at the purse in her lap, then lifted it and offered it to Sam.

He smiled as he took it from her grasp and set it on the table next to the sofa. Then he scooted a bit closer to Eleanor and took her hands in his. He took slow, deep breaths as he stared at Eleanor, continuing to smile.

His hands were warm.

"Do you want me to close my eyes or anything?" she asked.

"If you want to," Sam replied. "Just relax." He guided Eleanor through a series of deep breaths, and she started to let go of some of her stress.

"Is he here?" Eleanor asked. "Is Ben with us?"

Sam smiled and nodded.

Finally, Eleanor returned Sam's warm smile and sighed with relief. The rest of her anxiety melted away. "What is he saying?" she asked.

"Not much," Sam replied. "I get the feeling he wasn't a very talkative man."

Eleanor laughed. It always was a struggle to engage Ben in a conversation more than three words long. She had always assumed that since he had passed, he had become chattier because of her sessions with Harmony and other mediums. But now it felt like she was closer to Ben than she had been in a long time without exchanging a word. It reminded her of the moments—especially before Nate came along—when he would come up behind her when she was preparing dinner or doing the dishes, wrap his arms around her, kiss her ear and whisper, "I love you."

"He just whispered something in my ear," Sam said. "He says you know what it was."

Eleanor broke at that point. Tears welled up in her eyes while at the same time she smiled with joy. "Oh, Ben, I miss you so much."

"He's always with you," Sam told her. "You just have to remember those moments that make you feel like this."

"How can I do that without you?" Eleanor asked. "I don't have your gifts."

"You have the greatest gift of all. Life. Live it. Enjoy the people and experiences you can gather right now, and then you can take them with you when you join Ben—hopefully well into the future. He'll always be there waiting for you."

Sam laughed again. "He doesn't say much, but what he does gets right to the point, doesn't it?"

Eleanor looked at Sam. "What? What did he say?"

Sam squeezed her hands. "A boy needs his mother."

Eleanor lifted a hand to her mouth. Those were the last words Ben had spoken to her in life as she held his hand in the hospice bed, and he closed his eyes for the last time.

"Thank you," she said to Sam.

"Thank you," Sam said back to her. "I hope I find a relationship like you and Ben have." He looked briefly over at Jennifer.

Eleanor noticed the glance. She stole a look over at Jennifer, who appeared to blush.

"Well, I'm sure you'll find someone someday," Eleanor said, patting Sam on the hand. "Thank you again for your time. I'm sorry I was late. I must be keeping you from… something."

"No, not at all. If you like, that rain check for dinner is still available," Sam offered. He turned to Jennifer. "I believe Chef is making your favorite, *duck à l'orange*."

"Really?" Jennifer asked with a note of interest.

"That's really nice of you," Eleanor interjected, "but Dr. Daye and I have to be going." She turned to Jennifer. "I really need to get home. I have the crock pot on."

"All right," Jennifer said. "Another time, Sam. Thanks again for everything."

"Feel free to come back anytime, Eleanor. It was nice seeing you again. And meeting Ben."

"I'll think about it," Eleanor promised. "Thank you." She rose from the sofa and took Jennifer by the hand, dragging her to the front door.

Sam rushed ahead to open the door for them.

Eleanor smiled politely and pulled Jennifer out of the house and back to the van.

CHAPTER FORTY THREE

Marcia tidied up Danny's room a bit as he slipped into bed and under the covers. She picked up the clothes he had discarded on the floor and placed them in the hamper in his closet, then picked up a crumpled napkin and made a note to vacuum the crumbs under his desk in the morning.

"Do you want a story tonight?" she asked Danny.

"That's okay," he answered. "Maureen said she'd tell me one." Danny looked toward the foot of his bed.

Marcia followed Danny's gaze and stared at the empty space where he was looking, willing herself to see what he saw, hoping that there really was a ghost and that her son wasn't experiencing hallucinations. She worried about what that might mean. One of the more frightening possibilities she found online was that he had a brain tumor.

She shook it off and forced herself to smile at Danny. She leaned over and kissed him on the forehead. He was at the age where he was just starting to find this to be "yucky." In a few years, he would be a teenager. That was hard to fathom. A few years after that, he'd be driving, and it wouldn't be long before he was off to college.

But until then, she would kiss his forehead every night until he made her stop. "Good night, Danny. I love you."

"Love you, too, mom," he said in a way that foreshadowed a time not too far in the future when he would be reluctant to say that to her out loud as well.

Marcia switched off the light as she walked out. She left the door open a crack, so she'd be able to hear if he called out to her in the night. Then she lingered just outside, listening.

"Tell me about the gold mine," Danny said quietly to Maureen.

Maureen moved so she was sitting on the side of Danny's bed. "Again?" she asked. "Don't you want to hear something else? I remember a story about a boy who finds a giant peach in his yard."

"Please," he begged. "It's better than a story 'cause it's a real adventure."

Maureen smiled. "All right. I'll tell you about how my friend Joanna got lost."

"Did you find her?" Danny asked, a note of concern in his voice.

"Yes, we did. The story has a happy ending," Maureen assured him. "You see, me and my friends liked exploring the woods and the mountains. We had a lot of secret places where we would play. The gold mine was just one of them."

"That's so cool," Danny said, fighting off a yawn.

"We thought so. It was my older cousin, Jeremy, who actually found it. And one day I heard him telling his friends about it, so I told my friends and we decided we would follow Jeremy to find out where it was. We were good at sneaking around in the woods. Me and Joanna and Carl from the next farm down used to play hide and seek all the time, so the next time Jeremy and his friends sneaked off to the mine, we followed them. Then waited for them to leave before we checked it out ourselves.

"If you didn't know what you were looking for, you would pass it by. The entrance was narrow and hidden behind some bushes. Part of it was a natural cave. There was a big area just inside. The miners had leveled out the floor with dirt and had started digging tunnels into the side of the mountain.

"Jeremy and his friends had taken some old lawn chairs and a small ice chest and set them up in there. I think they were scared to go into the tunnels. They were kinda small and tight. Carl had taken a gas lantern from their barn, and I had managed to get a bunch of candles and matches. There were two tunnels off the main chamber, and we explored as much of it as we could. Part of it was filled with water, and we imagined there was a sea monster living there, so we stayed away."

"Good," Danny said, relieved.

Maureen smiled. Danny had confessed he didn't like monsters, and that there might have been one living under the stairs at their old house, so she steered clear of telling him the particulars of the creature she and her friends had imagined lived at the bottom of the mine.

"We also found out that the two tunnels actually connected to each other, and we found a wide spot in one of them and made our own little hideout that Jeremy and his friends didn't know about. We brought in some blankets and set up the candles. Carl had the idea to bring some hammers, too, so we could do our own gold mining."

"Did you find anything?" Danny asked, fighting to keep his eyes open.

"Not really. But we dreamed about what we would buy if we did. Like new bikes."

"How did Joanna get lost?"

"Well, one day after we were doing a little mining, we were heading home and Joanna realized she had left a bracelet behind and wanted to go back and get it. I gave her a box of matches and the candle we used to get in and out, and we waited for her.

"But after about ten minutes, she didn't come back. Then it was fifteen minutes, then thirty."

Danny's eyes had been closed for a while, but now they were wide open.

"What happened to her?"

"We didn't know. We decided to go back and see if we could find her, but she had the candle, and we couldn't go very far before it got too dark to see. We called out to her, but she didn't answer."

"What did you do?"

"Well, we were scared. So we ran back to my house and told my mother. And she called the police. We were so afraid we were going to be in trouble. Then she called Carl's mom and Joanna's dad and pretty soon there were a whole bunch of grownups there. They made us show them where the gold mine was. They brought in flashlights and lanterns and searched the whole mine, but she wasn't there."

"What happened to her?"

"Well, a little while later, some of the grownups who were searching the woods around the mine found her. She was scared and confused, but other than that, she was okay. She was inside the mine and tripped and dropped the candle and the matches. She couldn't find them, so she tried to get out by feeling her way along the floor and walls. Eventually, she found her way out through a hidden entrance, but got lost trying to find her way back to us."

"Did you get in trouble?"

"A little. Mostly it was my cousin, Jeremy, who got in trouble. And he was super mad at me for spoiling his hideout. The grownups got together and sealed up the entrance with cement so no one else could go in there and get lost. But we found the secret way in that Joanna used and played there the rest of the summer."

"What about the monster?" Danny asked.

"The monster?"

"In the water."

"Oh, well, he'll never get out now. I don't think we need to worry about the monster."

"Okay. Good," Danny said, relieved. "Maureen, can I ask you a question?"

"Of course you can," she said.

"How come I'm the only one who can see and hear you?" he asked.

Maureen considered his question. It was one she had thought about herself. She had no idea why they had whatever connection they had. But being Danny's friend was... comforting. "When I was a little girl, I would always dream about when I would get married and have my own family. And one time, I made a wish at a wishing well, that someday I would have a little boy. But since I died before I could have my own son, I guess being friends with you is the answer to my wish."

Danny thought about her answer. "I like that. I'm glad we're friends."

"Me, too," Maureen said.

Danny let his eyes close, and he drifted off to sleep.

Greg climbed the stairs and saw his wife leaning against the wall outside of Danny's room. She looked at him and he offered her a reassuring smile. "Is he doing it again?" Greg asked.

Marcia nodded.

"You're worried."

"He is so convinced she's real."

"Well, Dr. Daye did say—"

Marcia cut him off with a look.

"I'm just saying, it does explain his behavior."

"What if it doesn't?" Marcia asked. "What if there's something wrong with Danny? I want him to see a professional. A medical professional."

"A psychiatrist?" Greg asked.

Marcia nodded.

"Okay," her husband agreed. "I'll call Dr. Thorpe in the morning, see if she can refer someone."

"Thanks," Marcia said, reaching out to Greg for an embrace.

He held her for a moment, then led her down the hall to their room.

CHAPTER FORTY FOUR

The last light went out just before eleven o'clock.

Dale watched the house from a spot on the hillside in the woods behind the Foreman's home. It was a spot where he used to hang out when he was a teenager, waiting for Maureen to be able to sneak away from her family. It was accessible by a fire road higher up on a ridge. The location was fairly flat, and Maureen would bring a blanket with her, and they would snuggle under the stars and talk about their dreams for the future. Dale had big plans. He wanted to start his own construction company. He saw the potential to develop the valley and figured he could get in on the ground floor and buy up some of the land off the highway and parlay it into a small development empire.

Maureen would listen, smiling as Dale detailed his schemes, and she would in turn imagine how she would stay at home with their children, and pursue her dreams of being an artist. She wanted four kids, and they would live in an enormous house Dale would build for them, high on a hill overlooking the valley.

They would make love, passionately and frantically, the way teenagers did, then gaze up at the stars, or the moonlit clouds.

Of course, life didn't turn out the way they had planned. Dale had partnered with a man he had met while working for another contractor. The man had contacts, people who might be willing to finance

Dale's business plan. But he turned out to have his own business plan, one in which he leveraged the company they had built for his own benefit, excluding himself from any liability. In the end, Dale had lost his investment and found himself hundreds of thousands of dollars in debt.

It was devastating. Maureen had tried to reassure him that he could come back from this. People didn't blame him, they knew he had been swindled. But Dale saw no way forward without declaring bankruptcy, and he couldn't imagine how anyone would give him any money after he had so spectacularly failed.

And then he met Liam.

Dale had taken to spending much of the money he was making as a workman at a tavern downtown. He usually sat by himself, absently watching whichever sporting event was on the television behind the bar.

Liam sat down next to him one night, complaining about his own life, how his old man had borrowed the money he had been saving for a down payment on a house for what he claimed was a medical expense. His father took the money and disappeared. Liam's wife left him shortly after that, and a friend got him the job working for the local police department.

Their gripe sessions became a daily occurrence. Some nights they would stay until the place closed, wondering what they were doing wrong, what made them different from the millionaires, and the people for whom it seemed so easy.

Based on their experiences, the answer was obvious. The "winners" in life were all crooks. They were the kind of people who just took what they wanted—what they deserved.

What Dale and Liam needed to do was stop being suckers and start being takers.

Inevitably, the conversation would take a turn. They conceived of various plots to do just that. To just take what they wanted. Intercept cash coming from or going to an armored car. Grab the loose gems from the back of a jewelry store. Rob a bank.

Dale never took these fantasies too seriously. There were nights when he and Liam would be so drunk that it almost made sense to Dale. Why not? People got away with stealing from others all the time. That's why there was insurance.

Then one evening, Liam brought a guest. The guest had no name and wore dark glasses and a hat. Dale suspected that the man was disguising his voice too.

Liam called him the Mastermind.

The reason for his subterfuge became clear. He had a plan. A plan to rob a bank. It was foolproof, he claimed, but it required a team. Two people in the bank, and a third who could manage the response to the silent alarm.

There was a flaw in the system the Mastermind had uncovered. The bank had all the sensors and alarms a responsible financial institution should have, but the bells that rang in the bank could be easily circumvented. The alarm would still be triggered, and the hard line to the police station would still be activated, but the ear-splitting ringing that was designed to scare the burglars away would remain quiet.

All it would take to give the burglars time to break into the safe would be to intercept that silent alarm in the station and prevent the police from taking immediate action.

And Liam, as a police officer, was in a position to do just that.

Dale was reluctant. He had no idea how to break into a bank vault. But the man behind the dark glasses assured him he had access to all the equipment and know-how required to do the job. Dale's construction experience would be all he needed. It was just a matter of employing tools he was already familiar with in a specific manner.

The Mastermind left them.

Dale pressed Liam about the stranger, but Liam was hesitant— perhaps fearful—about revealing anything about the man except that he seemed to be well connected and knew the ins and outs of the Danville Bank and the Police Department intimately.

Dale wasn't sure what to think. All those evenings Liam and he had kicked around grand schemes were just far enough on the other side of fantasy as to not be something he needed to take seriously.

But now there was a real plan, an opportunity to give an outlet to his feelings, to make right the wrongs that had been done against him. But could he really do something like that? Rob a bank?

Over the next week, Liam slowly pushed Dale to consider the plan. It was the perfect crime. Every angle had been considered. The Mastermind had inside information that would make it well worth the risk.

Eventually, Dale agreed to move forward with the plan, but he still had one reservation. He didn't know the Mastermind, and he wasn't sure he was comfortable breaking into the vault with someone whose name he didn't even know.

Liam told Dale that he didn't have to worry about that. The man in the hat wasn't going to be a part of the execution of the plan at all. Dale was confused. Liam was responsible for diverting the silent alarm at the police station. Who was the other bank man going to be?

"You trust that lady of yours, don't you?" Liam asked.

Dale was stunned. How could Liam think he would risk involving Maureen in something like this?

But then again, who else could he trust?

Maureen had met Liam previously. They had dinner together a couple times, and on one occasion Liam had brought a date as well. Liam had even joked on one occasion that he and Dale were spending all that time together planning a heist.

Maureen sat and listened to the plan. The more Dale explained it to her, the more absurd it sounded to him. He expected her to laugh and accuse him and Liam of playing a bad joke on her.

Instead, she considered it for a moment, then said to him, "Yes, I'll help."

Dale was shocked. Maureen had always been smarter than he was, but also more sensible and optimistic. The fact that she didn't even question the sanity of the idea took him by surprise. Maureen interrogated Dale about the plan, about the Mastermind and the role Liam would be playing.

In the end, her last question was simply, "When?"

"Are you sure?" Dale had asked.

"Dale," she said to him, taking his hand, "I believe in you. And I've seen you slipping away from me these last months since you lost your business. If this is what it takes to get you back, then yes, I'm sure. But I have one condition."

"What?"

"Afterward, we leave this town. We go somewhere else, somewhere new, where we can have a fresh start. I want to have a family. With you," she said to Dale. "Will you promise that we'll go as far away as we can?"

"China?" he asked jokingly.

"Well, maybe Maine," she answered with a smile and then a kiss.

It was at that moment that Dale thought his life was finally back on the right track.

But then it had turned into a complete train wreck.

Fifteen years of his life, and all of Maureen's were gone.

And now here he was again. Following the plan of the man who had led his life so astray.

But what if it was true? What if it was Maureen the boy was talking to? And what if she could tell him where she had put the money? Maybe she wanted him to find it? To get that fresh start they had talked about. If nothing else, maybe he could tell her he was sorry.

Dale waited another half hour before making his way down the wooded hillside toward the house. There was only a sliver of a moon in the sky, but it was enough to negotiate his path through the trees.

When he got to the yard, he walked slowly and quietly to the back of the house. He didn't head for the door. Despite being somewhat remote, everyone kept their doors locked these days. But Dale knew something the Foremans didn't. The high, narrow window in their pantry, that they didn't bother to replace when they renovated the old farmhouse, had a latch that was fairly easy to undo from the outside with a thin blade.

He approached the window. When he was a teenager, it was easy for him to squeeze through the skinny opening, but he should still be able to wriggle inside. It turned out he didn't need the knife he had brought with him to unlock the window. The latch wasn't closed. But the window didn't open as easily as he had expected. It had been painted shut.

Dale carefully cut through the hardened latex until his blade could move easily between the entire edge of the casing. Then he slowly pushed up on the sash with increasing pressure.

The window didn't move. Perhaps they had painted it shut on the inside as well. He tried again, pressing his thumbs on the underside of the top rail of the bottom sash.

It didn't move.

He looked closer at the upper sash, noting that it was a double-hung window. Perhaps lowering the top part of the window would work better than trying to raise the bottom. His blade once again sliced through the paint sealing the sash to the frame, then he pulled on the outside rail, slowly applying more and more pressure until he felt like he was hanging on it with his full weight.

The window snapped free with a crack.

Dale lost his grip and tumbled to the ground.

In his ears, it sounded like a truck had crashed into the house.

He stayed on the ground unmoving, watching the upstairs windows to see if any lights came on.

None did.

He rose to his feet and put his face to the opening he had created in the pantry window and listened. There was no sound. No footsteps, no curious voices. The occupants of the house remained undisturbed.

Dale breathed a sigh of relief. He briefly considered trying to free the bottom sash so he could more easily enter through the window, but he didn't want to chance making any more noise. He looked around and saw a couple of milk crates by the door to the back porch. He grabbed one and set it below the pantry window.

He slipped off the knapsack on his back and climbed up onto the sill on his knees. There was enough light for him to see that there was still a shelf right below the window, but it was covered with boxes of cereal and other food. He reached inside with his gloved hand, pulled the boxes out, and dropped them to the ground outside the window as quietly as he could.

Once it was clear, he dropped his knapsack through the opening, then stepped up onto the sill with one foot and lifted his other over the sash and inside onto the shelf. From there it was a matter of contorting his body through the opening slowly and carefully, an inch at a time until he was in the pantry, standing on the shelf with both feet and hanging onto the edges of the window frame.

He lowered one foot to the floor, then the other. He pushed the window closed, but then remembered that he had left the food boxes outside. If he had time, he would take care of that. No need to make the police's job any easier. His main concern was to make sure he didn't leave any trace of himself behind.

He noticed he had left some dark smudges on the shelf under the window. Shoe prints. He found a roll of paper towels and a spray cleaner and wiped it down, then cleaned the bottoms of his shoes and carefully returned everything back to where he found it.

The pantry door threatened to squeak as Dale pulled it open. A little upward pressure on the knob shifted the weight of the door enough to prevent any sound. If he had thought through the plan more carefully, he would have brought along a can of WD-40, but he was past that now.

Dale stepped into the kitchen. The Foremans had completely redone the entire room. Gone were the Formica counters, chipped cabinets and the old, outdated appliances. In their place were granite and stainless steel, and cabinets with glass panes in the doors. It looked nice, the kind of kitchen Maureen had always dreamed of having.

He paused and looked around, peering into the shadows. "Maureen? Are you there?" he asked. "If you can hear me, if you're here, give me a sign. Please, I miss you so much."

He waited for a reply, but none was forthcoming. He had sincerely hoped that if her ghost was here, she would be waiting for him, and he could apologize and explain.

But there was nothing.

His fantasy of seeing her spectral form in the old house, being able to talk to her and find out where the money was so he wouldn't have to do what Liam had convinced him was necessary, turned out to be just that. A fantasy.

"I'm sorry, Maureen," he whispered, then crossed into the living room and moved silently to the stairs. He kept to the left side of the steps leading to the landing, knowing from many a late night sneaking up to Maureen's room when they were kids how to avoid the creaks and groans of the old house.

The boy's room was easily identifiable by the neatly lettered sign taped to it reading, "No girls allowed (that means you, Daisy!)" It was ajar.

Dale waited a couple of minutes, making sure his presence hadn't alerted anyone. Liam had assured him there were no pets in the house. From his knapsack, Dale pulled out a full respirator mask and slipped it over his face. Then he took out a bandanna and a dark brown glass bottle. He opened the bottle and soaked the cloth with its contents. Armed with the chloroform-soaked rag in one gloved hand, he gently pushed open the door to Danny's bedroom with the other.

Maureen didn't sleep. At least she didn't think she did. At the very least, she didn't dream. And why should she? Wasn't dreaming something her physical body did? But it didn't matter. Since the passage of time didn't affect her the way it did when she had a body that needed food and sleep, waiting the hours between when the Foremans went to sleep and woke up felt like the blink of an eye. She was never tempted to wander, even though she now knew she could do so without losing her connection to Danny. She simply waited in a corner of the boy's room for him to wake up in the morning.

She didn't have the same senses she did when she was alive. She didn't hear with ears or see with her eyes. It was almost as if she relied on people around her to lend her their senses—though she was still aware of her surroundings when there was no one around.

When Danny fell asleep, her perception of the world dimmed. So when the door to his room slowly opened, she didn't notice it at first.

But there was something stirring in her consciousness. A presence.

Then it became clear to her. There was someone in Danny's room.

It wasn't Greg or Marcia. She knew what they felt like, but it was someone familiar.

All she could perceive at first was a large, dark shape creeping toward Danny's bed.

"Danny," she shouted, "Danny, wake up."

Whoever had broken into the house and into Danny's room didn't hear her—which wasn't surprising. Only Danny had that ability. But could Danny hear her when he was asleep? So far, he hadn't even stirred.

"Danny, you have to wake up. There's someone in your room. Wake up, Danny! Call for your parents. Scream!"

Danny shifted on the bed, turning from his side to his back.

He yawned, but his eyes remained closed.

The figure in the room stopped, waited, then moved closer.

"Danny," Maureen screamed with all her might, "Wake up! Wake! Up!"

Danny's eyes fluttered, then opened.

Suddenly, Maureen saw what he saw. A monster reaching toward him, two large round eyes in its face, and in place of a mouth, an insect-like appendage.

"Scream, Danny! As loud as you can," Maureen shouted.

The boy sucked in a breath to do just that, but as he did, the monster covered his mouth with something in his hand, a cloth of some kind. Danny managed to struggle a bit, but his scream was smothered, then his eyes closed, and his body went limp.

The monster waited a few seconds more, then removed the cloth, shoved it into a plastic bag and tucked it away in a pocket. He lifted the respirator up away from his face.

It was Dale.

The name was filled with so many feelings and memories, so many emotions, but not one of them the fear she felt right now.

Why was he here? What was he doing to Danny?

Dale looked around and grabbed a pair of slippers beside the bed.

He pulled back the blanket Danny was sleeping under, picked up the boy easily, and draped him over his shoulder.

"Dale, please. Whatever you're doing, stop," Maureen begged.

But Dale didn't hear her. He made his way out of the room to the stairs, then slowly descended, keeping to the quiet side of the steps. Of course, Dale would know about that. This had been their house before…

Her thoughts shifted to Danny. Where was Dale taking him? Why was he taking him? Should she follow them? "Please, someone, hear me! He's taking Danny, you have to wake up!"

But no one heard her. The lights upstairs didn't come on. Danny's parents didn't wake, nor did his little sister, Daisy.

Maureen sobbed as she watched Dale carefully sneak into the kitchen with Danny's limp body slung over one shoulder. She knew from her experience tracking down the parapsychologist Greg had called that she should be able to find Danny just by thinking of him, but she wasn't going to take that chance. She decided she was going to follow them, find out where Dale was taking Danny, then find some way to communicate with someone. If she could talk to Danny, there must be other people she could talk to.

There had to be.

Dale stopped when he reached the back door. He stared at the keypad on the wall. There was an alarm system in the house. He looked at it for a moment. The screen was blank, but there was a single red LED glowing in the upper right-hand corner.

While in prison, he had listened in on the conversations between the inmates, swapping tips and tricks for breaking and entering among other crimes. For many inmates, their time incarcerated was an opportunity to earn the equivalent of a master's degree in larceny.

Some alarms were true deterrents, but others were mere window dressing. This one looked like one of those do-it-yourself systems. The bad news was that it was likely connected to the alarm company using a cellular connection.

The good news was that it was designed to keep people out, and

Dale was already in. Lucky for him, the Foremans hadn't thought to put a window sensor on the small pantry window they had painted shut.

Maybe he could go back out the way he came in, but that meant he would have to somehow lift the boy through the window and lower him to the ground. That didn't seem very realistic.

The kid was small, but the longer Dale held him on his shoulder, the heavier he got.

He carried the boy back out to the living room and laid him down on the sofa. Danny didn't stir. Dale didn't know exactly how long the chloroform would last, and he didn't want to risk giving the boy another dose.

He went back into the kitchen and studied the keypad. He pressed one of the numbers and the display lit up. The word "ARMED" showed up on the screen. He looked around to see if the Foremans were careless enough to leave their code nearby, written on a sticky note by the keypad, or maybe stuck on the refrigerator, or tucked in a nearby drawer. He came up empty.

Then Dale located the pair of small, white rectangular boxes at the top of the back door. The smaller one, stuck to the door itself, was a magnet, and the larger piece was the actual sensor. As long as they were lined up, the system was happy. But if someone were to open the door while the keypad was armed, unless the disarm code was entered within sixty seconds, an ear-splitting siren would sound and a call would be made to the police.

He inspected the sensor. The cover of the large piece came off easily so the battery could be replaced. Dale didn't know what would happen if the sensor suddenly lost power, but he assumed it would result in the same condition as if the door had been opened.

The magnet was simply stuck to the door with double-sided foam tape. Dale gave it a little wiggle. As cheap as it looked, it was stuck on fairly well. He looked around, then remembered one of the drawers he had opened looking for the disarm code was a junk drawer filled with odds and ends and various tools. One of them was a pocket saw. He grabbed it and a roll of duct tape.

Dale placed a strip of tape across the sensor and the magnet to hold them in place while he used the hacksaw-like blade to cut through the adhesive pad. He soon realized it was also fastened with a screw. The screw was behind the battery, so he had to keep sawing through the metal as well, but eventually the blade cut through the last bit of adhesive holding the sensor in place.

He glanced at the keypad. The display had gone dark again, and the red light was still shining brightly, but there was no alarm.

Dale wrapped some more tape around the sensor and its magnet, then tucked them into the junk drawer along with the tools he borrowed. He unlocked the back door and pulled it open.

Nothing happened. He let out the breath he had been holding and started to depart before remembering that he was about to leave behind what he had come for.

The boy was laying in the same exact position Dale had left him on the sofa. Dale put his ear to the boy's mouth, relieved to hear breath sounds. He had spent a lot more time in the house than he had planned on and half expected to see the rest of the family groggily coming down the stairs for breakfast.

Outside, it was still dark. Dale lifted the boy back over his shoulder and carried him through the kitchen and outside. He gently closed the door, then made his way through the screened in back porch and out into the yard.

He froze when he heard footsteps.

Someone was dragging something across the yard. Had they seen him?

Slowly, Dale turned toward the sound.

Red eyes glinted back at him in the moonlight.

A family of raccoons had come to claim the treasure trove of food Dale had left behind when he had crawled in through the pantry window.

Dale took a step toward them, and they grabbed the boxes in their mouths and scurried off into the trees. Once they were gone, he waited another minute to make sure one last time that he hadn't woken anybody, put the milk crate back where he found it, then started into the woods toward the spot a quarter mile away where he had parked the car Liam had gotten for him.

Maureen couldn't believe this was the same Dale she loved. He was older, that much was obvious, but there was also something very different about the way he acted.

The Dale she knew was compassionate. Kidnapping a child was not something he would ever consider doing.

What had happened to him to bring him to this point?

And where was he taking Danny?

CHAPTER FORTY FIVE

Marcia woke up when Greg's alarm shattered the quiet of the morning. She pulled the covers over her head while her husband rolled out of bed and padded toward the shower. Since she worked from home, she didn't have to worry about getting dressed and commuting, so she usually took advantage of the extra time to make breakfast for the family and lunch for the kids and Greg.

However, this morning she felt more tired than usual. She had a memory of dreams disturbing her sleep, but couldn't remember any of the details. She tried to convince herself that if she could just get in five more minutes, she'd be ready to start the day, but after a few seconds cocooned under her comforter, she threw the bedding aside and squinted at the window revealing the start of a bright sunny day.

Marcia pulled on her robe and stepped into her slippers, then padded out of her room. "Danny, Daisy, time to get up," she shouted down the hall as she made her way to the stairs.

The kids were usually pretty good about getting themselves up. Some mornings she would have to help Daisy change her outfit, as she had a tendency to mix her school clothes with her pajamas.

Marcia didn't feel like doing anything complicated for breakfast. She scrambled a half dozen eggs and threw some precooked turkey breakfast links into the microwave. She set the table and pulled out cartons of milk and orange juice.

It was nice to have a family breakfast. Before they had kids, Marcia and Greg often found themselves in a flurry of separate activities each morning. Now, starting the day off together was a welcome routine.

She crossed into the living room and shouted up the stairs, "Danny, Daisy, breakfast!" She waited for a moment, and then when she saw Daisy pop out of her room, she returned to the kitchen just as the microwave beeped. She grabbed the sausage and set it on the table.

Daisy entered and hopped onto one of the kitchen chairs. "Juice, please," she said.

Marcia smiled at her daughter, then filled the glass before her with orange juice.

"Thank you," Daisy added before taking a satisfying sip.

Greg entered and popped a pod into the coffeemaker and placed a mug under the spout. He put a hand on Marcia's arm as she passed him and gave her a quick kiss on the cheek. "Good morning."

"Good morning. What is your son up to?"

"Convenient how he's my son when he's late for breakfast," Greg observed. "Is there cereal?"

"In the pantry."

Greg stepped around the table to the pantry door. He opened it and went inside, then emerged a few seconds later, a confused expression on his face. "Don't see any."

"It's on the shelf in front of the window."

Greg stuck his head back in the pantry for a look. "Nope, there's nothing there."

Marcia rolled her eyes, then joined Greg at the pantry door. She looked inside, and much to her surprise, the shelf that she was sure was stocked with cereal, pancake mix and other boxed foods was now completely clear. "That's strange," she said.

"No biggie," Greg said. "I'll go check on Danny."

"Thanks," Marcia replied. She scanned the shelves on either side of the pantry, but the cereal boxes were nowhere to be found.

Greg jogged up the steps. "Danny, what's taking you so long?

Your mom has breakfast on the table," he said loudly. He reached the landing and saw Danny's door open a crack. He pushed it open, but the room was empty. His bed was still unmade, and his homework was still spread out on his desk.

Greg went back out to the hall and approached the bathroom. The door was closed. He knocked. "Danny, are you in there?" There was no answer.

He tried the door. It was unlocked. He opened it and found the bathroom as empty as Danny's bedroom.

Greg became anxious. He checked Daisy's room, then his and Marcia's, and finally the empty spare room at the end of the hall. All were empty.

"Danny? Where are you, son? Time for breakfast," he said, trying not to let the growing anxiety he was feeling creep into his voice. "Danny?"

His question was met with silence.

Greg ran down the steps, two at a time, nearly tripping halfway down. He looked around the living room, then crossed to the front door. He keyed in the disarm code to the keypad on the wall, opened it and stepped out onto the front porch. "Danny!" he shouted to the empty yard. His breathing quickened and his pulse raced as he went back into the house through the living room to the kitchen, trying to mask his panic with a smile.

"Daisy, did you see Danny this morning?" he asked.

Daisy, her mouth full of sausage, shook her head.

Marcia shot him a concerned look.

Greg walked past her toward the back door. He turned the knob and pulled. The door was unlocked. He exited to the back porch, then to the yard. "Danny, are you out here?" There was no reply.

"What's going on? Where Danny?" Marcia asked.

"I don't know," Greg answered. "Did you see him when you woke up?"

Marcia shook her head.

"He's got to be in the house," Greg said. He turned to go back inside, but Marcia grabbed his hand to stop him.

"You don't think he ran away, do you?

"Why would he do that?"

Marcia felt herself starting to cry. "Maybe he heard us talking last night. About seeing a doctor."

Greg pulled her into a hug. "No, he wouldn't do that. I'm sure he's around here somewhere. Come on, let's split up. I'll check in the basement, you go through the house, see if he's curled up in a closet or something. You remember when we first moved in and we thought he disappeared? Turned out he had made that stack of boxes into a fort and fell asleep inside."

Marcia almost laughed at the memory. Greg was right, he was probably hiding somewhere. Maybe he had a test or something at school and he wanted to stay home. "Okay," she said.

They walked back into the house, each squeezing the other's hand with hope and fear.

CHAPTER FORTY SIX

Nate stared at the large whiteboard covered with photos, headlines and articles surrounding a list under the heading, "What Danny Knows About Maureen Everly."

Each item, such as her name and address, what she looked like, where she went to school, where she used to hang out were connected with various colored lines to the different information sources Nate had independently found on the internet, and the photo stash that had been discovered in the Foremans' attic.

Not a single item on the list was without a matching source from Nate's cursory search. The topic of the robbery had been rehashed on several news sites, and even a couple of cold case and treasure hunting forums and podcasts had picked up the story on the occasion of Dale Everly's release from prison. So, most of the digging up of information about Maureen and Dale Everly's lives had already been done by others, trying to find some clue as to where Maureen had hidden the missing cash and valuables from the daring heist.

Dave entered the office with the day's mail. He paused when he saw the fruit of Nate's research laid out on the board and let out a low whistle. "Wow, looks like you have everything covered there."

"Occam's Razor," Nate replied. "The simplest explanation..."

Dave shrugged. "Well, if you were to ask Dr. Daye, the simplest explanation is that Danny got all this information talking to

Maureen."

"I said Occam's Razor, not Occam's Fantasy," Nate countered.

Dave walked around the large desk and approached the white-board. He picked up one of the markers laying in the tray beneath the eight-foot-wide board and wrote another item at the bottom of Nate's list.

"Location of missing loot."

"Danny didn't claim that Maureen had told him that," Nate said.

"I know," Dave answered, "but I don't see it in any of the bits and pieces you found, so, if he does come up with where Maureen Everly hid that duffel bag of treasure…"

Nate considered Dave's point but didn't answer.

"You really think a ten-year-old boy with limited computer privileges could really dig up all that information on his own?"

"Kids are very internet savvy these days," Nate answered. "And we only have his parent's word that he has limited access. Plus, who said he's working on his own?"

"You think Greg and Marcia are putting him up to it? His mom didn't seem too happy about the attention they were getting."

"Yes, but the father was all in on the whole ghost thing," Nate countered.

"But what's his angle?" Dave asked. "I mean, he might get some tabloid money for an interview, but he's also going to bring down a lot of interest from the treasure hunters—not to mention Danny's going to get a lot of teasing at school."

"All I can tell you is what I learned from my time as a policeman. People do strange things for all kinds of reasons. We live in an era where people become millionaires by making videos. Money is a strong motivator."

"Speaking of which," Dave said, nodding at the stack of envelopes he had left on the desk.

"More bills?"

"Yeah."

Nate sighed and started shuffling through the mail.

"Be honest with me, Detective Raney," Dave said. "How much

longer can we keep this going without any paying clients? I know you and Dr. Daye aren't telling us how bad things really are."

Nate looked up and met Dave's concerned gaze. The graduate student had been through a lot with Jennifer. Even though she was a popular professor at the university, the Dean of Anthropology was not a fan, and she struggled to gain academic respect. The focus of her research on the paranormal was at odds with many in her department, despite being popular with the student body.

"I can float us for a while longer," Nate assured the younger man, but Dave didn't seem comforted.

"So what you're saying is we should get busy making viral videos on TikTok," suggested Emily.

Dave and Nate looked over at the doorway where Emily was standing, leaning against the door frame, eating what looked like a green burrito.

"What's TikTok?" Nate asked.

"Don't sweat it, geezer," Emily replied. "You just keep thumbing it on that Blackberry of yours."

Nate shook his head. He actually had the latest phone from Samsung, complete with eight-K video. "Don't you have work to do for Dr. Daye?" he asked.

"She's teaching today."

Nate still felt embarrassed about that night he had dropped her off after dining with his mother. He had convinced himself that her flirtations were more than just her usual extroverted personality, but now he knew she didn't have feelings for him beyond being business partners. That was fine with Nate. He was glad to know where he stood. Besides, he was certain her interest lay with a certain psychic who likely moonlighted as a male model.

But if his relationship with Jennifer could help repair his relationship with his mother, that was all that mattered.

CHAPTER FORTY SEVEN

The lecture hall was quiet. Jennifer stood in front of the class, leaning on the wooden lectern, staring out at the crowd of students.

Images appeared on the large screens behind her. One was a scene from Hamlet, when the tormented prince is confronted by the ghost of his father. Another portrayed Ebenezer Scrooge's encounter with the chained specter of his deceased partner, Jacob Marley. A third showed a still from Akira Kurosawa's Rashomon, as the ghost of a murdered samurai tells the tale of his own death through a medium.

Jennifer spoke in a slow, measured tone. "Ghost stories," she began, "have been around since man has been telling stories. Literature from every culture is filled with tales of the consciousness of deceased persons visiting the living.

"And it's not just the books, plays and films of western and eastern civilization. Wherever and whenever there have been people on this planet, there has been the concept of ghosts, spirits, phantoms... dementors."

Her Harry Potter reference garnered mild laughter from the students.

"The ancient Egyptians believed that life was only the beginning of their journey to the afterlife. They believed the soul was made up of three main aspects. The Ka, which represented the life force. The Ba, which embodied the personality. And the Ahk, which in some versions of Egyptian spirituality unified the Ka and Ba—though there are other interpretations. It was their belief that the physical body was an integral part of their immortality, which led to the practice of mummification. If a family didn't have enough money to pay the embalmer for the deluxe Osiris burial package and went with the bargain plan, they ran the risk of their loved one's Akh, their immortal transformed self, returning and complaining. Nice reason to push that upsell for grandpa's mummy."

Amid the laughter, a hand shot up in the front row of the audience. "Yes, Miranda?"

"Professor Daye, have you ever seen a ghost?"

Jennifer smiled. She paused before answering, scanning the faces of the students, watching as some of them leaned in, waiting for her reply.

"Yes," she said. "I have. A few times."

She waited for the inevitable wave of follow-up questions. Several hands were raised. Jennifer pointed to a student in the middle of the room.

The young man wearing a red hoodie stood up. "Did you get any pictures?" he asked, then remained standing, a smirk on his face.

Jennifer recognized the look. A skeptic. And for a good reason. "No, no selfies with a ghost. The simple fact of the matter is we don't really know if cameras can even capture what we perceive when we 'see' a ghost.

"I've been in places that were known to be well traveled by specific spirits, but not everyone can see it when it does make itself known. This leads us to believe that it's not the usual photons impinging on the retina type of sensory experience.

"It's something extra-sensory. Which, if you think about it, makes sense."

"How does that make sense?" red hoodie asked.

"Well, if you're a disembodied consciousness, you don't have a physical body. You're just a psychic presence. And just like some people can see better in the dark, or hear sounds of higher or lower frequencies, there are people who are more receptive to receiving the impression the ghost is sending out. And just like there are people who are more able to perceive a ghost, there are likely ghosts who are better at making themselves known to the living."

The skeptical student sat down, seemingly unconvinced. He reminded her of Nate, that condescending look he would sometimes give her that meant he had already made up his mind and wasn't going to change it no matter what she said.

More hands shot up. Jennifer scanned the crowd and noticed a familiar face sitting off to one side. Helen Abara.

The bell rang, signaling the end of the period. An audible groan of disappointment rose from the students.

"Don't forget your reading!" Jennifer shouted over the din. "And get started on those midterm papers!"

As the students filed out, Helen made her way to the front of the room.

"How long were you sitting there?" Jennifer asked.

Helen grinned. "Long enough to be reminded why I worked so hard to get your course through the curriculum committee."

Jennifer sighed and then walked up to Helen and gave her a hug. "Thank you, Helen. I really appreciate your help."

"Well, don't thank me yet," Helen said.

Jennifer shook her head. "What is it now? Some sort of super-secret dean veto over the curriculum committee?"

"No, quite the opposite. He fast-tracked a number of courses, bypassing the committee completely."

"So, my course hasn't been denied," Jennifer asked, confused. "What am I missing?"

"There are only so many courses allocated in the budget. And Dean Patterson has already filled all the available slots."

Jennifer laughed. She had to. What was the alternative?

"I'm sorry, dear. Next year," Helen said. "Why don't you join me and Heather for lunch? Let us tell you how wonderful you are. It just might cheer you up."

"Okay," Jennifer replied. "That sounds nice. Thanks."

CHAPTER FORTY EIGHT

Marcia paced while Greg sat on the sofa, staring at the man across from him.

Chief Lewis took careful measure of the distraught family. A missing child was not rare in this part of the state, but when it did happen, it was usually an older runaway.

"Why are we just sitting around?" Marcia asked with frantic urgency. "Shouldn't we be out there looking for him?"

"Every officer on the force has Danny's description," Lewis assured her. He looked over toward the front door where Liam McDonald was standing. The officer gave an affirmative nod. "The best way you can help is to tell me everything you can about Danny, where he liked to play, who his friends were, places where he felt safe."

"You're talking like he ran away," Marcia said. "Shouldn't you be considering that someone took him?"

Chief Lewis rose.

Marcia stopped her pacing to look him in the eye.

"We are considering that, Mrs. Foreman, we have detectives on the case, but I have to be honest with you, there's no evidence to support that. You have an alarm system, and it wasn't tripped."

"But Danny didn't know the code for the alarm," Greg said.

"Even if you never told him the code, a smart kid like him, it wouldn't be hard to watch you key in the numbers."

"The alarm wasn't disabled," Marcia asserted.

"He could have turned it back on when he left," the chief said. "You keep telling me how bright he is. And the fact that there is food missing, just the kind a young boy might take with him, is something we would typically see in a runaway situation."

Marcia turned away, shaking her head.

"You yourself told me he was upset about you wanting him to see a psychiatrist for these hallucinations of his," Lewis added.

"He wasn't—" Marcia cut herself off. She could feel her frustration rising. They weren't listening to her. They were treating Danny as if he was some disaffected, unhappy kid. She took a deep breath and looked at the chief calmly. "If he was upset, he would have talked to us about it. He wouldn't run away."

"Okay," Lewis replied. "I believe you. But then tell me who would want to take him? Remember, it would have to be someone who knew he was here and knew the code for your alarm. And from what you've told me, that's a very short list and all of them are in this room."

"Maureen," Greg said from the sofa.

Liam tried not to react.

"Maureen?" the chief asked.

Marcia looked at Greg.

"It's the ghost Danny talks to," he said. "She used to live in this house."

The chief took the revelation in stride. "Ah, yes. I do remember hearing there was a boy in town talking to a dead bank robber. You think she took him?" he asked, confused.

"No," Marcia said. "But if you've heard about it, who's to say that someone else didn't hear as well and took it seriously? Maybe they think Danny actually is talking to her. All you see on the news lately is speculation about what happened to the rest of the money from that robbery. What if someone thinks Danny can lead them to where it's hidden?"

Lewis looked over at Officer McDonald. Liam remained stone-faced. He returned his gaze to Marcia. "Does he know?" the chief asked.

"Does he know what?"

"Does he know where she hid the money?"

"Of course not. There is no ghost. There's just a boy with an overactive imagination," she answered, casting a cautionary look at Greg.

"There's not much else we can do without any additional information," Chief Lewis told her.

"What about that bank robber? The one that just got out of jail?" Marcia asked. "What if he thinks Danny can actually talk to his dead wife?"

The chief nodded, then addressed Liam directly. "McDonald, go pay Mr. Everly a call, see what he has to say for himself."

"You got it, Chief," Liam responded, then let himself out of the house.

"Thank you," Marcia said.

"While we're on the subject, what about this psychologist you said came to the house?"

"Parapsychologist," Greg corrected. "Dr. Jennifer Daye, she teaches at Cal State East Bay."

"Did she believe Danny was talking to a ghost?" Lewis asked.

"She didn't reach any conclusions. She was investigating."

The chief pulled out a notebook and jotted down the name. "I see," he said.

"You might want to talk to the detective she was working with as well," Greg suggested. "Nate Raney."

Lewis raised an eyebrow. "Yes, I imagine I would."

CHAPTER FORTY NINE

The phone rang.

Emily was perched on Jennifer's chair, organizing slides on her computer for her next lecture. She looked at the phone. It was the business line Detective Raney had installed for the agency, the number printed on their business cards and posted on their website.

And up until today—as far as Emily knew—it had never rung.

"Detective Raney, phone," she said, barely raising her voice to a shout.

There was no answer. Then she remembered he had said something about taking Madge for a walk.

"I'll get it," Emily sighed. She picked up the phone and answered in her typical monotone. "Raney Daye Investigations. How may I help you?"

She listened for a minute.

"I'm sorry, Dr. Daye is out of the office right now."

The caller said something else.

"Detective Raney is walking the dog." Emily rolled her eyes. "Yes, an actual dog. He picks up her poop in little plastic bags and everything."

"Emily? Who's on the phone?" Nate asked from the door.

Emily held up a finger. "He just walked in. Who may I say is calling?" After she got her response, she placed her hand over the mouthpiece and answered, "Chief Lewis, from Danville."

Nate stepped forward and took the phone from her. "Chief, this is Nate. How can I help you?" As he listened, his expression changed from curiosity to concern. "Yes, we'll certainly do what we can. I'll round up Dr. Daye and meet you there." He hung up the phone and stared at it for a moment.

"What's going on?" Emily asked.

"Can you make a copy of the tapes and videos from the Foreman investigation?"

"Sure," Emily answered. She stuck a thumb drive into Jennifer's computer and moved the mouse around. "What's going on?" she asked again.

"What time does Dr. Daye finish her class?"

Emily checked her watch. "She should be finished right now."

Nate patted his pockets and looked around the office. "Where did Dave put my car keys?"

"They're hanging on the hook in the kitchen. The one you told him to always put them back on. Like a million times."

"Right."

"What's going on?" Emily asked one more time.

Nate stopped in his tracks and looked over at the whiteboard, covered in lists, clippings and photos. He focused his gaze on a family photo of the Foremans.

"Danny is missing."

CHAPTER FIFTY

Jennifer forgot about her troubles—for at least a little while. Sitting and laughing with Heather and Helen was just what she needed.

At first, she was distraught and suggested that maybe she should try to find a position at an institution with a more open-minded mission.

But the idea of that pompous ass, Dean Patterson, winning, was untenable to all of them, and walking away would be a victory to his small mind.

Besides, Helen reminded Jennifer, there was Dave to think of. If she walked away now, that would likely be the end of his thesis.

Jennifer hadn't confided her temporary living situation to her colleagues. She was hoping the tiny bump in salary she would get from teaching another class would help subsidize Dave's stipend. But now she would have to come up with something else. If Raney/Daye Investigations didn't take off soon, she might have to go back to performing as a magician.

Her phone rang.

The cheery ring tone echoed loudly, startling Jennifer. She rummaged through her bag to find the phone and check the caller ID. It was Nate.

"Excuse me," she said to her lunch companions. "It's my business partner." She rose, stepped away from the table, and answered the call.

"Hey, Nate, what's up?" she asked with an upbeat tone. But the smile quickly fell away from her face as she listened to what Nate had to tell her.

"Do they know how long he's been missing? Are there any leads?"

Nate's response caused her to gasp.

"Yes, of course. We should do whatever we can."

Jennifer pressed the phone against her chest to speak to Helen and Heather. "I'm sorry, I have to go. Thanks so much for lunch." She got up, slung her bag over her shoulder, and put the phone back to her ear as she hurried out of the cafeteria.

"I'm on my way," she said into the phone. "No, don't bother. I'll drive up myself. I'm sure they can use your help as soon as possible. Let me know if you get any updates."

She ended the call and placed her phone back in her bag.

Then she stopped mid-stride, pulled the phone back out and hit the speed dial on one of her contacts. She was visibly relieved that her call was answered.

"Hi, Sam, it's Jennifer. I need a favor."

CHAPTER FIFTY ONE

Maureen stood by the door to the dingy motel room where Dale had dragged Danny. The boy was still unconscious from the chloroform and laid out on the bed. Dale had zip-tied his wrists and ankles, covered his eyes with a rolled-up bandanna and placed some tape over his mouth. He had positioned the boy with a pillow under his head. It pained Maureen to see Danny bound like that, knowing there was nothing she could do.

Dale paced back and forth at the foot of the bed. Maureen didn't have a good sense of time, but she judged by the number of beer bottles Dale had emptied that they had been here for quite a while. As each minute passed, Dale became more and more anxious. He considered using the smelling salts he had to try to wake the boy, but he wanted to wait for the chloroform to wear off on its own.

Maureen had tried talking to Dale. Communicating with Danny was effortless, and she was surprised that she didn't have that same connection with her husband. They had spent years together, forming an intensely emotional bond. Danny was just a boy who happened to move into her old house, but he could see and hear her as if she was alive.

Dale was waiting for someone. But who? And what did they want with Danny?

She looked over at the boy, making sure he was breathing, relieved to see the gentle movement of his chest up and down. She fought the temptation to try to wake him. She didn't want him to be awake, to experience the fear she imagined he would feel when he realized he had been taken from his home and held by a stranger.

Danny moaned.

Dale stopped his pacing and directed his attention to the boy.

"Go back to sleep, Danny," Maureen said softly. "No need to wake up. Just go back to your dreams."

But if Danny heard her, he didn't take her advice. When he discovered he couldn't see or open his mouth, move his hands or feet, he panicked. He tried to talk, but the tape over his mouth turned it into a muffled scream.

"Danny, it's Maureen. Can you hear me? Danny?" Maureen asked as she moved to the side of the bed.

Danny nodded, feeling a little better knowing that Maureen was with him.

"Don't make a sound, kid. If you do what I say, you'll be back home before you know it," Dale promised.

Danny whimpered. The voice was strange and menacing. But Maureen was here, so he wasn't afraid.

Dale sat on the side of the bed and reached over to slowly peel back the tape covering Danny's mouth.

"Danny, Danny, listen to me," Maureen said. "Do what he says. I'm here with you. We'll get through this together."

Danny calmed down. He winced as the tape pulled at his skin, but he didn't cry.

"So," Dale said to Danny, "people say you can see and talk to my wife."

Danny seemed confused. He didn't know this man, so how could he know if he had ever talked to his wife?

Dale sensed his confusion. "Maureen Everly. Can you talk to Maureen?"

Danny nodded.

Dale took a deep breath. Was it true? Was this boy really able to talk to Maureen? "Is she here with us right now?" Danny turned his head.

"I'm here," Maureen assured him. "I won't leave you."

Dale watched Danny. It was clear that he was reacting to something—or someone. He looked around the room, his gaze passing right over Maureen, but seeing nothing.

"And you can talk to her?"

"Uh, huh," Danny answered meekly. "She says, 'Hi, Dale.'"

Dale spun around to face the boy. How did he know his name?

She was here.

Somehow, some way, it was true.

A wave of emotion swept over him. All the tears he had held in since he heard the news of Maureen's death seemed to rush out of him at once. He tried to speak, but only a wordless breath escaped.

Danny scooted himself backward until he was sitting up on the bed against the headboard. "Are you going to kill me?" he asked.

"No," he assured the boy. "I'm not going to hurt you. I just need you to help me talk to Maureen. Will you do that for me?"

Danny nodded.

"Can you ask her where she hid the bag from the bank?"

"She can hear you," Danny said. "I don't need to say everything you say."

"Okay, good." Dale looked around the room. "Can you help me, Maureen? Can you tell me where you hid it?"

After a moment, Danny answered for her. "She can't remember."

Dale sighed. His head dropped against his chest. "It doesn't matter," he said. "It wouldn't be the same without you, anyway."

Maureen looked at Dale. She reached out to touch his face, but she felt nothing, and he didn't react. "I don't remember much about that day. I remember dying, but that's all," she said to him.

Danny relayed her message.

Dale looked back up. "Why did you go back to the house? You were free? You got away? Why?"

"I don't remember why," Maureen told him.

There was a knock at the door.

Dale crossed to the window and peeked between the gap in the curtains. He undid the chain on the door, flipped the deadbolt, and opened it.

Liam entered.

Dale quickly closed the door behind him.

Maureen looked at the man from her past. The sight of him unlocked more memories, unpleasant ones.

"Well?" Liam asked in a low voice. "Is the kid really talking to her?"

Dale looked to the space where he imagined Maureen to be, then turned back to the officer and nodded.

"Shit, really? Holy crap. So, where is it? Where's the loot?"

"She doesn't remember."

Liam looked confused. "What?"

"I asked her, and he said she doesn't remember."

Liam laughed. "That's it? You asked the kid what the ghost knows, and he tells you she doesn't know, and you believe him?"

Dale shrugged. "It's over. It was our last shot, and she doesn't know."

Liam took off his hat and walked over to where the boy was sitting. He spoke in a low, gravelly tone, trying to disguise his voice. "You really can see and hear her?" he asked Danny.

Danny nodded, shrinking away from the officer.

"And she's here right now? And she can hear me?"

"Yes," the boy answered.

Liam smiled, then turned away from the boy. He spoke in a whisper, too soft for Danny to hear. "If you're really here, Maureen, then listen carefully. If you care about this boy, if you really care about him, then know this. If you don't tell us where you hid that money, if you think you can jerk me around and keep me from what is mine, you're sorely mistaken."

Liam was facing slightly away from where Maureen was standing, but his words were as loud to her as if he was speaking directly into her ear.

"So, you tell me where you put that bag, or your little friend here is going to disappear for good."

Maureen could sense the anger in him. It was intense. Liam turned back to the boy.

Maureen realized he was waiting for her to tell Danny something. To answer him.

Why couldn't she remember?

Her memories of that day were like shadows floating past her. Impossible to catch, to hold on to. Maybe she needed to focus? Like when she wanted to travel somewhere. If she could focus on a time as well as a place…

But nothing happened. She didn't have a starting point.

There was nothing to connect to.

The robbery.

The bank.

Suddenly, she remembered. She could picture herself in the bank, looking at the vault, watching Dale use his tools to drill through the steel. It had taken them most of the night.

Dale opened the enormous steel door. They filled bags with cash, then emptied the safe deposit boxes.

Then something went wrong. The police were on their way.

Maureen managed to get out, to get to her car.

And then she was at the house.

No, no, there was something missing. The bag. What did she do with the bag?

The woods. She remembered being in the woods. Carrying the bag over her shoulder.

"The woods," Danny said. He must've picked up on what Maureen was thinking. She looked at him. He reminded her of someone.

Carl. Her childhood friend. The one who had played in the old, abandoned gold mine with her when they were kids.

"The gold mine," Danny whispered.

Everyone turned toward the boy.

"What gold mine? What is he talking about?" Liam asked.

Dale knew instantly. Maureen had told him stories about the mine she and her friends had used as a kind of hideout. "There's an old abandoned mine in the hills behind the house, about a mile and a half in. Maureen showed it to me once."

"So, no one would think to look there for the loot," Liam said, thinking. He turned to Dale. "You know where it is?"

Dale nodded. He knew exactly where it was.

"Okay, you take the kid up there. Get her to tell you where she stashed it."

"Do we still need him?" Dale asked.

Liam cut him off. "Take the kid," he ordered. "I don't trust her." Liam looked around the room, trying to guess where Maureen was. "If she really loved you, she wouldn't be playing these memory games. She'd just tell you where it was."

Dale found it hard to believe Maureen was purposefully trying to mislead him.

"You don't think she blames you for her death?" Liam added.

That hit Dale hard. He blamed himself for her death and wished he had the courage to ask for her forgiveness.

Liam checked his watch. "Okay, I checked in on you. You were at the halfway house, no sign of the kid. That should give you a few hours to find the loot. Then we can get the hell out of here."

"The mine was sealed. With concrete," Dale recalled.

"Well, she got in there somehow. If you have the boy, I have a feeling she'll remember. I better get back. If they start organizing a search party, I want to make sure I steer them away from where you're going." Liam pulled out his phone and pulled up the satellite map of the area around the Foreman's house. "Where's the mine?"

Dale looked at the screen, then manipulated it with his fingers, zooming out till he found the area where the mine was hidden. He pointed at it. "There," he said.

Liam took note of it. "Okay, get the loot. We'll meet at the rendezvous and make an anonymous call about the kid. They'll be so glad to find him, we'll be long gone before they realize who took him."

"And what about the Mastermind? It won't take long for him to learn that we found the loot."

"I've been planning how I'd make a getaway for fifteen years,"

Liam said. "I'd like to see him try to find me. Just make sure no one sees you with the kid. You have any chloroform left?"

Dale nodded.

"Good. Don't screw this up."

Liam opened the door, checked to make sure the coast was clear, then left.

Once he was gone, Dale bolted and chained the door again. He turned to Danny. "Looks like we're going to have an adventure."

CHAPTER FIFTY TWO

Nate knocked on the Foreman's front door. It was answered almost immediately by a Sheriff's deputy. Evidently, Chief Lewis had called in the county's law enforcement agency to help in the search.

"Who are you?" she asked Nate.

Nate was surprised by her brusqueness. "Nate Raney, I'm, um…" He tried to think of how to describe his relationship to the family. "I'm a private detective, working with the family on another matter."

"What matter is that?"

"Is Chief Lewis here?" Nate asked, hoping a little name dropping might get him past the scrutiny of the deputy.

"We're working a possible kidnapping, Mr. Raney," she said, emphasizing his civilian status.

"Kidnapping? Has that been established? Has there been a ransom?"

"Deputy, would you stand aside and let Detective Raney in, please?" said a voice from inside the house. Chief Lewis waved Nate into the living room.

Nate recognized the trappings of a missing child investigation. There was equipment to record incoming phone calls on both the land lines and the cell phones, a topographical map laid out on the coffee table and nearly a dozen uniformed officers from both the

Danville police and the county sheriff's office, milling about, half of them on their phones.

Greg and Marcia sat on the sofa. There was no sign of Daisy.

Nate shook the chief's hand. He pulled the thumb drive Emily had made for him from his jacket pocket. "Here's all the recordings Dr. Daye's people made during their investigation."

"*Their* investigation?" Chief Lewis asked. "I thought you two were partners."

"Their portion of the investigation. I'm more of a devil's advocate in the process."

The chief handed the thumb drive to a middle-aged man wearing a police windbreaker, but not in uniform. An evidence tech, Nate assumed. "See if there's anything useful on this," Lewis ordered the man.

He nodded, then scurried over to a corner, where he plugged the drive into a laptop and began inspecting its contents.

"Need an extra set of eyes?" Nate asked.

Chief Lewis shrugged. "Why not?"

"What do you know so far?"

"The kid went missing sometime during the night. The alarm was set but didn't go off. No sign of forced entry. Our best guess is he ran away. The parents say he didn't know the alarm code, but—"

"That's what they said about his mother's computer password," Nate countered.

"Password?"

"He's a sharp kid. I wouldn't assume he didn't know the code."

The chief nodded. "Yeah. Several boxes of breakfast cereal were missing. The kind of thing a kid might take with him if he was—"

"Packing supplies," Nate finished. "But why? He seemed pretty well adjusted other than the ghost thing."

Chief Lewis cast a glance at the parents, who had a guilty look on their faces. "The parents think he may have overheard them talking about taking him to a psychiatrist."

"So why all the kidnapping gear?"

"Just covering our bases. There's a chance someone got wind of the whole bank robbery connection to the alleged ghost. We're getting ready to start a grid search."

Nate nodded. "Okay if I look around?"

"Do your thing," the chief invited.

Nate looked over at the Foremans and gave them what he hoped was a reassuring nod. "Daisy's okay?" he asked.

Marcia nodded. "She's with a friend."

"Don't worry, we'll find him." Nate promised.

He looked around the house. The living room looked much smaller with all the people crowded into it. Nate pushed his way past them, ignoring the questioning stares from the officers wondering who this guy was traipsing through a potential crime scene.

He made his way to the kitchen first. There were a few people crowded around the small table, writing on another topographical map, this one with a clearly delineated grid drawn on it with colored Sharpie markers. Nate smiled when he saw one of the officers working on a list of potential sites where Danny might have gone to.

The door to the pantry was open. Nate went inside. It was filled with both the types of food you would expect for a family with young kids, as well as baking supplies and a collection of high-end appliances. He spotted the empty spot in front of the narrow window where he guessed the breakfast cereal was kept, easily reachable by the children.

Nate ran his finger along the empty shelf. He didn't feel any dust, but when he lifted up his finger, there was a small speck of something stuck to the tip. He looked closer. A fleck of paint? Nate looked around the window frame to see if the paint was peeling, but it was clearly recently repainted.

He leaned over and checked the latch. It was locked. He undid the simple lock and opened the window.

A few flecks of paint fluttered onto the sill.

He poked his head through the window and looked at the outside. The window had clearly been painted shut, but recently someone had forced it open. It looked like they had even cut through the paint with a knife. Had the police noticed this? Had they asked the Foremans if they had done it? The window was narrow, but still big enough for a man to fit through. But could he have gotten out this way?

No, it might have been that the latch was undone when the window was painted shut, but he wouldn't have been able to latch it after he left.

Nate left the pantry and looked around the kitchen. He inspected the windows. They were newer ones with vinyl frames. Their latches were also locked, and in the upper corner of each one was a pair of small plastic rectangles. Nate recognized them as wireless alarm sensors. Inside one of them was a triple-A battery, while the other housed a magnet. As long as they were close to one another, the alarm system would report the window as closed. He recognized the system as one of the do-it-yourself kits they advertised on TV.

Each window that was capable of being opened had a sensor on it—except for the one in the pantry.

He checked the back door.

There didn't seem to be a sensor there, either.

Nate left the kitchen and crossed back out into the living room until he had a view of the front door. There was a pair of sensors at the top of the door frame. He returned to the kitchen and took a closer look at the back door. In the spot where the sensors should have been, there was a pair of faint rectangles of adhesive residue and a cut off screw.

Nate opened the back door and left it that way.

He returned to the living room and approached the Foremans.

"Greg, Marcia, do you have alarm sensors on the back door?"

"Of course," Greg said.

"And you didn't take them off for some reason?"

Greg and Marcia exchanged a puzzled look. Chief Lewis overheard the exchange. "What did you find?"

"I think someone broke in here last night."

"How?" Marcia asked.

"Through the pantry window," Nate said.

"We checked that. There's no alarm sensor on it, but it was

locked."

"We've never opened that window," Greg added.

"Yes, it was painted shut. But someone forced it open. Do you know if it was latched before last night?"

Greg shrugged.

"I think he left through the back door."

Marcia shook her head. "I have the alarm configured so that if one of sensors has a low battery or can't be detected by the base station, it sends me an alert." She pulled out her phone and opened the alarm app. "It says the back door is online and closed and has been all night."

Nate looked through the doorway to the kitchen and to the back door, which was wide open.

The Foremans and Chief Lewis followed his gaze.

"Well, that puts a whole new spin on the situation," Lewis said.

"Someone took him? Someone took Danny?" Marcia asked, stunned.

Greg put a comforting arm around her. "Why haven't we heard from them? What do they want?"

"They obviously want to talk to Maureen," Jennifer said.

The four of them turned to find Dr. Daye standing in the doorway, pushing her way past the overeager deputy. Sam Lightman followed her.

"That's just a theory. We don't know that for sure," Chief Lewis said.

Nate found himself disagreeing with his old captain. "You did say the word was around town. Seems the most likely motive—whether or not Danny can actually communicate with a dead woman."

Marcia and Greg exchanged guilty looks. "Oh my god, what have I done?" Greg asked. "I told the guys at the barbershop about it. Half the town must know."

"It's not your fault," Chief Lewis assured them.

"What about her husband, Dale Everly?" Nate asked. "Have you checked him out?"

"Yes, I had an officer check in on him. He's living in a halfway house just outside of town. No sign of the kid."

"He could have kidnapped him and put him somewhere else," Marcia insisted.

"Possibly," the chief acknowledged. "But he has to check in and out of the halfway house. They keep pretty close tabs on him."

Nate found the chief's remark curious. Even the best halfway house may do a bed check at night, but usually didn't keep track of the comings and goings of their guests. Why would he dismiss Dale Everly as a suspect so casually?

"The good news is we can narrow the search," Nate said.

"Why's that?" Chief Lewis asked.

"If we go with the assumption that it's someone who's chasing after the missing money, they're going to be in the area. From what I've read about the case, there was a limited amount of time she had to stash the loot, so wherever they took Danny is going to be nearby, and likely between here and the bank."

"Right." The chief barked commands at the officers gathered around the kitchen table. "Prioritize the areas between here and downtown. And let's get that search started. Only armed officers on the front line. Put volunteers in as backup."

"Chief, I may be able to help you narrow it down a bit more."

All eyes turned to Sam Lightman, who had kept quiet until now.

"And who might you be?" the chief asked.

"This is Sam Lightman," Jennifer answered.

"That doesn't help me because I don't know who you are, either, or why you're here."

Nate stepped in. "This is Dr. Jennifer Daye."

Lewis nodded. "Ah, the ghost hunter."

"Parapsychologist," Jennifer corrected. "And Sam is a very gifted psychic. He's helped the police find missing children before."

"Is that a fact?" the chief asked.

"I understand your skepticism," Sam said, "but it can't hurt to let me try, can it?"

"I want to know what he can find out," Greg said, rising to his feet.

Marcia grabbed his hand, trying to pull him back down. He shook her off.

"What do you need?" Greg asked.

"Well, if I can handle something that belonged to Danny, something personal that he has a strong connection to, that would help."

Nate looked away. Part of him was furious at Jennifer for bringing Sam with her. These parents didn't need any more psychic mumbo jumbo.

"I'll take you to his room," Greg said, then headed for the stairs.

As Sam and Jennifer passed, Nate met her gaze. "Give him a chance," Jennifer pleaded.

Nate said nothing. He waited for the chief and one of his officers to follow, then brought up the rear.

Marcia stayed on the couch, staring at the phones on the coffee table.

Greg opened the door to Danny's room. There was no need to turn on the lights. The afternoon sun was pouring in through the window. The bed was still a mess. Danny's backpack sat on the chair by his desk.

Greg went straight for a stuffed snake tucked between the side of the bed and the wall. "He likes it because it's the only stuffed animal his sister won't touch," he explained as he handed the bright green serpent to Sam.

Sam held it in his hands. He closed his eyes and slowly took a deep breath.

It seemed like everyone else in the room breathed with him.

Sam shook his head. "No, I'm not getting anything." He looked around the room, went over to the desk, and started picking up various items. Rocks, a Lego pirate ship, the collection of colored pencils he used for his drawing. He touched them like he was reading Braille.

Nate took the time to look around the room himself. He saw Danny's shoes next to his closet. How did these police think he ran away without his shoes? It made him furious to think of how much they had overlooked. They had made that initial assumption that Danny was a runaway and were only looking for evidence to support that theory.

He couldn't stand to watch the show Sam was putting on for the others. Instead, his eyes wandered over some pictures Danny had taped to the wall. There were illustrations of pirate battles, drawings of spaceships and monsters—typical for a boy his age.

"I'm not getting anything on Danny," Sam reported.

Greg sighed with disappointment. "Thank you for trying."

"What about Maureen? Can you make contact with her?" Jennifer asked.

Sam shrugged. He looked at Greg. "Do you have anything that belonged to her?"

Greg thought for a moment. "The photographs." He left the room at a run, then returned a few moments later with the shoe box Danny had found in the attic. He handed them to Sam.

The psychic took the box and sat down on Danny's bed. He opened it and placed his fingers on the loose photos.

Nate ignored Sam, focusing instead on the pictures on the wall. One of them was different from the rest. It had a boy in it, a boy who looked like Danny. And a woman—but not Marcia.

It looked like they were in space, with yellow stars surrounding them.

No, not space. They were standing, not floating. And there was a tool in Danny's hand. It looked like a large pickaxe.

It wasn't space. It was a cave. A cave speckled with golden nuggets and with what looked like wooden beams above them.

"Is there a gold mine nearby?" Nate asked.

Then he realized that Sam had asked the exact same question at the moment he had.

Jennifer looked at Nate.

Greg looked at Sam.

"I think Maureen is telling me about an old gold mine nearby," Sam explained.

Nate pointed at the drawing. "Kind of like this one?" he asked.

Everyone in the room focused their attention on the picture taped to the wall.

"There used to be a mine up in the hills," Chief Lewis said. "It was sealed off a long time ago. Some kids got lost in it."

"Well, Chief," Jennifer said, "maybe that's a good place to start."

CHAPTER FIFTY THREE

Dale carried Danny as far as he could after driving the rental car down the old fire road. After a half a mile, he set Danny down.

"Do you think you could walk for a while?" Dale asked.

Danny didn't reply.

"Look, I don't want to hurt you. I just want to find what Maureen hid and then go away. I promise you'll be okay, and you'll never see me again." Dale removed Danny's blindfold.

Danny squinted into the evening light.

"I believe him," Maureen told Danny. Everything she remembered about Dale assured her that he didn't mean Danny any harm — despite Liam's threats. In fact, he probably saw the boy the same way Maureen did. He was about the age their child might have been if things hadn't gone so wrong that day.

Danny nodded. He was scared, but was glad that Maureen was with him.

Dale looked around the woods. He had taken them as far as he could without being exactly sure where they were headed.

Maureen had taken him up to the old mine once. He remembered it was walled off with concrete, but she had told him they had found a secret entrance. That must've been how she managed to hide the duffel bag from the bank inside.

"Could you ask Maureen which way?"

"You don't have to ask me to ask her," Danny reminded him.

It was still hard for Dale to believe that Maureen was with them. He wished he could see her, too. But for whatever reason, his only connection to his dead wife was a ten-year-old boy who he had bound with zip ties.

Dale unfolded his pocketknife.

Danny started to back away.

"I'm just going to cut your feet free," he said. "You promise you won't try to run off?"

Danny nodded meekly and watched as Dale sliced through the plastic strips holding his ankles together. He paused for a minute, then also cut free the ties binding Danny's wrists.

For a second, Danny thought about running, but he figured the man looked pretty strong and would probably catch him if he tried. Besides, Maureen had told him everything would be okay, and he trusted her.

"This way," Maureen said, pointing toward a gap in the trees.

Danny copied her gesture, indicating the spot she had shown him.

Dale looked over in the direction he was pointing, then he reached out and offered Danny his hand.

The boy tentatively placed his small hand in the man's rough grip, and they started off into the trees.

Maureen led the way. Danny marveled at the way she moved. He couldn't quite see her feet, and at times it seemed like she was skating through the tall weeds without bending or moving them as she passed.

They continued deeper into the woods until they reached a trail that followed the contour of the mountain. Dale recognized the path now and knew they were close.

The path opened up to a view of the valley below. It was on the opposite side of the ridge where Maureen's house was, but close enough for adventurous kids to discover and explore.

The mine entrance was nothing more than a wide spot in the path. It was overgrown with shrubs and vines, but it was the spot Dale remembered. He pushed aside some of the plants. There was a concrete plug blocking the narrow entrance.

"Over here," Danny said. He continued walking down the path, following Maureen, who led them to into a thicket of bushes. Danny let go of Dale's hand, dropped to his knees, and peered into the dark undergrowth. "She says there's another entrance here. It's small, but we should fit. It's the one her friend found that time she got stuck inside without a light."

Dale remembered the story. He set his backpack down and pulled out a flashlight from one of the outside pockets. He turned it on and got down to ground level, where Danny was looking.

The beam of the flashlight swept across where the ground met the rock of the mountain and Dale saw the triangular-shaped opening that swallowed the light. "You first," he said to Danny.

Danny looked over to Maureen, who gave him a reassuring smile.

Dale handed him the flashlight, then pulled out a lantern from inside the pack, along with a canteen. He watched as the boy wriggled through the bushes and into the hole. For a moment, Dale wondered if he was going to fit. Obviously, Maureen had managed to get in all those years ago, and he had grown lean and fit in prison, but he wasn't a small boy or a slender woman.

After Danny had disappeared inside, he called to him.

"Danny, are you all right?"

"Yeah, it smells funny in here."

Dale didn't want to speculate what could be the source of the odor. Perhaps a dead animal? Or maybe just the damp mustiness of a cave. He pushed the lantern and canteen ahead of him, then rolled over onto his back and reached in with his left arm. By stretching his left shoulder ahead of him, he was able to make himself skinny enough to squeeze his torso inside, pushing with his legs.

But then his hips got hung up on the narrow opening. He tried to twist himself, but there wasn't an angle that allowed him to slip through, and he had lost any leverage with his legs.

"Help him," Maureen said to Danny.

The boy walked up to the stuck man and offered his hands. Dale reached up and took hold of Danny's arms just above the wrist. The boy leaned back and pulled, his feet sliding on the dirty floor of the mine. Dale wriggled his hips, and after a few tugs, finally slipped through.

He took a moment to collect himself, then looked around.

They were in a small space that narrowed like a funnel toward the opening they had crawled through. Dale detected the odor of wet rock that Danny had complained about. The chamber was just tall enough for Danny to be able to stand, but Dale only had room to get to his knees.

"This way," Danny said. The boy headed into a passageway that was about the size of a tube you'd find in a playground. After eight or ten feet, it opened into a larger shaft that was likely the main tunnel for the mine. There were telltale tool marks and bore holes in the walls.

Dale opened the canteen and offered it to Danny.

The boy drank thirstily, spilling some of the cool water, soaking his shirt. Dale drank a bit himself, then—catching himself before asking Danny to ask Maureen—said into the air,

"Well, which way now?"

Danny looked at Maureen.

She peered into the darkness that enveloped the mine in both directions. "I don't know," she said, a note of fear in her voice that made Danny nervous. "I can't remember where I put it."

Danny relayed the message to Dale. He didn't seem disappointed. "Well, I guess we just pick a direction and start looking."

Maureen shrugged in answer to Danny's inquisitive look. "You choose," she said to Danny.

Danny shone his light down one end of the tunnel, then the other, and decided they would start with the one that looked bigger. "Let's try this way."

"All right," Dale said. "I guess this makes us prospectors, huh?"

Danny smiled at the notion. Although part of him was still afraid he might not see his family again, he imagined he was in search of a hidden pirate treasure.

Maureen followed behind them. She thought she heard something, a voice. But it wasn't Danny. "Dale?" She asked. "Was that you?"

Dale went on, ignoring her question.

Danny looked back at Maureen and shrugged.

She waited for them to go ahead, listening in the dark.

There it was again. Definitely a voice. She remembered hearing it when they were on the way to the mine, asking her where they were. Not across-the-room faint, but like a faraway echo. She had told it they were going to the gold mine.

This time, it wasn't asking her a question, it was trying to tell her something.

The words eluded her, but then she was able to catch a couple of them, two words that gave her a feeling of hope even though she didn't know who was saying them.

"We're coming," it said.

She didn't know what it meant, but she instantly felt Danny was going to be okay. No matter what else happened, that was all she was hoping for. And now she had a reason for that hope.

"Hurry," she whispered back to the voice. "Please, hurry."

CHAPTER FIFTY FOUR

Nate followed Chief Lewis's car through the curves of the fire road. It was the same stretch where he had been run off the pavement and nearly killed. Part of him expected to see the gray Hummer looming in his rearview mirror.

Eventually, they reached a turnoff that led to a clearing.

Nate pulled up behind Chief Lewis' car and another police cruiser that had arrived before them.

"Maureen wants us to hurry," Sam said from the back seat.

Nate sighed and glanced sideways at Jennifer.

She returned a warning glare.

Nate opened his door and stepped out into the oncoming dusk. Chief Lewis was conferring with his officers as they unloaded a collection of sledgehammers and pickaxes from the trunk of the police car.

Nate recognized one of the men. He was the one he had met when he first arrived in town and gave Lewis a courtesy visit. McDonald was his name, he recalled.

One of the other officers pointed at a spot in the woods. "Looks like we're not the only ones out here."

Nate saw what he had noticed. The telltale path of a car that had driven off the road and into the tall grass. The trail led to a thicket of trees that almost completely concealed a car parked there.

"Go get the plate number," Lewis ordered. "If it's unlocked, take a look inside."

One of the officers finished unloading the last of the demolition tools out of the trunk and trudged off into the weeds to check out the car.

"That trail looks fresh," Nate observed.

"Yeah, five will get you ten that's our guy. Looks like your psychic friend was right."

"He's not psychic. I was able to pick out the same clues in Danny's room that he did."

Lewis shrugged. "Maybe, but where did Danny get the idea of drawing a picture of a gold mine in the first place?"

Nate didn't have an answer for that one, but whatever the explanation, it wasn't important now. It was increasingly likely that Danny had been kidnapped by someone who was convinced the boy could lead them to the missing money.

And aside from Sam Lightman stating the obvious, they needed to hurry.

CHAPTER FIFTY FIVE

Dale and Danny reached the end of the tunnel. At their feet was a pile of rubble. Dale shone his light at the ceiling. The overhead timbers that stretched across the top of most of the mine shaft were absent, which explained the mound of rocks and dirt.

He poked around the debris. Did Maureen have time to bury the duffel bag? Dale set the lantern down and dug through the shards, cutting his hands on the sharp edges as he furiously moved the broken stone out of the way.

Then he felt something that wasn't rock or dirt. It was a piece of what looked like canvas. He moved the lantern to give himself a better view.

There was something there. He dug some more, brushing aside the debris, his excitement growing.

"Did you find it?" Danny asked.

"I don't know. There's something."

Dale had uncovered enough of the fabric now that he could grab it in his hand. He pulled.

At first, whatever it was didn't want to come out. Then it gave way and Dale fell backwards, smashing his head against the hard floor.

He saw stars for a second. Then he held the scrap of fabric up in his hands. It wasn't one of the duffel bags they had acquired to carry away the cash and contents of the safe deposit boxes. It was thicker and smaller, a khaki color instead of the black of the bag Maureen has escaped with.

Dale looked at it closely. It looked like it was a cover for an old canteen. He threw it against the wall, then crawled back to the pile of rubble on his hands and knees throwing stones aside frantically, revealing only the fact that the missing money wasn't there.

Was Liam right? Was Maureen playing with them?

"Where is it?" he asked in a low, menacing voice.

Dale turned and looked directly at Danny. The cheerful air he had presented earlier, almost as if he wanted to be Danny's friend, was gone. He was looking at Danny, but he was speaking to Maureen. "You can't do this to me. I need that money. If I don't find it, they'll kill me."

Maureen was shocked by his revelation. "Who?" she asked. Danny repeated the question.

"Who do you think? Have you forgotten everything? We had partners. And they have been waiting fifteen years to get their hands on that loot. Do you think I really care? No bag of money is going to bring you back."

Maureen kneeled down beside Dale. She didn't know what to do. She still had no memory of hiding the money, but if what he was saying was true, then Danny was in real danger. She was sure Dale wouldn't hurt him, but what about the other man from the motel, Liam? Or the mysterious Mastermind?

Why couldn't she remember where she hid the money?

She needed to remember. Maybe if she went back to the bank and retraced her steps, something would trigger the memory—but she didn't want to leave Danny. She couldn't do that. But she had to do something. They had to get out of there.

"Danny, tell him I remember something. There's an air shaft in the ceiling, about halfway back to the entrance. I think I pushed it up there and wedged it in place with a piece of wood."

Danny repeated Maureen's words.

Dale looked skeptical. But he was running out of options as well. "Give me your flashlight," he said to Danny.

Danny handed over the flashlight to Dale.

Dale stood up and picked up the lantern. "Stay here," he said. "I'll be back." He turned and started walking down the tunnel, using the flashlight to illuminate the ceiling. But soon, he reached a bend in the tunnel, and the light was soaked up by the dark rock of the mine until it was just a hint of a dim yellow glow in the dark.

Danny started to cry.

Maureen still had awareness of her surroundings. She knew where Danny was in the darkness.

"Danny, can you hear me?"

"Yeah," he said softly.

"Can you see me?"

Danny peered in the darkness in her direction. "Kind of," he answered. He had a sense she was there, but since he couldn't see the floor or walls, it was as if she was floating in a big, dark, empty space.

"Okay, stand up, and walk toward me with your hands in front of you."

Danny followed her instructions.

"Reach out to your left. Do you feel the wall?"

Danny moved his arm out to his side and rapped his knuckles against the stone. "Ow," he said, then started crying again.

"You're okay," Maureen assured him. "Everything's going to be okay. Just put your hand against the wall and walk slowly toward me. Okay?"

Danny nodded. He reached out slowly with his fingertips until he felt the wall, then started taking small steps, letting the fingers of his left hand glide over the rough stone while he kept his right hand out in front of him.

"You're doing great," Maureen told him. "You're so brave."

Danny sniffled and wiped away his tears with the sleeve of his pajamas, and focused on Maureen as he continued walking slowly into the dark.

The voice Maureen had heard earlier was back, still faint, but closer. "Where are you?" it asked.

"The mine," she replied, "we're in the mine. Please help."

"Who are you talking to?" Danny asked.

"Someone who can help us," she replied.

She hoped that was true.

CHAPTER FIFTY SIX

The officer who had gone to investigate the car hidden in the woods returned with an envelope with some pink and white pages sticking out of one end. "It's a rental," he reported, handing the documents in his gloved hand to the chief.

Chief Lewis pulled the papers out by a corner and spread them out on the roof of his car. "Looks like someone from out of state."

"Or using a false identity," Nate suggested.

"Yeah, probably," Lewis agreed. He addressed his men, "All right, let's grab the gear and head out." He turned to Nate, Jennifer and Sam. "Wait here."

"What? No way," Jennifer said. "We're going with you."

"I can help," Sam insisted.

"This is as far as I'm willing to take civilians. I can't be responsible for you."

"You don't have to be," Jennifer said. She turned to Nate. "Can he keep us from going?"

Nate answered plainly. "Nope, this is public land." He wasn't sure that was exactly true, but he wanted to give Lewis an excuse to back down.

The chief looked at Nate. "If you get lost, you're on your own."

"Fair enough," Nate agreed.

"Let's go."

The chief led the way. After a short time, they picked up the path that Danny and his kidnapper had trampled down and met up with the trail that hugged the side of the mountain.

They arrived at the entrance to the mine. Someone had obviously torn away some of the overgrowth and discovered the cement plug.

One of the officers shined his light on it. "Doesn't look like anyone's tried to get in this way," he reported.

"Okay, so much for that theory," Lewis said, casting an annoyed look in the direction of Nate and Sam.

"There's another way in," Sam said.

"And you know this how?" Chief Lewis asked.

Sam raised his eyebrows as if to say, "How do you think?"

"Did our ghost happen to tell you where this other entrance is?"

"That part is kind of fuzzy. Just that they had to squeeze in."

Nate shrugged. "Assuming that car does belong to the kidnapper, where else would they have gone?"

Lewis turned to the older officer, McDonald. "Head back to the cars just in case they somehow double back another way."

Liam tipped his hat in a casual salute. "You got it, chief."

"You two start knocking that out," the chief said to his other officers, indicating the cement plug. Then he turned to Nate. "We'll split up and look for another way in. I'll take Psychic Sam this way. You take the Doc that way."

Nate looked up the trail in the direction the chief had pointed. It disappeared around an outcropping of rock jutting out of the mountain like a fin.

The chief tapped one of the officers hefting a pickax on his shoulder. "Give him your radio."

The officer handed the device to Nate, who made sure it was turned on and caused the chief's radio to squelch when he pressed the transmit button. He clipped it to his belt.

"If you find anything, radio it in. It's going to be dusk soon. It'll get dark quickly."

Nate nodded, then stepped aside as Sam left Jennifer's side to join the Chief. He noticed a look pass between the two of them. One of concern for each other, solidifying in his mind that there was something more than a professional relationship between them. "Come on," he said to Jennifer. "I guess we're looking for a small hole in a big mountain."

The two younger officers started pounding away at the cement as Nate and Jennifer started down the path, scanning the rock face up and down, looking for any sign of another entrance to the mine.

They rounded the outcropping and discovered a barrier of trees and shrubs between them and the rock face. Nate glanced down at Jennifer's feet and saw her ever-present Vans. "I knew I should have put on my hiking boots."

Jennifer smiled teasingly. "You really should stop dressing like a cop."

"I dress like a grown man."

"Well, you do look good in a suit," she said to him with a wink. "I'll crawl around in the weeds. I'm smaller anyway." She tightened her ponytail and looked for a way past the first group of trees.

"It shouldn't be too hard to get to if it's there. See if there's any broken branches around, or marks in the dirt."

"Nothing so far," she reported.

Nate watched her through the thick foliage as she examined the stone for any cracks large enough for a person. It was really starting to get dark, and even darker still among the trees. Jennifer pulled out her phone and put it in flashlight mode to aid her search.

Nate had a strange feeling. There was something wrong, but he couldn't put his finger on what it was. Probably Sam's presence coupled with Jennifer's casual flirtation.

And what did she mean he looked good in a suit?

He stopped that train of thought and returned his attention to the task at hand. Jennifer Daye was a mystery he wasn't likely to unravel anytime soon, nor was he sure that he wanted to.

Nate turned on his own phone's flashlight and scanned the area around the trail, looking for any sign that someone had been there ahead of them. It was too dry and hard to hold footprints, but perhaps Danny had the presence of mind to leave a clue.

And then he saw it. Tucked under a bush. A small hiker's backpack.

"Jennifer," he called out without taking his eyes off the pack, fearful that if he looked away, he would lose it.

Jennifer rustled through the bushes until she emerged next to Nate. "What is it?"

Nate pointed at the pack. "Do you see that?"

Jennifer swung the light from her phone in the direction of his finger. It was clearly a backpack.

They advanced and Nate was careful not to touch it as he moved the branches away. It wasn't dirty or wet, so it likely hadn't been there long. He carefully lifted the flap and looked inside. There were snacks and bottles of water.

Jennifer used her light to scan the rock behind the bushes where the pack was hidden. She found a dark triangle at the foot of a slight crevice. "I think we found it," she said.

Nate looked over at the spot Jennifer was illuminating. He added his own light, and it was obvious that there was more than just a depression in the rock. And there were clear scrape marks on the ground where someone had squeezed themselves inside. Danny likely wouldn't have had much trouble, but anyone Nate's size would not make it without widening the hole. "I'll call the chief," he said, reaching for the radio clipped to his belt.

"I think I can get in," Jennifer said.

"Hang on," Nate said. He clicked the transmit button on the radio and spoke into the device. "Chief Lewis, this is Raney, come in, over." He released the button and listened.

Nothing.

He tried again. "Chief Lewis, this is Nate Raney. I think we have the back door. Come in, over."

Still nothing.

"Anyone, come in, over."

This time, there was the hint of a voice amid a cloud of static.

"Can anyone hear me? Over."

More static.

"We better go back," Nate said, noticing that the sky was already purple from the sunset. Total darkness was not far behind.

"Are you kidding?" Jennifer asked. "What if they sneak out while we're gone?"

"Okay, you go and let them know we found another way in. I'll stay here and keep a lookout."

Jennifer didn't seem satisfied with his suggestion. "No," she said resolutely.

"What do you mean, 'no'?" Nate asked.

"We're responsible. If we hadn't taken on this case—"

"No, this whole treasure hunt thing has been going on for a decade and a half. If they hadn't called us, they would have called someone else."

"I'm going in," Jennifer said.

"That's not a good idea."

Jennifer ignored him and dropped close to the ground so she could get a better view of the entrance. "There's a ten-year-old boy in there, scared, tired, cold…"

"They could be armed."

Jennifer looked back at Nate, a challenging look on her face. "If you thought you could fit through that hole, you'd be inside already."

She had him there. "Be careful," he said.

Jennifer nodded, then scurried into the opening. She made it through—though not easily—reaffirming to Nate that if she needed him, there was no way he would be able to follow.

CHAPTER FIFTY SEVEN

Dale shone his flashlight up at the ceiling of the mine, searching for the air vent Maureen had mentioned—if she actually had. How could he be sure they were her words and not something the boy was making up? Regardless, he had no choice. There was nowhere else the money could be. It was clear that Maureen could have made it up to the mine to stash the loot, and if she had left it somewhere else, it would have been found by now. It had to be here.

He continued walking, keeping his eyes focused on the ceiling as the wide beam flashlight illuminated the stone. His foot caught on a ridge on the mine floor, and he tumbled forward. He dropped the flashlight and lantern as his hands spread out to break his fall. Both of them shut off as they impacted the hard ground, and Dale couldn't keep his face from smashing against the dirty stone.

It was pitch black.

Dale lay still for a moment. He could feel something warm and wet dripping down over his mouth and could smell the blood. He reached out, deliberately and systematically, searching for the flashlight or the lantern. He found the latter first and fumbled for the switch.

Nothing. He felt around to the bottom and discovered the battery compartment had opened up and the batteries were now spread out in the darkness as well. He got to his knees and realized he had smashed the left one in the fall and putting weight on it created an explosion of pain. He sat down instead, massaging the joint until he could flex it comfortably.

Then he heard something in the dark. Someone knocking? No, it was more of a pounding, as if there was a hammer being smashed into the wall in the distance.

Ghosts? he asked himself. Had Maureen asked the spirits of dead prospectors to scare him, or maybe even harm him? Was she mad that he had left Danny alone in the dark? He was able to cover more ground on his own. And if the kid closed his eyes, it would just be like he was sleeping.

The banging was constant, almost insistent, and the vibrations seemed to be coming from everywhere at once.

Was it possible there was someone besides himself and Danny in the mine?

Or trying to get *into* the mine. Someone trying to break through the cement blocking the main entrance?

Which way was that? He had lost all sense of direction at this point. If it was someone coming in, that meant they knew—or at least suspected—that they were here. Had Liam betrayed him? He had said he was going to steer the search away from the mine, but here they were.

Dale started reaching around, continuing his search for the batteries or the flashlight. Once he had finished the area in his immediate vicinity, he shuffled forward and repeated the process. When he had gone what he guessed was about ten feet, he gave up and turned around, starting to search in the other direction.

Was he imagining it, or was the pounding getting louder?

His hand bumped against something that rolled away from him in the dark. Dale leaned over, slapping his hand against the ground, trying to find what it was. His hand finally landed on the barrel of the small flashlight. He reached for the button on the back. Again, nothing happened. He felt up and down the length of the flashlight, but it seemed to be intact. He grabbed both ends and gave it a twist, checking to make sure it was securely fastened, and the bulb lit up.

Dale sighed in relief. He used the flashlight to find the batteries for the lantern and restored it to working order. He slowly got to his feet and tested his weight on his injured knee. There was a little discomfort, but it wasn't broken.

He could hear the pounding a little louder now, but still couldn't tell which direction it was coming from. Was it getting closer? Or were his ears playing tricks on him?

He picked a direction and moved steadily forward, still inspecting the ceiling, but taking care with his steps.

CHAPTER FIFTY EIGHT

Jennifer found her way to the main tunnel of the mine through the small passage that connected it to the chamber she had crawled into. The light from her phone barely penetrated the darkness.

There was no sign of Danny or his kidnapper. She wanted to call out to the boy but was afraid of alerting his captor. Her best chance was to surprise them. What she would do after that was something she really hadn't thought about. She would probably start with a strong front kick to his groin and then move on to some more conventional martial arts moves. Hopefully, she would be able to disable him enough to escape with Danny.

Then again, if there was more than one of them, or they had guns... she didn't want to think about that.

She wasn't sure which way to go, so she chose the direction that led deeper into the mine. She kept her light low to the ground, trying to see if she could spot any sign of life in the distance.

She heard something before she saw anything. A faint voice.

"Hello?" it asked, softly.

"Danny? Is that you?"

"Yes," he answered.

Jennifer hurried down the tunnel, then rounded a slight bend and saw Danny Foreman standing there, his left hand reaching out to the wall, clad only in his pajamas and slippers. His face and clothing were smeared with dirt, and he looked like he had been crying. She rushed up to him and grabbed him in a hug.

He hugged her back.

"Are you all right?" she asked.

"Uh huh," Danny said, nodding. "Maureen's husband brought me."

"Her husband?"

"His name is Dale."

Jennifer recalled the name from the conversation at the Foremans' house. "Where is he now?"

"He's looking for the money," Danny replied.

"It's here?" she asked.

Danny shook his head. "Maureen just told him that so we could get away. She said somebody told her they were coming to help us. She didn't know who."

"Sam must've gotten through," Jennifer said. "Do you know what direction Dale went?"

"No. It was dark. He left me at the end of the mine."

Jennifer shined her light down the tunnel but couldn't see the end. "How did you get here?"

"Maureen helped me."

Jennifer looked around, hoping the circumstances might make her more receptive to perceiving the ghost, but she saw nothing but the rough walls of the mine. "Okay, let's get you out of here and back home. Do you want me to carry you?"

"I can walk," Danny insisted.

Jennifer shined her light back down the way she had come from, looking and listening. She noticed something she hadn't heard before. A rhythmic pounding as if someone was hitting the rock with a big hammer.

The officers breaking down the cement plug.

If Dale heard it, too, he might decide to make his way back out the way he came in. At least she knew there was only one kidnapper. She had to decide whether to try to make it back to where she had come in, or head for the main entrance.

"This way," Danny said, pointing in the direction they were going. Jennifer looked at him.

He peered back up at her. "Maureen says if we go this way, we can get to the main entrance, while Dale goes the other way. She says the mine is kind of a big loop."

He said it so casually, so matter-of-factly, that she instantly believed him. "Okay. Sounds good," she said.

Danny led the way.

CHAPTER FIFTY NINE

The officers smashed away at the cement. It was thick, but hadn't been properly cured, so it was fairly crumbly and disintegrated with each strike of the sledgehammers and picks they were using.

One of them stood back and set his hammer with the head resting on the ground and leaned against it for support while he took a short break.

The other reared back with a pickax and struck the dent they had made in the cement.

The steel spike pierced the plug, throwing the officer off balance. He pulled the tool back. There was a hole opening into the darkness of the mine.

The officer who was taking a break grabbed his radio and broadcast a message. "We're through, chief."

A second later, the chief replied. "All right, we're heading back. Did you let Raney know?"

"Haven't heard from him," the officer replied.

"Copy that," the chief answered.

The officer clipped the radio back to his belt and grabbed hold of the hammer. Now that they had an opening, they were able to make quick work of the cement as large chunks broke away with each blow.

A short while later, there was a light bouncing down the path and

Sam came jogging into view. The chief followed shortly thereafter.

"Stay back," the chief warned Sam.

Sam stepped aside as the chief approached the breach in the cement plug and shined his light inside. He took a step back, shocked and surprised when a face appeared in the opening.

It was Dr. Daye.

"Jennifer!" Sam called out.

Jennifer examined the hole they had made. "Can you give me a hand?" she asked.

She disappeared back inside, and then two slipper-clad feet appeared in the opening. The officers rushed forward and pulled Danny out as Jennifer lifted him through the hole into the arms of the men. Then Jennifer crawled headfirst through the hole and Sam stepped forward to help her.

"Are you all right?" he asked.

Jennifer wrapped her arms around Sam's neck and leaned on him while the officers helped extract her from the mine. Sam stepped back and her feet cleared the hole in the cement, and she slammed into him. He stood fast, holding her tight. Jennifer's feet found the ground, and she pulled back, offering a grateful smile to Sam. Then she turned her attention to Danny. "Tell Maureen thanks."

Danny rolled his eyes and sighed. "I don't have to tell her what you say. She can hear you."

Jennifer smiled. It was obviously not the first time he'd had to explain this to someone.

"What happened to the kidnapper?" the chief asked.

"He's trying to get out the other way," Danny explained.

"It's Dale Everly," Jennifer said.

Chief Lewis grunted. "Where's this secret entrance?"

"That way," Jennifer said, then, with a note of concern. "Nate is there by himself."

The chief nodded to one of the officers. "You stay here in case he doubles back this way." Then to Jennifer and Sam, "You two stay with the boy."

Nate was getting nervous. It had been over fifteen minutes since

Jennifer had disappeared into the crack in the rock. And his attempts to use the radio had continued to prove fruitless.

Then he saw a light coming out of the tunnel. But instead of Jennifer's head poking through, it was a man's, with short cropped salt-and-pepper hair. Nate turned off the light on his phone and watched the man struggle through the narrow opening. He managed to get one arm and then his head through, then he snaked the other arm out. The man grabbed onto some of the nearby branches in an effort to pull himself the rest of the way through, but he couldn't get his hips past the opening, and obviously he couldn't push his way out with his feet from the other side.

"Damn it!" he exclaimed. "This is all I need."

Nate turned his light back on. He recognized the man instantly when he turned his face toward him.

Dale Everly.

"Evening, Dale. Need a hand?" he asked.

Dale looked up at Nate, surprised and then confused. "Who are you?" he asked.

Nate smiled. "The guy who you need to assure you didn't hurt the kid or the woman who went in after him."

"What woman?" he asked. "Are you talking about Maureen?"

So, it was true. The guy believed Danny had a hotline to his dead wife.

"Dr. Daye is just fine," Chief Lewis said from behind Nate.

Nate spun around and saw the chief and one of his officers walking up to them.

"The kid's okay, too," he added as he shined his light on the ex-con stuck in the hole.

The officer laughed. "He looks like Winnie the Pooh."

The chief gave him an annoyed look.

"My kid loves that book. Especially the part where they draw a face on his butt."

Nate and Chief Lewis ignored the officer. "I guess we should pull him out," the chief suggested.

Dale tried to push himself back inside. Nate grabbed one of his arms, stopping the attempt. The chief managed to get a grip on the other arm and together they pulled. Dale screamed in pain as his back and hips scraped against the sharp edges of the crack he was stuck in. They heaved and nearly fell over as Dale popped out like a reluctant cork. The officer rushed forward with a pair of handcuffs and before Dale could manage to get his balance, his hands were linked behind his back.

"Dale Everly, you're under arrest for kidnapping, parole violations and probably trespassing," the chief announced.

They marched him back to the mine entrance, where Jennifer and Sam were sharing a candy bar with Danny.

"Hi, Dale," Danny said.

The man grunted at the boy, obviously frustrated that his plan ended with him in handcuffs.

Jennifer approached Dale, her face inches away from his. "What kind of man kidnaps a boy from his home, drags him out to an abandoned mine and leaves him alone in the dark? You should be ashamed. I hope you spend the rest of your life in prison."

"We'll see to that," Chief Lewis promised. He eyed the hole made in the cement plugging the entrance to the mine. "I guess we better get some people up here to knock the rest of that out and give the mine a good search."

"It's not in there," Dale insisted. "She lied to me. I can't believe she lied to me."

"You threatened the boy," Sam answered.

Everyone turned to him.

"For whatever reason, Danny can see and hear her. They've formed a bond, a friendship. She probably has maternal feelings toward him. Never come between a mother and a child—even if they're not related."

"Even if she's dead," Jennifer added.

"Let's get Danny back to his parents," Nate suggested, hoping to change the subject.

"And this guy into a cell," the chief added.

CHAPTER SIXTY

Liam sat in the car, keeping an eye on the rental tucked away in the trees. No one had come by, and nothing had happened except for the sun setting and darkness descending.

It seemed obvious at this point that Dale had failed to find the loot and likely would be caught. It would only be a matter of time before the ex-con turned on Liam. He had an exit plan, and was tempted to just take off right now, but it was likely Dale would wait to give them Liam's name, hoping he could use it for leverage.

Then he heard faint voices on the radio. He couldn't make out everything they said, something about "breaking through." He tried to contact the chief or one of the other officers, but the mountain made that nearly impossible, and no one answered his queries as to what was going on.

Eventually, he saw lights dancing in the distance, heading toward him along the path they had left on.

When they broke out of the trees, he could see one of the officers escorting Dale, followed by the chief, the detective, and the parapsychologist and her psychic friend. He could see the man who claimed to be able to speak with Maureen carrying something. Then he realized it was the boy.

Liam got out of the car, trying to make eye contact with Dale.

Dale avoided his gaze.

Once they reached the cars, Chief Lewis walked over to Dale and patted his pockets. He found what he was looking for, a set of car keys. He tossed them to one of the officers. "You drive that rental back to the station. Make sure you wear gloves." He turned to the other officer. "You ride with Detective Raney and take the boy to the hospital. As soon as you have a cell signal, call his parents and make sure they meet us there." Then he turned to Liam. "You and I are going to take him to the station."

Liam nodded his understanding. He opened the door to the police car and helped the other officer squeeze Dale into the back seat.

Sam carried Danny to Nate's SUV. He and Jennifer got into the back with Danny, while the officer Chief Lewis had assigned to accompany them rode shotgun.

Nate was the first one to turn his car around and head back down the fire road.

The officer in the rental followed.

Chief Lewis sat behind the wheel of the police car, watching the other vehicles disappear in his rearview mirror.

Once they were well and gone, he turned around and looked at Dale. Then he turned and looked at Liam. "So, which one of you fuck-ups wants to tell me what the hell you were thinking, dragging that boy into that mine?"

Liam tried his best not to betray his surprise at the chief's accusation.

Dale looked at the chief, studying his face, remembering.

There was something about that voice… "It's you," he said.

Liam looked at Dale, wondering what he was talking about.

Dale seemed surprised that it wasn't obvious to Liam. "Our silent partner. The Mastermind."

Liam looked again at the chief. The man they had met with had worn dark glasses and a hat, and spoke in a very deliberate fashion, but now that Dale mentioned it, it was clear that the man who had provided them with the plan and the means to rob that bank all those years ago, and Chief Lewis, were one and the same.

"You really think I'd take an SFPD pension and then put up with all the bullshit of this small-town police department for my health? I knew this knucklehead was getting out, and that you were still hanging around waiting for him. But I didn't think you would do something so monumentally stupid that I'd have to clean up after you. If the money's in that mine, you better tell me now, otherwise the crew I'm going to send in is going to find it and we all get nothing."

"It's not in there. I looked. It's not that big, not that many places she could have stuffed a large duffel bag."

"So, the boy was making it up."

Dale shook his head. "He knows things, things only Maureen would know. But apparently ghosts don't have photographic memories."

"Okay," the chief said, calmly. "Here's what's going to happen. Officer McDonald and I are going to take you to the station, and you'll be booked into custody. You will say nothing. You won't even ask for a lawyer. When the time is right, you'll get a chance to escape. Nod if you understand."

Dale nodded.

Then he addressed Liam. "You stick with me. After we drop him off, we'll head to the hospital. If somehow this kid does know where that loot is, we need to move fast."

The chief didn't wait for a reply. He started the car, then backed up and swung back around onto the fire road.

CHAPTER SIXTY ONE

Marcia and Greg rushed up to the emergency department recep-
tionist. Liam was waiting there, and before they had a chance to ask
about Danny, he stepped up to them. "This way," he said, waving
them toward a set of large double doors.

"Is he okay?" Marcia asked.

"He's fine," Liam assured her. He led them through the doors to
an examination room. Danny was perched on the edge of the hospital
bed while a doctor examined his eyes.

Marcia rushed to him and grabbed him in a hug, ignoring the
presence of the doctor. "Are you all right?" she asked, smothering
him to the point where he could barely answer her.

The doctor replied instead. "He's going to be fine. A little dehy-
drated, but no injuries aside from a few scrapes."

"He was very brave," Jennifer said.

Marcia responded to Jennifer's comment with a glare. "He
wouldn't be here if you people hadn't —"

"It's no one's fault," Nate insisted. "Once Dale Everly got out of
prison, it was inevitable he would come snooping around the house
where he used to live. The important thing is that Danny is okay."
Nate absently rubbed his bad shoulder. He had tweaked it when he
and Chief Lewis had yanked Dale Everly from the hidden mine entrance. He desperately wanted to take one of his pain pills, but he

had left them in the car.

Marcia appeared to settle down. She cast another look at Jennifer that was likely the closest thing to an apology she was going to get.

"Are you all right?" the doctor asked Nate, indicating his shoulder. "Did you hurt yourself?"

"No, it's an old injury. I just tweaked it." He cast a glance at Jennifer's arm, where some abrasions were crusted with dried blood. "She might need some antibiotics, though."

Sam reached out and held her arm as if it was a fragile vase. "Does it hurt?" he asked.

Jennifer shook her head. "No, it's fine."

Nate looked away from the couple, focusing instead on Danny. He noticed Officer McDonald standing just outside the door, listening attentively. "Chief," Nate said, "I don't mean to step on your toes, but it probably would be a good idea to ask Danny a few questions about what happened while it's fresh. We don't know if Everly was working alone or not."

"Can't we do this later?" Marcia asked.

Chief Lewis exchanged a look with Nate.

Nate assumed the chief wanted to balance the needs of his investigation with the well-being of the Foreman boy. But he couldn't ignore the gut feeling he had that there was more to the story. Jennifer would probably accuse him of being clairvoyant. But he knew the kind of scrutiny an ex-con on parole is under. He would have needed someone to arrange the rental car, for one thing.

"Just a few questions," Chief Lewis said to Marcia. "I promise it won't take long."

Marcia sat down on the bed next to Danny, putting a protective arm around him. "Okay, just a few."

Greg moved to stand next to his wife and son in silent solidarity.

"What's the first thing you remember?" Chief Lewis asked Danny.

Danny took a moment, thinking back to the beginning of what was a very long day for him. "I woke up in a big bed. My eyes were covered and there was tape on my mouth and my hands and feet were tied with those plastic things. Dale wanted to know if I could really talk to Maureen, and he wanted her to tell him where she hid his treasure."

Nate smiled at the word Danny had used, "treasure."

"Was there anyone else?"

"There was a man who came by and asked Dale a bunch of questions. I couldn't hear him very well, though."

Nate noticed Liam leaning into the room, his eyes focused on Danny.

"Did you see him?" the chief asked.

Danny shook his head. "No, Dale didn't take off my blindfold until later."

Liam seemed to visibly relax.

"But Maureen saw him," Danny added.

The chief didn't know what to make of that answer. He shot a glance at Nate, then Dr. Daye, before returning his attention to Danny. "She did?"

"Uh-huh."

"And does she know who it was?"

Danny raised a hand and pointed across the room at the officer standing in the door. "Officer Liam," he said.

All eyes swung around to Liam—except Nate, who was watching Chief Lewis. The old cop didn't seem at all shocked by the accusation, just as he wasn't surprised to see Dale stuck in the hole at the mine.

Liam became defensive. "When I saw Dale, he was at the halfway house, and there wasn't any kid in his room."

Everyone continued to stare at him.

"You can't believe a kid who says some ghost saw me," he said, laughing off the allegation.

Sam lifted his chin, cocked his head as if he was listening to something. "Liar," Sam said. "Maureen says you're lying."

"He's the one who shot Maureen," Danny added.

Liam laughed. "Chief, seriously?"

Chief Lewis didn't answer. He stared a warning at Liam.

Liam's expression shifted from mild amusement to fear. He took a step back and then bolted down the hall.

Nate instinctively made a move to chase him, but he was all the way on the other side of the room. Sam reached the door before he did and started chasing after the officer. Nate followed in a close second. Liam didn't stand a chance against Sam. The psychic was extremely fit and obviously no stranger to cardio. It didn't take him long to chase down the frightened officer. Nate slowed his pace when he saw Sam reach out and grab Liam's arm. The officer spun around, lost his balance, and smacked his head into a concrete block wall. Nate could hear the sickening crack the man's head made.

Liam collapsed into a heap. He was unconscious for a moment, but then opened his eyes, obviously disoriented.

Nate approached them and disarmed the officer, then grabbed the man's handcuffs from the small holster at his back and clamped his wrists together.

A crowd of hospital employees gathered.

Blood streamed out of a cut hidden somewhere behind his hairline. A nurse approached and inspected the wound with a gloved hand. "What happened here?" she asked.

"He fell," Nate replied simply.

By then, Chief Lewis and Jennifer had caught up as well. Two more officers arrived, likely summoned by the chief. "Take him back to the station," he ordered.

"He should be looked at. He might have a concussion," the nurse insisted.

The chief considered, then nodded his okay. The officers lifted Liam to his feet and followed the nurse to a nearby examination room.

"Make sure you read him his rights," the chief added. "He talks to no one until I have a chance to interrogate him. You understand?"

The officers nodded.

Lewis turned to Nate. "Thanks for catching him."

"Don't thank me. Sam's the one who chased him down. I just slapped on his own cuffs."

Maureen watched as Liam was escorted away. She was relieved that both of the men who had threatened Danny were now in the hands of the police, but also sad that one of them was Dale. But what had really shaken her was the memory that had come to her when Liam had smugly dismissed Danny's charge.

It was the day of the robbery. She had returned to the house to get some of her things and some cash so she could get away.

And then Liam had shown up. To warn her, he had said.

She made her way up to the attic where she stashed the photos and left a note for Dale, then climbed out onto the branch of the old oak. If she could make it to the woods, she could get away. Liam would stall them, redirect their attention to someplace else.

Maureen could hear other cars and officers arriving as she crawled through the boughs of the giant tree. She looked back to make sure no one was watching.

But there was someone coming around the front corner of the house. She was relieved to see it was Liam.

He smiled up at her. The same sly grin he had made when Danny accused him of being in the motel room with Dale.

Then he lifted his gun, aimed, and fired.

It was Liam who had killed her. He had ended her life and, with it, all of her dreams.

She looked over at Danny, safe in the embrace of his parents, and recalled another memory.

Before they had ever thought of robbing the Danville Bank, shortly after they had been married, Maureen and Dale had been walking in the woods behind the house. She had just shown him the mine where she had played as a child and took him down into a valley where there was an old, dry well she had discovered when she was a kid. It wasn't as interesting to her friends as the mine was, but she believed it was magic.

A wishing well.

And it was there, with her hand grasping Dale's, that she wished with all her heart that she and Dale would have a family filled with children.

Maybe a little boy like Danny.

"I know where the treasure is," she said to Danny.

Danny looked up at her, his eyes lighting up with excitement. "You do?"

"Do what, honey?" Marcia asked him.

"Maureen says she remembers where she put the treasure."

Jennifer, Sam and Nate appeared in the doorway, catching his last statement.

"She does?" Jennifer asked, curious.

"She does," Sam confirmed.

"Well, don't keep us in suspense," Nate said, the note of sarcasm clear in his voice.

"It's in the wishing well," he said.

Maureen smiled.

Her wish had come true.

CHAPTER SIXTY TWO

Dave and Emily focused cameras on the volunteer spelunker, who Chief Lewis had recruited to check out the bottom of the abandoned well. It was exactly where Danny had told them Maureen had said it would be. Emily seemed nonplussed by all the events—though a little put out by being dragged into the woods. "I don't do nature," she had told Jennifer. But even Emily had trouble saying no to Dr. Daye.

Dave was fighting off a swarm of gnats buzzing around his head and slapping at mosquitoes attacking his neck and arms. "How come the bugs aren't bothering you?" he asked Emily.

"They wouldn't dare," she said flatly.

Jennifer approached, the Foremans close behind, this time with both of their children. "This is exciting," Jennifer said. "Make sure you get a closeup of them dropping into the well."

"Got it," Emily replied, holding up a handheld camcorder. She pushed her way through the weeds up to the police tape the officers had strung around the site.

"Seriously?" Dave said, noticing that no one else except him was battling the bugs. "Can I go back to the van?"

Jennifer had spent part of the night unloading her personal belongings from the van into one of Sam's garages. He didn't ask her any questions but had offered to let her use a guest room for as long as she needed. She told him she would think about it.

"You can't miss this, Dave," Jennifer said. "There could be a million dollars in that well."

"I'll watch the tapes later," he said.

Jennifer changed the subject. "Have you seen Nate?"

Dave scanned the crowd of people and saw Nate standing behind a group of cops. "He's over there."

Jennifer was surprised Nate had yet to remind her that his prediction had come true. Maureen *had* left the final clue to where she had hidden the money where Danny could find it.

The note she had left for Dale, and the message, "*Wish* you were here," with the word, "*wish*," underlined. And now they were here, at the wishing well.

"Do we get to keep the treasure?" Danny asked.

Greg smiled at the question. "Well, it doesn't really belong to us. But the chief said there might be a reward."

"Cool," Danny replied.

"Can I get an American Girl doll?" Daisy asked.

"If there's a reward, it's going straight into your college funds," Marcia said.

The kids groaned.

"Looks like they're getting ready to go down," Jennifer announced.

At the well, the spelunker checked his harness, made sure his line was secure, then lowered himself down into the deep hole. It was about six feet in diameter, so he was able to walk his way down the stone wall of the well.

Jennifer had managed to talk the chief into allowing her to mount one of Bits' portable sports cameras on the man's helmet. Whatever he saw, they would have a front-row seat.

The cave diver disappeared down the well. It was nearly thirty feet deep, according to the preliminary inspection. They had found the site overgrown with weeds. There had been some loose boards over the top of the well, whose walls extended only a few inches above ground level. If they hadn't been looking for it, they would have missed it completely—as had probably countless treasure hunters over the last decade and a half.

They had cleared out the area and had to hike in the equipment they needed about a half mile, as there wasn't even a fire road leading to the site.

Everyone held their breath as they waited for word from the spelunker. "There's something here!" he announced.

They dropped a second line down with a basket on the end of it. Several minutes later, the spelunker tugged on the rope, and the officers at the top of the well carefully hauled it back up.

Emily managed to get a good angle with her camcorder.

Jennifer and the Foremans crept up as close as the police tape would allow.

The basket appeared, in it was what looked like a pile of dead leaves.

They set it on the ground where they had spread out a tarp, and carefully dumped the contents of the basket out.

Among the leaves and twigs was a dark bundle.

The size of a large duffel bag.

It was frayed, and there were holes in the fabric.

A rat scurried out of the pile.

Daisy shrieked at the sight of the creature and buried her face in her father's leg.

Jennifer cringed as well.

"Awesome," Danny said.

"Yeah," Emily agreed.

An officer wearing a pair of purple nitrile gloves poked at the bag, making sure there weren't any other surprises inside. He found a zipper and pulled on it. Instead of unzipping, the zipper pulled free from the fabric of the duffel bag, creating an opening. He reached inside and pulled out what looked like shredded newspaper.

Emily zoomed in on the paper in the officer's hand.

It was money. Chewed into bits over the years by whatever creatures had made the well their home, and the years of weather that had soaked it with rain.

"Oh, well," Greg said. "At least we have a good story."

The officer kept digging. There were a few bills that were partially intact, but none of it seemed redeemable. He also found a few coins, items that had been stored in the safe deposit boxes Maureen and Dale had dumped into the duffel.

Still, nothing of any life-changing worth. It looked like Dale and Liam's quest for the lost loot would have been fruitless, even if they had been successful.

Then he came across a small, flat wooden box. It, too, had been chewed on, but was mostly intact. When he picked it up, it fell into two pieces, and inside, nestled in a lining of black velvet, was a string of sparkling diamonds.

The officer carefully lifted it up for everyone to see.

It was the necklace, the one that had been the focus of years of speculation. Had it been in the bag Maureen had made off with? Or had the owners made a false insurance claim?

The answer was shining brightly as it hung off the officer's fingers.

"Whoa," Marcia said, awestruck by the sight.

"Looks like it's Harvard for you and Daisy," Jennifer said to Danny.

"What's Harvard?" he asked.

"Okay, let's get this bagged up," the chief ordered. He leaned over the well. "Anything else down there?"

"Looks like just some animal skulls and muck."

"All right, come on back up."

The officer slid the necklace into an evidence bag. The chief took it and grabbed a manila envelope from the evidence collection kit. He dropped the necklace into the envelope, sealed it, and set it into a larger paper bag. He addressed a nearby officer. "Make sure you don't lose that," he warned. He turned to the rest of the crew. "I'm going to head back to the office. I think the owner of that necklace is due some good news."

He trekked off into the woods, following the recently trodden path back to the road where they had left the vehicles.

Jennifer looked around for Nate. He had been strangely avoiding her all morning, insisting on driving up on his own.

Now he seemed to have disappeared.

"Arrggh!" Dave shouted, waving his arms around his head. "Can I go now?"

Jennifer looked at Dave. He was alternately swatting whatever was biting him and scratching his skin all up and down his arms.

"He's funny," Daisy observed, laughing.

Danny joined her.

"All right, looks like we have what we need," Jennifer conceded.

"So, what happens next?" Greg asked. "I mean with you."

Jennifer shrugged. "Nothing. I think we'll put together a video and some written accounts. And then we'll put it away in our files. We'll be sure to keep your names out of it."

"I'm not sure how much good that's going to do," Marcia said, waving at the crowd of people around the well. "I don't think we're going to be able to keep this quiet."

"I wouldn't worry too much," Jennifer said. "They'll be some other story that comes along and before you know it, you'll be old news."

Chief Lewis made the half-mile hike back to the side road where he left his car. When he got there, he was surprised to see Nate Raney waiting by his vehicle, leaning against the driver's side door. "Hey, Nate, didn't see you leave. Thanks for your help with this. If you're open to working in Danville, I can certainly spread the word. Maybe get you a little business."

"Thanks," Nate said.

The chief approached his car, but Nate didn't move. He smiled awkwardly. "Something else I can do for you?"

"Turn yourself in," Nate said.

Chief Lewis seemed confused. "Turn myself into what?"

"I know you're connected to Everly and McDonald. It never made sense that they could have pulled off that robbery by themselves. But I guess even a mastermind like yourself couldn't account for a little girl wandering off in the middle of the night."

The chief laughed. "Mastermind? Nice one, Nate."

"Come on, you must be dying to tell someone," Nate goaded. "All those years, planning the perfect robbery, only to have those incompetent idiots you partnered with drop the ball."

The chief shook his head, refusing to concede to Nate's accusations. "Everly had all the skills he needed to pull off that job."

Nate shrugged. "Maybe, but he needed that inside man to make sure the silent alarm remained silent. Couldn't get away with that in a big city like San Francisco, but a place like Danville? All it took was a disgruntled cop and a desperate, unemployed sap beaten up by the system. Unfortunately, that young woman got caught up in your scheme and paid with her life.

"Tell me, was it your idea for Liam to shoot her before he got his hands on the loot? Or did he come up with that bone-headed idea on his own?"

"I don't know what you're talking about, Nate."

"I'm talking about the fact that I heard you took early retirement over an internal affairs investigation."

"Really? A good cop like you believing gossip? I thought you were above such things."

"Well, I wasn't ready to put much stock in that rumor until I noticed your reaction when you saw it was Dale Everly crawling out of the mine."

"I don't think I reacted at all."

"No, you didn't. Even though officer McDonald had told you he had spoken to him earlier and had dismissed him as being involved."

The chief laughed. "Wow, you certainly can read a lot into nothing."

"And then when we returned to the cars, you and McDonald took Everly back to the station before heading to the hospital. I imagine you had quite a conversation with them. What did you promise Everly? A chance to escape?"

"You're really testing our friendship, Nate. Move aside. I have business to take care of."

"Okay," Nate said. "Just hand over the necklace and I'll let you go."

The chief sighed. "The necklace is in an evidence bag back at the well."

"I saw the switch. What did you drop in there? Your handcuffs? The necklace is in your pocket."

"I offered to help you out, Nate. Now you're just throwing away all that good will." Chief Lewis pulled his gun from its holster and aimed it at Nate. "Move aside."

"Or what? You'll shoot me? How long do you think you'll be able to protect your stooges if you do that? It won't take long for Everly and McDonald to flip on you if they're charged as accomplices."

"Those fools won't flip. They know if they try to throw me under the bus, there's no place they can hide."

"So, you're just going to take off with the loot and leave them to rot in jail?"

Lewis laughed again. "You think this ends with me?"

"What does that mean?" Nate asked.

"You were right. That Hummer did run you off the road. But I'm not the one who sent it. Can't you see that this is bigger than a small-town heist? I thought you were smarter than that."

It was Nate's turn to smile. "You're right. I am."

Chief Lewis heard something behind him. He turned to find two Deputy Sheriffs, their firearms drawn and pointed at him.

He lifted his hands into the air.

Nate took the gun from the old chief, then fished the evidence bag from his left pocket. He held the diamond necklace up so that the late morning sun hit it inside the transparent bag. "I think you should probably read Chief Lewis his rights," Nate suggested.

The deputies did so as they handcuffed him. The necklace was now evidence in the case against him. Nate handed it off to them as a county sheriff's car pulled up, and they stuffed Lewis into the backseat.

"We'll be in touch," one of the deputies said to Nate.

"You'll want this, too." Nate pulled a pen out of his jacket pocket, clicked it and handed it to the deputy, who raised an inquiring eyebrow. "It's a spy pen. I've got our whole conversation on there. I'm sure your tech guys will know what to do with it. Just make sure you send it back to me when you're done. Those things aren't cheap."

The trooper dumped the pen into another evidence bag and left Nate with a handshake.

As they drove off, Jennifer, Emily, Dave and the Foreman's emerged from the woods.

Jennifer noticed that the chief's car was still there, but there was no chief. She turned to Nate. "Did we miss something?"

CHAPTER SIXTY THREE

Nate sat in the office he shared with Jennifer and stared at the shrinking balance of his bank account on his laptop screen. When they had started this enterprise all those months ago, he was in a different place in his life. He was recovering from a career-ending injury and had nearly died himself saving Jennifer's life at the end of their first case together. She was being persecuted by the university administration, and her staff was without a home. It made sense to combine their resources and share expenses.

Although he hadn't actively participated in the publicity that case had engendered, he was confident at the time that it would generate business for him as a private investigator. But most of the cases that dribbled in were people convinced they were being haunted or possessed or were getting psychic messages from aliens. His friends from the force had thrown him some work, but nothing major, nothing that required more than a day's worth of effort.

Now, after more than six months, the money was still going out faster than it was coming in. He had always been a gadget freak, so when Jennifer would drop hints about some new camcorder or motion sensor that Bits had recommended, he more often than not added it to the assets of the business, expecting that once they had a few more high-profile cases under their belts, there would be a solid return on the investment.

But those cases never materialized. And in addition to the office equipment and investigative gear, Nate's grocery bill had skyrocketed as he found himself providing a couple meals a day for three college-age kids.

Nate reached into his jacket pocket and pulled out his prescription bottle. Up until about a month ago, he left it in his medicine chest, but after the last surgery, he kept it nearby so he could knock back the pain when it became too much. And since he had aggravated his shoulder yet again a couple of nights ago manhandling Dale Everly, it was becoming more and more difficult to keep the pain at bay.

He opened the bottle and tapped a pill into his palm. He stared at it for a moment, then added three more and tossed them into his mouth. He followed them with some coffee, then sealed the bottle and slipped it back into his pocket. He'd see his doctor, he promised himself, just as soon as things settled down.

Something cold and wet brushed against his left palm. He looked down and saw Madge sitting beside him, expecting him to devote his attention to scratching behind her ears. Nate obliged, and Madge squeezed her eyes shut with pleasure. "Maybe I should send you off to drug-sniffing school so one of us can earn a few bucks," he suggested.

Jennifer breezed into the office, a smile on her face. Nate automatically assumed she had spent the night with Sam—not that she didn't have every right to date whomever she wanted. He just wished it didn't bother him. Jennifer was very extroverted, and connected with people easily, the near polar opposite to Nate. He always approached people with suspicion, an occupational hazard from his time as a police detective.

She started humming.

"You seem like you're in a good mood," he noted.

"It's a good day. We helped save Danny, and the Foremans have agreed to let us do some follow-up interviews when things settle down." Jennifer looked at Nate and noticed immediately something was weighing heavily on his mind. "What's got you down? I thought you'd be happy. If it wasn't for you, Lewis and his accomplices would have stolen that necklace. Again. And probably disappeared into the wind."

"Yeah, I put the guy who was going to try to throw some P.I. work my way in jail. I think I need to work on my business plan."

"I'm sure things are going to turn around for us," Jennifer said.

"Yeah," he said, unconvinced. "How's that new course of yours coming along?"

"I guess you've been talking with Dave."

"He does most of the talking."

"Well, to be honest, it was really bothering me, but even though it won't be an official class, a couple of colleagues are going to help me set it up as a non-credit seminar—which is already part of the department budget, so the dean can't stop it."

"Good for you," Nate said. "I'm glad everything's working out."

Jennifer could sense there was more going on behind Nate's sarcastic façade. "What's really going on?" she asked.

Nate wasn't planning on having this conversation today, but maybe this was the right time. Maybe it was time to admit that this… experiment just wasn't going to work. He could get his life and his home back. Maybe he could apply to one of the large investigative firms in the city. He heard they paid ex-cops very well.

The phone rang.

Probably the press, Nate assumed. He wasn't interested in taking a spin on another one of Jennifer Daye's paranormal carnival rides.

"Aren't you going to get that? It could be another case."

"Let it go to voice mail," Nate said.

Emily appeared. She answered the phone. "Raney Daye Investigations," she droned.

Nate brought a hand up to his face. This wasn't going to be easy.

"Uh huh," Emily said into the phone in her usual monotone, betraying nothing about who might be calling or for what reason. "Yes, Dr. Daye is here. Hold on." Emily handed the phone over to Jennifer. "It's Marcia Foreman."

So much for a new case, Nate thought. They probably were going to send him a bill for Danny's pajamas.

Jennifer took the phone handset from Emily. "This is Dr. Daye," she said. After a moment, she added, "That's wonderful news. Congratulations." She covered the mouthpiece so she could fill Nate and Emily in on the news. "They heard from the company that insured the necklace. Apparently, there was some sort of reward."

Nate remembered seeing something about a ten-thousand-dollar bounty in the research he had done into the case. A nice start to the kids' college funds.

Jennifer kept listening, but stopped giving Nate and Emily updates about the other end of the conversation. Her eyes widened, and she collapsed backward into her chair. "Yes, of course. Thank you. We really appreciate that."

"Appreciate what?" Emily asked.

But Jennifer ignored the question. "I'll tell him. Thanks again." She handed the phone back to Emily, who returned it to its base. She looked at Nate and appeared to be struggling to speak.

"That's a first," Nate joked. "Jennifer Daye at a loss for words."

"So, technically, it's not a reward," she began. She swallowed before she continued, as if her mouth had dried out. "It's a finder's fee. Ten percent of the insured value of the item."

"How much was it insured for?" Emily asked, her tone betraying curiosity.

"Ten million dollars. The Foremans are getting one million dollars for finding it." She looked directly at Nate and smiled. "And they're giving us half."

"Half of what?" Nate asked. He hadn't quite fully registered what she had said. And his mind had trouble accepting that it could be real.

"Half a million dollars," she replied.

"Holy cow," Emily answered. "That's a lot of Hot Pockets."

"Half a million dollars," Nate said.

"Half a million dollars," Jennifer confirmed.

Nate mentally subtracted the expenses Raney/Daye Investigations had incurred since its hasty inception, then divided that sum into the remainder of the figure. They could easily keep going for years with that money. Even if they didn't get any more paying cases. They were set.

"What was it you were going to say?" Jennifer asked.

"What?"

"You were going to tell me something. It seemed important."

Nate shook his head. "Nothing. I just wanted to ask how things had gone with my mother and Sam. You never filled me in."

"Yeah, well, that's your fault," Jennifer said. "You've been acting weird lately."

"Hello!" called a voice from the kitchen.

Eleanor poked her head into the office. She had a couple of grocery bags in her hands. "Here you are. I was ringing the bell forever. You really should keep that door locked, dear," she said to Nate. "Someone could dognap Madge."

Madge whined at the sound of her name.

"What's in the bags, Mrs. R?" Emily asked.

"Lunch. I thought I would make all of you my famous lasagna. Dr. Daye told me you mostly eat meat pockets."

"Hot Pockets," Emily corrected. She turned to Nate. "We're out of pepperoni," she reported.

Jennifer shot her a reproachful look.

"What? It's not like you guys can't afford it."

"Well, today you're getting lasagna with freshly made pasta. Can you give me a hand, Nate?"

Nate was still in shock that his mother was here and not complaining about him cutting her off from her psychic friends.

"Sure," he said. Nate got up and took the bags from Eleanor as she led him back into the kitchen.

"I assume you have a pasta roller."

"I do," he said. He set the bags on the counter, then pulled out a stainless steel pasta maker from one of the cabinets.

"What's all the excitement?" Eleanor asked.

"A case," Nate said.

"The one with the little boy who can talk to ghosts?"

"Ghost," Nate corrected, then added, "allegedly."

Eleanor laughed. "Your father always said you were stubborn," she remarked.

Nate didn't notice it at first, but there was something different about how his mother referred to his father. Usually, it was in the present tense, something like, 'Your father always says you're stubborn.' But now she wasn't acting as if she had just been talking to him. She was recalling a fond memory.

"I get that from you," Nate pointed out.

"Yes, you do," she said. Eleanor turned to Nate. She stared at him lovingly. "But you got your eyes from your father. And your sense of honor and loyalty, and that annoying habit of always putting others before yourself."

Nate felt his eyes starting to tear up. He'd never heard his mother talk about him like that before. He always felt that his resemblance to his father only served as a reminder to his mother that her husband had passed away.

"You were right," she said.

"About what?" Nate asked.

"Well, not about me being able to talk to your father. I know I'll never be able to convince you, but I've accepted that." She reached out and wiped away a tear that was rolling down his cheek. "You were right that I shouldn't be spending all of my time—and money—to do it. I've been spending so much effort trying to hang onto my relationship with Ben that I forgot I was neglecting my relationship with you."

Nate reached out and grabbed his mother in a tight hug, mostly to hide the torrent of tears now streaming from his eyes. "I love you, Mom."

"I know, dear. I love you, too. Now let me go. I can't breathe."

The two of them laughed as Nate loosened his grip.

"Should I come back another time?" Dave asked. He was standing at the entrance to the kitchen with his backpack slung over one shoulder.

"No, come on in. You're in for a treat today. My mom's making us lasagna," Nate told him.

Dave held up his phone. "Emily texted me that we got some good news?"

"We're getting a foosball table," Emily announced.

Nate turned and saw that Emily and Jennifer were standing at the opposite side of the kitchen. Jeez, had everyone been watching him cry with his mom?

"We're not getting a foosball table," Jennifer countered. "But we are getting a share of the million-dollar finder's fee the Foremans collected for recovering that diamond necklace."

"No kidding?" Dave asked.

"Half a million dollars," Jennifer said.

"What?" Eleanor asked. "You didn't say anything about a million dollars," she scolded Nate.

"Does this mean you can finally stop living out your van, Dr. Daye?" Dave asked.

All eyes turned to Jennifer.

"What is he talking about?" Nate asked.

"Who told you?" Jennifer asked Dave, ignoring Nate's question.

"I'm not an idiot," Dave answered. "I've almost been a Ph.D. for over five years now."

"You don't live in your van. You have an apartment in that building off campus. I dropped you off there."

"Jeez, some detective you are," Emily said.

Jennifer shrugged. "I didn't know how to tell you. And I know you've been worrying about money."

"Well, hopefully with this reward, you don't have to worry about such silly things. Honestly, I wish you two would get a room already," Eleanor said.

"Mom!" Nate said.

"We're with you on that one, Mrs. R.," Emily added.

"She has a boyfriend," Nate said to Eleanor.

"I do?" Jennifer asked.

Nate turned to Jennifer. "Sam," he said. "Aren't you two—"

"Friends?" Jennifer asked rhetorically. "Yes, we are. I've known him for years. He's a nice guy, but he's not really my type."

"I just assumed…" Nate added weakly. He addressed his mother. "We're business partners, Mom. There's nothing else between us," he said, then turned to Jennifer for confirmation. "Right?"

Jennifer took a second to reply, feeling all the eyes in the room on her. "Right," she agreed. "I guess I'll get started on looking for a new apartment—assuming we can use part of the finders' fee for Dave's stipend."

"Of course, that goes without saying," Nate added, glad the subject had been changed.

Eleanor was the one who finally broke through the awkwardness she had created. "All right, if none of you have anything better to do, you can help me make lunch."

Nate stood back and watched as Eleanor started assigning tasks to the staff of Raney/Daye Investigations. How quickly things had turned around from just a few short minutes earlier. He had been on the verge of calling the whole thing off, and now they were closer than ever. Not only did he have his mother back, but this old house that had always been filled with family when he was a boy was once again bustling with excitement and love.

Jennifer was slicing tomatoes. She glanced over at Nate, with that infectious smile on her face that exuded eternal optimism.

Nate resolved to never doubt her again.

Besides, even if Raney/Daye Investigations did turn out to be a bust, they could always open a restaurant.

EPILOGUE

Greg and Marcia sat on either side of their children, all of them crammed onto the sofa watching a movie while Danny and Daisy ate popcorn from a big bowl perched on Daisy's lap.

"I know what's going to happen," Danny said teasingly.

"Don't tell me, that's not fair," Daisy protested.

"Danny, don't tease your sister," Greg warned.

"How can you possibly know what's going to happen? This movie is twenty years old." Marcia said.

Danny looked at his mother, then over at one of the empty armchairs.

Marcia turned her gaze over to the chair. "Maureen, what did I tell you about secret conversations with Danny?"

"She says she's sorry," Danny reported.

Marcia ruffled Danny's hair, then put her arm around him and squeezed.

Maureen smiled as she watched Marcia try to hold on, as Danny struggled to squirm out of her grasp. Although it was something she would never do with her own child, she enjoyed the vicarious experience, nonetheless. She was grateful that the Foremans had accepted her presence. Sometimes it seemed that Daisy almost could hear her, and she wondered if in time, that the little girl would see her as Danny did.

The guest room was now officially Maureen's again. Marcia had framed and hung some of the photographs from the box Danny had found in the attic on the walls and set them on the dresser so she could enjoy them whenever she wanted.

Set prominently in the middle of all of Maureen's memories was a family photo of the Foremans, standing in front of the old farmhouse.

She had finally gotten the family she had always wanted.

Jennifer and Nate will return in

FAR SIGHT
A Raney/Daye Investigation

Visit https://raneyanddaye.com for more information.

AFTERWORD

In the scheme of things, most people don't distinguish between what we, versed in studying the paranormal, call ghosts and hauntings. You see a figure standing in front of you, or hear voices coming out of nowhere, or even sense a presence or feel like something is off in a space you've just entered. You say the place is "haunted" and might even say that there are "spirits" present.

But over the 140 years since the scholarly and scientific study of all things psychic phenomena related was officially started with the founding of the Society for Psychical Research, we've naturally learned a thing or three about many things considered "ghostly" and "haunted."

First of all, there is a difference between a spirit of someone who has died—what we typically call an apparition (less cultural baggage than the term ghost, though they can be used interchangeably)—and a place or object that is haunted.

If we are truly talking about an apparition, ghost or spirit, we're talking about someone's consciousness surviving the death of their brain and body and having the capability to still be aware of and interactive with our physical world, and us. Consciousness is paramount here for the understanding of what a ghost is, and interactivity and at least apparent self-awareness supports the entity being conscious.

When using the term haunting—often used with a qualifier and stated as residual haunting by some of the paranormal reality show folks—we're not using the term to refer to a conscious entity. The concept is that the environment, the land, the house, or object store information of activity and emotions that happen in and around them.

Living humans—and we think animals, of course—have the capability to pick up snippets of this recorded information from the environment. The information gets interpreted by our perceptual processes and added to our normal perceptions, kind of like adding a background on a Zoom call. Whether this is a form of ESP or some biophysical thing happening between our brains and something in the environment has not yet been determined.

People experience this information residue in many situations without ever saying the place is haunted. One example being when we go house or apartment hunting. We walk into a place and get a vibe, a sense of good or bad emotion and "energy"—nothing to do with the décor or smell. That emotional imprint comes from the people who lived there, or even still live there. If it's "bad vibes," we leave and continue our hunt for a new place to live.

The information can be translated in our heads to emotions (the most common) or visuals or sounds or voices, even smells and physical sensations. Objects can also hold such emotions and other information for us to perceive. For what is a house? It's a big object we enter instead of touch or hold in our hands.

One last important point about the "recording" that hauntings hold: the Living leave the imprints, not the Dead. Yes, many places we call haunted are old and no longer have people living there, with the people who used to live there perhaps being long dead. And yes, places where a murder was committed, or a suicide happened, can be haunted by the emotion—and even other kinds of perceptions—related to the murder or suicide.

However, just because someone died there does not mean the death or manner of death was responsible for any information residue.

Consider a movie like *Frankenstein*, released in 1931 (I'm a sucker for the old Universal monster movies). When the movie was filmed, everyone in it was fully alive. However, since then, the majority (if not all) of the people on screen have died. Yet I can watch that movie whenever I want on DVD or streaming. I am watching a recording of people who are dead, yet who made that recording when they were alive.

It's the same with a haunting. The information we pick up was imprinted into the environment by living people, though for some it's from living people in the process of dying (but not dead yet). There are hauntings on record of people even seeing ghostly figures which turn out to be images of themselves!

One last point before I move on to discussing the main phenomenon of this novel, apparitions.

The word "haunt" refers typically to places. It is not uncommon to hear a character in an old detective mystery movie say something like, "we need to check the killer's old haunts." Living people haunt their regular hangouts (you're even haunting your own home and place of work or business). Regular customers of bars and restaurants are technically haunting the place while alive. Norm and Cliff haunted the bar on the TV sitcom *Cheers*. In other words, anyone who spends a lot of time in a place is technically in their "old haunt."

So yes, apparitions—ghosts—can haunt a place, but we don't call that a haunting per se, mainly because that seems to be a choice. Apparitions can and do move from place to place on occasion, but at least in the US and other western countries, they hang around in places where they had a real emotional connection when alive.

What that means is that when someone dies and sticks around after death, they seem to stay with their home or appear in a place they had an association with when alive. In most cases, that's a positive association and, other than their former home, could be a bar, restaurant, hotel, or other place they might have spent a lot of time. Whether they died there or not is irrelevant. It's about the association from life, so if they died in that bar or restaurant, they might hang out there after death, or might head home.

I do want to mention a few more tidbits here before moving on to discuss the case I had that inspired the main ghostly interactions in the story you have just read (or maybe are about to read).

An apparition is our personality (or spirit, soul, consciousness, mind or whatever you want to call it) surviving the death of the body, and capable of interaction with the living (and presumably other apparitions). It is pure consciousness. Apparitions are seen, heard, felt or smelled (thankfully, not tasted!) by people through the process of ESP, ExtraSensory Perception. Not a "sixth sense," but rather something extra, a perceptual process that does not involve the physical senses. It seems our own ESP allows us to perceive them in different ways. And yes, we all have some degree of ESP unless we're totally blocking it, usually related to fear and/or belief.

The model of an apparition is that it is consciousness without form. As the apparition has no form, and no sensory organs or normal ability to communicate, he or she essentially connects to the minds of living people. The apparition essentially broadcasts sensory information (what he or she looks, sounds, feels and smells like) to the minds of us living folk. Our minds process the signals and add them to what our normal senses are picking up. Some people do better with visual input, some with auditory or other kinds of information. Some can process combinations. It's an individual thing.

But because they have no physical form, they are not seen with the eye or heard with the ears, as such. It's why in a crowded room with lots of living people and a ghost some see the ghost, some hear him, some feel his presence, some smell his cologne, and some get different combinations of those perceptions. And of course, lots of people in the room may get nothing at all. This is also why ghosts generally can't be photographed—they don't reflect or give off light to affect our eyes or cameras.

If a ghost could appear in a picture, it would be because the apparition consciously affected the film or digital media, not because they simply appear in a bright flash (which is absolutely not the case). In other words, the apparition affects the picture media with his or her mind. By definition, this is psychokinesis (PK), or mind over matter.

PK is also how an apparition could move an object or even create a recording of a voice inside a voice recorder (what's called electronic voice phenomena, or EVP).

When one sees or otherwise perceives a "ghost," we in parapsychology have to figure out if what's perceived represents an actual conscious entity or is a haunting. The distinction is related to interaction, since recordings typically do not react or interact with us or show any indication of self-awareness.

One way I can get this point across is to bring up the old ghost stories.

Let's say we have that old haunted Scottish castle, where the Lord of the manor (who died some 300 years ago under tragic circumstances, of course) appears on the parapet every night at midnight (playing his bagpipes, naturally). You see him coming towards you—needless to say, you're starring as the intrepid investigator here. He reaches your position, then walks right through you. And night after night, he goes through the same motions (playing the same tune). That's either a haunting—a replay from the past—or a very boring ghost (perhaps he has OCD).

Should he stop one night, however, and ask if you have any favorite songs you'd like to hear (on the bagpipes!)... well, you've got yourself a real "live" ghostie.

One important additional bit of information about apparitions is that there are numerous reports of apparitions of still-living people. Often those people are having an out of body experience at the same time as they're being perceived as apparitions, or they're having dreams about visiting the persons who see them as apparitions. Sometimes, the apparition is generated by a person in some sort of immediate danger or crisis. It's as though the apparition is projected to get help for them.

It is clear that the vast majority of encounters with apparitions happen at or within a couple of days of the moment of death of the person represented by that apparition. After that, they're gone to whatever the next stage of existence is (called the afterlife or the other side by most people). Some few seem to stick around longer, and there are a number of personal reasons why this might be, a range of reasons that reflect the individual person.

After being around this field for over forty years, coupled with my own investigations, those of my colleagues, and the reports in our century-plus literature, I am of the opinion and belief that a personal desire or other reason to stay is not enough. Otherwise, I think we'd have a lot more such cases to investigate. It's likely that there are some connections to the physical environment at or after the moment of death, such as to the Earth's magnetic field.

We also cannot eliminate that there may be something spiritual or even divine, that a greater power has something in "mind" for us, individually, when we die. Science cannot research such things as God or gods, due to them being "unknowable" in nature. I don't personally believe this is the case or not the case. But it is something to consider.

One other important piece here that is completely ignored by "ghost hunters," it seems (except those who do have the curiosity and motivation to learn from the field that has been studying the paranormal since the 1800s): Ghosts have ESP, too.

Without some form of non-sensory perception, apparitions could not perceive ("see" or "hear") us or the physical world in general, since they do not have physical sensory organs to gather information. They don't physically make sound, otherwise everyone present could hear them and recordings could easily be made of those sounds or voices. No voice box, no physical voice.

Apparitions perceive the world and communicate using non-sensory—or extrasensory—means.

As mentioned earlier, since they have no physical form per se, anyone "seeing" an apparition is perceiving some kind of self-image of that apparition. Since, with rare exception, we in Western culture think of ourselves as wearing clothing, and ghosts are people too, naturally that psychic image people pick up on has the apparition wearing clothes. And often, the ghost looks much healthier, younger and even fitter than the people they were at their time of death. Close your eyes and get a picture of yourself in your mind and you'll get what I mean.

In communication with apparitions over time, people who have communicated with them, whether "normal" people or psychics or mediums, have learned that they don't have a real sense of the passage of time. After all, they have no body-clock, no real need to eat, and apparently no need to sleep (I say "apparently" because the ghosts in the wonderful CBS and BBC TV shows *Ghosts* do apparently sleep at night, but that's pop culture for you).

In some very few cases, the apparitions have learned to move things or otherwise affect the physical world. As they have no bodies with which to do this, we can say they're interacting with the physical via mind over matter—psychokinesis, or PK. As a pop culture example, I point you to the 1990 film *Ghost* with Patrick Swayze, Whoopi Goldberg, and Demi Moore, in which Swayze's character has to learn from another ghost how to move something.

On to the apparition case at hand...

First, for a complete write-up of this case, please see my chapter "Interactive Apparitions" in Leslie Kean's 2017 book *Surviving Death: A Journalist Investigates Evidence for an Afterlife*, available in multiple formats.

The intriguing call came into the office of the Graduate Parapsychology Program at John F. Kennedy University in the San Francisco Bay Area, where I was on faculty. This was not long after I received enormous national publicity in the fall of 1984 as a "Real-Life Ghostbuster." (NOTE: The Graduate Parapsychology Program ended in the late 1980s, and, as of 2021, JFK University has been folded into National University. I continue to teach Parapsychology online through the Rhine Education Center, www.rhineedu.org, and Atlantic University, www.atlanticuniv.edu)

The call came from a woman named Pat in Livermore, a city east of Oakland, California, less than an hour's drive from where JFK University was. Pat was an attorney who lived in Livermore with her son and her husband. Her mother lived nearby. The call was prompted by her learning that her son had been having conversations with the ghost of the previous owner. She also learned that these almost-daily conversations had been going on for well over a year, since shortly after they moved in.

Pat's attitude was refreshing, as was her story. They had purchased the 70-plus year-old home in an estate sale a couple of years after the death by natural causes of the owner. The woman who was that previous owner had lived in the house since her birth in 1917 until her death in 1980. Since moving in the house, Pat, as well as her husband and her mother had seen the apparition of a woman appearing and disappearing in the house, but until her son mentioned his daily communications with the ghost, the others had not even admitted they'd seen her too. In other words, they'd all seen the ghost, but kept the sightings to themselves. Pat grew up in a family environment that acknowledged psychic experience and was not afraid of the ghost.

One day, Pat's 12-year-old son Chris began talking about the origins of some of the antique furniture and some of the porcelain dolls they had also purchased in the estate sale. Pat asked if he had found some kind of paperwork about the items. Chris simply replied that "Lois told me." Lois was the name of the late owner. Chris also let her know that the ghost, Lois, had told him that the other family members had seen her but were not talking about the experiences.

After Chris's revelation, Pat spoke with her husband and mother, and they all admitted to one another that they, too, had seen the ghost on several occasions. But it was Chris that Lois apparently felt most comfortable around and appeared to every days.

Pat was curious about having a ghost in the house with a growing pre-teen. In fact, by the time of her call, she had already taken her son in to see a local psychological counselor to make sure he was "okay" and that it was not damaging to have him continue conversing with the ghost. With the family's permission, I had lunch with the therapist, who, he admitted, was a bit of an agnostic when it came to ghosts. However, he was convinced that Chris was well adjusted and not prone to making things up—consciously or otherwise.

I agreed to come check things out myself, and I was quite excited to do so. Pat stated that Chris was able to get verifiable information from Lois. This was a rarity when it comes to apparition cases.

Pat did pass along a concern of Lois's about my visit, however, that Chris had passed on from Lois. Apparently, Lois watched television quite a bit with Chris and had seen a commercial for *Ghostbusters*. She was worried we'd bring along "blasters" to get rid of her. I assured Pat that this was not the case.

Driving with me from the University to Livermore were Joanna Rix and one of the Transpersonal Counseling students, Kip Leyser. As we drove to Pat's place, we talked about a number of things. A few, in particular, came back to "haunt" us in a way. The car I was driving was giving me problems, and I expressed ideas for a new car. Joanna was seriously contemplating quitting her job that week. Kip, we learned, had been a professional dancer for ten years before coming back to school at JFK University.

We arrived and were greeted by Pat, her mother, and Chris. Pat's husband was out of town at the time. As we were invited in, I got the impression Chris was giving us the visual once over to make sure we had no ghost traps. We started a tape recorder and walked around the house, discussing the sightings of the ghost they had all had.

Pat and her mother had seen the ghost on brief occasions. She always appeared as an elderly woman. Chris had been seeing her almost every day for more than a year. He told us she didn't always appear as an old woman to him. She often looked like a teenager, a six-year-old, a woman in her thirties, and sometimes middle-aged.

"Did her clothing change often?" I asked.

"All the time," he replied. In fact, Pat and her mother also admitted to seeing Lois wearing different clothing. This was important to me, as was the appearance of Lois at different ages.

I asked Chris how that was possible. He told us Lois believed she did not have a "form." She believed she was some kind of "ball of energy" that was able to communicate by "projecting her thoughts" to others. These thoughts included visual and verbal information that she would "project into the minds of others" so they would "see" and "hear" her as if she was really there. Remember, this was coming from a twelve-year-old.

This meant that Lois was aware that she was literally "telling" Chris's mind what to "see" and "hear" about her. They were not really seeing or hearing Lois. They were perceiving her, and both Lois and Chris were aware of this.

"Why was Lois appearing in different forms and clothing?" I asked.

"Because that's how she felt that day," he replied. In other words, as indicated earlier in this Afterword, it was Lois's own sense of self, her perceptions about the way she viewed herself that day—at a particular age in particular clothing—that shaped her "projection" of herself.

We finished touring the house, hearing about some of Lois's furniture and her doll collection, about the city of Livermore, and about Lois herself when she was alive. For a twelve-year-old, Chris was an articulate purveyor of anecdote. In fact, I had little trouble believing someone else was feeding him the information.

Was Lois there with us? Apparently, she was by Chris's side the whole time (or so he said).

As we ended the house tour, we asked whether we could ask Lois some questions. We sat down in the living room, facing Chris, who was seated next to an empty chair he identified as Lois's favorite spot to sit. According to the boy, she was sitting there with us all.

So, the three of us pitched questions at an empty chair as a young boy looked and listened to "someone" sitting there, repeating or translating "her" answers. There was a surreal feel to the situation, like we were in some weird situation comedy. While Joanna and Kip asked questions more related to Lois herself, I pretty much kept to questions related to her current incarnation as an apparition.

The answers we all got were specific and to the point. More and more information came out about Lois, giving us the picture that she was a local social butterfly, often hosting parties at her home throughout her life. Most of her relatives had died, but we were informed on one who was still alive.

For me, Lois related—through Chris's excellent translation—more description of her form and ability to communicate on a telepathic level with Chris. She declined to appear to us. She still didn't quite trust us, she said, and admitted she wasn't even sure she really could. She related that others seeing her might also have to do with their current attachment to the house and how psychic they were.

Most of what Chris told us Lois said about her form as an apparition was more than a bit familiar from my readings in parapsychological literature—not from books for the general public. This was not something I expected from a twelve-year-old boy who, according to his mother, had never read anything on ghosts.

One of the more enlightening questions I asked was why Lois was still hanging around her old house, why she had not passed on. The answer was that she had done much socializing, had many parties in her life, and had not been an avid churchgoer. A believer in heaven and hell, she thought too much partying and not enough church might see her to hell, so she figured why not stick around rather than take the chance of ending up there? Besides, she told us, she liked the new family and felt very happy with them, especially Chris.

From this, one cannot conclude that there is a heaven or hell, only that Lois believed there was. However, we could infer that her belief and her desire to remain somehow enabled her to stay as an apparition in her home. As mentioned above, it is unlikely it's only a desire on the part of all who die that's enough to allow everyone to be here as a ghost, as there were also most likely some environmental factors and some person-specific factors that allowed Lois to stay. Otherwise, we would have many more apparition cases than we do.

I finally asked if Lois had any questions for us. Lois decided to show off. Chris looked at the empty chair and then asked us each a question.

"Loyd, she wants to know if you've decided on a color for that car you want.

"Joanna, have you really thought about the kind of job you want after you quit the one you have?

"Kip, how long were you a professional dancer?"

I think our jaws probably hit the floor at the same time. We each, in hollow voices, answered the questions. Then, after telling Pat and the others that the questions related to our in-transit conversation, I asked how Lois knew to even ask the questions.

Chris looked over at the chair, then back at us a bit sheepishly. "You're probably not going to like this, but Lois wanted to make sure you weren't bringing blasters to get rid of her, so she hitched a ride with you here and eavesdropped."

We all got a big—though nervous—laugh out of that. Kip was especially shaken, since the only place Lois could have "sat" was next to him in the back seat. We got up to leave, promising continued contact and follow-up.

We did go through the tapes to listen for any indication that we somehow told them about our previous conversation. We concluded that either Chris—or Lois-read our minds, or that my car was bugged, or that Lois really caught a ride with us. To this day, I'm sorry it didn't occur to me to ask how Lois got to JFKU to get into my car in the first place... did she hitchhike there? Take a bus? Fly?

Sometime afterwards, Lois's only living relative was tracked down. I spoke with the elderly gentleman, who was able to verify the tales of Lois's youth as true, as well as information and stories about the family and Lois's house that Chris came up with.

In case you're wondering, Pat did thoroughly check to see if Chris had somehow found diaries or other papers Lois might have left behind. None could be found.

Chris continued to see Lois on a daily basis for a while, but then lost interest as he grew and discovered—and was discovered by— real girls, though he apparently asked Lois for advice on many occasions. I continued to follow up with Pat through the early 2000s, and Lois was still in the house, still seen on occasion by members of the family, and still apparently happy to be staying in her lifetime home.

This case is my favorite on many levels. First, the verified information was enough under the circumstances to convince me that normal sources of information could be ruled out. Lois was there, or perhaps Chris was some kind of super-psychic who was able to pick up the information from the house itself through clairvoyance or retrocognition. That there were other witnesses to Lois puts heavier emphasis on the former possibility rather than the latter.

Second, the information about how Lois was able to appear and communicate was far beyond what most people would be able to read about easily at the time, let alone the kind of information that a twelve-year-old would spout about ghosts.

Third, that the family called us in because they, too, were curious about apparitions was refreshing and enabled us to ask the kinds of questions I like to ask about the "how" and "why" of apparitions.

Finally, that the family was well-adjusted, seemingly without psychological issues about the ghost was very encouraging to someone like me who so often encounters people whose first impulse when they see a ghost is to turn and run.

Lois showed herself to be a person first, and a ghost second. She proved my adage that "Ghosts are people, too."

Cases like this exist all over the world, though unfortunately my colleagues and I rarely get to visit and dig deeper into them. Most people wouldn't think to call for a parapsychologist (or other paranormal investigators) when they have a friendly ghost or even a positive-imprint type of haunting. It's generally only when one is afraid, angry, annoyed or otherwise put out that one calls for "help" with psychic experiences or encounters–or for plumbing, for that matter.

One last thing: that "squirrelly" case Jennifer Daye investigates in this book is also based on one of my own experiences.

In the actual case, I sat on the rough attic floor waiting for something to happen. It is one of the only cases I've ever done where I did so at night with the lights out, as that was the condition of the attic when the couple heard the "ghostly" footsteps from the floor below.

I actually heard scratching and light thumping sounds across the attic from me, sounds that were coming closer. At the same time, the male owner of the home yelled up to me, "do you hear footsteps?" I turned on my flashlight and shocked the squirrel rolling a big nut across the floor. He (or she) scampered away through a hole I found. I then found a pile of nuts nearby.

It seems odd acoustics were to blame for the bouncing nut to be heard as footsteps. To test my hypothesis, I rolled a nut across the floor. "Footsteps!" yelled the owners. To further test, I grabbed a handful of the nuts and rolled them all across the floor at once. The couple responded with more yelling (and a little screaming), asking if I was "okay."

I came down from the attic, at which point they looked at me suspiciously. I explained the acoustics and had to take them up one at a time (the other remaining below) to show them how it all worked, as well as to point out the squirrel's entry point.

You may wonder why I did the test with a handful of nuts, especially since it was going to freak out the homeowners (and did, of course).

Sometimes you just have to do something to entertain yourself in these investigations.

—Loyd Auerbach, January 13, 2023

FOR MORE INFORMATION

If you're at all interested in finding out more about psychic phenomena in general, psychic abilities, ghostly encounters, and research on all of this—the kinds of things that Jennifer and Nate encountered in this book, in the first in the series, NEAR DEATH, and in future investigations—check out these organizations as your starting points. They are credible, provide excellent information and learning opportunities, and are ones I am proud to be part of (or a member of, in the case of the SPR).

Rhine Research Center: www.rhine.org

The longest running lab and educational organization in the United States, this is the legacy of the Duke University Parapsychology Laboratory founded in the 1930s. The Rhine has a huge media library—videos of lectures by researchers, psychics, and others presented over the last few years. There are a few that are free, but you are encouraged to join, not only to gain access to the media library and get discounts on webcasts of new lectures and discounts on classes and other things, but mainly to help support the work of the Rhine.

The Rhine Education Center (www.rhineedu.org) offers online courses throughout the year (Loyd Auerbach is one of the main instructors and loves teaching through the Rhine).

The Society for Psychical Research: www.spr.ac.uk

The SPR is the oldest psychical research and parapsychology organization, founded in 1882. Lots of good info here for free, especially the Psi Encyclopedia (https://psi-encyclopedia.spr.ac.uk/)—an ever-growing resource on psychic abilities and research.

The Forever Family Foundation: www.foreverfamilyfoundation.org

Free to join, this non-profit supports the work of evidential mediums in the family grieving process and supports scientific research into experiences suggestive or supportive of the concept of Survival of Consciousness (and Loyd Auerbach is the current President)

Follow Loyd Auerbach on Twitter @profparanormal
Subscribe to his YouTube channels at:
www.youtube.com/user/loydauerbach/videos
www.youtube.com/user/profparanormal/videos
Or you can reach Loyd Auerbach via email at:
profparanormal@gmail.com

AUTHOR'S NOTE

If you've read *Near Death* (and if you haven't, you should), the Author's Note shares the long history of Nate Raney and Jennifer Daye from pitch, to pilot script, to novel, in detail. (It's also available on our website, RaneyAndDaye.com) Rich, Loyd, and I have been thrilled with the response to the first book, which included several comments that the project would make a great streaming or television series. Huh? May have to look into that.

There was a huge sense of completion when *Near Death* was finished, but now *After Life* is here, bringing Nate and Jennifer and their colleagues to new places. It's an exciting step that opens up myriad possibilities and brings Raney and Daye to life in a way they never have been before. After almost three decades, they are investigating a new case, albeit an old new case, fitting for their own history. And they will soon be back in their third adventure, *Far Sight*.

We hope you continue to follow their investigations, and that their experience, and ours, is living—and dying—proof, that almost anything is possible.

ESPecially,

—Arnold Rudnick, January 13, 2023

ACKNOWLEDGMENTS

My ongoing gratitude to the earliest fans of the Raney and Daye novels who continue to help shape and refine the story and characters into something I hope you all enjoy. Thank you to Kathryn Rudnick, Sheila Smith and Jenn Mier.

Also, huge thanks to Nina Henderson for all her time and effort to make this a better book.

For *After Life*, we also recruited a "launch team" of fans of the first book to help us spread the word about this latest volume. You all know who you are, and I am extremely grateful for your enthusiastic help. If you're interested in getting early access to the next Raney/Daye Investigation and participating in reader outreach, contact us on Facebook @RaneyAndDaye, or at RaneyAndDaye.com.

If you want to keep up to date on the next book in the series and other Raney and Daye news, sign up for the email list on the website, and we'll send you a free bookmark!

I also want to thank the Readers' Favorite organization which sponsors an annual contest in addition to publishing excellent reviews. We are honored to have received a Bronze Medal in the category of Supernatural Fiction for the first Raney/Daye Investigation, *Near Death*.

I had the opportunity to accept the award on behalf of myself, Ar-

nold and Loyd in November of 2022 and met a lot of interesting people, including a gentleman who was kind enough to relate his own
near-death experience, elements of which may just find their way
into a future story…

—Rich Hosek, January 13, 2023

After Life would not exist if it weren't for our lead author, Rich Hosek, who forewent sleep and numerous hours of binge television to
handle the heavy lifting on this book, and whom I must acknowledge
first and last.

We are also indebted to Loyd Auerbach, not only for his creative
input, but for his paranormal expertise, ensuring Nate and Jennifer's
investigations never make the reader wonder, "Would a ghost say
that?"

Like any creative project, I cannot imagine its birth without the
support of my wife, Kathryn, not only for her moral support, but for
proofreading and bringing an immense knowledge of literature, to
ensure our books deliver to the most discerning of readers.

It takes a village to build a book, or a movie, or a building for that
matter, and there are many more who made this book and series possible, but the final acknowledgment is to you, our readers, who make
this worthwhile.

—Arnold Rudnick, January 13, 2023

First—and once again—I must acknowledge my two co-authors:
Rich Hosek and Arnold Rudnick (especially Rich, for taking on the
huge task of writing).

I also need to acknowledge my mentors and influences who are
gone from our plane of existence: Martin Caidin, Annette Martin,
Marcello Truzzi, D. Scott Rogo, Alex Tanous, Karlis Osis, my uncle
Herb Norman, and my father, Dick Auerbach, and one that's still
here, thankfully (Ed May). All of them—and a litany of others—had
real influence on my career in Parapsychology (and often on my par-

allel career as psychic entertainer "Professor Paranormal"), as well as my work with the media.

I also have to thank:

—John Kruth, Executive Director of the Rhine Research Center, for his continual support and friendship, especially when it comes to the online courses I teach for the Rhine Education Center, as well as my Rhine students (many of whom support my every-other-week Facebook Live sessions with their attendance and questions).

—The Executive Board and Certified Mediums of the Forever Family Foundation, especially Bob Ginsberg and Leigh Harris, for their incredible work with this all volunteer non-profit organization

—and all my other colleagues in the field of Parapsychology and the world of Psychic Entertainment

Whew!

—*Loyd Auerbach, January 13, 2023*

RICH HOSEK

Rich has written for numerous television series with his writing partner Arnold Rudnick including, *The Fresh Prince of Bel-Air*, *Star Trek: Voyager*, and *The New Addams Family* for which they won a Leo Award for Best Writing for Comedy or Variety. More recently he has been focusing his efforts on novels and short stories. He is a fan of Legos and *Doctor Who*, and now that there is a Doctor Who Lego set, his life is complete. Be sure to check out his other novels at RichHosek.com, his short story fiction podcast, *Bedtime Stories for Insomniacs* at https://BedtimeStories.studio, and follow him on X @RichHosek and on Facebook @Written by Rich Hosek.

ARNOLD RUDNICK

Arnold studied film and accounting at the University of Illinois, Urbana-Champaign, then moved to Los Angeles, where he worked in feature development at Paramount Pictures and Gary Lucchesi Productions. Arnold and Rich have collaborated on numerous scripts for film and television, including The Fresh Prince of Bel-Air, Star Trek: Voyager and The New Addams Family. He has also written children's books, including ESPete: Sixth Grade Sense—which won a silver medal in the Moonbeam Children's Book Awards and Reader's Favorite Awards and was a pick in Danny Brassell's Lazy Readers Book Club—and Little Green. He and his wife live in Los Angeles, California.

LOYD AUERBACH

Loyd Auerbach, MS, is a world-recognized paranormal expert with thousands of media appearances and the author or coauthor of nine paranormal books and one on publishing and publicity. He is President of the Forever Family Foundation (since 2013), and Director of the Office of Paranormal Investigations (since 1989). He is on faculty at Atlantic University and JFK University (National University) and teaches online Parapsychology courses through the Rhine Education Center. He is on the Board of Directors of the Rhine Research Center and the advisory board of the Windbridge Institute. He is a past president of the Psychic Entertainers association, and besides working as a parapsychologist, he performs as professional mentalist Professor Paranormal (and occasional chocolatier). Follow him @profparanormal on X.

www.ingramcontent.com/pod-product-compliance
Lightning Source LLC
Chambersburg PA
CBHW072313020726
47501CB00002B/493